COLD MAGIC

Also by Martyn Carey

GREY NEIGHBOURS SERIES

Grey Neighbours

Passing Shadows

The Bone House

ORDINARY WIZARDS SERIES

Ordinary Miracles

Other Heroes

OTHER BOOKS

The Queen of Brighton's Daughter

SHORT STORY COLLECTIONS

Snow

Broken House

COLD MAGIC

Ordinary Wizards

Book 3

MARTYN CAREY

For my children, my friends and other unavoidable distractions

1

The cold wind battered the trees as the heavily wrapped man struggled up the steep wooded slope, fighting against the broken ground and the brambles that tore at his legs and threatened to trip him with every step. The tree branches scratched at the late autumn sky, seeming to cut furrows into the clouds, and the snowy wind had teeth that bit deep through his coat.

His rucksack dragged at him and he winced as a hard edge dug into his lower back. It was too late to repack it, even if he'd had the inclination to stop for that long in this weather. He paused to catch his breath as a wave of pressure rolled down the hill towards him, a pressure that had nothing to do with the atmosphere. There was a strong feeling that something that didn't want him to do what he was going to do. *'There is no other way to do this'*, he thought, as if trying to reassure himself, *'and it's not for the want of trying.'* Even his thoughts sounded petulant.

He didn't know precisely where he was going, but he knew he could locate the right place once he was close enough because although he couldn't see it he could *feel* it. He ignored the cackling crows and the pheasants that sprinted away from him as he searched the slope, hunting for that one particular place.

The tall trees thinned slightly then closed in again, and he felt himself drawn toward an isolated stand of ash trees. Then he found it, even though it looked like any other patch of ground. It was covered in brambles, coarse whippy grass and was still dusted with snow, despite being fractionally sheltered from the weather by the close-standing trees.

He swung his pack to the ground, pulled out a gardening hook and tore away the undergrowth to expose a patch of bare earth, grunting when a low branch sprang back and hit him in the face with disturbing accuracy. He reached into his rucksack again and pulled out a small folding shovel then, swearing under his breath, sketched the outline of a hole and dug in short hard movements. He was hunched over uncomfortably but still grateful that the exercise was helping to keep him warm.

By the time he'd finished digging he was feeling sick, but it had little to do with the exertion. He was increasingly spooked by the feeling that he was being watched, overlooked by something that didn't want him there. But he had to do this, because this was the only way that he could get out of the mess he had found himself in.

He had expected some resistance but he'd hoped it to be something more passive, not this feeling of being stared down by something that really, really didn't want him there. He wasn't even sure he'd be able to complete what he was doing before whatever it was managed to stop him.

He pulled a metal tube out of his bag, not quite a metre long and a handspan across, and slid it into the hole, tamping the earth down around it so that it wouldn't move. He flexed his fingers against the stiffness, then extracted a ceramic vessel from deeper in his bag, which he slid carefully into the tube. He would have offered a prayer if he'd bought into that particular fantasy, and he was relieved to see a purple glow develop at the bottom of the hole after a few seconds. The light seemed to soak into the ceramic like water penetrating a sponge and he smiled into his scarf. The device was working. Everything was going to be all right.

He slipped the metal cover onto the tube then scuffed the earth and brambles back over it, the better to hide it from anyone who might come across this spot. He marked a nearby tree before repacking his gear and heading down the hill. The wind was brutal now, battering at him as if it were trying to drive him away, and he hoped that the weather wouldn't be quite as unkind when he came back to retrieve it in a couple of weeks.

Instead of being relieved as he descended the hill he became increasingly frightened, and the fear grew until it was like a great beast hovering over him, glowering, waiting for the moment to strike. Then, almost without realising it, he was running, bouncing off trees in his haste. Panting, he threw himself through the wide wooden gate at the bottom of the slope, scrambled into his car and, close to panic, started the engine.

The car growled and complained as it lurched out of the muck when he set off, wheels spinning and coating the shiny blue paintwork in mud. He barely paused when he reached the main road, turning sharply north into the traffic to the noisy disapproval of a lorry coming down the steep hill toward him. He had made it as far as the causeway over the river when the force that had been louring unseen struck. It slammed into the back of his car and he swerved hard to avoid broadsiding a tractor, corrected only just in time and then sped away as fast as the glutinous traffic would let him.

*

We first realised that something was wrong when Clara forgot how to make coffee. She just stopped, staring at the cafetiere on the draining board as if she had never seen one before.

"Do you know," she said conversationally, "I have no idea what I'm supposed to do with this." I could feel her confusion and her hands were none too steady, so I quickly got up from the big table in the living room and went over to her. She was shaking, so I took her hand. Sam, who was also here, was equally concerned.

"Are you all right?" I will readily concede that this was a bloody stupid question. She looked at me, grey faced and distressed, so I gentled her into a chair by the big table. Her colour improved but her confusion didn't, so we moved her onto the big squishy couch where she lay back and shut her eyes. Her breathing became ragged and laboured, seeming to catch in her throat, and the tattoo on her left arm glowed slightly, but this faded as her skin went from pallid grey back to its normal soft brown.

"I'll call a doctor," said Sam, sounding worried. This was beyond our meagre first aid skills and we were wise enough to recognise that.

"No," said Clara faintly. "No. I'm just... tired. I need to... sleep." She drifted off, her face becoming smooth and slack as her breathing became more even and regular. The big room fell silent, apart from the crackle of the stove at the far end of the room and the delicate 'whump' of the wind gusting against the big picture window. We watched for a moment as she moved in restless distress.

"I'll take her up to her room," said Amy softly. She raised her hands in front of her, palms up, and Clara rose from the couch on a cushion of air, still horizontal and mostly asleep. Amy moved her up the broad staircase that wraps around the big main room of the farmhouse and up to her bedroom. Without getting up from my chair I exerted myself a little and the fire in the wood burning stove at the far end of the room, which we'd lit against the unseasonably freezing October wind, quietly fell into ash.

"Why you do that?" Sam asked, sounding a bit cross.

"I thought we were all going to bed now." It was just after nine thirty in the evening, not an unusual time for us to do that.

She shrugged. "OK. We tidy first." I didn't argue. Sam may be slight and short, but she's more capable than me and I'm a tiny bit scared of her. And if you tell her that, I'll pull your molars out through your ears.

Our house – Whim Hill Farm - is in the hills north of Nottingham, not far from the village of Linby. Normally it's just me and my fiancée Amy who live here, but both Sam and Clara come here so often that they have their own rooms and a basic selection of clean clothes. We all go to a college in

Nottingham, itself a part the university, where we study magic rather than geography or history or creative apathy or whatever.

If you study Sports Science you need a place to practise, somewhere you aren't going to put a golf ball through a window or get run over when you go jogging. It's the same with us; we needed somewhere to do what we do without it causing problems for other people. So we have a big house, a converted barn in fact, way out in the countryside.

So yes, we are wizards, although we prefer the term 'mage' so people don't get us confused with Harry Potter, Harry Dresden and Harry bloody Houdini, none of whom are actually mages. And contrary to what some people think, magic is not just a way of turning superstition into money.

Amy came back down before we'd finished shutting things down. "She's asleep. I don't know what's happened."

"Are you sure that we don't need a doctor?" I asked, because Clara is as fit as any dedicated athlete and had never shown signs of this sort of illness before.

"No. Well, not tonight anyway," she amended thoughtfully. "I'll stay up and keep an eye on her. It doesn't feel like anything that needs immediate action so you should get your head down for a bit." Amy and Clara are magical partners – *erdikide* is the technical term – which means they have an unusually strong connection. It means that they are aware of what the other person is feeling, if not what they are thinking, far more than non-magical people are. Sometimes it can make life... uncomfortable.

"OK."

"I'm not sure about that," Sam said to Amy. "I think she really is very ill. She went a very funny colour."

"I saw that too," she replied, frowning. At that moment we heard Clara cry out upstairs. Sam got there first. Clara was sitting up in bed, staring wildly around, eyes bright with tears.

"What's, what's...? Where am I?" She started to shake. "Why isn't she here? Where is she?" Sam tried to gather her into a hug, but Clara pulled away. "Who are you?" Her voice was rising in panic.

Amy stepped forward and laid a gentle hand on Clara's forehead. "*Loaren.*" That's a medium strength sleep spell and it worked quickly, so I helped lower Clara back onto the bed, profoundly and untouchably asleep. I left the girls to put her back into bed properly and headed for the telephone.

"Doctor?" Amy asked me when she slowly came down the stairs.

"The ambulance is on the way and I told them the symptoms resembled transient global amnesia."

"Don't try to do their job for them dear, doctors don't tend to like it," said Amy. I smiled. She says things like that as a form of bleak humour, which is a bit lighter and more Dickensian than black humour.

When the doctor arrived we lifted the spell but she found that Clara was still confused and less than fully coherent, and so insisted that she went to the hospital. As this was urgent but not an emergency it took the ambulance ages to arrive, finally pitching up in the small hours. I don't know why they're called 'small' hours because they're bloody huge if you have to stay awake through them.

Sam decided to stay at home with me while Amy went to the Queens Medical Centre in Nottingham. It's only about 7 miles away but it seemed to take forever. Clara's parents were visiting her brother on St Lucia when she fell ill, so if anyone was going to be going to the hospital with her it was going to be one of us. We would have gone anyway, of course.

*

Sam and I arrived at the hospital just after 10 a.m., right at the start of visiting hours, even though Amy had been sending us reassuring texts since some indecent hour that morning. The walk from the very distant Car Park 3 – the only one with any spaces in it, even that early – seemed to take us on an unguided tour of the whole site, which did nothing for my anxiety levels or my aching feet.

"Hello," said Clara brightly when we finally appeared in the over-populated and under-resourced ward. "How are you doing?"

'Knackered, worried sick and bogging for a coffee' was what I carefully didn't say. "Concerned about you," I replied, an understatement that was like saying that sticking your hand into a meat grinder is probably an unwise thing to do.

"I am, apparently, fine," said Clara, glancing at the other beds in the room, which contained people who very obviously weren't.

"You weren't fine last night," said Sam.

"I know - or, at least, so I've been told. I've no memory of anything after getting up from the table after dinner to make the coffee."

"The young lady was in a deeply confused state when she was brought in," said the doctor who was looking after her. His badge said 'Dr Pierce', and he looked to be in his fifties, with greying hair and trustworthy spectacles. "Amy briefed us on what happened once we had got Clara to sleep. My initial suspicion was that it might have been a TGA, but once she woke we realised that her accessible recollections were too recent. A TGA normally affects the memory for the last several months, but Clara has lost just a few hours."

"I see," I replied, trying to sound intelligent and well informed and doubtless failing miserably. "So what do you think happened?"

"To be completely honest, we are not at all sure. We thought perhaps a TIA, a mini stroke, but we've done all the tests, scans and so forth that I can think of and everything is normal, apart from slightly raised adrenaline levels. They're too low to be diagnostically relevant, and the levels of adrenochrome and adrenolutin are unremarkable. There are no more test that we can usefully run."

"Oh. Good, I think. When can she leave?"

"Oh, within the hour, all being well," said Dr Pierce. "I trust you brought a change of clothes? The ones she came in are a bit... tired." He didn't elaborate, and I thought it might not be tactful to ask.

"Oh, I didn't..." I started, but Sam was indicting a holdall that she had put next to the bed. I hadn't thought to bring more clothes for Clara, nor wondered what was in the bag. Amy would say that was typical, which reminded me...

"Where is Amy?"

Clara pointed to the corridor. "She's gone to the loo."

"However," the doctor went on, his tone suddenly heavy and serious, "I would recommend, in the strongest possible terms, that she is not left alone for the next few days."

"As in 'I would make this an order if I were in a position to'?" I asked.

"As in," he replied with a slight smile.

"She can stay with us," said Amy, coming back into the room. "We've got the space. Can she go into college as well?"

"Yes," said Dr Pierce after a moment's thought. "She should continue her activities as normally as possible, but you mustn't let her get too tired nor anxious."

"I'm sure we'll manage," said Sam.

"And if she has another episode, or displays even the slightest sign that something is wrong, one of you must contact me immediately whilst someone else calls an ambulance." He handed Amy a business card.

When we left the hospital Clara curled up under a blanket in the back of my battered old VW, chatting with a bright brittleness that I didn't quite like. I had carefully briefed the people at the college about what had happened and warned them of the possible consequences. They were properly concerned but couldn't offer more than bland reassurances and a promise to help if we needed it.

*

Her next attack was two otherwise normal days later, thankfully while we were all at home. This time her distress was so severe that the paramedics who rushed to the farm had to sedate her before they could even get her into the ambulance. Dr Pierce was impatiently waiting for us when we got to A&E, and fortunately we were able to circumvented the irritably patient waiting room queues.

This time it also had a marked impact on Amy, not only because they are *erdikide* but also because they're close friends. Sam and I also suffered, but much less than Amy. Or I think so anyway, because when Sam decides she's going to do the whole inscrutable thing it's hard to tell.

It was especially disconcerting because of the complicated way that the four of us are connected. We all have magical 'Talents', abilities very loosely tied to earth, air, water et c., and these are part of the connection between us. But, like so many things involved in magic, it's not at all straightforward.

While the girls are at the height of their skills and power, I have recently suffered some setbacks that mean I have very little access to the magic I have in me. It also scrambled my connection with the others, and Clara's condition had left me feeling slightly dizzy, like I had a mild case of Labyrinthitis. I'll admit it does occasionally get me down.

Amy, looking pale and wobbly, sat by the bed and held Clara's hand – white skin, dark skin, concern beyond anything mere friendship could create. I felt tears, and blinked them away. My emotions about the girls are... complicated.

"What was she saying this time?" I asked the doctor, by way of a distraction from what was going on in my head. Same doctor, same ward, same worries.

"She kept muttering 'she's gone'," said Dr Pierce. "She was very distressed. Has she recently lost her mother, sister, or other female relative?"

Amy raised her head slightly, looking out through a cloud of completely white hair that she was distractedly running her fingers through. "No. Her mother was fine when I spoke to her yesterday. She has only one sibling, a brother. He lives on St. Lucia and he and his family are fine too."

The doctor nodded. "And she hasn't lost any female friends recently?"

"No." Amy sighed. "You seem extremely concerned about this."

"Only because Clara was. People in distress say strange things, but she said it over and over. It almost seemed to be causing her physical pain. Her anxiety was so great that she even had difficulty breathing at times."

Clara had a nasal cannula, an oxygen feed pipe under her nose, which hissed gently as he spoke and we waited because there wasn't anything else we could do. I sat down on another of the hard plastic chairs near the bed and sighed, which made Sam glance at me anxiously. I really was feeling awful, a sort of strange, sick dislocation that could only have some kind of magical origin. Sam touched my shoulder and gave me some *indar*, magical energy, then snatched her hand away like she'd been stung.

Clara stirred and cried out in her sleep, an incoherent sound of loss and pain, and the doctor turned to look at the monitors. I found myself breathing out the urge to do the same. I rubbed the tattoo on my left forearm, a simplified representation of the dragon tattoo that runs the full length of her arm. Clara is strongly connected to an earth power known as 'the Dragon', and we both bear its mark.

"She kept doing that too, rubbing her arm," said the nurse. "We wondered if the tattoo was recent and perhaps it was giving her pain?"

I shook my head. "It was done more than a year ago and hasn't caused any problems so far." Clara's tattoo is a beautifully detailed picture of a classic dragon, coiled down the whole length of her arm. Mine is only on my forearm, is a much simpler and more stylised image and, man alive, it hurt. Then the pain sudden got worse, and I felt sweat starting on my forehead. Then, just as abruptly, it stopped. Clara slumped back onto the bed and her breathing returned to normal.

"That's happened before," said the doctor. "She will sleep now, probably for several hours, and we'd very much like her to do that. We'll call you when she wakes up."

"I'll stay," said Amy. The doctor shrugged and I noticed that the nurse had already put a comfortable chair next to the bed. I'm using the word 'comfortable' in the loosest sense, you understand.

"I'll take him," said Sam, lifting me by the arm – actually using a very basic spell called *jaso*, which needs quite a lot of power for someone my size – and physically propelling my reluctant self out of the room.

"What's up with you?" We were in the car – thankfully in a closer car park this time - and she had taken the driving seat without consulting me. I explained what was going on in my head. "Is this something to do with the Dragon? Has something happened to it? How?"

I didn't laugh, although I felt like it. What could happen to such a fundamental force as the Rockingham Dragon? "No, not the Dragon - I think it's the connection between them that's the problem. I... need to... investigate." I had to breathe deeply between each word, and I was suddenly so weary that my eyes kept closing by themselves.

"No," she said, starting the engine. "*We* need to investigate. I wouldn't trust you to drive in the right direction just now."

I gave in. I do that a lot. The women in my life are so powerful and so frequently right that I'd long ago given up arguing. It's like having three rather bossy big sisters. It was a 20 minute drive from the hospital to our home and I don't remember a moment of it.

*

I woke the next morning hoping that yesterday hadn't happened. I was gripped by the urge to investigate our connection to the Dragon, but I was too tired to do anything but eat toast I didn't make and fall asleep on the couch. It wasn't worry or magical interference that had worn me out, but a deep-seated and illogical exhaustion that wouldn't let me alone. It took most of the day to wear off.

Clara came home the next morning – well, when I say home, I mean to stay with us, even though this isn't strictly her home. She spent the whole of the day lording it over us – perhaps that should be 'ladying' it over us – from the couch, demanding tea and sandwiches and foot rubs. We all went along with it, taking it in turns to be the obsequious servant, sycophantically attentive to her every need, but by mid-afternoon everyone was worn out, so we all slept until I made a late supper of smoked salmon and cream cheese on home-made sour dough rolls at around 9.30.

Clara and Amy spent the next day at home, while Sam went into college to track a developing weather pattern in the Mediterranean. I studied satellite images of a possible illegal dump of toxic waste off the coast of north Devon. Sam is a meteorologist of some note and I'm an environmental scientist, and sometimes that requires our attention, probably more often than you might think from these inane ramblings.

The next day Clara decided to go back to college and we hoped that whatever it was had passed. I took her in even though she had recently got a new car, this one actually larger than a roller skate, but we wouldn't let her drive it just in case. Everything was fine for nearly three days.

*

This is probably a good time to explain a bit more about magic. People are born mages (we don't use 'wizard' because I'm not Dumbledore, or 'sorcerer' because I don't make ketchup) and we go to one of the two dozen or so colleges around the country to learn how to make the magic do what they want it to. Mage skills focus around six 'Talents' – air (which Sam is), water (which Amy is), earth (Clara and me, usually), fire, Healing and *kemen*, this last being the direct manipulation of the energy that's behind magic. Not everyone makes it as far as the senior ranks, but age, ethnicity, gender, sexuality and preferred flavour of milkshake have no bearing on capacity. In fact we have absolutely no idea what does, despite literally centuries of research.

The physical effect spells such as push, pull, lift and so on are based on changing things like gravity, momentum and the like. The control of these and other forces comes with experience, training, age and whether or not you are suicidally impatient. They can also be combined to create greater and more complex effects, but that is not something lightly or simply done because such magic is both difficult and inherently dangerous.

I could go on, and on (and on, according to Amy), about the basis of magic – the manipulation of the EM spectrum and the ability to interfere with light, inertia and so on – but I won't because you're already starting to glaze over and I'm too concerned about Clara to be able to concentrate properly.

My problem was that I am a weird thing called an *'euste'*, which means someone who can use spells from outside their own Talent provided a mage possessing that Talent is within range. It's quite a rare ability, appallingly difficult to do, extremely unreliable and proving to be a damned nuisance. Doing magic in this state is like trying to tattoo a soap bubble with knitting needle.

Just remember that magic is a set of skills no more mystical than playing the violin, although the violin is less dangerous to your health when you're first learning how to do it. Well, probably less dangerous.

*

The next 'episode' Clara had was while she was actually in college and before we'd had a chance to check out the Dragon. That meant that, fortunately, there were some very senior mages around to help, but it was still well scary.

The college common room, despite being full of mages of every rank from *Iksale* 10 (the lowest student grade) to the upper reaches of the *Jaun* grades (which denotes the senior ranks, like having a black belt in karate to something), looks like every common room you can think of. It is known, with a wearying lack of originality, as The Leaky Cauldron.

Stackable chairs, battered melamine tables stained with coffee rings and a servery that doles out drinkable coffee, appalling tea, halfway decent meals and some of the most unappetising snacks that you can imagine. Not that you'll ever see an active mage who is anything more than slightly tubby – casting spells relies on energy from the mage themselves, so you can eat like a tunnelling machine and not put on any weight. And that's my excuse and I'm sticking to it.

My little group, not that they are 'mine' in any meaningful sense, are connected at a very deep level even for mages, so we all felt it when Clara started to go again. Sam sat by her to reinforce the familiar, Amy applied a spell called *lasaitu*, which is a kind of tranquilizer, while I went to get help.

It arrived in the form of the head of the Nottingham college, Professor Terry-Anne Wicks. She's American, which isn't her fault, and Professor Gowan, the boss of the earth Talents, who is extremely Scottish. We'd briefed them about the situation in advance, of course, so they brought a Healer with them, a wispy sort of chap called Bo Hinxman.

Apparently it's short for Baudelaire, so you can see why his boyfriend insists he shortens it. I have a blurred memory of an inadvisable amount of beer one evening and him applying a hangover cure the next morning that was so powerful that I managed to stay awake through an entire lecture on the protocols for dealing with restricted interaction with civilian authorities in non-emergency situations, which is normally more effective than a tranquilizer dart in the neck.

We got Clara to the college medical section and made her comfortable, and then the professors got to work. It was disconcerting, even for us; they just stood by the bed with their fingers tips touching Clara's head, while Bo monitored her vitals from a little way off by more conventional methods. There were a lot of magical control systems in the medical section, but despite that it looked uncannily like the ward she had been in at the Queen's Medical Centre.

Clara, by now almost entirely asleep, shifted uncomfortably and then began to talk in a voice entirely unlike her own. It wasn't long before I saw that the dragon tattoo on her left arm was glowing, a sign that she's drawing directly on the power of the earth, which doesn't happen very often. Then the much smaller one on my forearm started to hurt too. It felt like someone was using a pull-through on my arm bones. I started to sweat.

Clara began speaking, but it wasn't her speaking, if you see what I mean. "I will not lose what is mine." There was a pause. The voice was harsh and somehow metallic, the words hesitant but imbued with enormous power. "I will not permit her to be taken."

By now Professor Gowan was breathing as hard as if she had sprinted a mile, and Professor Wicks was shaking. Bo was frowning because the monitors now suggested that Clara's temperature was -30°c, her pulse was over 250 beats per minute and her blood pressure was comparable to the centre of the sun. I ignored them as the words echoed in my head, just half a beat behind Clara's voice.

"I will not suffer this." Now the voice was filled with so much anger that I felt like hiding. "There cannot be another. The *ahots* and the *ahots* will not be taken from me. I will not... permit." I was light headed, full of fury and acid determination and oh so very much power. "I will *deuseztatu*."

As Clara cried out in pain I felt a shaft of agony run up my left arm and we both passed out.

*

I have no intrinsic aversion to medical facilities, other than that you have to be ill or have snapped something to take up residence in one. I have been to several, usually in a horizontal position, and however brilliant the staff are the best thing about those places is the prospect of leaving.

I managed to get cleared to leave medical fairly quickly but Clara didn't nor, scarily, did Amy. Clara was profoundly unconscious, almost comatose, her brain activity not much more than a torpid trickle, so they'd asked for a specialist Healer to look after her. Amy, who had passed out at the same time, was sleepy and confused, and her neural traces were abnormally sluggish. The Healers couldn't work out why they had both been affected at the same time, unless Amy had been pushing *Indar* into Clara when it had happened, which was possible.

Professor Wicks tried to get me to leave, as did Professor Gowan, but Sam didn't bother to even try - she just sat with me as I watched and waited. The pain in my left arm faded to merely very fucking bad, but I barely noticed. Pain is an old friend, or maybe a familiar enemy, to be greeted with resignation rather than panic.

The hospital rooms were just like any others I could think of, smelling of antiseptic, sweat and oddly, cinnamon. Amy was very still, far more still than she is when she's sleeping normally. All right, I'll admit it, sometimes when I'm wakeful I'll get out of bed and just sit and watch her sleeping. She sleeps beautifully, her face soft and young, and she rarely snores. Shut up laughing.

Bo had stepped back from them when the senior Healer, Dr Steph Collingham, arrived. Most senior Healers are also doctors and I gathered that she was *Jaun* 6, so very powerful and very skilled and Bo told me that she normally worked as a senior consultant at a hospital in Manchester. Before she arrived I had been firmly but politely ejected, and I wasn't allowed back in until after she had left, so I got all my information from Bo who seemed to like her, or possibly was frightened of her.

Our fear was that Clara was in a fugue, a state of withdrawal into the mages' *gogoan*, their own mental realm, from which they never, ever, recover. I was relieved beyond measure that Steph was confident that it wasn't a fugue. She didn't know what it was, but it wasn't a fugue. Definitely. That should have been a relief, like waking up on a freezing cold morning and realising its Sunday and you don't have to get up, if I'd been sure I could believe her.

People came and went, testing everything for some clue about what had happened. I felt nothing magical, but I rarely feel anything magical these days. It's because of some unwelcome things that had happened to me in the soaking heat of the previous summer, a summer that was now a distant and precious memory in this time of icy winds and machine-gun hailstorms. I no longer have access to any significant magical power because I am stuck between two conditions. Liminal states have always fascinated me, but this was just a monumental pain in the arse.

I was a *Jaun* 5 earth Talent but then I had become *euste*, which is not the same as a 'eunuch', thank you very much. Then an accident took away even that, and I became *isilak* (which loosely translates as 'silent'). This is someone who is so imbued in magic that they probably glow in the dark but they have no access to it apart from some very basic stuff that most mages can do by reflex. So maybe a little bit like a eunuch after all.

It's like, if it's like anything, no longer being able to feel the temperature on your skin. You're aware that you should be feeling something but the somehow the message just isn't getting through. I am probably the most powerful utterly powerless mage you'll ever meet, and it's a horrible state to be in, like a world-class sprinter suddenly confined to a wheelchair. It's so frustrating that even beer won't cure it, and that's saying something.

It was Sam who noticed the change to the tattoo on my arm. She saw it before I did because she's my *erdikide* and not because I wouldn't notice a brass band standing behind me playing Wagner when I'm worried about Amy. Honest.

She touched my arm, and for a second I thought she was trying to hold my hand. "Your dragon," she said, bending her gaze to my forearm.

I looked at it. Normally the tattoo, a flowing shape in a style like the Uffington White Horse, suggested rather than stated a coiled Chinese dragon. The sinuous dark purple lines occasionally glow when the light is dim, but now they were ash grey shading into silver, and with no power in them. I showed this to Bo, and he checked Clara's. It was the same.

"That would do it," said Bo. "I've been talking to your professors and I understand how profound your connection to the Dragon is. The fact that it's been the thick end of two years since it was created means it's fully integrated by now, as much a part of Clara as her bones and blood. To have that forcibly removed would be very traumatic and that could easily explain her current state."

"Removed?"

"Yes. Her connection to the Dragon has been disrupted. That's probably what's behind all this." He gestured to Clara, who was blinking torpidly.

"How?"

"No idea."

"So what can I do?"

"Go and find out why the connection has been broken and re-establish it. There's nothing you can do here." Bo rested his hand on my shoulder reassuringly. "I don't want you to worry about her – I'm doing enough of that for all of us."

*

There was only one place to go: The home of the Dragon, the place where we first met it. If the solution to this lay anywhere, it had to be there.

I should say that it isn't actually a dragon, as in a big scaly lizard that farts and eats sheep; that's just the image that's applied to this particular quasi-conscious manifestation of an elemental force. It just wouldn't be the same if was a pelican or a woodlouse, would it?

We had first encountered it about two years before at Rockingham Castle, which overlooks a wide river valley not far from Corby. It's a beautiful pile of stones commissioned by William the Bastard and occupied pretty much continuously ever since. And just to cement it into history, it's on the top of an Iron Age hillfort that was later used by the Saxons. After it was modernised in the late 14th century – the term 'modern' is quite a flexible one in Britain - it housed nearly 3,000 people. It's no wonder the magic was so strong there – at the time the 4,000 acre estate was at the heart of the then largest forest in England, and forests have a great deal of power of their own.

The castle is one of the 'places of power' that are scattered around the country. They are in locations like St Paul's Cathedral in London, the island of Lindisfarne, the cathedral at Southall, southern parts of the Lake District, the Norfolk coast, the stone circle at Avebury and so on. They are in any place where the natural magic of the earth is more accessible and more open to direct contact. Nobody is clear why this happens where it does. Theories abounding, suggesting it could be anything from the local geology to the colour of the lord of the manor's socks.

But two years ago we'd needed a lot of power very quickly so Clara, *Jaun* level earth Talent, had made direct contact with the Dragon. The problem is that once you have that level of contact you can never break it – unless you're like me and you've had all of your magical circuits disabled. I hope it's temporary.

The castle was open to the public that day, which it isn't very often, and that meant that I could drive right up to the castle itself and get properly close to where the Dragon lives. The castle really is spectacular, with high walls, proper turrety turrets, a lovely rose garden, a genuine tilting field, the most wonderful view over the valley of the river Welland and a splendidly idiosyncratic tearoom. I sometimes think that if I could find the right door in the cellars I might be able to see the Dragon, curled up like a CGI image from a fantasy film. I don't know what the dragon's name is, but I'm pretty sure it won't answer to Viserion, Smaug, Eragon or bloody Toothless.

I know I drink too much coffee, and I certainly talk about it too much, but what I felt when I arrived made me really need one. The Dragon is the power at Rockingham, and it pervades every inch of the hill, the castle and it's grounds. It protects the area in all sorts of subtle but powerful ways, and I promise you would never want to pick a fight with it. Aura readers say that the castle looks like it has a golden volcano at its heart. Almost everyone can feel it, and earth Talents grow in power just by being there.

Clara's connection to the Dragon, which was the thing that woke the magic in her in the first place, is profound, although most of the time you wouldn't know it. They think as a pair, work as a pair, and fight as a pair, and sometimes they let me come along for the ride. It has become an essential, fundamental and irremovable part of her.

And it had vanished.

2

Which is, technically, impossible. Earth scientists - not the pseudo-scientific eco-green vegan Gaia mob, but the 'science is true even if you don't want to believe it' version - can tell you exactly how the earth creates power. The different rotational speeds of the liquid core and the solid core creates electro-magnetic energy. Magic, being a perfectly explainable physical phenomena, can be explained equally well.

I'm unclear why the power is stronger or more available in some places than others, but it's very definitely not because they are sacred sites. Quite the opposite in fact – places *become* sacred sites because the power is more easily accessible there.

Rockingham has been one of these places since forever, which is probably why the castle is there. I'd never heard of a place of power losing its energy, other than because of a major tectonic event like an earthquake or catastrophic subsumption. A flood that leaves a lot of standing water can also do it, but it usually recovers when it dries out. Even though this was one of the wettest and coldest autumns on record and the countryside around the castle was well soggy, there hadn't been a flood or an earthquake, so I doubted that this was a natural effect.

It was also clear that this was way beyond something I could deal with by myself, or even bloody understand for that matter, so I wandered back to the car, found a seat out of the glacial wind and called Richard Slater. He's one of the trio that are in charge of the Central College in London and so, notionally at least, all the mages in the country. It doesn't actually work like that, but never mind.

Richard told me to go home and that he would get some sort of expert to contact me as soon as possible. Instead I went to see how Clara and Amy were doing, because that was way better than going to an empty farmhouse.

*

They were coping… differently. Amy was better, in fact almost recovered. This meant her being cross with whoever had hurt Clara and threatening dire consequences. I used to describe her as a psycho in training, and being stuck with an idiot like me hasn't ameliorated that one bit.

Clara was still unconscious but was resting more easily than before. Her tattoo was still greyed out like buttons you can't press on a computer screen, and just as frustrating. Despite the improvement, Bo and other Healers had made it quite clear that Amy would not be coming home tonight, and probably not for even longer.

I stayed with her for ages, because nothing promotes recovery like having your boyfriend hanging around like a bad smell, getting in the way of the nursing staff and annoying everybody.

Clara's parents had visited her, of course, but couldn't offer much more than moral support. Her mum, who is a senior radiologist at the hospital in Corby, had no illusions about how little we knew, but accepted our assurances that we would tell them as soon as anything happened.

Eventually it was Amy who sent me home, citing the need for me to make sure the house was all right, and because she needed to sleep. I don't think the last was true; I think she just wanted to be rid of me. Bo was certainly relieved when I left. I didn't sleep very well that night.

*

The earth power expert arrived at college the next morning, bringing with him some of the strongest autumn snow showers in a decade, yet more of the irrational weather patterns that climate change continues to cause. I just hoped it didn't get any worse.

I was the first one to meet the expert, and he struck me as odd straight away. He looked 18 going on 35 and train spotters would have described him as boring, even if they could remember what he looked like. His clothes were unremarkable with shoes that were only vaguely polished and hair was smoothed down with a colourless, odourless product. Even his glasses were plain, with suspiciously low power lenses. In fact he looked so unremarkable that I knew that he must have done it deliberately.

"Hello," I said.

"Mike Frost?" I nodded. "Oliver Gunn." His grip was strong and dry, but also brief and insincere. "Shall we get on?"

Oliver, it turned out, was a senior earth Talent who specialised in places of power and the ways that mages interact with them. I had thought, if I'd thought about it at all, that what Clara had was unique, or damn near. I said so.

"She's not unique, no," he said slowly. "Very, very unusual, but not unique." Even his voice was grey, and he looked like his smiling muscles had atrophied with underuse.

"So what about people like me, who are just ligging on to the connection?"

"Honestly I have no idea. You are an anomaly because I haven't heard of anyone doing something like that before, at least not to this extent, and certainly not without them being *erdikide*."

"Do you know how it happened?"

"I didn't come all this way to talk about you," he said. I couldn't help but feel slightly offended. "I'd like to see Clara."

"Sure." I took him up to her room and watched carefully while he looked at her. Bo Hinxman had come in with us because Clara was in such a fragile state that nobody was allowed to be in there without a Healer being present. Oliver touched her hand for a moment and then brushed his fingers over the tattoo on her arm. It seemed to twist under his touch, almost as if it were in pain, and the greyness faded where his fingers rested but reasserted itself when he moved his hand.

She stirred but didn't wake and her face changed as the tension drained out of her body. Amy, drowsing in the next bed, woke with a gasp. I leant over and squeezed her hand as another Healer came in to see to her.

Meanwhile the little grey man had finished. Clara's colour slowly improved and her breathing became easier, becoming much more like natural sleep than the dragging torpor of illness or the numbness of exhaustion.

"She should rest better now," said Oliver. "Part of her mind was constantly searching for the Dragon; I've stopped her doing that."

"You've broken the connection?" I was startled – I didn't think that was possible, and I had been trying my damnedest to restore it.

"No, nobody has ever managed to do that. I've just stopped her searching for the dragon, that's all."

"I see," said Bo. "Is there anything else you can…?"

"Perhaps. I have several things I need to do as soon as I can." He steered me firmly out of the room and I didn't have a choice because his grip was like iron. I managed to stop in the reception area of the medical centre by pulling out of his grip and turning to face him.

Reception was a small space with a desk, a lot of phones and a bank of computer screens which were displaying a variety of things, all slightly worrying. Because being a mage is often hazardous to your health, and occasionally very hazardous, all colleges have well equipped medical facilities. Ordinary schools used to have the nurse's room, where poorly pupils would be taken to be treated for nosebleeds or wasp stings until their parents could collect them. This was the equivalent, but for mages who have accidently re-wired their neural circuitry, set fire to their hair or frozen some part of their anatomy. These are common problems, especially with first year students. I still have shiny burn scars on the back of my hand and one eyebrow that's a mite shorter than the other.

"Mike," said Oliver firmly, "I need three things. The first is that I need a shower – I drove up from Bristol this morning and the heater in my car is either on full blast or it's completely off. I really need to wash and change."

"No problem."

"Second, I need tea and something to eat."

"We can do that."

"And thirdly I need to visit the source of the power."

"Now?" It was mid-afternoon, already coming dark and the castle is the fat end of 50 miles away.

"No," he said after a moment. "Tomorrow will do." He made it sound like a magnanimous concession.

"Good. Have you got somewhere to stay?"

"Yes."

"OK, shower then." I took him to the changing rooms, pointed out the route to the common room, told him I'd meet him there and then went back to be with Amy. She was asleep again, but now a much more natural asleep.

Bo was reassuring. "Whatever the problem was, it's stopped. She's just asleep now, but it's taken a lot out of her. Normally I would ask her *erdikide* to give her some *indar*, but... well, not in this case."

"Can someone else do it?"

"Of course, and it's already been done. All being well she should be able to go home tomorrow. Or possibly the next day," he added. I nodded. The farm where we live is a good place for quiet recuperation, and Bo knew it – he had been at our housewarming and had displayed an alarming fondness for cocktails like Manhattans and Corpse Revivers and, the next morning, paracetamol.

"How about Clara coming home?"

"I don't know, but it certainly won't be soon. She's suffered significant harm and we must give her time to heal. She is really unwell." Bo is a proper doctor, so I had no doubt that he was right.

"Can she stay with us, or will she need to be somewhere special?"

He thought for a moment. "There's no reason why she can't go to the farm. There is no gross physical damage that needs a mundane hospital to fix." Mundane, in this context, meant non-magical. "Don't worry, we'll contact you straight away if there are any changes. Her parents are coming back later," he added. Mages getting damaged is fairly common because magic is dangerous all the time and very dangerous far too often.

When I got back to the common room I couldn't see the little grey man, but there was an unfamiliar face behind a stack of food big enough to feed Sam for about a week. It was quite a transformation - Oliver now looked about the same age as me, with spiky hair, a diamond stud in his ear, jeans, no glasses and a t-shirt with a picture of Karl Marx on it and the legend 'I told you this would happen'.

"Sit," he said around a mouthful of something. "Coffee." He pointed to a mug on the table opposite him.

I sipped it. Just how I like it. "How did you know…?"

"I didn't. They did." He gestured to the staff behind the counter and one of them smiled at me. Clever sod.

"So why the disguise?"

"I needed you to take me seriously."

"Why did you think we wouldn't?" He been sent as an expert to assist, so this puzzled me.

He snorted around a mouthful of sandwich. "Looking like this?"

"So why did you go so far the other way?" It seemed like a very odd thing to do. "Why not go with smart casual or something like that?"

He snorted again. "Smart casual doesn't cut it, so I use the grey man when I'm in a new place because someone with my skills can't look like this. People expect me to be older and have more gravitas. To be more boring and conventional. More… traditional."

"Tradition is just peer pressure from dead people," I said, more for want of something to say. Obviously Oliver Gunn had a fucking great chip on his shoulder about something, and I just didn't want to get involved in it. All I wanted him to do was fix Clara and then piss off.

He pushed one plate away and grabbed another. This one had three pastries on it, one of which I stole. Yes, it was a challenge. He looked cross for a moment but then it faded. "What level are you?" I asked.

"Six." I nodded. That made him one level higher than I would have been if my magic had been working. Mages are graded as students (*Iksale*) from 1 to 10, then *Ikasberri*, the single apprentice grade, and then the *Jaun* levels, which are the 'master' grades. I was *Jaun* 5, the same as Sam, Amy and Clara. You might not believe it, but we're actually good at this.

Real magic isn't 'wave a wand and fix everything' like in Harry Potter. It's complicated and often hard to do and at higher levels, or when it's much more complicated, it rarely does exactly what you want and often just plain doesn't work. It can also be rewarding, and occasionally it's a lot of fun.

"So what are you going to do now?"

He slurped his tea and belched slightly. "That's better. I had breakfast before I came, at about 5 o'clock this morning, and I didn't managed to get much lunch, so I was fucking starving. Tell me about the Dragon."

So I told him about Amy being kidnapped and how we'd needed to access a much more powerful source of magic to find her. He nodded. "It's frequently something like that, often when someone is lost or needs medical help beyond what is available," he said. "From what I understand the Dragon could well be the most powerful direct source of magic in the country. That is going to make this interesting, and potentially difficult."

"Why difficult?"

"Because I have to make at least some connection to it before I can help Clara."

I nodded. He'd obviously read the report that we'd eventually written. "Do you have to go to the exact site to make the connection?"

"No," said Oliver. "'Close enough' seems to be good enough."

"And how close is that?"

He nearly rolled his eyes. "Depends on the strength of the source and skill of the mage, of course."

"And how long does the link last?"

"That depends on the thing that you're trying to make contact with."

I sighed. I'm not a fan of that much imprecision. "No, not getting that."

"Well, the energy at Lindisfarne, for example, appears as a protective dome, so an abstraction, so although you can draw on it for power you can't get very much." I wasn't so sure about this – we'd been to Lindisfarne not long before and the amount of power there had been prodigious.

"What Clara is connected to is a personification, which is where the power seems to have sentience. It's unclear if it actually does, because we've never got one to hold still long enough to do the Turing Test. The mage and the source develop a relationship of sorts, which makes the link much more long lasting and harder to break. Lifelong, usually." He paused for a moment. "Some of us think that it means that the power source can also be drawn on by other mages without the connected mage coming to any permanent harm." He used the word 'permanent' in a way that suggested it wasn't of much importance.

I grunted. "The evidence suggests otherwise, in this case at least."

He shrugged. "Well, we're still working on that part of the theory. These events further support for that point of view," he added as Professor Wicks joined us at the table.

"Hello Oliver," she said. She didn't seem overly pleased to see him, but it's hard to tell with her some times.

"Hello Professor. He's got himself a load of troubles, hasn't he?" He gestured toward me with a Belgian bun, shedding pastry and sticky white icing over the table.

"Yes, and it ain't for the first time neither." My – our – rise through the grades from the lower *Iksale* levels to the dizzying heights of the middle *Jaun* ranks had been frankly meteoric - things catching fire, animals fleeing, dinosaurs dying out, that kind of stuff - so we were still catching up on all the background developments that would have come naturally if we'd got there at a more normal rate. The fact I was also an unresolved *isilak* turned something that was already tricky into something potentially very dangerous.

"So what have I done now?" I asked.

"You ain't done anything," said Terry-Anne. "It's just that what's hurting Clara is also hurting you." I made to protest, to deny it, but she stilled me with a gesture.

"You also have the problem," interjected Oliver, "that you've got this huge reserve of magical power building up inside you, and you've no outlet."

This was true. People who are magically capable but don't know that they are, of which there are a surprisingly large number, can cause weird effects when they 'leak'. I was, not to be too graphic, magically constipated, and when it let go it was likely to be spectacular.

"Am I going to explode or something?"

"I don't know," said Oliver. "It might be that once you've got all the power you can hold you'll stop producing it, or that the pressure will keep of building until something gives," he finished, sounding slightly smug.

"And you guys don't know."

"Nope," said Terry-Anne. "Even Gronk can't find anything other than unreliable hearsay and folk memory." Folk memory, in this context, means something that someone made up a long time ago, as opposed to rumour and speculation, which are things that people have made up quite recently.

Gronk is our fairly newly installed college librarian *cum* archivist *cum* brainbox of the first water. Even though he's from Norfolk his name is something polysyllabically Germanic which nobody but he and Sigrún, our senior air Talent, can pronounce. She's from Iceland, and if you can pronounce that then German is a breeze. We just call him Gronk, with such invective or pejorative additions as the circumstances warrant.

"That is not reassuring," I said.

She grunted, like a distant warthog after a dodgy piece of fruit. "I ain't trying to reassure you Mike, I'm trying to warn you. And him," she added, glancing at Oliver.

"Why does he need to know that I'm both powerless and likely to explode at any moment?" I was trying for irony, but Professor Wicks didn't notice. Americans tend not to be too good with that sort of thing.

She sighed. People do that a lot when I'm being gloomy or obtuse or, for some reason, telling jokes. "You're a clever bloke Mike," she said, "for all that sometimes you're as thick as a bucket of porridge. Your value right now is your knowledge, not your ability to do magic. Some of the things you've done…"

"And screwed up," I added bitterly.

Terry-Anne looked at me steadily. "Oliver," she said, not even glancing at him, "could you give us a moment please?"

"Why?"

She glared at him until he left then sat down, looking at me curiously. "So, ya feeling useless again?" I could have cried. Professor Wicks is the head of the whole of the Nottingham college, which is one of the top five schools of magic in the UK and the top twenty in Europe. So pastoral care for individual students is way down on her list of priorities, only slightly above making sure the toilets are cleaned and the bins are emptied.

"I should be *Jaun* 5 now, which is a higher level than I ever dreamed I could achieve," I began.

"Really? I always had you tagged to be at least *Jaun* 4."

I smiled bleakly. "Then all that stuff with Professor Weaver happened." She nodded, tactfully not mentioning that I'd had to kill one of her senior lecturers. "And everything has just gone to rat shit ever since."

"It's a point of view," she replied carefully. "Why do you say that?"

"Because I should be helping Clara, using my knowledge to establish what's wrong with her and what I can do to fix it. But I can't do a bloody thing."

"Is that why you've been so down recently?" She sighed. "Other people are dealing with it Mike. It doesn't always have to be you, even if it makes you feel guilty when it isn't. But I get that it's frustrating."

"Very."

She thought for a moment. "When was the last time you went to karate?"

"Couple of weeks." Couple of months, actually.

"Go to the next class. Smash some bricks or summat. That hollow feeling in your gut is just the dregs of an adrenaline burden that you keep topping up on things you can't do anything about." It was my turn to grunt – I knew this even if I wasn't ready to admit it, even to myself. "And the fact that you've also lost contact with the Dragon, something which you seem to be trying to ignore, has got to be unsettling for you too."

"I just feel like I've done something wrong all the time."

"Oh, that's just normal randomised guilt," she said, waving it away with a faint grin, "'less you actually have, of course."

"That's not helpful."

"I know. But you've got to work with Oliver on this. However…" she trailed off. "If anyone can sort this crap out it's you two." She strode off, leaving me flat and confused. Oliver had vanished, so I tried to see Amy and Clara, but Bo told me to go away because they were both asleep and definitely wouldn't be coming home tonight.

I would have liked to stay with them, but I couldn't. I would have liked to stay with Sam, but I couldn't because she shares a house with her brother Zang Wei and his fiancé Lian. With everyone speaking Mandarin at full speed I get a headache in minutes just trying to keep up. I contemplated going to see mum and dad, but that would have meant spending the night in the same house as my brother Simon. Frankly I would rather drink lager and watch football than do that – and that's saying something.

So in lieu of an actual decision I went for a curry. I tend to go for the milder and more flavourful ones, what I call 'curry without consequences', but today that wouldn't be enough so I chose something that was described as 'strongly flavoured without too much chilli'. I was just becoming certain that I had found a non-surgical way of getting my tonsils removed when my book, which I had been reading as an alternative to thinking, was flipped shut without anyone touching it.

"Fuck me, you're a hard man to find," said the person who sat down opposite me. From his hair - which needed a wash - through his shirt which had seen better days - most of them that week - to his disreputable trainers, he was not someone it was easy to misidentify.

"Hello Gronk," I said warily. "Why are you trying to find me?"

"Sheesh, would you listen to this guy?" He said it to the room, but it paid no attention to him. "Why do ya think, ya lunk? I got some griff on what's been happening to your lady friends."

From the way he talks you'd think he came from the lower East Side of New York, but he's actually from a place in Norfolk he calls Dead-End-Next-The-Sea, a collection of boats and salt-blasted shacks on a mud flat halfway between Salthouse and Cromer.

"So what have you got?"

"Ya mean apart from a raging thirst?" I signalled the waiter, expecting Gronk to get a beer, but instead he ordered a whole meal and told them to stick it on my bill.

"So what have you got?" I repeated as he forensically disassembled half a chicken, baked red and spicy in a tandoor.

"I found two references to earth magic... stuff," he prevaricated. It doesn't do to admit that you're a mage in some places because you can't always be certain of the reaction. Although the curry shop wasn't crowded there certainly were people within earshot and he wasn't talking any more quietly than usual.

"Was that in the third or fifth edition of the Dungeon Master's Guide?" I asked, slightly too loudly, and suddenly everyone assumed we were talking about Dungeons and Dragons or some other MMRPG. Now we could be completely open because they think we're nerds rather than mages. I'm not quite sure which is worse.

"That was clever," he said after a moment, thankfully a bit more quietly. "Anyways, the first was from the time of Elizabeth the First, her of the red hair and famously grumpy dad; ya know her?"

"Not personally."

"You're funny, you know that? Anyways," he went on, pulling a sliver of chicken out of his teeth, "this was a guy called Maskelyne."

"Now him I've heard of."

"Not his one you ain't. This is the famous one's some-number-of-greats grandfather. He was supposed to have had protection against the 'malignities of the universe' because of a ring he had brought 'from a mountebank in the Roman city of Vannes.' Leastways that's his version. I suspect he nicked it."

"So why does this…?"

"There's an account in *Diversis Rebus Magicis*. It isn't quite clear, but it mentions a couple of things that could be relevant." *Diversis Rebus Magicis* is one of the oldest, most comprehensive and least reliable books on magic that has survived from the 16th century. It's also written in not very good Latin.

"Is it reliable?"

He snorted. "Not even remotely. But John Damysell, the bloke who wrote it, didn't have the imagination to make up most of this stuff. You can tell the bits that he did invent 'cos they're loaded with sea monsters and maenads and arse-licking about the queen." He snorted. "Didn't do him no good anyhow."

"What happened to him?"

"The *Diversis* said that he was 'cruelly slain by sorcerous magics that '*ignem in animo*,' which roughly translates as 'put fire into his mind'."

"Stroke?"

"Nah. There are court records that say he was discovered in a 'most improper state' with Harriet, his housemaid, and his wife stabbed him through the eye with a poker straight out of the fire."

I laughed. I shouldn't have done, but I did. "So what did the adulterous Mr Damysell have to say about the unlamented Mr Maskelyne?"

Gronk started on the next dish, something I couldn't identify which smelled like liniment and looked like luminous green wallpaper paste.

"'Upon no sound cause the ring did one day cease to function, giving much distress to Mr Maskelyne. He said that it had been but one day since he had met a *homo diversae cognitionis* – 'a person of diverse knowledge' – who had given great interest to the matter of the ring'."

"Right. Er... do you think you could stop quoting the Latin – you know perfectly well that I don't understand it. We both know that you're smarter than I am."

He grinned. I reckon Gronk is about 35, so maybe ten years older than me, but he dresses in jeans and a hoodie like a teenager and has the hairstyle of someone who hasn't noticed that he's thinning on top. I don't really care about most of that but he will not be permitted a comb-over. I am prepared to put up with a lot for other people but I will not give myself a hernia trying not to laugh every time I see him.

"Yeah, whatever. Anyway there's only one other reference to this here person. He uses the term *'magicae fur'*, which could be a 'magic thief', someone who uses magic to steal things, or it could be someone who steals magic. I reckon we gotta think it's the second."

"So there was a person who drained the magic from a static shield generator. That's not really..."

He held up one finger. I waited. He belched and then drank more beer. "Damysell quoted Maskelyne, who he did actually meet, who described the person as *'divinum esse'*. His Latin is well dodgy, but that roughly translates as 'a divine being'."

"Maybe he was talking about the lovely Harriet?"

"Ya trying to be funny again Mikey?"

"No Gronk."

"That's the general term that Queen Lizzie's people used to describe a mage."

"Who drained a protection ring," I added impatiently. This sort of thing is not uncommon – a ring, necklace, bracelet or whatever holds the spell in a kind of statis until the mage, who doesn't even have to be wearing it, puts power into it. It's like a torch – it retains the capacity to create light, but doesn't actually do so until a battery is installed and it's switched on.

"Nah, that ain't it." He looked at me. "I ain't gonna get into all the details right now, but the term 'malignancies of the universe' was used for everything from bad luck, peculiar diseases and smelly feet to thinning hair, being attacked by footpads and losing your shirt playing cards. It ain't stuff that a shield spell would be able to do anything about."

I nodded. If this was earth power protection it was the Lindisfarne model rather than the Rockingham version. "He got it in Vannes…" My grasp of French geography is far from firm, but this rang a bell. "That's near… oh, Carnac, of course." Carnac is one of the strongest places of power in the world – with vast and ancient stone alignments that were erected in antiquity to control and direct the rampant energy. If that ring – the equivalent of Clara's tattoo, I suppose – was connected to that then he would be immune to buildings landing on him, let alone any tonsorial inconvenience. "What about the other one?"

"This is where it gets real interesting. This is a later record, from around 1650, from the Welsh Marches."

"You're not going to starting talking Middle Welsh at me are you?"

"You gotta be kidding me. I don't speak Welsh."

"Me neither."

"It was written in Latin too," he said smugly.

"Oh do fuck off Gronk. What have you found?"

"Won't."

"Gronk, there's many a time that a man's mouth broke his nose," I said wearily.

"You ain't no kind of fun no more," he replied, sticking his bottom lip out in a dramatic manner. He looked like one of those Amazonian tribesmen doing the whole 'disc in the lip' thing that makes you wonder how they eat without dribbling.

"I bought you dinner," I said, gesturing at the field of debris in front of him.

"Oh, all right then. The document is a load of notes and journal entries compiled by a doctor who retired to Wales in later life. He told this stories to a local magistrate who wrote it all down and from the way it was written I suspect it was over several glasses of port. His name was Octavius Bush."

"Seriously?"

"Different times buddy, different times. Anyway, Dr Bush was treating the Earl of Easterholt, a man he described as being of 'dissolute and inappropriate habits'. The Easterholt account books suggested he was trying make his way through the family fortune as fast as possible. He spent three quarters of it in five years on wine, women and song."

"What did he do with the rest?"

"I suspect he wasted it." He delivered this line with a perfectly straight face. "The problem was that the Earl – one Nathaniel Carlton – signally failed in his efforts to dissipate himself to death, and the good doctor couldn't work out how the hell he'd managed it."

"Solid yeoman stock?"

"Carlton had what was probably TB when he was a child and he wasn't expected to live into his twenties. He was nearly fifty when he called on the doctor to deal with a troublesome bunion."

At this point we were interrupted by a waiter, who offered us the opportunity to either order something else or piss off. I paid the bill, which made my eyes water more than the curry had, and we took ourselves to a bar where the music wasn't quite loud enough to make your ears bleed.

"So what happened to the Earl?"

"According to the good doctor Carlton was fine unless he left the area around Easterholt for too long," he said, making inroads into yet another pint. "If he got more than about ten miles away he became ill and weak and prone to fits of mania and melancholy."

"What was the house called, Ballybran?"

"Easter Lodge," he said, sounding puzzled. "Does it matter?"

"Never mind. Was the source of the earth power the house itself?"

"Somewhere near the house rather than the house itself, but yes. Somehow Carlton, who otherwise showed all the magical talent of a shoe box, had managed to get himself attached to it."

"And I'm guessing that the source of the power dried up and he died."

"Not quite." Gronk took a long pull on his pint - and I took a small sip of my orange juice. He lives staggering distance away, but I still had to drive home. Then he held up his glass, which was empty, so I got it refilled. This was hard work, because Gronk was milking this for all it was worth. Next time, he'd be paying.

"Enlighten me Gronk," I said, holding the pint out of his reach, "before you're too pissed to make sense."

"Oh all right." I wouldn't say he was steaming drunk but he certainly wasn't sober, and the lower East Side accent had faded into something that definitely had wisps of straw in it. I didn't know why he wanted to sound like a New York wide boy, but it's less weird than some things that I've seen mages do.

"But by then the Earl of Easterholt had nothing left but a pile of bad debts, the home farm and a country house in an advanced state of crumbling, located somewhere south of Newstead Abbey. So he sought out a 'cunning man' to help, I 'spect because he wanted to be able to flee his creditors without dying before he crossed the channel."

"OK."

"The 'cunning man', who was actually a woman named Joyce de Despenser, told him that his soul was 'inextricably entwined with the land' and only by severing the connection would he be free to leave."

"Oh, I get it. He was so strongly connected that once he was out of range…"

"Yeah. Nowadays we train people how to connect to the earth without becoming a bound-in part of the matrix. It means they can move around freely." I vaguely remembered doing that in the first year at college. They had explained to us why it was necessary, but when you're new a lot of the things that the professors say sound like someone translating Chaucer using a Japanese-Arabic dictionary. I hadn't really understood what they were getting so het up about it, let alone why I needed to do it, but the professors still made sure we did it. OK, so now I got it.

"But he didn't have that."

"Nope. So now you know why hermits have to stay in one place for decades – they can't leave."

"Is that true?"

"No idea – I just made it up, but it sounds reasonable."

I resisted the urge to sigh at this classic Gronk-ism. "So what happened to the Earl in the end?"

"The cunning woman promised that she could detach him from the power by means of a ritual. An expensive ritual, as it turned out."

"Do I smell a rat?"

"Maybe not as much as you think. de Despenser did perform a ritual – we got no details of it – but instead of detaching him from the power she appears to have broken the link by stopping the power almost completely."

"She killed a place of power? Fuck me – I didn't think that was possible."

"I've only found references to something like that happening two other times, and I ain't entirely sure 'bout either of them. But here it something definitely happened because the Earl was able to leave the area without falling ill. He was real happy 'bout that."

"So what happened to the Earl and the power?"

"Well, his Earlishness had got so used to being invulnerable that he didn't adjust his lifestyle. He died, probably of alcoholic hepatitis, about a year later, whilst on a spectacular bender in Cheltenham, of all places."

I nodded. He didn't notice. "And the power?"

"It got moved, but I the 'cunning man' didn't do a very good job because there are some accounts that suggest that a little bit got left behind."

"Moved? Someone told me that the power comes from where it does for mostly geological reasons. Is that not right?"

"Yeah, well, you would think that."

I sighed. I was getting a headache. "Why don't *you* think that, Gronk?"

"Earth Talents have never understood how these places are created."

"True, but I'm not an earth Talent," I said. I wished I could have that drink now, because that had reminded me that I have all the magical power of a hat stand, and that I was going home to an empty house. I knew I was tired because the second half of the thought left tears touching my eyes.

"No, you're *isilak*, which makes you I don't know fucking what," he replied. "You're the only one I've even met." He drank more beer, blinking owlishly.

"What happened to the power Gronk?" He held up his empty glass. "No more refills until you tell me."

"Maybe I won't tell you unless you do." He was definitely sounding a bit slurred.

"Maybe I'll come round your house at 6 o'clock tomorrow morning with three road drills and a brass band."

"It vanished," he said heavily, "and then it reappeared."

"Where?"

"Southwell Minster. That's why they built it there."

"How? Was it immediate?"

"Don't know and no. It seemed to take a couple of years, or possibly slightly longer."

"Is there a ritual that allows you to relocate a place of power?"

"Yup."

"But you don't know what it is?"

"Nope."

I sat back. It sounded like someone had rediscover the ritual and was using it to try to move the Dragon, or steal the Dragon, and they were trying to cut the connection to me and Clara so that they could. But the Dragon had objected.

I finished my drink, bought Gronk another pint and walked back to the car. The air was cold and sharp, and it woke me up. Before now we'd dealt with someone who had created a magical source of power that didn't work properly, and when he decided he wanted to misuse it for his own ends he killed people to keep it to himself. That hadn't ended well for anyone.

And then just a couple of months ago there was a mage who was losing his power because of something he didn't understand. He did whatever he could to get it back, up to and including theft, murder and betraying his wife. It had been like watching an aging actor reaching for the Botox because he had bought into the delusion that it made him look better. It hadn't worked out for him either.

But this was something else, something really big and serious, something that could be a problem for a lot of people, especially if it got out of hand. There were so many questions – like how it was done; were they intending to move just the Dragon or would they go for other things later, and, of course, why were they doing it? None of which I had the slightest clue about, of course. All I knew for sure is that it threatened Clara and, to a lesser extent, the rest of us. Big picture be blowed - they had made it about Clara, so this was now personal.

I don't really remember the drive home, just the dark tunnel between the hedges and the flurries of snow that streaked past as I drove. It looked like I was jumping into FtL travel in the Millennium Flacon. There were lights on at the farm, but I already knew who was there, so I put my car in the barn next to the Vauxhall something or other that Sam was driving and she met me at the door. She knew I couldn't stay at her house and that I didn't want to be alone, so she'd come here.

When Professor Wicks was kind I had nearly cried. When Sam hugged me I did cry, and she held me until it passed, then gave me the stiff drink I'd needed ever since I'd found out that Amy wouldn't be coming home tonight. All this isn't as odd as it sounds to outsiders because magical partners have a connection between them that is profound. It isn't telepathy but they share feelings and certainties, fears and confusions. They can also transfer energy – *indar* – and keep each other strong when things get rough.

Erdikide live inside each other's heads and, however weird it sounds to outsiders, for mages it's completely normal. It's slightly awkward for Sam and I because my *erdikide* is not the same gender as me, which happens less than 0.01% of the time. So Sam is my *erdikide*, my magic partner, but not any other kind. Amy and Clara are magical partners, even though Amy and I are engaged, so I'm outnumbered by women most of the time. My friends Ambrose and Jerry try to help with that, mostly by dragging me to the pub.

That is what an *erdikide* is – they are the part of you that just knows, whatever it is. We talked for an hour, by which time it was nearly midnight, and she sent me to bed. I got reassurance from her and peaceful sleep from Amy, although Clara was still profoundly unconscious. I was still turning fretfully an hour or so later when I heard the bedroom door open and Sam came in.

"You sleep now," she said softly. "You need to sleep."

"I know," I said, my eyes stinging and gritty, "but my brain just won't shut up."

She climbed into the bed, held me close and kissed me, an intimacy that we didn't often share. As her lips lifted from mine I heard the word '*lo*', felt the powerful sleep spell land and the whole world went away.

3

The next day dawned far too bright, but thankfully not excessively early, and I was the first person awake. The whole world had gone white outside because the flurries I had seen on the drive home had become a major snowfall. The way it changed the world held me for a moment; fog hides but snow buries, a different way of making things not be there anymore.

In a fog you can feel that things are there, that if you can just get close enough you will be able to see it, but with snow you could be standing on it and still not be able to. It's a different kind of concealment, and the sudden realisation that 'hidden' doesn't always just mean 'hidden' struck me as idiotically profound, even though it's probably just profoundly idiotic.

I had too many thoughts and they were too confusing, so I needed to empty out my head. Lacking one of those magical washing up bowls that Dumbledore had, I wrote them down, a list of questions that I didn't have answers for, and scattered the paperwork across the big table. By the end of it there was one big, fairly obvious thing that wasn't clear - if you have the ability to move a place of power, where would you move it to?

Which led me on to why – not just 'why move it', but why move it to that particular place? Presumably because you wanted the power exactly where you wanted it, but the amount of effort involved meant that you must *really* want it to be there. It wouldn't be something you would do on a whim, unless you're a complete head case or you don't know what the word 'whim' means.

But I agreed with Gronk – I didn't know how places of power were created. If the cause was geological, then destroying them seemed impossible other than by a major event that even a numb-nut like me would notice. Sam, who I had left genteelly snoring, lent over my shoulder and hugged me while I scanned the pages. She chuckled.

"You look like my father used to," she said. "When he had to sort his schedules he would leave his papers everywhere. Drove my mother mad." Her father had been a distribution manager for a glass manufactory before his death, which was about a year before I first met her. "Very good. Makes sense. Any idea what's to do next?"

"Get Amy home, then see what we can do for Clara."

"No." She shook her head firmly. "Get the Dragon home. That's what's making all this happen. Clara and Amy are sick and you rattle like a dice box."

"How can we get the Dragon home? Rather, *can* we get it home?"

"Oliver says we can. Maybe not soon, but…"

"You've spoken to Oliver about it?"

She nodded. Her expression said 'of course, you idiot'. "When you were with Amy. He said it was possible, sometimes. He wasn't happy to talk about it, which was a bit odd. Jealous of his specialism perhaps? Afraid you might steal his lightning?"

I shrugged. "Gronk told me of a case, not far from here actually, where it took nearly two years for it to steady down."

"OK, so first we stop Dragon leaving, then we find out who behind this."

"Sounds like a plan."

She frowned. "It is a plan, silly."

She went off to take a shower while I called the college. Amy was still asleep but Bo said she was much better and needed no further intervention. They said they were glad about that because two second years had done something deeply unwise of a vaguely sexual nature with an icicle spell and they needed a lot of attention while they were being treated for frostbite of the extremities.

I also found out that Clara's condition hadn't improved, and that her extremely intermittent pseudo-boyfriend Ben had arrived from London. I decide to go down to the college but Sam wouldn't let me out of the house until I'd had a shower and some breakfast.

"Stinky boy, you shower now," she said, almost pushing me up the stairs. I left her melting the snow off the ramp that leads up to the front door, and then carefully drying the water that inevitably ended up on the floor inside. Slippery floors are a nightmare for Amy, with her dodgy hips, her sticks and her wheelchair, so we have to be very watchful. Her mobility is normally good enough that she can get herself upstairs to bed, albeit sometimes quite slowly, but we can't ever stop being careful.

I came down to toast and coffee, plus a large hug that set me up nicely for a day of worrying unnecessarily about things I couldn't change.

*

While all this was going on Oliver Gunn, without bothering to mention it to anyone, was doing something that Professor Wicks later described as 'unwise going on bloody stupid'.

Presumably thinking along the same lines as us, he had decided that someone was interfering with the Dragon. He concluded that part of the interference was being caused by whatever was trying to detach it from whatever was making it be where it originally was. So while I was with Amy and Clara he took himself off to Rockingham to see if he could work out what was happening.

The castle sits above the wide, damp valley of the river Welland, which is surmounted by a causeway that connects Rockingham to the village of Caldecott, barely over a mile to the north. The river normally wanders along its course in a fairly unobtrusive manner, but because of the persistent autumn rain which then got snowed on, the water level was very high and the causeway looked more like a floating pontoon.

From what we could piece together, Oliver had gone onto the castle lands and made his way the edge of the forest between the castle and the river and did… something. He had then made his way back to his car and started to cross the causeway, apparently at some speed. For some reason or other Oliver's car was knocked clear off the causeway by a lump of power the size of a small bus that rolled him over just as he was halfway across it.

Normally being turned upside down in a river is not good for your health, but thankfully Oliver didn't have to rely on just holding his breath. Even if semi-conscious, mages have a sort of protective bubble that they cast almost by instinct, with even the least levels of consciousness. Fortunately three vehicles behind him on the road was a large and powerful tractor that was carrying towing straps. The farmer managed to get one of them around the rear axle – the car caught on the river bank when it's spoiler dug in, so it was only partially submerged, and they'd dragged it clear of the water before Oliver ran out of air. The ambulance arrived not long after.

He ended up in hospital, soggy, frayed around the edges and unresponsive for no reason the doctors could work out. His car, rather predictably an electric blue Subaru Impreza with gold wheels, was taken to a scrapper.

*

While he was doing that I was getting things ready for Amy to come home. This meant bringing her clean clothes – yes, I thought of it this time – and being very patient while Bo finally conceded that some domestic recuperation would be better for her than clogging up one of the beds in the college medical centre.

Ben was there too, sitting by Clara's side, looking concerned. He is Scandinavian pale, even though he comes from Worcester or somewhere over that way, and he's a fire Talent who works at Central as a bodyguard *cum* fixer. We shook hands, but I couldn't think of anything to say that didn't seem obvious, fatuous or unhelpful.

I had thought that their very brief interaction last summer, which I don't think ever got further than a bit of surreptitious snogging, had been no more than that. But now he just kept turning up like a particularly persistent virus and I suspected that he wanted to get more serious – or at least more horizontal - but Clara was having none of it. She resisted his advances, often resorting to scorn as a defence against his insistence. She's far more powerful than he is, but as their Talents don't clash at least that side of things had been going fine so far. Sadly 'fine' is the best I could say for it, and I was certain it wouldn't last.

Bo told me that Amy had spent the night sleeping soundly, if not necessarily peacefully, and that she wasn't to exert herself much for a few days. Further, she was to avoid using magic because her injury had largely been caused by her being Clara's *erdikide*, so the more time she spent letting that particular wound heal the better. This was like telling someone with a broken leg to avoid walking, a bit of a 'no shit Sherlock moment', but I smiled and thanked him for his advice.

She seemed a bit washed out when we met in the entrance to the medical section. "You picked out these clothes, didn't you?"

I nodded. "I tried to bring things that would be comfortable." Her expression told me I'd done something wrong *again*. I was getting a bit fed up of it, to be honest.

"Hmm. A yellow sweatshirt with peach trousers?" I looked blank. "I sometimes wonder if you're colour blind or if you've just got no taste."

I felt all my energy drain away. "No dear, it's because I'm extremely fucking stupid. You obviously can't trust me to do anything right, so I'm going to dig a great big hole in the ground and hide in it."

I was suddenly really upset; I'd been awake half the bloody night, sick with worry, done my best to make everything as good as I could – there were even fresh flowers on the table at home – and I got criticism for a greeting. I could have said more, but words said in anger cannot always be repented at leisure, so I didn't.

Instead I walked off, leaving her standing flat-footed and astonished in the middle of the room, and the turning heads suggested that I might have said that a tiny bit too loud. I went down to one of the practise rooms, the magically shielded spaces in the basement that closely resemble a large school gym or a physiotherapists torture chamber.

I spent some time using the spell *zirta* to create sparks that circulated randomly around the room, generally referred to as 'sprites'. Then I employed tiny fireballs and other ballistic magic to knock them down, blow them up or otherwise inconvenience them in some way. I kept going, getting more violent, destructive and loud until I no longer had the urge to do it anymore. I felt like I'd been in there for days, but it was probably not much more than half an hour.

It wasn't until I left the room that it realised that, as an *isilak*, I shouldn't have been able to do any of that. As *euste* I can draw on another person's Talents, but being *isilak* meant that I shouldn't have been able to do any magic. There is a significant emotional content in magic, so I wondered if it only worked when I was angry, like the Incredible Hulk. I hoped I wouldn't have to do the whole turning green thing, because finding trousers that magically treble in size at just the right moment could be tricky. I hate shopping for clothes.

Out in the corridor I tried another sprite, to see if anything felt different in the casting, but nothing happened at all, which didn't improve my mood.

*

Amy found me sitting in the car, watching the snow and thinking about nothing that I'd care to repeat. She very quietly opened her door, put her bag on the back seat and then sat in the front next to me. There was a long, snowy silence. Eventually she stirred.

"Sorry," she said in a small, quiet voice that made her sound like a contrite six year old. I put the car in gear and took her home. I don't suppose we exchanged four words all the way, and once I'd put the car in the barn I went to bed – in Clara's room.

I was upset and exhausted and I had no idea how long it would take me to get to sleep. I couldn't expect Amy to use the couch, and I expected Sam to turn up later, so I was the one who had to be displaced so that nobody else would be inconvenienced. It felt like I came last and it always seemed to be that way. It's probably because I'm weak or insecure or not selfish enough, I suppose.

The room smelled of Clara, of clean hair and shea butter and that citrus perfume she likes. I don't think that Clara has ever been soppy or girly in her life, but that doesn't mean she can't be feminine when the mood is on her. She has dangly earrings, but they're made of barbed wire, and steel toe-capped boots with flowers painted on them. When she has cornrow plats in her hair they aren't lines of vegetables, they're ammunition belts. It will take a better person than Ben to make her happy, and his growing disgruntlement suggested he was finally realising that. I would take someone extraordinary to make her happy and I knew that, even if I were single, it couldn't be me. I fell asleep immersed in the smell of her.

Mages dream a lot – it's partly how we process our world and its extraordinary complexities. Some dreams are vague and silly, involving llamas with punk hairstyles, talking trees and being chased by a squad of cheerleaders made of chocolate – or is that just me? Others are sharp and vivid and so real that you think you could pick a flower in the dream and still have it in your hand when you wake up. I dreamt of Clara and the Dragon, which is a good name for a kid's book (a modest commission would be acceptable, cash in small denominations only), but thankfully without most of the extraneous rubbish that so often gets in the way.

Clara was in a pixelated landscape, one that was familiar without being exactly anywhere in particular. Hillside, river valley, causeway – you get the idea. She was trying to pull something out of the ground, or push something into it, but I couldn't quite make out what it was.

I guessed that she was trying to free the Dragon, who was trapped, or to remove something that was doing something to it. I'd expected a magical field or a spell or something along those lines, but what I saw in the dream was something silver, metallic, solid, a made thing. Dream Clara noticed me and came over; she looked pretty much like she always does, but with a tightness around the eyes crumpling her face in the way that I recognised as frustration and pain.

She looked back across the stylised landscape and indicated the shiny thing, then said something that sounded like *'danjé'*. I had no idea what that meant, or even if it was a real word, and I started to wonder if I actually was dreaming at all.

`

We walked, floated, teleported or whatever to the side of the valley above the most silent torrent I have ever come across. It foamed like the Niagara Falls but made less sound than a snowflake falling on feathers. Don't you just love the weird shit you get in dreams?

On the side of the bank below the – oh look, there's a castle up there – was a bare patch that had been stripped of most of the vegetation and, what a surprise, there was a bright silver something or other in the middle of it. I tried to touch it, but Clara grabbed my arm and pulled me back.

"*P'òkò touché, tèt wèd,*" she said, sharp and admonishing. I had no idea what that meant, other than it sounded faintly French and, knowing Clara, it wasn't necessarily very polite. But her family is from St Lucia, where they speak English even though there is a common patois that is based on French. And she was brought up in Corby, where what they speak closely resembles English, so why she would be speaking this French-sounding stuff rather than plain English I had no idea. Then she grabbed me by the scruff of whatever I was wearing and pulled me down to where she was crouching.

"Find it," she grated. "Get rid of it. I can't hold this for much longer. *Soukou.*" Then I became aware of the smell of coffee and frying bacon, and I knew that this possibly-dream had finally let go of me and that in reality someone was making breakfast.

The snow was coming down again but it was even harder than yesterday. I knew that Amy was awake, and Sam too, and that my contact with Clara somehow felt different. I also knew that I urgently had to do something, but apart from visiting the toilet I had no idea what it was.

"Morning," said Amy when I came down the stairs, her voice carefully neutral. "Help yourself – bacon's on the Aga." I went over to the top and was about to lift out a sizable portion of pig when the closed lid of the plate next to it made me stop. A shiny silver disc, embedded in a dark green surface. I made the bacon into a sandwich with the rye bread I'd made the day before and chewed it thoughtfully until the memory came back with a bang.

"Oh bollocks. We have to go to Rockingham. Now."

They objected, of course, citing the time of day (it was barely 6am), the weather (foul), breakfast (unfinished), the objective (unclear) and my sanity (no comment). So I told them about my dream. Mages pay a lot of attention to dreams – not the ones where the chairs are made out of custard, obviously – so they were less inclined to doubt the value of what I told them, even if they didn't understand it any better than I did.

That said it was still more than half an hour before we left, and the specious nature of some of the delays made me wonder if they were just making sure that everyone got through the shower first.

The snow was still filling the dark sky when we set off and the wipers, even going at full speed, were barely able to keep up. On the tiny roads near the farm there were snow drifts that could have swallowed a small horse, but they flew into fragments when Sam glared at them. I wasn't sure if she was using a spell or just frightening it to death.

Then she threw a heat cloak over the car and extended it about a hundred feet beyond the bonnet, so we were driving in our own snow-free bubble. Someone managed to get a video of it which decorated the front page of YouTube for, oh, nearly a whole minute before being superseded by yet another cute cat.

We managed to get to the causeway at Rockingham in just over an hour, which is faster than I'd thought we could - I guess the roads being almost empty helped. The world was a swirl of white and only the stupid or desperate would be out on a day like this. There were a surprising number of them, most driving without switching on their lights or, apparently, their brains.

"You seriously think we can achieve anything useful in this?" Amy asked as we pulled up. I knew from the dream that we didn't need to go to the castle itself but into the woods on the north side of the castle hill, so we'd rolled down Cottingham Road, sandwiched between the flood plain, which was living up to its name, and the big hawthorn and maple hedge that lined the ploughed and now fallow lands below the castle.

There were a couple of muddy gateways, and Sam pulled into the second one while she could still see it. By now the snow had that settled-in look that was making us doubt that we could do anything right now. Sam raised the same question.

"Clara was asking for help," I said, trying not to sound uncertain. "She said she couldn't hold on much longer. She didn't say what she needs us to do, but it sounded urgent and serious."

"I know," said Amy. The interior of the car was very muggy now, and the windows had steamed up. I made to wipe them but then stopped, because there was no point unless we were just going to give up and go home. "Clara's very weak," she added.

"Then let's get going," I said and pushed the door open. The wind almost slammed it on my head and the snow swirled in clumpy confusion around us as we got out. It was bloody freezing so we hastily zipped up our coats then donned gloves and hats. But however uncomfortable it was we were still going because none of us was a coward, the sort of person who never makes the same mistake once.

"I'll help," said Sam. I felt a spell rise, an old, deep spell, not flashy but wide and powerful. I'm sorry about the vague terminology, but I'm trying to describe things that are very hard to describe. Anyway, the snow eased slightly and the visibility improved, but the cold became deeper and more penetrating. "The balance of the weather is with me now," she said. Her voiced was strained. "I will hold this until we're done."

With our heavy coats, heavy boots and heavy thoughts we set off up the hill toward the castle. It wasn't long before we were properly cold, cold enough for it to be a problem, and I cursed the fact that I was the only fire Talent there who could warm us up but I had no access to the power. Sam's spell was corrugating the clouds and the wind pressure was rising. Don't get me wrong, I'm not saying this was like a trek through the arctic or something – I could almost see the roof of a pub from where we were – but it's still not something I would do for fun. The wooded hillside would have loomed over us menacingly if we'd been able to see it through the snow flurries.

"That's odd," said Amy as the snow tumbled through the branches. She was struggling to walk against the wind, even using both her sticks. "It's almost like I can feel Clara somewhere ahead of us."

"So that's where we need to go," I said, completely unnecessarily, as she had been steering us sideways across the heavily wooded bank for several minutes.

The walk became a trudge once we got deeper into the ankle-grabbing vegetation and leaf litter beneath the trees, and I was concentrating so hard on keeping Amy upright that I sort of lost track of where we were. Then we passed into another thicket of trees – probably ash, but I couldn't be sure - and a snow-laden branch slapped me in the face and that brought my concentration back to the job in hand.

"There," said Amy, pointing to a patch of snowy grass that looked exactly like every other patch of snowy grass. I found her a tree stump to sit on – I could tell that her hips were really hurting after the struggle over the rough, steep ground, but typically she wasn't saying anything about it. I looked at Sam.

"I'll hold the snow," she replied, only a tiny part of her mind on me. This beast of a storm was getting upset because it wasn't being allowed to play in this part of the valley, and that was making it very hard work for Sam. She was diverting it around us rather than trying to keep it back, but the amount of effort that required seemed to be enormous.

I got a long branch and raked it through the grass, top to bottom of the slope, all the while trying to keep my feet against the gusty wind. It could have been comic, but I was hurting with the cold and not inclined to laughter. The low temperature was a physical force by now, one that should have been faced with specialist clothing not just heavy coats and woolly hats. The effect encompassed the whole Rockingham area and was later described as an 'extreme microclimate', which is meteorologist for 'we have no idea why this happened'.

All I knew was that despite boots, our warmest coats and skiing gloves it was bloody freezing, and the snow was starting to overbear whatever power Sam could still muster. I really wished Jerry Denton was here, or that I was wherever he was, because it would undoubtedly be warmer.

It took me a couple of minutes to find it, a disc of some silver metal about the size of a hub cap, tucked into the ground so that just the top was visible. I could feel the power coming from it even before I touched it, and there was even more from the protective field that surrounded it. I guessed that it would react to any attempt to do anything magical to it, but as *isilak* I knew I should be magically impervious so I could be do stuff like this without suffering any ill effects.

Boy, was I wrong about that. What I was doing was actually more like walking on a broken leg when you're so full of morphine that you don't realise the extra damage that you're doing.

I grabbed the metal plate and pulled, and because it wasn't attached to anything I was able to lift it clear in a single movement that toppled me over backwards. That earned me several scratches on my face and a deep ragged cut on my arm where a branch managed to jam itself up my sleeve.

In the hole there was a hard to focus-on purple glow coming from the metal-lined hole which the cover had fitted on to. I touched the lining and the magic grounded from it, passing through my hands. It felt like I'd been bitten by a snake, one with serrated teeth that wouldn't let go. It bloody hurt but I ignored it, bar quite a lot of swearing, and kicked the cover away into the snow. Despite the deep tremors of cold running through me I turned back to the hole and looked into it. Amy joined me, leaving Sam sweating and swearing in Mandarin. In the bottom was a ceramic container a bit like a canopic jar, round and glowing purple, resting on the bare earth.

"No idea," said Amy over the wind.

On any other occasion I would have stepped away and got a specialist in to deal with this, but we were running out of time. So with the boldness reserved for the profoundly ignorant I reached in, paying no attention to the arching electrical discharge that scorched my gloves. I hadn't thought my hands could hurt any more than they already did, but I was wrong. Just bending my fingers made me break out in a sweat, which then froze on my face.

I grabbed the pot and pulled it. It didn't come out easily and when it did I ended up flat on my back, feet aimed at the top of the hill, which gave me a huge head rush. This was lucky, even though my arm slamming hard into an unseen boulder, because a shaft of purple light shot out of the hole, splashed onto the overhanging vegetation and punched a hole through it that was framed by burning branches until the snow extinguished it.

"*Bing*," Sam cried as her spell collapsed. The clouds sprinted back up the valley toward us, the wind howling and pushing a wave of ice before it. Amy fell over and blued the air with her displeasure. I clutched my left arm, which was agonising after the fall, with a hand I only knew was there because I could see it. This was not, I thought, turning into a fun day out.

I knew we had freed the Dragon, but I also knew that we needed to get into proper shelter soon. I could feel the numbness of frostbite digging into my earlobes and fingers, and I doubted the others were in a much better state. '*Bing indeed*,' I thought. It's the Mandarin word for ice.

The purple light faded from the air and concentrated in the pot I was still holding. Without any clue why I smashed it on a rock, the same one I had landed on, and it felt like revenge. The vessel cracked in half and the deepest purple light, almost black, blew out of it like smoke and scattered without any reference to the wind, before diving back into the hole like a rat up a drainpipe. I hadn't thought about it for long enough to understand how appallingly dangerous doing that could have been.

Amy raised her head. "Clara's free."

Sam picked up the remnants of the pot, which had a mechanism inside it, so I grabbed the cover, helped Amy to her feet and we made to leave. We'd managed two steps against the growing ice storm when the Dragon arrived, weaving through the trees like a snake on steroids and settling in front of us. Then, to my astonishment, it bowed to us.

"*Ahots*, you have my thanks." I was going to say 'it said', but the words just appeared in my head – and evidently in Sam and Amy's too.

"Er… glad we were able to help."

"The one who did this must be stopped. You must do this."

"I will. Do you know who it was?"

"No." The Dragon turned its head, weaving slightly on its long neck, looking quizzically at me. "Why are you not using your powers?"

"I am *isilak*, I have no access to magic."

The Dragon laughed, even though it didn't move. "*Ahots*, you have so much magic."

"I know, but I can't reach it."

"Yes, you can. You will find a way." The pressure of its will was like a breeze block settling on my chest.

"I have been trying."

"You cannot be mute, you are my *ahots*. Find a way."

"Nobody knows a way."

The Dragon was silent for a while, it's head still weaving slightly, hypnotic as a snake. Despite its size, we started to relax. Although it had a very big 'voice' it was like being shouted at by a kind person.

"I see *kea* around you," it said. "It takes the magic you have. You must become one with it to be free of it. I will *arindu*." The word translated as 'relieve', but I had no idea what it meant in the here and now. It looked directly at Amy. "You share his burden. You have my respect." Amy looked stunned.

Then it turned to Sam, and bowed again. "My Lady. The sky gives you greeting. Be well and wise, for your skills will be needed soon." It turned back to me. "I name you *lurra kea* and charge you to protect my *ahots*. She has greatly harmed herself to keep me safe from this. She has my gratitude." Then it rose into the sky, a coil of glowing purple like a contrail and plunged into the hillside.

"Fuck me," was Amy's considered verdict. "No wonder Clara isn't afraid of anything." She hugged herself against the bitter, cutting wind which still funnelled down the valley. "If it respected us that much it could at least have given us a bit of heat."

Then the whole world went purple and we found ourselves back at the car. We put the artefacts in the boot, climbed inside and turned on all the heaters whilst the wind tried to blow the car across the road.

Amy got on the phone to college. Even though it was barely 8.30 in the morning everyone who needed to know was already there. It seemed that Clara had woken with a jerk when I pulled the pot out of the hillside. She was weak but coherent, which made the Healers very happy, but possibly not as happy as the rest of us.

4

Our interaction with the Dragon was noticed, of course, in the same way that you would notice machine gun fire in a library. So it was no surprise when, having battled our way through foul and freezing conditions back to the farm, we were joined around lunchtime by Nadia Hussain and Richard Slater, who had come all the way from the Central College in London despite the grim weather. They brought another man with them, a cadaverously thin bloke called Hugo something that I didn't quite catch. Another of Nadia's apparently endless supply of specialists, I thought he was probably another senior earth Talent brought in to replace the still-dormant Oliver.

And they all needed to be fed and watered and, due to a considerable worsening of the weather mid-afternoon, be found somewhere to sleep. Fortunately, if you see what I mean, Clara was still in the hospital, and Sam had gone to the college to see Sigrún, the head of her department, and would go home from there. They needed to sort out what had happened to the weather at Rockingham and, more importantly, what the consequences of Sam's actions might be.

The people who built the farm knew that the snow can fall like a custard bomb, so all the pipes were buried, the huge Calor gas tank is in a shed in the back garden, the wood store can be reached without going outside and every window is triple glazed. Whatever we were talking about one or other of us would be stealing glances out of the big window that looked down the valley, like school kids constantly distracted.

As usual, Nadia was steering the conversation. "Most of what happened is clear," she said, with an optimism that bordered on insanity, "but there are three things that we still need to resolve."

"Only three?" Amy asked faintly. Her hips were giving her a lot of pain after this morning's escapades and she was pretty much confined to her specially designed high-seated chair, the type that helps you stand up by gently tipping you forward. There always came a point when her refusing to give in to her condition finally became her recognising that she really had to. She always did this slightly too late, and that meant that if we wanted to go anywhere for the next few days she would probably be in her wheelchair. But that was the life we had chosen and nothing to be concerned about.

Nadia ignored her, but with a smile. "The first is the level of consciousness, cognition even, displayed by what you call the Dragon. The energy involved is very like *indar*, but it's created directly from the earth. As you know it manifests in many ways, like the protection over Lindisfarne, the coastal barrier off the Arran Islands, the porous landscape of the southern Lake District and so on, but in every case they were not known to be sentient. What it does is part of how and where it is created, and how it appears to people is just the imagery that they put on it to be able to interact." We all knew this. "So how is it that the Dragon was able to hold this conversation with you?"

"It first spoke when Clara was taken ill," I said. "It called Clara and I *ahots*, which Sam says means 'voice', and then it threatened to destroy anyone who tried to separate it from us." I rubbed my arm, where the stitches that closed the long cut were itching under the bandage. Bo, fed up with dealing with what he called my 'endless avoidable injuries', hadn't been very gentle when he'd put them in. Presumably he hoped this would make me more inclined to be cautious. Yeah, right.

"We thought that was just Clara voicing her own fears," said Richard, in his elder statesman sort of way, "but that appears not to be the case."

"So we need to do some work on this," said Nadia, "because if some of the places of power are genuinely sentient we'll have to rethink a number of our basic assumptions."

"I imagine that's what Hugo is here to do," said Amy, shifting uncomfortably again. The big downstairs room was warm and the kitchen end smelled nice, but she was in a lot of pain, and not just from the frostbite we had all nearly got. I had given her all the help that I could short of using the spell *sorgortu*, which is a kind of magical morphine. It does remove the pain, but when I do it she tends to fall asleep so she'd asked me not to for the moment.

"No," said Richard.

"The second consideration is the reason it was being attacked, and whether this was directed at the Dragon because it's sentient, or if that was just coincidental. Then it's just the matter of who and how."

"Just?" Amy said faintly.

"And why," Richard added.

"What about the device?" I asked. The muscles in my hands still ached from the electrical discharge, but there had been no lasting damage.

"Well, the cover was just that, a protective cover."

"Could that device have been what hit Oliver?"

"No. The residue on his car showed that it was a direct casting by someone at the scene, but we don't know who. The metal tube was just that. It's the pot and the thing inside it that interests us. I asked one of the technical support staff from your college to retrieve the pieces and they examined them while we travelled up from London."

"Good," replied Amy, wincing as she shifted her weight. I quietly started moved things off the sofa so she could stretch out if she needed to. "We were somewhat curious about it too."

This made even Hugo smile, albeit briefly. Nadia nodded. "We've only had it a few hours, but it seems to be a simple *garraiolari*, a magical storage device. But there has to be more to it than that if the objective was to move the Dragon."

"The urge to be sarcastic," said Amy, "is bordering on overwhelming at this point."

Richard chuckled. "I'm fairly certain there will be further developments on that front in due course."

"Oh goody," she replied.

Meanwhile I was watching Hugo, who had made no contribution to the discussion. Richard caught his eye and nodded.

"I wish to speak to you concerning not just the fact that the Dragon spoke, but what it said." His diction was precise, his accent possibly slightly French and his movements a little pedantic. Everything on the table appeared to be several inches to one side of where he thought they should be, and he moved them as he spoke.

"Hugo is a *kemen* Talent who specialises in the interactions between fundamental forces and mages," said Nadia.

"Indeed. Your recall of the words used gives me reassurance that the greater part of the dialogue was as you reported." It took me a moment to untangle that. "However, there are two things that are of concern to me. The first is the term '*ahots*'. This Sam you spoke of is correct, in that the literal translation of the term is 'voice', but he failed to recognise that there is a greater meaning to it, one that the context makes me believe may be appropriate."

Nadia looked at me. "He'll get there," she mouthed.

Hugo ignored her. "The second term concerns me, and very much more concerns me than *ahots*. It is the word *kea*, especially in the form *lurra kea*." He stopped.

"Let's sort out *ahots* first," suggested Richard.

"Very well. On the face of it the term *ahots* suggests that the person is the voice of the er... Dragon, that they speak the words of the Dragon. But it also implies that they are able to speak – and by extension act – *for* the Dragon, that they are its representative and advocate. I suspect that this role was supposed to be taken by Miss Downing, with Mr Frost acting as her second."

"That seems reasonable," said Nadia. Unlike most previous occasions, when I got the idea she knew everything that was going to be said in advance, this was obviously news. Their arrival here had been so soon after we reported the incident that they'd had only the journey here to prepare, to read the report that our technician had written. This was clearly a serious matter, and not just because of the effect on Clara.

"The term *kea* – which literally translates as 'smoke' – is more troubling. *Lurra kea* just means 'earth smoke', and I believe it is simply a form of emphasis based on your Talent. As an *euste isilak*, Mr Frost is in the unenviable position of having the capacity to use the abilities of any appropriate and proximate mage, but has been unable to bring this to fruition. *Kea*, to be in the smoke, explains this." He stopped, looking around expectantly.

I used to have a maths professor who had a magic button called 'therefore'. He would write an equation on the board, put ∴ and then write another equation, which seemed wholly unrelated, underneath it then look at us with the same expectant expression. I never had a clue what he was going on about either.

The air took on a feeling of glutinous anticipation, which Amy broke. "I have no idea what you're talking about," she said politely. "As I am a water Talent, and have no connection to the Dragon, you'll need to explain everything to me in really simple terms." Which was excellent, because all I could think of were fatuous questions and expressions of mulish incomprehension.

"Very well," said Hugo. "To be 'in the smoke' is to be separated from your abilities by something powerful but insubstantial – unable to proceed normally, as if obscured by fog, if you will."

"I see. And how do we, ah, dissipate the smoke, as you might say?"

"That entirely depends on the nature of the smoke," he replied primly. "The word *kea* is a generic term, and so is of scant assistance in identifying it. Until the precise nature of the er, smoke, is found it will not be possible to effect an elimination."

"I see." So far, so opaque. She tried again. "And how would you go about ascertaining its true nature?"

"Why, by testing, of course." Hugo seemed startled that she'd even asked the question.

"And how do we test it?"

"Interactive sequencing." We all looked blank. "By using fractional wavelength analysis to construct a formative matrix. Then we plot the failure indices against their corollary activity points." Yes, I know; I hadn't the faintest idea either.

"Or, in English," Richard interjected, "Hugo gets you to do a whole load of magical things and writes down which ones don't work. With the results he can work out what, if anything, we can do for you." I didn't much like the 'if anything' bit, but I had to be realistic.

"That's what I said," responded Hugo stiffly.

"Not really," replied Richard with a slight smile, "but we understood you well enough. How soon will we be able to start doing the tests?"

"In approximately two weeks, all things cooperating to achieve the sought for optimal outcomes."

"I understand. Please get that set up as soon as you are able. Meanwhile," he glanced at the big window, where the drifting snow was covering the bottom third in a dense white haze, "I have no confidence in our ability to reach our car, let alone civilization."

Amy sniffed. "My home counts as civilisation, thank you," she snapped, then softened it with a raised eyebrow. "But not to worry, we have a well-stocked freezer and an emergency generator, and we will be able to find places for you all to sleep. Meanwhile I will leave you in Mike's capable hands because I have to go upstairs for a bit." Richard nodded absently as Amy rose stiffly. He was sending a text to his partner Jill, who had apparently been expecting him home that night. I thought that her optimism was a bit unrealistic, bearing in mind the weather.

Nadia helped Amy up to our bedroom, gave her some of the magic morphine and she was deeply and painlessly asleep in a matter of moments. While they were doing that the rest of us just sat looking at each other, unable to think of a single thing to say. After a few moments we were spared the silence by the phone ringing. It was Steph, the Healer who was looking after Clara, who I'd gathered was overseeing Oliver's recovery as well.

"How is everyone?" I asked.

"Oliver is no longer soggy, although he is still groggy, and he's spectacularly cross. Mostly about his car, it seems. He should be able to leave tomorrow."

"Do you know where he's going to go? Home?"

"London, he says. The artefact he is interested in has been transported to Central and he is anxious to examine it. He seems extremely… keen."

"I understand. And Clara?"

"Is recovering. She is very weak and tired but otherwise quite well."

"When can she come home?"

"Come *home*? I was given to understand that she had her own accommodation, and that you live with Miss Deerborn?"

"Well, yes, that's true, but when any of us are unwell, in need of some peace and quiet or have something complicated that they need to work on, they tend to come here."

"That is reassuring. I would be unhappy if she were to return to her flat alone. To stay with you would be substantially better for her. However she will have some basic needs that she may require assistance with. I assume that Miss Deerborn will be available to provide that help?"

"Of course. And if she isn't, it's likely that Miss Lee will be here a lot of the time too."

"No other males?"

"No, just me, unless we have visitors."

"And none of you are Healers?"

"No."

"Hmm." Silence for a moment. "I would like to see you, personally, before I let Miss Downing come to you."

"OK. Er... you do understand that I am *isilak*, that I have no access to magic?"

"No I don't, because you aren't."

"I'm sorry?" I know she's *Jaun* 6, but...

"I read the preliminary report of your er... misfortunes during the summer, which lead me to read other things. You are not *isilak* Mr Frost, you are *kea*, 'of the smoke'."

I was startled – this was exactly what the Dragon had said. "Have you encountered this before?"

"Yes."

"Oh. I thought it was extremely rare." I felt slighted, as if I'd had my uniqueness stolen or besmirched.

"I have been a Healer for many years Mr Frost, and I've met only two others."

"Oh. What happened to them?"

"One recovered. The other one died, but that was caused by ill-advised velocity on a motorcycle in wet weather. It was nothing to do with being *kea*."

"I am deeply confused."

"And I am required elsewhere. Come here tomorrow at 10, weather permitting, and be prepared to stay for some hours." And then she just hung up. I recounted the gist of the conversation to Richard, Nadia and Hugo, who kept nodding like a small bird picking up seeds one at a time.

"Yes, of course, that makes sense," he said. While we spoke I started to prepare dinner, a rich stew made of local wild boar served with baked potatoes and broccoli. I like to cook, although I don't get to do it as often as I'd like.

"What do you mean?" It was barely four in the afternoon but there was no light from the outside at all, although thankfully the wind had faded from a malicious howl to a discontented muttering that shuffled around the outside of the building like an impatient burglar trying to find a way in.

"You are a Dual Talent I take it?" Hugo asked stiffly.

Nadia cleared her throat. "The last time we looked he was *euste* across five Talents." Which isn't the same as having five Talents – it just means that I can briefly hijack other people's abilities.

This wasn't the same as the last time we went digging about in that part of my mind. On that occasion there had been six things in there, each representing one of the Talents that were lodged, inaccessible, in my psyche. Skills locked behind glass, tantalizingly untouchable.

"Oh. I see. The doctor may be referring to a Talent extra to those being er... shrouded and so therefore theoretically accessible, even now."

"So I have Talents that the 'smoke' is preventing from working, but that's apparently not all of them," I said and he nodded. I turned to Nadia, who was looking thoughtful. "Is this smoke stuff normally what's behind the whole *euste* business?"

"No. It's normally a blockage in the energy flow, the part that allows the Talent to interact with the outside world." She shook her head. "I always knew you were a bit of a strange one."

*

The next morning the snow had finally stopped falling, but the whole world seemed to be hip deep in the stuff. The weather was due to warm up a little the next day, but that didn't stop people pointlessly panic buying food and toilet rolls. It did affect the trains, because they still can't cope with 3 inches of snow on the line. The gritters had been out since early, but the road up to the farm were never treated.

But Nadia and the others needed to leave, and I had to see this Healer so I could get Clara home, so we applied a bit of magic to the problem. I mean, what's the point in having these skills if you don't use them? So, bacon sandwiches in hand, Nadia and Richard banished the snow from outside the house.

I would have melted it, which probably would have flooded the farmland downhill of us, but they just made it go away. The spell, Nadia told me later, was *kendu-elurra*, the magical version of sublimation. *Kendu* is a generic term that means 'remove', but they'd modified the spell to remove only the snow, otherwise everything – cars, grass, walls, oxygen – would have gone too. Please don't ask me to explain how it works, unless you really want a wearisome lecture on thermodynamics. She did explain it to me but I stopped listening, OK, understanding, about halfway through.

Then they climbed into their car and drove down the lane, pushing a bow-wave of magic ahead of them that cleared the road completely, like a giant hair dryer.

I won't bore you with my drive, but it took the best part of an hour and a half to get to the college in Nottingham, by which time I was starving. The college canteen is a seven day a week operation, so I could get a substantial if not remarkable feed before I had to see anyone else. Steph had agreed to wait until I'd eaten.

"Mike, are you worried about being in smoke?" Sam asked around a mouthful of what they claimed was Eggs Benedict. She'd joined me as soon as I'd arrived, having had a much shorter and easier journey than me.

"I think I'm more confused than worried."

"You get confused about which shoe goes on which foot some days," she replied.

"Yeah, and I love you too."

She smiled. "So what are you confused about?"

"I'm *euste* across five Talents, yes?" She nodded. "But last time we went into my *gogoan* there were six." The *gogoan* is the heart of a mage's inner world, a place where their magical Talents have a discernible and occasionally manipulable representations.

"I remember. Why you not mention it to Nadia?"

"I don't know."

"Have you got an inhibition again?"

"No, it's nothing like that." I couldn't look at her, even her, because I couldn't admit that what I was feeling was *ashamed*. I'd decided quite early on that I wanted to get deeply into magic, to go beyond just the ability to use it, because I wanted to help. As an earth Talent I'd assisted in reviving poisoned landscapes and purifying water. When I'd witnessed a horrible train crash I'd been able to help, to Heal, to save lives. And now I could do nothing, or that's what I thought.

"Which Talent is now free?"

"After what Dr Collingham said I suspect it may be Healing."

"That's very good," said Sam. "If you use all your power as a Healer you could be a lot of help to a lot of people."

I suddenly wasn't that hungry any more. "And what if I can't? What if I'm stuck in the smoke forever?"

"You said that Dr Collingham told you that one Talent that was in the *kea* had also been revived."

I couldn't think of a reply that would allow me to cling onto my self-destructive mood. "Yes, you're right. You ready to go?"

"We go."

We went.

*

Although I had spoken to Steph several times this was the first time we had met. I know a voice can't give you much of a clue about a person, but when I saw her I was surprised, even though I shouldn't have been.

Based on her last comments Steph had to be at least seventy, but she looked about forty and wouldn't have been out of place in a shot-put team. When we shook hands I'm sure I felt small bones grinding together. Sam didn't even try.

"I go and see Clara," she said and left, which was an unusual display of cowardice.

"Mr Frost, pleasure to meet you. I have read a great deal about you."

"Anything good?"

"Indeed yes."

"Don't believe a word of it," I replied with a grin.

She frowned. "Why not?"

"Never mind. What did you want to see me about? The facilities for looking after Clara at the farm?"

"No. I have spoken to her about the physical circumstances required for her recovery at your home, and I am satisfied that provided there is a way that she can reliably summon you without having to come down the stairs then your home will be more than adequate to the task."

It took me a moment. "A big bell?"

"Would be adequate. An intercom system would be better."

I nodded. I was sure that I could get a walkie-talkie from a toy shop on the way home. "So what…"

"Please come with me." We left the reception area of the medical centre and went down the corridor to what I thought would be her office. It wasn't.

The room was a lab full of testing equipment like ECG and EEG and other things ending in 'gram' and 'graph' that bleeped a lot. Everything in there had bundles of leads attached, drooping like creepers on a hot day, each tipped with coloured tags. They all had screens that were currently displaying flat lines that would doubtless wiggle excitingly once someone was plugged in to them.

I sighed, not because of the prospect of the tests but because the sticky pads that hold the sensors to my torso always pull out hair when they come off, which is uncomfortable and makes me look like I've got the mange.

"Please sit." She indicated a bed with the head raised. I sat. She dabbed bits of my head with a sticky goo and was about to cover me in wires when I stopped her.

"I'm sorry, what are we doing?"

"You are sitting still and I am doing some tests."

"Yes, I understand that, but for what?"

"To investigate the er… smoke." She frowned. "Dr Swithering told me that he'd briefed you on this."

"Dr…?"

"Hugo Swithering. He was at your house?"

"Oh yes. He said it would take a couple of weeks to set things up."

She smiled. "He wanted to test you all your Talents at the same time. I am intent on testing you as a Healer, nothing more. I don't need to wait for him to 'get his act together'."

"Oh. I didn't think I had an independent Healer Talent."

She looked at me oddly, like she was talking to someone seven feet tall who maintained that they were quite short. "Of course you do. Have you never Healed anyone?"

"Well, yes, of course. I learned as much Healing as I could, to be able to help people. The lecturers at college encourage everyone to do it."

"And have you ever Healed someone more than you believed you could?"

I thought back to the train crash at Paddington and the people I'd helped that terrible night; the teenage girl with her leg torn open, the young mother who seemed to be dead but then wasn't, and the man, who I now knew to be a *Jaun* 4 mage, who I had failed to save. "Perhaps," I said quietly.

"Have you learned *sorgortu*?" I nodded. "Have you ever been able to use it at full power?"

"Yes. Bev Hinch taught me it." I gave her a flicker of the spell. "There were times when that was all that stood between Amy and agony."

She looked at me steadily. "You are aware that you have to be a Healer, and at least *Jaun* 2, to be able to cast it like that?"

"What?" I felt a brief flash of annoyance. "Why didn't anyone tell me that?"

"Why would they?" She sounded genuinely puzzled. "A non-Healer can do a version of it of course, but it's like using aspirin instead of morphine. Did anyone know you were doing it at full power? Who have you used it on?"

"Amy mostly, when her hips are very bad. On myself once," I added, suddenly remembering.

"Yourself? Under what circumstances?"

"I'd been hit by a partially deflected fireball." I remembered the moment and closed my eyes for a second.

"Do you have any scarring?" I shook my head. "Remarkable. May I see?"

With some reluctance I removed my trousers, displaying my heavily muscled but intermittently hairy legs. I touched a spot on the outside of my right thigh.

"I see." She made a gesture and muttered something like *kalte* and my leg changed colour. The impact site of the fireball went dead white, fragmented striations in a linear patch, like a scrape through old dirty ice. "I see. Well healed and almost entirely by magic. How long did it take to heal it like this?"

I thought back. "From injury to immediate treatment, emergency first aid, was under a minute. It was properly dealt with by a Healer about half an hour later, along with a lot of other injuries," I added, remembering pain.

"Ah, this was the building collapse, yes?" I nodded. "By all accounts, even as protected as you were, you should have died."

"Well that's cheerful," I said. As I pulled my trousers back up I explained that Sam had given me enough *indar* to keep me going until I could get to proper medical treatment.

She frowned at that, laying her hand on my chest and pressing me back onto the bed. After a few silent moments, she raised her head. "It wasn't just *indar*. She was Healing you. I can still feel it, just. To still be detectable after such a long time it must have been an extraordinarily powerful spell."

"But she's an air Talent. She can do good first aid, but that's all. I was actually crushed," I said.

She nodded. "I know, I can see the damage. But you wanted to be healed, didn't you?"

"Bloody hell yes – I'd have been burnt alive otherwise."

"You were trying to Heal yourself, even though you weren't consciously aware of it. She reflected it and gave you the power that you needed." Suddenly that all made sense – I'd been very seriously hurt but had recovered ridiculously quickly. Light finally dawned on me like sunrise over the arctic – very, very slowly.

"So I can Heal." It seemed extraordinary. "As in I am a proper Healer?"

"Of course you are. You always were, but you were too busy with your earth Talent training to notice." She paused. "Which is odd, and something that we should look into at another time, because your tutors should have spotted it straight away." She made that sound like that was deeply suspect, like believing anything you read on social media or not wanting to punch Donald Trump. "Now lie still and let me do things."

I couldn't be bothered to make the obvious remark so I leant back, closed my eyes and drifted. Well, right up until she turned on the machines that beep, at which point I would have had more luck trying to sleep in a roller disco. It went on for several thousand years, or at least that's what it felt like - it was actually about an hour. I did drift off after a bit, into a sort of dream that involved Amy, black lace and ice cream... no, sorry, that's a memory. Anyway, by the time she'd finished I was as washed out as a dish rag and had no urge to do anything except sleep. So, of course, that was the last thing I managed to do.

"Please get up," she said. I did, but not at all steadily. "Your Healing Talent is no longer suffering from er... smoke damage." A tiny smile touched the corners of her mouth. "You will need to be properly trained of course, but in terms of power I have no doubt that you will be graded at least *Jaun* 2. However you will need to be *Ikasberri* to an experienced Healer before you are, er, let loose upon the world."

"You?"

"I already have one, and he is more reliable than you, so no."

"Oh well."

"Please return to the college. Professor Wicks wants to see you and then it will be time to take Clara back to your house."

"OK. Thank you."

"You are most welcome. I hope you enjoy being a Healer."

"Right. Me too." With her just looking at me I left.

*

Terry-Anne Wicks is usually scary enough that you'd be wise to run away, so seeing her smiling is a rare and unnerving experience. "Ah, Michael, glad to see you're being rehabilitated," she said. "How did it go?" This was, on the whole, an altogether too genial remark, and I frowned suspiciously.

"Dr Collingham seems to think that I've become a Healer all on a sudden."

"That was the one Talent you never showed any sign of. I wonder why that happened?"

"No idea, but…" I shrugged. "At least I'll be able to do something useful for once."

"Oh, you've always been useful," she replied warmly, "although not in obvious ways. Anyway, there is a little thing I need you to look into."

"OK." I replied cautiously. I regard comments like that with considerable trepidation these days, as they are never actually a 'little thing'. So far they have resulted in a Detective Sergeant vomiting on her shoes, Clara being concussed by a karate trophy, my brother nearly being immolated in a pub in Newcastle and a museum curator's husband being knocked over by a tree.

"Yes, just a quick thing... er... we believe that someone is trying to move another place of power."

"How truly fucking joyous for them. Why do you need me?"

"Because you sorted the last one."

"I found a metal tube with a ceramic vessel inside it, which I broke. I have no doubt that any half-wit with a metal detector could have found the cover plate and the rest was just mindless violence which, I will concede, seems to be something that I'm quite good at."

"We've tried that but nothing was found, even using the magical version of a metal detector. Yet the drain, just like the dragon thing, continues."

"OK, fine, where is this happening?"

"On the coast of Norfolk, a place called Morston."

"Never heard of it."

"I'm not surprised - it's not very big." She chuckled. "Our local contact says that while it isn't actually the end of the world you can probably see it from there."

I sighed. "Presumably this came from Nadia at Central?"

"Yeah."

"So why doesn't she send one of her specialists to deal with this?"

"She is sending one of her specialist Michael. She's sending you."

"But I don't work for Central. I don't get paid to do this sort of stuff."

"Very few of them do," she replied.

"Oh." That should have occurred to me – at least enough to ask about it – some time ago. "We can't really go – Clara needs looking after."

"Her boyfriend has been cleared by Central stay here and do that while you're away, and Ambrose is around as well."

Ambrose is another part of our little gang and was a vaguely innocuous Londoner that I haven't been able to shake off. "Ben's here again?"

"Yes. He's taking Clara back to her flat and he'll stay with her until either she's well enough that she doesn't need him anymore or you return." I was sure that Clara wouldn't be too happy about him taking care of 'basic physical needs' and that Ben must have exaggerated his position in her life to be considered an appropriate person to do that.

"How the hell long do you think we'll be there?"

"As long as it takes." Her voice was suddenly flat and more serious. "The power of place at Morston lacks the sort of focus that can be found on Lindisfarne, nor is it a personification like Rockingham, so you may have to do something extra to sort this out."

I sighed. "I am now an untrained Healer. Sam is an air Talent. Amy is a water Talent, which I agree could be useful, but this needs an earth Talent. Doesn't it?"

"Sure does. So Oliver Gunn is coming with you."

"Oh. I didn't know he'd properly woken up."

"As much as he ever does."

"Good. He'll be here some time this afternoon."

"OK." I hesitated.

"Someone will brief you in couple of hours – meanwhile, why don't you go and round up Amy and Sam? Take them to lunch. Be nice to them."

"I'm always nice to them," I protested.

"Fair enough, as you would say. Now go away, I'm busy."

On which encouraging note she went back to her office. I could see the door from where I was and there were two very nervous, very junior mages sitting outside, on what are colloquially known as 'the bollocking chairs'. I don't remember being that callow, but I have been in their place more times than I really should have been.

5

Lunch at a nearby restaurant was nothing to write home about, although the bill was worthy of an exclamation of protest, and we reconvened at college as the snow started again. What was a pristine white coating at home was gutters full of slush in the city and the whole place had taken on dispiriting sogginess. This was now freezing solid as darkness fell at some ridiculously early hour. We were briefed later in the afternoon by, I was surprised to see, Anne Collister, certified scary person and one third of the people notionally in charge of all the mages in the UK. Apparently she'd travelled up from London that morning on a train that had crawled the whole way through leaves on the line and sliding snow drifts.

"This is clearly another attempt to remove, or at least move, a source of power," she said as we sat attentively in front of her.

We nodded.

"We have been unable to locate a device like the one that was used at Rockingham, despite days of looking."

We nodded.

"So we need you to go to the area, find the device and neutralise it. If possible I also want you to find out who's doing this and why."

We nodded. She paused.

"What a talkative bunch you are today. Normally I can't shut you up." Anne is a 40-something widow, six feet tall with the clothes sense of a scarecrow. She is also *Jaun* lots, and she started out as a Healer, so now she was a little more interested in me than before.

"Tell us something we don't already know," said Amy, smiling. "Starting with how you found out about it in the first place, what investigations have been done so far and what support you can offer us."

Anne grinned. "I knew I could rely on you to ask sensible questions." She and Amy have always got on well. "It came to our attention when a local man, long retired from the active use of magic, noticed a change."

"Who is he?"

"Patrick Ashe, formerly *Jaun* 1 earth Talent, now *lotar*." The word literally means 'sleeping', but here refers to someone who has the lost ability to do all but the most basic spells. This normally results from ill health, advancing age, mental infirmity or an excess of contrary theology.

This last hasn't always been a problem because, in the old days, the local vicar would be at least *au fait* with the supernatural, the uncanny and the paranormal. But in these days of 'trigger warnings', flagging things in advance just in case some poor little darling is upset by the real world, everything has to be natural, canny and normal, so they're of even less use than they used to be.

"How did he become aware of it?" I asked.

"He helps out at an animal shelter near Wells, and he noticed that the source of magical power that he had been using had been compromised. Despite being *lotar* he has retained the ability to channel power even if he has no power of his own. You'll need to meet him when you get there, get the most up to date information."

"OK."

There was a long silence as we leafed through the briefing packs on the table. When I looked up Anne was packing up her notes. "Bye then."

Amy smiled. "Now we've got that out of the way, how about we go and get some dinner? We've found a new Thai restaurant that I think you'll like."

"That's more like it," Anne replied with a grin.

*

We left fairly early the next morning and the drive was lovely as the unseasonal snow stopped once we'd escaped the gravitational pull of the King's Lynn ring road. The route was a slow, narrow road through a parade of tiny attractive villages with wonderfully odd names like Holme-Next-the-Sea, Titchwell (I'm unclear how one Titches badly) and Burnham Overy Staithe.

We arrived in Wells, another Next-the-Sea, after about three hours. Oliver Gunn, for all his magical Talent, snores like a warthog with a heavy cold. I felt sorry for Sam, who'd had to endure the back seat with him the whole way.

Wells has been around since before Domesday and used to be a port of some significance, but it declined in the 1860's and it's only a small operation now. There are shops that face the water, most of them aimed at tourists, and a more conventional town centre a little higher up the hill.

Patrick said he wanted to meet us in a café at the eastern end of the waterfront, so once we'd found a place in an overcrowded car park we followed his directions to 'walk under the granary'. This confused us until we saw the long green gantry thing that stuck out over the road from the top floor of a waterside warehouse. It was doubtless used for unloading barges directly from the river into the building without disrupting traffic.

Once beyond that we, as directed. headed for a chandlery, a place where you buy things to chandle with presumably, and into the café on the other side of the road. It was a slightly over-warm but welcoming space with lots of blonde wood, a seafood-heavy menu and some really splendid coffee.

We had passed part of the journey speculating about Patrick Ashe. Once we'd stopped being silly – I didn't *really* think he was a retired spy who'd been given a new identity by MI5 – we'd concluded it most likely that he'd be a gentleman somewhat stricken in years, retired from a worthwhile but unexciting career, with a wife called Mary or Susan or, if her parents where particularly racy, Theresa. She would certainly sport a perm, but probably not a blue rinse. The matter of his facial hair was allowed to lie on file, but we were betting on him being a charming old buffer with a twin-setted wife and almost certainly a Labrador called Fido, Benson or, god help us, Rover.

You're probably expecting me to say that he was a 25-year-old punk with a pink Mohican, biker boots and a Rottweiler called 'Groinbiter' or something. He was, in fact, neither. Patrick Ashe was forty something, unhealthily thin and black, with cropped hair that was beginning to show some grey. He was accompanied by his husband, a plump, slightly balding white man of much the same age.

"My word, what a motley crew," was his opening remark. His handshake was firm and his palms rough, like he regularly did manual labour. "This is Gerard, my best beloved." He pronounced it with a French softness to the 'G'.

Gerard, who looked much more like a plain old Gerald to me, offered a smile but not his hand.

I made the introductions. Patrick nodded. "Gerard dear, do order us a lot of coffee and some of those lovely little cakes they do here, then you can go and do that bit of shopping. Buy lots of those organic vegetables you insist I eat." Without so much as a rebellious glance, Gerard did as he was asked.

"He's lovely and so kind," said Patrick, "but this sort of thing does upset him."

"He's not a Talent then?" Amy asked.

"Not so as you could notice." He smiled. "To answer the question you are carefully not asking, we met when he wrote off his car. In fact he drove his car into the back of mine. It's just that mine was a Porsche Boxster and his was a Nissan Micra, for goodness sake. I was amazed that someone who drives so much for his work – he's a Health and Safety inspector – had such a silly little car. So I bought him a new one and I've been looking after him ever since, or the other way around, or both." He paused to take a sip of his coffee, an oddly careful movement. "Anyway, you didn't come all the way here to hear about my dull domestic arrangements; you came to talk about the vanishing power off Morston."

"Mr Ashe," said Oliver, who didn't appear to have been listening, "as our current information is based on your perceptions we have to eliminate perceptual and confirmation bias, so firstly please tell us why you are *Iotar*."

Patrick's grin slipped a bit. "Well, you're very direct."

"Yes," Oliver replied.

"I was very ill," he said seriously. "Don't worry, it's nothing you can catch from having coffee with me." He laid his hand gently on my arm. Amy carefully put her hand next to mine, showing our obviously matching rings. "Oh well," said Patrick with a small smile, "it never hurts to ask."

By now I wondering why he was being such a cliché – the fingertip only wave to the man behind the counter, the loose-wristed gestures, the hint of a lisp. But this was the persona that he was choosing to present to the world, and who was I to question that?

"Can you describe what's been happening?" I asked.

He did, at length, with so many camp digressions I wondered if he was like that before he fell ill. With all the asides and snippy observations removed it amounted to this: He had, as was his habit, been helping at an animal shelter in Stiffkey (it's pronounced 'Stew-key', in case you were considering making jokes about things being stiff or anything as crass and obvious as that), drawing on earth power to help him while doing construction work on some new kennels. He had realised that the amount of power available had dropped sharply, and he was unable to discover what had caused it. So he contacted the college in Norwich, who had put him on to the people at Central, and that had ended up with us being sent to sort it out. Unsurprisingly he had no idea about the events at Rockingham, although he had at least heard of the place.

"So there you are, my dears. I'm just a poor *lotar* deprived of his last vestiges of power and forced to struggle along like an ordinary mortal."

"What was your job before you fell ill?" Oliver was being blunt again.

"Software. Terribly boring if it isn't something that you're into. I had lots of people under me." He stopped. "Now there's an image to conjure with. Anyway, then I fell ill, retired and came here to become a gnarled rustic." I found out later that he had worked for the Ministry of Defence doing something very hush hush to do with tracking submarines, hence his evasive answers.

"Where is the focus of the power?" Amy asked.

"Oh, there wasn't one dear – that's the problem. Go to St Paul's or Avebury or the like, and it's a specific place, almost a single spot. The Lake District does have a discrete source but it's expressed over a very wide area. Morston is much the same, but it had a lot less power to start with. It began around the high water mark and extended out across the marshes, over Morston Creek into Scalp Run and at least out to Blakeney Point where the seals haul out. Sideways it ran from Cabbage Creek to the Glaven at Cley, so it's a large area. The source being much weaker means that it isn't very strong in any place." Even though I had previously studied the maps it took me several minutes to work out the size of the area he described. It was big, about 15 miles long and 2 miles wide, so around 30 square miles, or 77km^2 if you have a metric head.

"So a little like the one on Lindisfarne," I said, then immediately wished I hadn't. Lindisfarne is less than 2 square miles.

"Distinguish between source and range," Patrick responded sharply. "The Lindisfarne source is small but powerful and its effect covers just the island itself. Here it's a single, weak source that is expressed over a much larger area." All the extravagant gestures vanished as he spoke and I could see the sharp and focussed mind that was probably what made him such a success in his work. "Go and visit – find out for yourselves." He stopped, leant back and blew out a long breath.

Just then his mobile pinged. "Now would you look at that, Gerard is getting twitchy because I've been with you lovely young men for so long."

"I can assure you he has no need to be concerned on my behalf," said Oliver stiffly. He looked like the very idea offended him, which I found amusing.

"Oh, I wouldn't be so sure dear," Patrick said, rising creakily from his seat. "I'm certain that there are lots of things that you aren't telling me." He suddenly looked very tired. "I have to be off now. You have my number. Call me if you need anything, but...," he took a slow, deep breath, resting his hand on the back of his chair, "not until tomorrow at the soonest." Gerard came in and, supporting Patrick under one elbow, lead him through the tables to the exit. That left me to pay the bill, but never mind that.

We sat in speculative silence as the card machine processed my payment. "So probably not called Rover then," I said. Amy smiled, but I suspect only to humour me.

"Hotel," said Oliver, carefully folding the receipt into his wallet, no doubt to claim it on his own expenses.

The suggestion was wise as the winter sun was already teasing the horizon when we got to Blakeney, another of the string of attractive settlements on the north Norfolk coast. Originally called Esnuterle, the current name

'Blakeney' is bang on because it means 'island in the marsh'. The village is in the heart of a 1,100 acre salt marsh that has been the home of fishermen, farmers, Carmelite friars and pirates for at least 3,000 years.

We had booked rooms looking out over the water at the quayside – another part of the anguine river Glaven, it turned out – which was lined with small boats, disconsolate gulls and hardy tourists. It was endearingly bleak and the wind, with nothing between us and the North Pole except the odd stray reindeer, was bloody freezing. It made us very glad of the sheltering warmth of the bar.

It's odd how sometimes you just can't relax, whatever you do. That evening was one of them, one when every one of us was unsettled but we couldn't quite work out why. Oliver seemed to be especially twitchy, almost cross, although he tried not to show it. He barely spoke until we pressed him about what had happened to him at Rockingham. It took Sam being understanding at him, and several drinks, before he would finally open up.

"I had to do something," he said eventually. "I could feel the power building up and I knew how much it was hurting Clara, so I just had to go there." He shrugged and looked at me. "You found the thing and broke it when I couldn't even find it. I had only got halfway up the slope when I got knocked down by some sort of defensive spell."

"Like *armarria*?" Amy asked. *Armarria* is a static shield spell rather than an active form of defence.

"No," he said slowly, "it wasn't a shield. It was something with more attack to it, so I think it was probably something from the *uxatzeko* group of spells." The word means 'repel', and it's often used to describe spells that are used to fend off floods, landslides or avalanches in emergencies. It differs from a standard lifting spell like *jaso*, because a lift has to be tightly directed – *uxatzeko* is more to do with generally preventing contact. More 'I wish you wouldn't do that' than 'stop it', but like many spells that are developed against movement, the harder you push the harder it pushes back.

"Whatever it bloody was it was too strong for me," said Oliver, "and whatever I tried I just couldn't get past it. The weather was totally shite and it was bloody cold, so I decided to give up and go back when I wasn't getting my ears blown off. Then there was all that business with the river, and my car." He wouldn't say any more about that, and I thought there might well have been some embarrassment being ineptly concealed.

"So what about here?" Amy asked. "Does it feel the same as at Rockingham?"

"No," he said slowly. "I can barely feel anything here." I nodded. It was the same for me, but I didn't know if that was to do with my peculiar disabilities.

"I wonder if we might if we got close enough to the thing that's draining the power," I said, wondering why we hadn't encountered this *uxatzeko* spell when we tracked down the thing at Rockingham. Maybe it had been a one-shot deal that had burned itself out dealing with Oliver, but I rather doubted it. If it was so all-fired important then I'm sure they would have put up something more reliable, or that at least would go off more than once. I shelved the thought when I realised that the room was silent and that everyone was now looking at me. "Hmm?"

"So are we going out to the marsh at first light tomorrow?" Sam said, clearly repeating herself.

"Um, no. We'll have to go mid-morning."

"Why?" I could hear the strained patience in Oliver's voice.

"Because what's doing this has to be far out in the marsh – if it were on land or even near land it would probably have been found by now."

"Oh, right. That's fair enough," said Oliver and drained his pint. "Bed." He left.

Sam had been uncharacteristically quiet during this rather wandering conversation and I looked at her anxiously. "Are you OK?"

"There is something strange here."

"Other than what we are here to do?"

She just looked at me. I know that look – it's the 'stop talking bollocks' one she reserves for me when I'm being particularly obtuse or conspicuously dense.

"Remember Lindisfarne, the feeling of being protected?" I nodded. We'd been on Holy Island not long before and the magical field around it had been a protective dome that had covered the entire island. "It's not the same here. There is… looking."

"The energy field is looking?"

She shook her head, irritated. "There is… searching in it." This kind of thing is so nebulous – from *'nebbia'*, which means 'fog' – that you always end up using woolly terminology and vague indications, because any attempt at a literal description makes you sound that you've been hitting the gin a bit too hard.

"I can't feel it," I said.

"No. This is not an earth thing. It feels like an air thing. There is something searching in the air."

"Is it an air Talent effect?"

"Not sure. Probably. Could be just an air talent doing it. Not sure."

"I'm getting nothing," said Amy.

"Just as Patrick said the source of this power is not a clear thing. I'm not sure if the searching is even to do with this. It is just… there."

"Maybe the person doing this…" I trailed off as a thought struck me. "The person who is doing this needs the power for some reason, like Peter Avery did. They tried at Rockingham and we stopped them, so now they're trying it here. But they haven't found the exact source of the power here so they're using a wide area collection because they can't find the exact place to put one of those ceramic pots."

"Yes dear," said Amy. "Had you only just worked that out?"

"Um." Sometimes I feel like I should be wearing a big pointy hat with a D on it. "Well, yes, but…"

"It's all right," said Sam. "We look tomorrow. Now we should all sleep. *Wân'ān.*"

"Good night." I echoed.

She smiled and went up to her room, leaving me and Amy in the darkened lounge bar, comfortably close to the fire. The moment was what used to be called a 'brown study', an instant where the memory sets everything in glass or aspic to create a frozen image that seems burned into the mind and can be recalled in almost perfect detail.

The hotel bar was doing a fair imitation of an old-fashioned gentlemen's club, with bum-polished leather chairs, dark wood tables and the nautical equivalent of hunting prints on the walls. They'd got the fire in against the chill that crept around the doors with icy, insidious fingers, and we were grateful to be able to relax into the wing armchairs, which admirably performed their designed function of keeping the chilly breeze off our necks.

By now Amy's hips were only stiff and a bit sore, and sitting still on the drive over had helped enough that we had risked not bringing her wheelchair, but her crutches were still with us, leaning inconspicuously on the side of her chair. I looked at her for a long moment, and I couldn't have reliably described what was going on in my head for all the tea in Twinings. I took her hand and gently squeezed it.

"I'm sorry," I said. I found that I had little strength in my voice.

"For what?"

"For being useless." I suddenly felt overwhelmed, exhausted, teary.

Amy looked alarmed. "You aren't. Why do you always think that?"

"You lot are so Talented and clever, and I just hang around doing grunt work but otherwise getting in the way. I feel like a roadie."

She started to cry, very softly. "My love, you aren't useless. You used to be so powerful and, yes, you've lost that, but only for the moment. But even though you can't do spells at the moment you understand magic so well. Your current value is your knowledge, not in what you can do."

Somebody else had said the same thing quite recently and I wasn't as reassured as I could have been because I was feeling thick as well as useless. "Logically that's true, but that's not way it feels." I'd never thought of myself as being clever. Moderately bright, perhaps, on a good day.

"Ah well, feels like, that's another matter," she said wiping her eyes on her sleeve. "You are an autodidactic polymath Mike, if not a polyglot, but your morale is almost undetectable."

I nodded. I've always been something of an introvert and it shows up in odd and sometimes illogical ways. "I suppose. We, collectively, can do all sorts of stuff, but I can't do any of it myself."

"Really?" She sounded a mixture of amazed and cross. "Who saved me and Sam from getting killed at Somerby Court? Who walked through a spell storm at Marchwood that should have turned you into a pile of smoking ash so that everyone else would be safe? Your bravery is amazing."

"Bravery is just being the only person who knows you're scared."

"OK then; who's just turned into a *Jaun* level Healer without even trying?"

I shrugged.

"My love, just because you can do something doesn't mean it's easy. I know you are *kea*, but has it occurred to you that…" She stopped abruptly and took a deep breath. "You're *euste* across five Talents, with a sixth that is free and operating fully. If Steph and the others can get you out of the smoke you'll be the only person ever who has been *mamua*, a mage who can fully operate all the Talents at the same time."

As bizarre as it sounds, this genuinely hadn't occurred to me. All I knew was that I had lost almost all of my original magical abilities, but had been given the consolation prize of being a Healer. I know that sounds awful, like I'm devaluing Healing, when in fact it's probably the most widely employed and generally useful of all the Talents. We sat in silence for several minutes. I registered that Amy had spoken to someone, but otherwise I was absorbed in my own thoughts until the barman returned with a balloon of brandy for her and a good whiskey for me.

"Drink," said Amy. We drank and, with my head full of conflicting thoughts, we went to bed.

*

The next morning, after a breakfast that would have fed Amy and I for two entire days at home, we climbed into the car and headed for Morston. Apparently its original name was Merstona, which means 'settlement in the marsh', so obviously the local environment hadn't changed all that much. It was not a nice day, although thankfully it was no longer blowing snow, but somehow the icy grey bleakness seemed appropriate to what was going on.

I'd sent Patrick Ashe a message but the reply, which was so stolid that it could only have come from Gerard, said that he wasn't feeling well and could we not disturb him today please. I would have liked to offer him some Healing, but I was sure that he'd already received all the help he could get.

We parked in an overpriced car park, actually just a patch of potholed and puddly ground which boasted some smelly toilets, a hut that sold ice creams and nasty coffee in the summer, and nothing much else. The cold bit and the air was full of the noise of gulls tumbling on the wind and the clank of poorly secured rigging rattling against the masts of yachts that had been pulled up out of the water.

The sky was huge and, from our position maybe ten feet above it, the marsh reached almost to the horizon. There was one deep winding channel running through it, yet another part of the sinuous and ubiquitous river Glaven, with weather-beaten jetties and several vessels slowly sagging to a lopsided rest as the tide withdrew. The rest was rivulets and gullies between high points that were covered in Marsh Samphire, Sea Lavender and other salt resistant plants.

The pattern of the muddy banks looked a bit like the surface of a brain, but it didn't smell like one. It reeked, the sour smell of estuarine mud, decaying seaweed and a hydrocarbon tang from a small dingy that chugged up the deeply cut main channel at a dignified putter.

It was the kind of scene that you can never take a decent photograph of. If I could have frozen that moment it would have made a splendid painting by Edward Hopper or Jack Vettriano, but not even John Constable could have made it beautiful.

Oliver grunted. "Well, I can feel the power."

Sam nodded. Amy looked troubled, but didn't say why.

"Can you locate the source?"

"Of course." He pointed out into the acres of soggy mud and submersible vegetation. "it's over there."

"Any idea exactly where?"

"No."

"I'll find it," sighed Sam. She didn't sound enthusiastic about the prospect.

"It's all right, I'll do it," said Amy softly. "It's bound to have more effect on the water than the air. It's just easier for me."

Sam shrugged. "OK."

Amy did exactly as I had expected; she sat at one of the tables by the wooden hut that doubled as a lookout post, and her face went blank, a slight glow around her for those with the skills to see it. The rest of us went to the tables on the other side of the hut, the better to not disturb her.

"So what should we do once we've located it?" I asked.

Oliver, who I thought should have been able to answer that question, just shrugged. He looked cross. "What you did last time I suppose," he said eventually, "although if you could preserve the device this time that would be helpful," he added, sounding oddly sour.

I didn't stare at him, although I felt like it. Smashing it was the only way I'd found to stop the damn thing working and it occurred to me that the pain in my hands had suddenly eased after I'd broken it. More Healing leaking out, presumably.

Preserving the thing was like asking me to take the yolk out of a boiled egg without breaking the shell – I'm sure that there's some clever bugger out there who can, but I didn't know how and, to be honest, I wasn't much interested in trying.

So I just nodded, leaving the whole staring thing to Sam, who mutter *'bái chî'*. This impugned Oliver's intelligence in a manner that I couldn't bring myself to disagree with.

Amy joined us a few moments later. "Found it," she said, sounding slightly uncertain. "There seems to be a single focus but I don't that it's the actual source. I suspect that there is a device out there, but I think it's submerged and... oh, it's hard to explain." She sighed and indicated a number of colourful buoys bobbing in the distant grey green water.

"I'm making a few assumptions here, OK, but the person who did this will need to retrieve the device, yes? They can't gather the power from it remotely." We nodded. "But getting it out of the mud unobserved would be pretty much impossible."

She was right – the marsh seemed to be bleakly empty, but when you looked more closely there were at least a dozen people in view whichever direction you were facing. They were all just going about their ordinary business, birdwatching, tending to their boats or just walking on the marsh enjoying the brisk, salt-laden air. If you lived in a city it would be nectar. To me it just felt soggy.

"So they must have attached it to one of the buoys," said Amy slowly, "and positioned so that it rests in one of the low points on the mud, out of sight, at low water."

We nodded.

"Which one of the buoys is it?" Oliver asked abruptly.

"I'm not certain at this range, but it's definitely on the other side of the deep channel, so probably closer to where the seals are." There was a collection of immobile lumps on a distant promontory of the mud, which was what I assumed she was referring to, so I guessed this was the Blakeney Point Patrick had mentioned, about 1½ miles away. "I think that has to be near where the focus of the power is too, otherwise why put the device out there?" Amy added.

We nodded but I was curious. Anne had said they hadn't been able to locate it, but we had managed it in minutes. Actually we hadn't - we'd just made an assumption, based on another assumption, which was that the person doing this had managed to find it the source. I presumed Anne must have asked Patrick, but he seemed to barely have the strength to breathe unaided, so it was no surprise he had been unable to maintain *maparen*, the standard locator spell, for long enough to pinpoint it.

"So now we have to go out there and lift the device."

"How do we do that?" Sam asked. We had watched a couple of people walk out to their boats and it was clear that the mud was shin-deep in most places, glutinous and as hard to shift as gum on a jumper.

"A boat, once the tide has come in," Oliver replied. "We obviously can't walk there."

"And where are we going to get one of those, and a captain who won't ask questions?" Sam asked, raising an eyebrow.

We all looked blank – hiring a boat around here wasn't too much of an issue, but questions are always a problem, because magic and the people who use it try very hard to remain a small and inconspicuous part of society. Like everyone who is different and has some sort of power, people tend to either be fascinated by us, frightened of us or treat us like freaks. I mean, look what a rough time the X-men had.

Despite all the good that we do, and the very little harm, we are not talked about in polite company, like cess-pit cleaners or tax inspectors.

You'll still hear people say things like 'they said it was done with, you know, *that stuff'*.

Healers save hundreds of lives a year, but not everyone thinks that what we do is even real. The conspiracy theories that try to explain magic away can be fantastically inventive and inventively fantastic, but they bear no resemblance to the truth at all. It's quite trying being considered as reliable as a homeopath when you can make a building explode just by thinking about it.

We don't live in the insulated world of Harry Potter – we are fully integrated into the real world at all times. Sadly, most people are only interested in us when something goes wrong, rather than when it goes right. You get huge headlines about a hospital when an operation goes wrong, but the same tabloid newspapers and social media whingers never mention the hundreds upon hundreds of operations that are carried out flawlessly every year. It's the same as that.

"And what about protection?" Oliver asked. "There were serious defences on the Rockingham device – how are you going to deal with whatever is out there?"

"I don't think there will be any defences," I replied, wondering about the certainty in my voice. "Once the tide is in there are boats going all over the place. Triggering a serious defensive spell when some random boat happens to pass over it would be rather obvious. I suspect whoever is doing this is relying on camouflage. Mind you, that's not to say they aren't watching us right now and won't attack us when we try to remove it."

"We can deal with that," said Sam. I believed her – she had recently perfected the spell *horma*, which creates a wall that nothing can get through, not just magic stuff. The sheer amount of power she can put into it makes the shield literally impenetrable. I couldn't create one properly, even when I could do magic, although I thought I was getting close.

"So," said Amy, apparently addressing the freezing marsh, "we'll need a boat then."

"I'm sure I can hire one," said Oliver quickly. "Can't be too sure how safe it will be, no questions asked." He glanced around. "I hope you can all swim," he added, and he didn't sound like he was joking.

"Yes, we can all swim," said Amy.

"Oh, OK," he replied. "I'll see if I can find something that won't sink as soon as we get on board."

"Good," I said. "You work on that, but right now we need to get out of this bloody wind." At that moment a wave of magical energy rolled up from behind us, not directed at us but like the bow-wave ahead of a very big ship that has no intention of stopping.

"Jeez, what a dump," said an awfully familiar voice, "smells like my socks."

I resisted a sigh. "Hello Gronk. What are you doing here?"

"Following you, ya lunk."

Oliver looked at him then glanced at me, his eyebrows making a question. "Sadly, yes, I know him," I said. "Why are you following me?"

"My stamping ground, right?" Gronk replied.

"Sure. Same question, ya podnuk." I think that's an American slang term, but I might be wrong. It should be, even if it isn't.

"'cos I'm all kinds of certain that you ain't got the least clue what goes on around here." He smiled, smugly self-satisfied. I wondered once again if he was displaying some sort of autistic trait or if he was just a git.

"Who is…" Oliver started, so I briefly explained who Gronk was and that he was apparently unavoidable.

"Us'n don't much like furriners, even ones down the city, so I thought I'd mow in with yer peerking." His accent had shifted to a blurred bumpkin archetype.

Oliver looked at me. "Have you any idea what he's talking about?"

"No. He generally either speaks Latin or Smartarse. This is a new one on me." The girls were looking equally mystified, so I turned back to Gronk. "I get it that you're here to help, but we're going to need you to speak English or you might as well be in Vladivostok."

"All right," he said grumpily.

"Hotel," said Sam. "It's cold here. We can ask about a boat." Gronk made to speak, but Sam cut him off. "Hotel," she said firmly. He wisely decided not to argue.

*

We took our usual place in the hotel bar just before the lunch rush – all of three other people – started. Gronk's usual *faux* American accent proved as reliable as a politician's promises, and within five minutes he was talking like a straw-chewing local again, much to the bemusement of the hotel owner, who had arrived here from Dunfermline by way of Bath.

We outlined the problem while Gronk drank his beer and mulled it over. "Well, you're right 'bout needing a boat. If'n the device is out on the point, there's no carnser will get you there."

"Carnser?"

He clicked his tongue. "A causeway through the marsh. No, you're definitely going to need a boat."

"I agree," said Oliver carefully. He was taking every exchange with Gronk in small stages, probably so he didn't frighten or confuse him. "I'm sure I can find one."

The staff came to tell us that it was time to eat, so we dutifully went into the dining room. Despite a reliance on the word *jus* when 'gravy' would have been more appropriate, it was splendid. Because of the other diners and the staff, who almost outnumbered them, we turned the conversation to more innocuous matters. In one of the pauses, Gronk thoughtfully said 'Jasper would do', before plunging into an unnecessarily erudite explanation of why 'blar' is the local word for crying.

*

'Jasper' turned out to be Gronk's boat, the name explained by a lurid yellow and black paint job. He explained, with his usual wearying smugness, that 'jasper' was the local name for a wasp. I held my tongue – this was typical Gronk; once he's established that he's cleverer than you he can relax and put his huge brain to work, at least until the pubs opened.

I won't bore you with the story of Gronk bringing his boat, which was not much bigger than a large truck, to Blakeney quay that afternoon. We'll gloss over the surreptitious baling, all the faffing around with life jackets and his heads up, horizon scanning pose as he drove the boat over the submerged marshes and round toward the point.

It was freezing out on the water, and Sam was looking more than a little green when we crossed the deep channel. Oliver was tight-lipped and visibly uncomfortable, whereas Amy just looked bored – she's been on dive boats a million times, so for her this was as exciting as a trip to the shops. I just sat there, wiping my nose and wishing I could do something. At least, I thought, offering myself a small crumb of comfort, if someone fell in I'd be able to Heal them, once I'd worked out what I needed to do.

I was trying to find something to break this bleak and defeatist mood when I felt a disturbance in the magical field around us, and no, it's not the bloody Force. We all felt it, of course, but I could see something like a corkscrew rising out of the wiggly sea.

Amy glanced at me. "Can you see it?"

"Yes." I gestured out over the water and made a spiral motion with my hand.

"Interesting," she said gnomically after a moment. "Professor Denisov did wonder if that might happen."

Denisov is the head of the water Talents department at Nottingham, although the amount of time his expertise requires him to be elsewhere means that his second in command, Mrs Abercrombie, is effectively running the place. Amy had been spending an increasing amount of time helping her, especially when her hips were bad and she was confined to her wheelchair. Admin duties were dull but necessary and, as she put it, 'at least I can do that sitting down'.

Gronk turned the small boat sharply before I could ask her to clarify, which soaked our shoes and did nothing to improve either Sam's discomfiture nor Oliver's temper. We edged our way over to the spiral and the engine dropped to a murmur as Gronk kept us on station against the current.

"How deep do you think it is here?" Gronk asked.

"Four foot or so," said Amy. She just knows that sort of stuff. She knelt by the side of the boat and leant over, so I shifted my weight to the other side to stop us tipping. Amy held her hand out over the water.

"Damn," she said after a moment.

"I'll help," said Sam and I felt the boat being pulled downwards on their side, then leap up with a pop as something on the sea bed responded to the combined force, lifted out of the glutinous mud and bobbed to the surface. The spiral flared and flattened, then spread out across the water with a ripple that would be barely have been enough to dislodge a teetering ice cream.

What arrived at the surface, attached to a grubby white buoy, looked like a large Tupperware box which had been sealed waterproof with glue and gaffer tape. It felt horrible and smelled like burnt plastic, the kind of stink that you just can't get out of your nostrils. So we dropped it in the bottom of the boat and headed back to shore as fast as the little wasp could take us.

That was when the first of the defensive spells hit us. Well, I say defensive, but they felt more spiteful than threatening and I thought it had to have been triggered because we had the smelly box with us. There wasn't enough power in any of them to actually hurt us, even if we hadn't got shields up. So this wasn't a Parthian shot in hope of a Pyrrhic victory, it was more like a small act of petty revenge. I suspected it was intended to make casual visitors uncomfortable enough that they would stay away from the area but without quite knowing why, rather than being defensive in the full sense of the word.

It struck with no more than a sigh and faded like lingering flatulence. Oliver grunted. "It wasn't like that at Rockingham." He looked at me. "Are you hurt?" Puzzled, I shook my head.

"It was automatic," said Sam. She pointed to a ripple like a frozen spall-mark in the water just ahead of us. As more magical energy was released another appeared just beyond the boat.

Amy sighed. "They're all around us in the mud." She stretched out her hand and a metal object the size a stubby beer bottle jumped out of the water and landed in the bottom of the boat. "They're like jump mines."

"Mines? Why don't we just leave them be?" Oliver asked, sounding plaintive. I guessed that he really wasn't enjoying being out on the water.

"They would be nasty for people who are on the edge of being able to use magic," said Gronk, "and the progress of the detonations would give the person who planted them a clue about the direction we went in."

"So what we do?" I asked. We had found the device but I had no idea what we were going to do with it, and I didn't relish being tracked by whoever was doing this.

Gronk, who had to be a *Jaun* level something, negligently waved his hand and about thirty of the damned things went off, all at the same time. Each location was marked by a column of oily bubbles that popped on the surface with a sticky percussion that just added to the turbulence. "Let's go back to Blakeney," he said.

We did, and while we were at it Sam and Gronk exerted themselves a bit and put the box and its contents under a dampening field. Gronk wasn't very focused on what was going on around us and he would have driven the boat straight into a skein of crab pots if Amy hadn't grabbed the tiller from his inattentive hand and set us back on course.

Gronk and his wasp went home almost immediately, but not without a certain amount of grumbling and demands for beer as payment. Oliver and the box did a bunk with almost indecent haste, heading for Central as fast as the local train service could get him there. We drove him the 10 miles to the railway station at Sheringham and he went via Norwich, Liverpool Street and the tube. It took him 3½ hours and I hoped the dampening field wouldn't fail because if it did he'd be a mess by the time he arrived. I wished him well for the journey at least.

That left me, Sam and Amy, and it was no effort at all to resist the urge to go straight home, mostly because it was dark, cold, rainy and, possibly more importantly, we couldn't be bothered. So we arranged to have dinner with Patrick Ashe and his Gerard.

"Oh, I can feel it's no longer being interfered with dear," said Patrick when we had settled in a quiet corner of a rather good pub restaurant not far from the windmill in Cley, yet another Next-The-Sea. I wondered if the people who name places in Norfolk are allergic to the word 'to'. "I knew whoever was doing this had tried to hide his device from the moment you started poking around, and now it's all as free as air." He smiled and waved one hand, but it was forced and he seemed a bit grey as he picked at an unseasonal salad.

"I'm glad it worked," said Amy quietly, looking at him with concern. "Will it make your life easier? I hope it will."

"Perhaps."

"Why only perhaps?"

Gerard stirred. "Because Patrick tried try to carry on as normal even when the power was diminished. It proved to be... unwise," he added sourly, glancing at his husband.

"How so?"

"He drew on his own resources to carry on when he should have had the wit to surrender to the inevitable."

"Er..."

"I appear to have gone beyond *lotar*. I have left myself almost without power," said Patrick lightly.

"Why?"

"Because I didn't want to let the people at the rescue centre down."

"It's not just that, is it?" Amy said sharply.

Patrick didn't look at her, but turned his eyes to his plate. The silence grew thicker until Gerard moved. "Patrick was already unwell, but doing that has made him worse. Now he barely has enough strength to keep his own heart beating."

"It's not that bad," said Patrick, his voice faint. He leant back and closed his eyes.

I'm never clear what the appropriate thing to do is on occasions like this. Do you keep eating, or do you stop and risk your food going cold if the pause goes on too long? Say something encouraging or maintain a tactful silence? Make a joke?

Gerard solved it for us by resuming his meal after just a few seconds. He looked at me. "I can't be much use to him if I'm fainting from hunger," he said quietly, touching Patrick's hand. He opened his eyes. "Can you eat a little more?"

"In a little while perhaps," he replied, sipping a glass of water which he was holding unsteadily.

"I take it," said Amy, "that the Healers have done everything they can for you?"

"Indeed. I spent many hours with the lovely people at the Norwich college, but they could do no more than this." He paused. "They even sent me to Central, but those folks couldn't help me either. Mrs Collister and Dr Hinch were quite upset about it. Miss Hussain just said 'looks like you're fucked then, doesn't it'?" He sighed and smiled crookedly. That sounded typical of Nadia, and if the Healers at Central couldn't help then there was no point in offering my thumb-fingered assistance.

Deliberately, and with the adroit assistance of Gerard, I turned the conversation to the latest amusing inanities of people trying to use, or blame, magic for things that went wrong. A far-right political candidate with the IQ of a party balloon was accusing the incumbent of using magic to 'make all his votes vanish from the ballot boxes'. A video gamer on YouTube – no doubt shouting excitedly about whatever he'd been paid to promote whilst wearing his hat backwards – tried to use a spell to increase the speed that he could press the keys, but mistook speed for power. His desk collapsed, breaking both his legs in the process.

There was also a *fromager* who asked an inexperienced French mage to speed up the aging process for his cheeses, the quicker to get them to market, only to find he'd got the spell remarkably wrong and had left him with a warehouse sloshing with rancid milk. As I've said before, the more advanced the magic, the more likely it is to go spectacularly awry.

The gathering ended before we got to pudding because Patrick was suddenly exhausted and grey, and we found ourselves back at the hotel earlier than expected.

"You remember that idiot who was stealing powerful artefacts to try to restore his own magic?" Sam and Amy nodded – that particular nuisance was still on remand in prison, awaiting trial for an interesting variety of offenses. "You don't think that Gerard is trying to do the same thing for Patrick do you?"

There was no point in even suggesting that Patrick was doing it himself. After he'd told us his story I had scanned him, another odd Healing-related ability that I had picked up from somewhere, and I found that he barely had the strength to walk up the stairs in his house. So the idea of him building all these devices and then planting them out in the marsh – and doing all that stuff at Rockingham too – was not even worth mentioning.

"He has no power," said Sam, looking at a glass of whiskey in a predatory manner.

"Maybe he just made the devices?"

She snorted. "He has no knowledge of magic."

"OK, fair enough. It was just a thought."

"Silly thought." She sank the whiskey in one mouthful. "We go to bed now. We talk in the car."

Amy and I were not far behind her on the stairs, but we didn't go to sleep immediately. When I finally managed to drop off I was so far down that it took her three goes to get me awake enough to go to breakfast.

I had this terrible fear that if I couldn't get out of the smoke, couldn't stop being *kea*, I might end up like Patrick, burnt out, powerless and reliant on other people for everything. The thought left me in a sombre mood.

6

The relief when Clara came home the next day was amazing, but not quite as amazing as the fact that it was Jerry Denton who brought her. Ben's inept and inappropriate attempts to care for her hadn't lasted even four hours, and once she'd thrown him out – literally, according to one version - she'd been back under the care of the Healers until we returned.

When we got to the farm Clara was sitting on the couch talking to a tall woman with very dark hair who treated Jerry like he was her property, from which I assumed that she was his fiancée Ariadne.

"We were there when they said she could leave, so we thought we'd give her a lift," said Jerry. He's a fire Talent, Jaun 3, and was doing some sort of research on the medical applications of fire spells, focussed on remote cauterisation, I think. "And there was something else I wanted to talk to you about too," he added in an undertone.

"OK, let's get Clara settled." She didn't need to be settled, she needed to be calmed down, because she was bursting with a bright and brittle energy that in small children would be described as 'febrile'.

"It's the relief," said Ariadne, who was skilfully directing Clara into unpacking her bags, making coffee, deciding what she wanted for lunch and then going to the barn to make sure her car was all right. "She came very close to death and people who come through something like that often become either depressed or euphoric. Clara has a euphoric personality type, hence this reaction."

"Well, yes," said Amy, "she's always been quite positive in her outlook. Er... please don't think me rude, but how come you know so much about this?"

Ariadne looked at Jerry. "You haven't talked about me at all, have you?" Jerry's a fairly burly sort of bloke, but he seemed to shrink slightly.

"Maybe not everything..." he prevaricated cautiously.

She sighed, turned to Amy and held out her hand. "Dr Ariadne Maris, Clinical Psychologist." She smiled. "I know you've been friends with Jerry for ages, so when he told me that Clara was in hospital and why, I thought I'd see if I could help."

"Thank you," said Amy.

"She's brilliant," said Clara, coming back into the room. Ariadne went straight into professional mode and gathered Clara and Amy into the kitchen area while Jerry and I, dismissed, shuffled off to other end of the big room.

"I know we've been busy mate," I said, "but what's all this?" I indicated Ariadne. "It's like she's already moved in, at least into your head."

"Things just got out of hand." Jerry mumbled. "She kinda swept me off my feet."

"You're that serious?" Even as I asked I knew it was a stupid question.

"Oh yeah. That's what I wanted to ask you..."

I guessed. "Best man or godfather?"

"It would be an 'oh god' father in your case, but right now I need a Best Man. But I can't find one, so I'm going to have to settle for you. We have talked about having kids, but she wants to practise a bit more...," he saw the grin I couldn't keep off my face and sighed. "Practise as in being a doctor, you dirty old man."

I raised my hands in surrender. "Whatever you say. When's the wedding?"

"In the spring. I'll let you know."

"Cool. You guys want to stay for lunch?"

Ariadne looked over at us. "I thought you'd never ask," she said, which proved that she'd been listening to every word. It felt nice to have a house full of people again, and lunch was a roaring success.

*

Three days later everyone had left. A serious meteorological problem was threatening an already desperate southern Europe, and the local Centre – a repurposed Palladian villa just outside the village of Itri, halfway between Rome and Naples – had put out a call for all appropriately skilled air Talents to pitch in. Sam was on the next plane to Italy.

Clara, now much better but still bobbishly energetic, had decided that she needed to study something arcane and complicated to do with the structure of the earth's crust, the better to understand the Dragon. She had hoped that she could do it at Central, but instead she'd been sent to a research facility at Thiézac in the Massif Central in France. Her French, I discovered, is idiosyncratically St Lucian – it was a French territory until 1814 - which occasionally leads to humorous misunderstandings, but she usually gets on fine.

Amy, meanwhile, had received a despairing message from one of her former students who was certain that he had located a significant Roman trading vessel that had sunk off the east coast of Ireland, but he couldn't do even a basic investigation because of the extremely muddy and turbulent water. Amy left the day after Sam, and none of them had any idea about when they'd be back. They could only be certain that would be a matter of weeks rather than days.

So I was alone, which for me Amy defines as 'being in bad company'. My parents were on holiday somewhere a good deal warmer and my brother Simon and his boyfriend Idris, who I didn't see often anyway, were too embarrassed by their clutter-bomb of a flat to invite me to visit, so I couldn't think of anywhere I wanted to go.

Nobody contacted me about anything. Nobody wanted me to do anything or be anywhere, so after a couple of days I took myself back to the college in Nottingham – oh, the sheer glamour of it – and signed up for training as a Healer. I had the Talent – as in it was now my only Talent – so I thought I ought to be able to do something useful with it.

I got through what would be considered advanced first aid training fairly easily, but once we got onto more doctor-ish stuff it all rather fell apart. Bone knitting is a basic Healer skill, one of the most important after stopping blood loss, maintaining cardiac function, supporting respiration and other things involving squishy bits. You use a push/pull spell combination – strictly *bultza* and *tira* - to separate them, then *irekia* – which means 'open' – to align them, and then *metxa* – 'fuse' – to join the broken ends together.

Done properly the technique also encourages the body to finishing the knitting process itself. But you have to make sure that the porous bits line up properly, plus the marrow and the associated blood vessels too, so it can all heal correctly. As a natural process it's called 'osteoblastic reconstruction', but Healers usually call it 'gluing'. It's all about using the right amount of energy in each spell in the right place for the right length of time, and that's very complicated and difficult. Or I found it so anyway.

My first attempt produced a solid, impenetrable, calcified lump like an ossified cannon ball. *'Too much power for the available level of control'* was the verdict of Alessandro Tahy, the boss of the Healers, who had decided to 'keep an eye on me'. The second attempt was way too porous and crumbled when I tried to lift it. Needless to say, we were using cow bones rather than live people, or live cows for that matter. I got frustrated with the next one and rammed the ends together so hard that it exploded.

That was when Alessandro politely but firmly ejected me from the class. She suggested I needed to study a bit more theory before going back to the practicals. On reflection the exploding bit may have been some of my fire Talent leaking out – the pressure on us was getting quite serious by this point and it was getting to me, even if I didn't realise quite how badly.

At which point they suggested that I focus on that because I was actually quite good at it and after that I only got to do the sort of thing that a paramedic would do rather than what a doctor would. There's no point in perfectly realign a broken arm if the patient bleeds to death while you're doing it.

But after a few days of rattling around at home, avoiding doing the housework and trying to learn Healing, I decided to find out what had happened to Oliver and the sandwich box, visit my favourite pub and maybe have a chat with my favourite Healer. As all of these things just happened to be in and around Central, I packed a bag and got on the train for London.

*

I've become quite fond of the whole Blackfriars area and the slightly odd things that surround it. My dad's from Kennington so we used to come down to London quite often and my cousin Juliet and I used to haunt many of the pubs, clubs and other dives in the capital, so even the Circle Line at chucking out time doesn't bother me too much. The fact that she's just been made a sergeant in the Met probably helps with that feeling of being safe whenever I'm around her.

The Blackfriars area is always insanely busy during the day, and almost as busy in the evenings, and I have never worked out why quite so many people want to cross the river just there at the same time. It also smells, both actually and magically, the latter probably because it's hard by St Paul's, which is one of the strongest places of power in the country. If anyone tried to drain that source like they did at Rockingham the backlash would probably empty the Thames.

The route from the underground to Central is simple and short as the tube station is less than 200 yards from the front door. The brutalist concrete block of the Central College, which the rest of London thinks is a BT building on Queen Victoria Street, is very familiar to me, as it is to most *Jaun* level mages. It started as a telephone exchange, then spent 15 years as a museum before apparently becoming BT offices. It's a far from attractive building, sprawling over the site like illogically stacked Tupperware boxes made of pebble-dashed concrete and sheet glass.

The only thing of note about it is that it stands on the site of a proper castle, Baynard Castle, which was destroyed in a certain conflagration in 1666, along with most of the rest of the city. Outside it, and unnoticed by just about everyone, is a cast aluminium sculpture not unlike a totem pole, called The Seven Ages of Man. Even close up all the seven ages appeared to be variations on the theme of 'grumpy'. I think it's rather splendid.

I'd spent far too long there over the previous couple of years, so I had a security pass and they always managed to find a room for me. I was met by one of the people who usually man the desk who took one look at me, sighed, allocated me one of the rooms overlooking the river – which I always prefer – and almost smiled.

I nodded to him and set off toward the lifts that serviced the annex at the eastern end of the building. My room was the same as most of them, like an anonymous mid-range hotel room with all the charm and style of a caravan park. Once I'd unpacked I did what I always do when I'm at Central by myself; I went to the pub. I love the Black Friar, a Grade II* listed haunt of CAMRA types finished in 1905. It's mostly dark wood with an amazing mosaic ceiling in the dining room and excellent beers, decent ciders and an almost unhealthy fixation with gin. I was happy to wait there until one of those three people came and found me, even though I hadn't told them that I was coming.

The Black Friar is a mage's pub in the same way that you get copper's pubs – a place you can be sure you won't see anything that requires you to be a policeman. The Friar has a big sign over the bar, written in a way that only mages can see, that says '*Magia Ez*', which means 'No Magic'. And trust me, it's not a suggestion.

In the end all three of them arrived at the same time. Nadia likes the beer, but Bev and Oliver Gunn seemed to prefer the gin, especially as I was buying it.

"It wasn't one of those things like Rockingham," said Oliver, halfway down his drink. He showed me a picture of the thing we'd dredged up in Norfolk. "That is a straightforward energy absorption device."

"We don't know who was trying to use it either," said Nadia, "but after what happened in Morston we took some additional readings from the Rockingham device. The thing you broke couldn't have absorbed more than a tiny fraction of the power that's there," she took a pull on her beer, "and the thing you pulled out of the sea was barely even doing that. It was mostly just throwing out a dampening field that blocked the energy enough to make itself noticeable."

"So somebody wasn't really trying to steal the energy from the marsh at Morston?" I asked, by now confused. "It was a decoy?"

"Yes. They were never going to gather much power, at least not with that device anyway." She started in on her second pint with a relish that reminded me of Gronk. "So I've no idea what that thing was even for. It's almost like someone put it there for the purpose of getting noticed – a decoy, as you might say. We've checked with other local mages and they aren't aware of anything that could be in any way relevant to this."

"So what was Gronk on about?"

Oliver snorted. "You asked him about places of power being stripped of their energy, so he told you everything he could find. What else did you expect from someone like him?" Grumpy sod. Accurate, but still grumpy.

"That's true enough," I sighed. Gronk is nothing if not literal, and I was increasingly certain he was on some kind of spectrum somewhere, probably in the far infra-weird.

"So what are you going to do now?" Nadia asked. She didn't seem to be overly concerned, which didn't seem normal. She's usually on top of everything she gets involved in, so this was... odd. Then I realised she was doing it again, seeing that I had a head full of questions and leaving me to work out the answers for myself. It was a habit she had picked up from Richard, and I didn't like it when he did it either.

"Nadia," I said wearily, "I just don't have the energy for this."

Bev, a Healer of extraordinary abilities who is a bit of a genius, and slightly a nutter, nodded. "He really doesn't," she said. "I don't know why, but his energy is seriously compromised, badly scattered."

I looked at her and took another drink. With my Talents in a complete mess odd bits of magic had been leaking out. For example I'd been able to 'read' someone the last time I was here, which is something I shouldn't have been able to do. I'd also been able to locate a powerful magical object by 'feeling' it. I'm sorry about the awful description, but it's sometimes hard to explain stuff like this without sounding borderline deranged. That sort of thing has been happening more and more, including me accidentally heating up things that should have remained cold, like ice cream, and gaining the ability to make people fall asleep just by talking to them. No, hang on, I've always done that.

"This wasn't just a misdirection was it? Get all of us over to Norfolk while something important was going on somewhere else?"

"Well, it could have been that," said Oliver, "but there's no sign of anything very similar happening anywhere else just now." There was something odd about the way he phrased that.

I looked at him. Oliver was jangling my nerves in a big way. "Nothing very similar, is it? So there's been something slightly similar? Vaguely along the same lines? Same sort of style of thing? Can you clarify that please?"

I put down my drink and covered my eyes with one hand, wiping my nose with the other. The slight headache that had lurked at the back of my head for the entire journey to London had now moved right to the front of my head and I was having trouble keeping my eyes open.

"Can we stop this? I just need to know…" Bev gave me a couple of small white pills and eased me to my feet.

"Walk with me," she said. Nobody argued. The air outside the pub, despite having so many car fumes in it that you could probably have folded it, still seemed fresher than inside. In silence we made our way across the front of the tube station, down the steps onto the embankment, and I felt a weight lifting from my mind like a fog bank shifting. We stood by the river, watching the lights of the South Bank glistening on the water. Queen Victoria looked down on us with a fixed, stern and slightly dyspeptic expression while trains swished through the covered bridge above us.

I watched an RNLI boat weaving around the tall red pilings that were all that remained of the old Blackfriars bridge, and wondered why coming here always made me feel better, more grounded, far more than you would expect just from the magic that emanates from Central.

"Oh hell Bev, what's happening to me this time?" I was wearily familiar with this – as soon as one of these bloody things starts to get complicated something horrible happens to me or my magic or both. I usually end up unconscious or having head-fucking dreams whilst confined in the medical department until it gets sorted out. I sniffed miserably.

She laughed quietly. "Have you got a headache? Feel really tired? Muscles aching? Been sneezing?" I nodded. "Mike, you have a cold," she chuckled.

"Is that all?"

"Yup. Sorry, it isn't a magical realignment of your Talents or some kind of premonition. It's just a cold."

"So why do I feel so spectacularly crap?"

"Man flu?" I looked at her. "OK," she laughed, "you know that part of getting you out of the smoke has been pushing you to do things you haven't been able to do before? I suspect this is your subconscious' way of objecting to that."

"Well, it isn't doing me any good, so can you make it stop?"

"We'll try. I think we should go back now because you clearly need to get some rest. Do you promise to get some sleep when we get back, or do I have to do something to make you do that?"

"I promise I'll rest," I said as I followed her in one of the back doors into Central, the one concealed in Blackfriars Passage, and on up to my room. I think she may have done something to me anyway, because once I'd had a brief text conversation with Amy I lay down in the bed and the whole world went away for the next twelve hours or so.

*

I wasn't capable of anything much until after lunch the next day, and even then I felt totally rubbish. I was hunched over another mug of coffee in the common room, chilly and unenthusiastic, when Oliver found me.

"Well, you look like shit," he said, sitting opposite me. I suspect that he was trying to be humorous, but instead it came out sounding like a criticism. I just grunted. "There's been another one," he said.

The canteen was the same as always, although they had made some effort to brighten it up by repainting it. They'd put up some jaunty posters, as well as the prices. It was still called 'Popina', which is the Latin word (via Umbrian), for a restaurant or bistro. Why anyone thought that was a good name was beyond me, and most people call it 'Poppy's".

"Another one what?"

"Power drain."

"I thought the last one wasn't a power drain?" I may have come across as a little testy, because he flinched a bit.

"It wasn't, but Rockingham was, so it counts as 'another'." He sounded exasperated.

"Whatever. How did you sort it out?"

"Why do you think that we have?"

"Past tense – 'been', not 'is'."

He glared at me. "You are altogether too fucking clever. What if that was just bad English?"

"You don't speak bad English Oliver. If you use the past tense then it's something that happened in the past."

There was a long-ish silence of the type that just itches to be filled by impromptu, sometimes inappropriate and often revealing remarks. I filled it with coffee and sniffing, waiting to see if Oliver had anything more to say for himself. He was looking uncomfortable and almost unsure if he was going to speak. "It was another device, but it wasn't spotted because nobody tried to access the power it was collecting," he finally said in a rush, as if he was reluctant to let the words out.

"Where?"

"An ancient site in Wiltshire, a place called West Kennett."

These days Amy is a marine archaeologist, but she started out as an ordinary archaeologist, and she had dragged me around lots of very old places all over Europe, inviting me to gasp in wonder which, truthfully, I rarely did. So I've seen all sorts of things, including a subterranean tunnel in Cornwall called a fogu - which really should be the name of a noxious cheese - part of a Roman bath complex underneath a motorway in Hertfordshire, the astonishing cathedral at Chartes and various bits of Hadrian's Wall, which really does warrant its reputation. I'd also been dragged around the British Museum many times – twice before Amy and I became a couple, which shows how deep she'd got her claws into me before I noticed.

Then there was an early Celtic salt mine at Hallstatt in Switzerland and the unremarkable humps of Sutton Hoo, which looked a bit like a nascent BMX track next to an excellent museum. There was a bit of a hike to a cave at Paviland in south Wales, a tour of the Roman fort at Porchester and more castles than even a Hollywood action hero could reasonably lay siege to. It had all started to blur after a while.

But I clearly remember the sacred landscape of Wiltshire because it was amazing and numinous in a way I couldn't describe, let alone understand. We went to Stonehenge, of course, but despite a splendid visitor centre it sadly has no energy left. Avebury stone circle, however, has so much power the glow is probably visible from orbit. Then there's the huge artificial mound of Silbury Hill, the henge boundary at Durrington Walls and... West Kennett long barrow. It's a long thin Neolithic burial mound from around 3,600 BCE, the resting place of about 50 people, and if it had any power I'd never felt it. So what Oliver was saying made almost no sense, but at that moment I felt so crappy that I didn't much care.

"Another device?" I sighed. "Did you manage to get hold of it this time?"

"We didn't find anything. One of the people in the area just reported the drain of power, that's all."

"Can't have been very much," I said. I wasn't interested; in fact, I just wanted to go to sleep, possibly because I was ill, or possibly because I was bored, or some combination of the two.

"No, but it proves the technique for drawing off the power works. Do you want to investigate?"

"What would be the point?" I sniffed and wiped my sore nose. "The deed is done, the power is gone and the consequences are something very close to zero."

"But Nadia told you to investigate these things," he protested.

"Nadia asked me to *look* into the thing in Norfolk, which I did. And it's just me at the minute, the one with sod-all power and a stinking cold, yeah? So what's the point in me even going there?"

That seemed to stump him. He opened and shut his mouth a couple of times and ran his hand through his hair, disarranging the pedantically deconstructed style. "Right, fine, don't bother," he snapped, slamming to his feet. "I just thought that you'd be interested."

I immediately felt slightly guilty, but with me being powerless and full of snot, it was like getting annoyed with someone who has a broken leg because they don't want to go for a walk. I looked around the common room, which was next to the door to Poppys. It had low tables, semi-comfortable chairs, river views and various newspapers and magazines lying around. The most popular of these was The Magic Circular, the trade paper for the noble and estimable Magic Circle. This occasionally produced hoots of laughter and the search for gigs to supplement the ungenerous wages that the junior staff at Central receive.

My phone pinged several times as I watched the barges and tourist boats sliding under the Millennium Bridge and past the location of the Globe Theatre, which isn't the same as the place where they built the replica. The first ping had been Sam, I knew. Something was changing with her, but I didn't know what.

'All good', it said. *'Home in 4 days. Sick of pasta'*. That made me smile. Despite not being much of a cook, Sam will normally eat almost anything - provided it's stopped moving - but a monotonous diet was not something that she was never very happy with.

The next was Clara. *'I'm coming back this weekend. Lots of reading to do. Will not be bringing Ben with me [more on that later], but I may need to occupy the farm for a while'*. That was fine; in fact I'd expected it and I didn't mind one bit. Mages have odd notions of privacy, probably because we are so closely linked. Oh stop it, you dirty-minded blighter.

The last was Amy. *'Damn the sea is cold here. Should be home in three days or so. I'll text flight details so you can collect me from the airport. Please bring my chair. We need a big gathering when we all get back. Love you.'* Yes dear, whatever you say, I thought, while typing a more tactful reply.

So I had two days to get home, refill the larder and make the house presentable. I had just resigned myself to the whole trip to London being a waste of time when Oliver returned, this time with Nadia in tow. She sat opposite me.

"You off then?" Nadia asked. Telepathy is not an ability that any mage has ever been known to possess, but with Nadia you would never know it.

"I just need to get the house ready," I replied, wiping my nose again. "Looks like they'll all be back in short order. I'm going to have a house full in less than a week."

Oliver's face fell like he was disappointed, or maybe cross. It suddenly occurred to me that maybe he was paying me all this attention because he fancied me. That didn't trouble me. In fact I found the idea slightly flattering, but it wasn't something that I could reciprocate. "Things have been very disrupted recently and I'm keen on having a bit of normal for a while." Famous last words.

"But you haven't sorted out this energy drain business, have you?"

"No, but I have some ideas I want to work on for a bit." I didn't, but I wasn't in the mood to be given anything else to do. "I'm sure Gronk will be delighted to help me."

"Seems a useful chap this Gronk, what with his boat and all that," said Oliver, his voice studiously flat and his face closed.

"He's very bright but, I will concede, he is a bit odd," said Nadia. Bearing in mind some of the extremely bizarre stuff that surrounds the world of magic, that was quite a statement. "He was the assistant director of the Archive before Nottingham got him." I hadn't known that. I wasn't sure if the remarkable Tanya Linden, the current Director of the Archive, would have been pleased to be rid of him or not.

Gronk had come to the college at Nottingham when our previous archivist/librarian, the magnificently named Elmore Hildebrand, had almost succumbed to a massive heart attack whilst trekking in the Cairngorms the autumn before. Elmore had survived but wasn't going to be well enough to come back to the college in the foreseeable future – *Iotar*, just like Patrick. How Gronk had taken to moving from a converted farm near Cirencester to urban Nottingham was not a question I had asked, nor was it one I particularly wanted to hear the answer to, mostly because I had other things I wanted to do this year. I looked at my watch.

"Well, I don't want to miss my train, so I'll have to be off. I'll be in touch," I added, looking at Nadia. "Goodbye," I said to Oliver, just so he was clear. He looked irritated but didn't reply.

*

It wasn't until everyone had been back for a couple of days – and I was feeling a lot better - that I started to wonder about the whole Norfolk thing, and especially Gronk's sudden, unexpectedly and suspiciously convenient appearance. He's not known for his altruism, nor for his fondness for most members of the human race, so the idea of him dropping everything and driving all the way to Morston – more than 3 hours when the traffic is good and even more in that ambulatory ruin he calls a car - just in case we *might* need a hand seemed about as likely as me taking up synchronised swimming by myself. Or at all.

Which meant he'd been sent, and that meant one of the professors at the college, or possibly someone at Central, had told him to join us. And that suggested that they suspected that something, or someone, might happen to us – or we would happen to someone else - and that we might need another pair of magically capable hands. Using Gronk, a Norfolk native, had been clever because it gave a vague suggestion that he was only there because it was his home turf. In criminal investigations it's called 'plausible deniability' – the rest of us call it 'a feeble excuse'.

"But the girls are so capable, competent and something else good beginning with 'c' that sending Gronk to help us didn't make sense. So I decided, on the basis of no facts at all, that it had to be Patrick Ashe, or possibly his best beloved Gerard, that they were concerned about. Otherwise the suspect person we had to fend off had to be one of our own team, or some miscellaneous Norfolkian, or whatever the word is, like the owner of the hotel or the nice lady who served us in the place where we stopped for lunch.

Neither seemed likely, and other than that it had only been the fleeting and transient interactions of everyday life. I raised the idea with Clara, not because I thought she especially wanted to know but only because she happened to be in the room when the thought occurred to me.

"It's an interesting idea," said Clara, her eyes distant while she drew a fine pencil sketch of a flower.

"Does it make sense?"

"No. Well, not really. Gerard is not a mage and Patrick has no power."

"I know that, but who else could it be?" She kept on sketching, something I knew she was good at but I didn't see her do often. She was very good, with a fine, delicate style. "Do you think it's any of us?"

That seemed about as likely as dropping an egg off a mountain and expecting it to bounce. "Of course not."

"Gronk? Oliver? Professor Wicks? Nadia?"

"No." I was starting to feel a bit silly now. "So it has to be someone else, doesn't it?" She was being aggravatingly reasonable, which was almost embarrassing, while delicately shading beneath the petals.

I shrugged. "I suppose so. You got any ideas?"

"Many, but not about this."

Sam and Amy came in at that moment, and as we had a mid-morning coffee break we found ourselves sitting around the big kitchen table in silence. This was an odd moment – it was very unusual that we had all been separated for more than a couple of days, and we still had some catching up to do.

Sam told us about the weather in southern Italy – warmer than here but suffering from some apparently immovable storms. It had taken the combined efforts of nearly twenty *Jaun*-level air Talents to break the pattern. They had also needed numerous water Talents to ameliorate the flooding and several equally powerful earth Talents to cope with the landslides, sink holes and habitat destruction, but it had still caused some serious problems.

It had, she said, been the largest weather project that mages had carried out in Europe for more than a century. The sudden cessation of the intense storms had left the local meteorologists reeling and unsure they would be able to make a reliable forecast for months. The effort had left Sam and the other air Talents exhausted and, in her case, craving some decent Chinese food. Sadly she had to make do with my attempts at it – I am better than I used to be, but my sweet and sour still tastes like deep fried pebbles in wallpaper paste.

Amy told us about the freezing cold water of St George's Channel and the Roman trading vessel that she'd managed to isolate from a swirling tidal flow for long enough for the bits to be recovered from the sea floor. The technical term for them could be flotsam, jetsam or lagan, depending on how the stuff ended up in the water which they couldn't know, so 'bits' seems to be the best term to use. They would probably be exhibited in the National Museum in Dublin after conservation, but that could take several years. Conservation, I'd recently learned, was not a quick process - they'd had to spray polyethylene glycol on the Mary Rose for 34 years before it was safe to let it dry out.

Clara was continuing her drawing, adding a second flower, this time a rose. I don't know what the first one was but it had been tall and spiky and was probably poisonous. "It was very interesting," she said, eyes remaining on the page when we asked about her time in France. "They found my accent confusing." She gave a bleak, twisted grin. "But I found out some very interesting stuff."

"And Ben?"

She still didn't look up. "What about Ben?"

"You said you wouldn't be bringing him back here."

"So? He lives in London."

Amy touched her hand, stilling it. The dragon tattoo shifted slightly. "What happened?"

"Why do you think…?" She stopped. Amy is her *erdikide* so it's virtually impossible to hide anything serious from them. "It was nothing."

Amy leant back and started to plait her hair in a marked manner. She used to wear it down to her waist but she told me that it had started to get in the way when she was diving, so she'd had a hairdresser in Rosslare trim it to shoulder blade length.

Clara lasted almost two minutes. "All right. Ben asked me to move in with him."

You might have expect us to offer congratulations, but she delivered it in the tone that you might use to disclose an undesirable diagnosis or confess to having joined the Ku Klux Klan.

"Not a… welcome suggestion?" Amy asked. I didn't feel qualified to comment because I hadn't actually asked Amy. She'd sort of ambushed me and I wondered, not for the first time, if this was a female thing. Usually I don't mind being surrounded by women but occasionally I feel a bit like I'm drowning. Amy sometimes calls me Captain Clueless, and I felt I was living up to the name at the moment.

"You didn't want to," Sam said. It was obviously not a question.

"No. He is *abèbè*."

"Don't understand that word," said Amy. Neither did I, but I'd got a pretty good idea what it meant.

"He asked me for the wrong reasons."

"The wrong reasons?"

She pressed her pencil into the paper until the point snapped and was ground into dark dust. "When I got back from France I met his friends. There were about ten of them and I was the only one who wasn't white. I realised that I was a trophy, a token, something they could parade around to prove they weren't racist. Sometimes I wonder who it was they were trying to convince. It seemed to be a foregone conclusion that I would agree to live with Ben, and for no other reason than because he asked me to."

I shook my head. Were there still people out there who thought like that? *'Nasty old men and stupid children'* I thought, wondering where they left their dinosaurs when they went to the pub.

"I won't be anyone's conquest, to be waved in front of his friends for the purposes of envy and imagination. I'm sure he's already gained lots of kudos by telling them he'd got me into bed, even though he hasn't." Her face flickered, a brief image of distaste, and I was certain his attempts would always be unsuccessful. She stood up. "I'm going for a walk."

Nobody tried to stop her and nobody tried to go with her. We could all feel how angry and hurt she was, how betrayed she felt. We also understood how little we could do other than just being there, for what that was worth – something, I hoped.

Amy and I looked at each other. "What a slimy bastard," she said.

"I knew it wouldn't last," I said, "but I didn't think it would end like this."

"It's sad," she replied, "but I'm not surprised either."

"Clara doesn't have much luck, does she?"

Amy nodded glumly. "I thought that Dominic might last, but you frightened him off good and proper."

"No I didn't," I replied indignantly.

"You remember Malta? The swimming pool?"

"Oh yes. I take your point. She deserves better than both of them."

"True." She paused. "Maybe different rather than better." She paused again, head on one side like an inquisitive puppy. "She's decided to come back." Clara had been gone about fifteen minutes. "You best start on lunch. Hopefully she'll want to eat something."

"OK." For no reason I could explain this discussion felt... awkward, as if we were skirting around something we didn't want to talk about, the famous 'elephant in the room', but I had literally no idea what it was. I never have any doubts about Amy's fidelity, even though she sometimes goes away for weeks on end, and I believed that she felt the same about me – I certainly give her no reason to think otherwise.

"Why does this feel odd?" I asked as I turned the oven on.

"I thought that was just me being paranoid," Amy replied.

"Oh, it's that too," I said, "but that's normal for you." Which earned me a clunk on the back of the head and a big hug.

"Something from the outside is doing this to us," she said, "and I don't think it's only leakage from Clara. Or maybe it is, and it's just sensitised us."

I touched her face, a tender palm on her cheek, and she echoed the movement. This also allowed us to reach into each other's minds a little, which reassured us that this feeling really was being imposed from the outside and hadn't arisen from anything that either of us had been doing, or was even seriously thinking about doing. It was also rather nice and we were being… cuddly when Sam came back downstairs.

We waited to see if she could feel it. She doesn't have a partner at the moment so it would be interesting to see how it affected her. It didn't appear to, probably because she arrived at the same time as Clara, and any subtle change was swamped by Clara's sadness and anger. And then, just to top it off, the phone rang, jarring the moment and releasing some of the tension.

"Hello," I said as the others started to get out plates and things for lunch. Sometimes we can be so domestic it's like a bloody soap opera.

"Mike, it's Oliver." *'Oh goody'*, I thought, putting it on speaker.

"What can I do for you? This time?" I coughed. The worst of the cold had passed but I still felt a bit crap.

"I'm going to need your help." For the first time he didn't even try to make it sound like a request.

"Still in the smoke, yeah? So what do you think I can I do?"

"You managed Rockingham perfectly well, so I don't see what your problem with being in the smoke is."

Except that without Sam to hold off the snow and Amy to locate the object, I would never have got near the damned thing, but I just couldn't be bothered to explain that to him. "What is it this time?"

"It's another energy drain."

"Not a dampening thing?" I may have sounded a tiny bit sarcastic.

"No. I did check." He sounded affronted, offended even, which made me wary. Something wasn't right about this, but I had no idea what. Oliver may have been a pain but my reaction to him seemed disproportionate, even to me.

"Where is it?"

"It's only about half an hour from where you are, near a place called Ironville."

"And if it's just another drain thing why can't you deal with it yourself?"

"You remember what happened to me? My car? The river?"

"Yeah, I remember." I also remembered that great big defensive spell you told us about that only went off the once. I began to wonder if he'd crashed his car because he'd lost his bottle and was running away. That could easily be true – anyone who can do that to the Rockingham Dragon must be awfully powerful. I made a mental note to find out just how powerful, but only if I could do it from a safe distance.

"I need your amazing ability to get through stuff like this undamaged."

"Trouble is," I said. "I used to do stuff relatively unscathed because I was *isilak*, and immune to magical harm." It struck me, not for the first time, that being immune had proved very useful. I was also aware that magic normally has an equal impact on magical and non-magical people, so exactly how I had been immune I wasn't entirely sure. Maybe 'immune' is the wrong word; perhaps 'shielded' would be better. I wondered if I would be able to go back to being like that.

"But now my Healing Talent is working I have to assume that I'm not safe anymore. I don't want to get hit by the same thing that got you."

He was silent for so long I thought the line had gone dead. "Mike, please come," his voice was suddenly interested. "I, I don't want to do this by myself, not again. Your Healing might come in useful too," he finished, on a note of near desperation.

"OK, I get the message. Did you ask Nadia to send some help?"

"I did. She said I should call you." That sounded just like her. "So you'll come?"

"OK. Er... give me about an hour – I've got some stuff to sort out before I can leave."

"OK, I'll see you there at around four thirty." He gave me directions and then hung up. The ladies were all looking at me.

"So are you going?" Clara asked.

"Yes."

"Where?"

"Ironville."

"And where's Ironville?" Sam asked.

Amy stirred. "It's one of those planned village places, the ones the owners built to house the workers in their mills. It's about 15 miles north east of Nottingham, so about half an hour away. It was developed by... er... Butterly, around... 1830 I think. It's somewhere near Cadnor Castle, on the er... Erewash."

"How do you know all this stuff?" I asked, frankly amazed.

"I don't know, it just sort of sticks in my mind."

"So I'm making lunch then?" Clara asked.

"No. I am." I paused. "And you're coming with me. All of you."

"Why?" Clara asked. She sounded puzzled but her anger seemed to have faded, or at least was no longer as obtrusive. At least my hastily improvised plan to distract her seemed to be working.

"Because I smell a very large rat indeed."

"You think Oliver's involved?"

I thought about his near desperation and the thick silence behind his voice. "I think someone might be forcing him to entice me there."

"So it's an ambush then?"

"I suspect so."

Clara clenched her fists briefly. When she opened them, there was a roiling ball of purple fire in each hand. "Good."

7

We didn't travel together. We didn't even travel at the same time. I let Sam and Amy get at least 20 minutes ahead of us before Clara and I set off up the A611. We had found that the place Oliver was talking about was a really old building, maybe as much as 300 years old, set in a semi-deserted location on the side of a wide valley above something that was technically called a river but was more like a stream on steroids.

I could see Oliver's car, a hastily purchased brick red Hyundai something or other, when I pulled up. I was pleased to note that I couldn't see Amy's car anywhere. The building was squarish, tallish, at least three storeys high, plus an attic under the eaves. I suspect it had once been a small mill building, and it seemed to have been partway through conversion to flats or offices when the bottom fell out of the property market, again, and work had stopped.

Oliver was leaning against the doorway, and was not at all please to see Clara, hide it though he tried – which wasn't very much. "Oh, I didn't think… hello Clara."

"Hello Oliver. Found another one, have you?"

"I think it might be another one," he prevaricated, not looking at me.

"OK, show us this suspect thing then."

"Um... do you want to wait here? I know you were quite poorly, so I thought you might... want to rest... No? Fine, you'd best come along then." The door was already open, and it seemed to have been forced – if by Oliver or someone else I had no idea. The smell of rat became even stronger.

"So where is the actual source of the power?" I asked as we trudged up the dusty, part-constructed staircase.

"The river," Oliver replied, resting his gloved hand on the banister rail as he turned to look at me.

"It can't be a major source," Clara said quietly. "I can't feel anything."

"No, but someone's still trying to drain it," said Oliver hastily. "I thought we might find some clues in here without any danger of getting deep fried by a defensive spell."

"Very thoughtful," I said as we continued to climb the stairs. The floors were empty, even of dividing walls, and the low afternoon sunlight made the interior look like it was on fire. If I had been looking for a renovation project this would have been very attractive.

"It's just up here," he said as we reached the top floor. By now the smell of rat was almost overpowering, because there was no logic whatsoever in putting a magical drain three floors up, especially over such a weak power source as the river.

In the far corner of the room, right over by the water, was a large wooden box, almost the size of a chest. The floor around it was heavily scuffed, although I hadn't noticed any footprints in the dusty wood shavings that littered the staircase.

"You should, er...," said Oliver.

"Yes, of course." I took a step forward while he continued to hover at the top of the staircase. I wondered if the floorboards had been sabotaged, cut through so they would collapse when I stood on them, but the lack of disturbance suggested otherwise. With me walking close to one wall, and Clara the other, we approached the box. It was plain heavy wood, just the size that's awkward for one person to pick up by themselves.

"I feel nothing," said Clara quietly, resting her fingertips on it.

"There's nothing in the box?"

"There's no power anywhere at all. I'll open it – watch out."

I stepped back and turned a little, which meant there was no part of the room I couldn't see. Oliver was still standing at the top of the stairs, his face a studious blank. "Are you all right?" I called out.

"Fine," he replied. "I just don't want to get caught... if anything happens. Somebody has to be able to rescue you," he added. He tried to smile but it looked like the rictus on a desiccated mummy.

"Do you expect something to happen?"

"Well, no, but, after Rockingham..."

'And if you're standing there out of general caution then I'm the scrum half for Manchester Rovers,' I thought.

Meanwhile Clara lifted the lid of the box. There was an odd shimmer across the dust on the floor, but otherwise nothing happened. Inside it was another wooden box, this one just big enough to hold a crash helmet. The smaller box was locked, but Clara broke the hasp with an abrupt gesture. It was empty too, as was the room when I looked up. The floor shimmered again, this time a clear concentric wave moving outwards from where we were standing, a ripple strong enough to raise the dust and almost deform the floorboards.

"What the fuck was that?" I asked.

Clara shrugged. "No idea. Come on – Amy is insisting that we leave now."

"Yeah," I said after a moment. "I'm getting the same thing from Sam as well."

Clara stopped when we reached the stairs. "Oh, there's a thought – we didn't really search the boxes, did we?"

"Shall I go and..."

"No." She turned back and blew them to splinters with a purple fireball the size of a fist that went off like it was stuffed with TNT. Several windows cracked, the shards of glittering glass twinkling as they fell. "Oops. Well at least, that proves that there wasn't anything in them."

"Feel better?" She grinned. "Now stop showing off and let's go."

We clumped down the stairs, try to ignore the increasingly strong urgings that Sam and Amy were pressing into our minds. They met us in the trees beyond the car park, and I noticed that one of them had moved my car and tucked it up the hill next to theirs.

Clara unapologetically explained about the small explosion while Sam continued to stare at the building. I could feel that she was concentrating hard, but I couldn't work out what she was doing.

"That was a trap," said Amy, leaning against her car and wincing.

"We guessed that," I said. "I wonder why it wasn't triggered? Maybe because Clara was there?"

"It was triggered, I suspect when you opened the second box," said Amy.

"But nothing happened."

"Only because Sam stopped it."

"Stopped what?" It was coming dusk in the deep valley now, and the old building loomed over the river as a block of darkness, broken only by the last vestiges of the light in the sky catching the windows.

Sam took a deep breath as Amy turned on the car headlights. The building sprang to life as a grey block against indistinct trees and the irregular glitter of the tiny waterway.

"This," said Sam, and let go. She had been using *eseki*, which very temporarily suspends the action of magic and the consequences of it, so she must have caught it really quickly. For a moment there was nothing, then a broad black crack like a knife slash grew around the corner of the building just where we'd been standing. The toothless grin widened rapidly as a series of loud bangs came from the side of the building that we couldn't see.

You wouldn't expect a structure that had withstood wind, weather, dereliction and developers to shiver, but this one did. Dust puffed out of the walls and the whole corner of the building collapsed, dropping directly into the valley bottom like a drunk missing an aimed-for lamppost.

It took less than three seconds for the rest of the building to notice that something had happened and fold up like a house of cards that's been sneezed on. It was all over in the time it took me to say 'fucking hell'. Even if we'd sprinted Clara and I would have barely made it to the stairs before the whole thing became a pile of rubble.

Amy held up her mobile. "I've made us reservations at a pub in Westwood. The next village to the east." This seemed an oddly nonsequitous statement until she called the police and reported that we'd been driving past and had just seen the building fall down. We waited for them to arrive while Sam got her breath back – she'd suppressed the disintegration of the building for nearly five minutes, which was an astonishing display of control, even for someone as powerful as her.

It took the police nearly half an hour to reach us, and with no reason to think that we were in any way involved, they took very brief statements before letting us go. Then, for the sake of verisimilitude, as well as the fact that we were hungry and a bit shaken, we went to the restaurant in the pub.

'Once more, but for the grace of Sam, I would be dead', I thought so we clambered out of our cars and headed for the door. *So would Clara.* It was a horrible understanding. If I'd been there alone... but then I wouldn't have walked into so obvious a trap alone. I might have brought the police with me, or just Amy or... but if it had been anyone except Sam I would probably still be dead.

I could say thank you, but she didn't need me to. As *erdikide* she felt my gratitude more powerfully than I could ever express with just words. This is what it is to be a mage – a collection of Talents that combine to do some things that are occasionally surprising, rarely malicious but often startlingly, unexpectedly, wonderful. Sam squeezed my hand when she felt my understanding.

We were waiting to be seated in the restaurant by then a place. It was called the Parrot and Trebuchet or something, and the staff were finding our conversation fascinating, to the detriment of the other diners.

Clara broke the moment. "Oliver's trap?"

Amy thought for moment. "He didn't wait to see if it had worked, whether he needed to finish you off. He just got you inside the building and legged it. Left half a wing's worth of paint on the gatepost in the process." Her statement to the police had mentioned a car leaving at speed and her description vaguely suggested Olivers, but she did not hint that she knew the identity of the driver.

"Maybe someone who's in a position to lean on Oliver is after us."

Amy nodded. "It has got to be to do with rescuing the Dragon."

"Why?" Sam asked. "We do other things but the Dragon."

"I know that, but we haven't got in someone's way that much for a while now."

She shrugged. "OK, so it was the Dragon."

"Unless you did something while we were away that you haven't told us about?" Amy asked, arching one eyebrow and tilting her head questioningly at me.

"I was an absolute paragon of dutiful virtue whilst you were gone," I said, trying not to sound smug.

"Really? That was unadventurous of you. I had expected you to be a parody of virtue. A couple of drunken late nights at the very least." OK, she was teasing me, but I didn't spot it just then.

"Who with?"

"Well, Ambrose, who you haven't spoken to for a month, even though he's only down the road. Jerry and Ariadne, who keep wondering if they've offended you in some way, or even Nicky Inglis and her wife. I know she's a Chief Inspector, but she doesn't bite. Well, not unless you ask her to."

"Um," was all I could manage. It was true – I had spent too long sitting at home missing Amy instead of taking my freedom, if that's the right word, and having some fun with it. I was going to claim I was too busy (which, despite the Healer training, was a lie), not feeling very well (also not completely true) or had a prior engagement (ditto), but instead I just shrugged.

"You need to think a bit younger," said Clara. "You're too much like someone twenty years older than you are."

"Well, he doesn't get it from his parents," said Amy, "and his brother is running at least minus five years, so… I don't know. I suspect he's just an old fart in a young body. But he's my old fart, so I don't mind." She smiled and patted my hand.

This made me a bit glum. I knew it was just stress-relieving badinage, but them taking the mick out of someone else for a change would have been nice.

"So what about this whole business with Oliver then?" I was trying to get them back onto the subject of what had happened, but they didn't want to, not just now. Nobody replied, so I tried again. "So did you wreak terrible revenge upon the obnoxious Ben?"

Clara chuckled, the first true smile since she'd come back from France. "Only slightly, but I couldn't do much. He is a *Jaun* 1 fire Talent who does bodyguard work, so he'd have spotted it if I'd started anything serious, but…"

"Tell me," said Sam. "Maybe I need some ideas."

Her last boyfriend, Sho, had been sniffing around again. It seems it hadn't worked out with the girl he'd left Sam for, and he was hoping. Fat chance. She'd probably turn him into a beetle and step on him. The waiter came to take us to our table.

"He's going to find that a number of his new contacts in the magical world are not quite as white, nor as compliant, as he thinks they should be," Clara went on. "Nadia has moved him into a specialist section – he thinks it's a promotion – where none of the four people in the hierarchy above him are Caucasian. Then it's Katherine Duncan and then Nadia. A short, sharp lesson in racial equality that he has to live with. Or, in Katherine's words, 'he can just piss off'."

Katherine Duncan is Nadia's right hand, an attractive red head with such a sweet smile that you could forget for a moment that a smile is just someone baring their teeth.

Then two mobiles rang at the same time. One was Sam's.

"*Wei?*" She started talking, quickly and quietly. The other was Amy's and it turned into one of those one-sided conversations that just itch to have you fill in the spaces. I gathered the person on the other end was driving.

"Yes? Oh, hello."

"Yes I did."

"No, we're fine."

"Probably. Not sure."

"Yes, we are."

"Not any time soon."

"Should be fine."

"Carpaccio?"

"OK." She killed the call and addressed the menu. Sam was still talking.

"Who was that?"

"Nky," she mumbled around a mouthful of a chewy, flavourful sourdough roll.

"Say again?"

She swallowed. "Nicky. We're all on the police system with flags, so when I reported the collapse it triggered an alert on her system."

"Oh." Nicky Inglis is a Detective Chief Inspector based in Rutland and is the local representative of an odd police department called 'Special Operations'. Their job is to deal with us weird magical types, and druids for some reason. The fact that her wife is a Healer means she doesn't try to get us sectioned every time we work together. "She got anything interesting to say?" I asked.

"She was concerned when her system lit up like a Christmas tree, so she wondered if it was something she should be taking an interest in."

I stopped and looked at my own roll, wondering why my sourdough never looked like that. "Oh yes, of course. The Rockingham business isn't something the law would be interested in, but knocking down a building is."

"Yes dear," said Amy.

"So presumably we'll have to talk to her about it at some point."

"We only need an informal conversation with her at this stage. The actual collapse will be dealt with by the local force, and we've already given them a statement."

We chatted for few minutes, and then Amy nodded to the waiter. "Could you lay a couple of new settings please – we have some people joining us shortly."

The staff shuffled a couple of tables around then put out more plates and glasses. Amy glanced at her watch. "They'll both have the Carpaccio for starters and we'll delay our mains until everyone has caught up." The door swung open and she smiled. "They're here – thank you." Sam was still outside on her phone.

The waiter soft-shoed away as Nicky and her wife wove through the tables, sitting down with warm smiles. Melanie is a doctor, tall, dark haired and firm of eye. Nicky is blonde, short and looks about 18, but is a firearms trained DCI with a brain like a computer and a smile that can melt toffee at ten paces.

"You've been having adventures again, haven't you?" Nicky said. "Let's hope nobody ends up in hospital this time." The last time we worked together someone ran her over, fortunately with no lasting consequences beyond a couple of small scars and an enduring mistrust of the Vauxhall Vectra in all its forms.

"Yes, let's try to avoid that," said Amy, half a beat before Melanie.

"So what can you tell me that you didn't want to trouble the local force with?"

Around the starters being cleared and the mains being served, we described the events that had led up to this. Nicky started out interested and ended up cross.

"You bloody idiot," she said to me. "You knew it was a trap and you walked straight into it. Why?"

"Because I knew Sam and Amy could take care of it."

"No you didn't," she replied sharply. "You *hoped* that they could. What would have happened if it had been a conventional explosive device instead of magic? Would Sam have been able to hold that?"

I looked down at my plate. I remember that it was fish of some kind because it was staring balefully up at me. The only thing I could think of was the useless *'but it wasn't like that...'*, the sort of thing people say when they don't want to think about what's going on.

Melanie rubbed my shoulder as Nicky did some violence to a steak. "Nik always gets cross when civilians do stupid stuff like that because it's always far more dangerous than people think it will be. Maybe the building collapse was just criminal damage, but if it had landed on top of you two it would have caused a mountain of paperwork."

Neither Clara nor I had thought to put up more than basic shields, and magical immunity, which I no longer had anyway, is no defence against a strategically lobbed brick, let alone a whole building. "Sorry," I said meekly.

"Talk to me first the next time, you plonker," Nicky replied, with a hint of a grin. "This is what I get underpaid for."

"That's more than I bloody do," I replied.

The main door opened and Sam came back in - she'd been on the phone the entire time. She looked grim, but it didn't stop her devouring several quick bites of her dinner before looking up. "Starving." After a moment she burped in a genteel way. "Better out than in, like Donald Trump in a lifeboat."

I frowned. I could feel Sam was really disturbed about something but she wasn't frightened so much as troubled. "What is it?"

"That was Nadia. There's a big problem at Central and they need to find Oliver urgently. I told her everything."

"What did she say?"

"Fuck." She picked up her drink as a slightly startled retired Colonel type and his blue-rinsed wife muttered about foreigners not using English properly. Knowing Nadia, Sam was using it extremely accurately.

"So what's happened?"

"It seems that Oliver's been working on a *blitzen*." This means 'collector', something that gathers up magic and can sort of store it. The search for a reliable, powerful and portable source of magical power is a big thing at the moment and this device was less for the storage of the power and more for access to it once it's been collected. "He needs to finish it, but he's not there."

Nicky looked at her once we'd explained. "I get the idea that's bad?"

"Not normally, but in this case it's very bad. Oliver was using a major earth power source to charge it – the one at St Paul's Cathedral in this case – but he didn't, er turn off the power drain. It's like he left a tap running and soon the bucket will be full. Once that happens it will spill."

"And that would cause a lot of damage," Clara added.

"Can't someone else just shut it down?" Nicky asked, obviously expecting the answer to be 'no'.

"No," said Sam. "It's an *erreka*."

"Damn," said Clara.

"What?" Nicky asked, sounding alarmed around a mouthful of something that smelled of garlic.

"That literally means 'stream'," Sam replied. "I read about these things. What he has done is like creating a pipeline between the source and Central, and then locked it open. That's fairly normal but he's the only one who's got the key, for want of a way to describe it – and he's vanished. Others can er… put a cork in it, but that won't shut it off properly. For technical reasons, it has to be Oliver who closes it down."

"And he's running," I added.

"Why do you think he's running?" Nicky asked sharply.

"Because he tried to drop a building on me." I said. I tried to make it light but it came out sounding grim. "If I'd done that, I'd be running."

Nicky chewed in silence for a moment, glancing at Melanie. "Mike, I think you could be conflating things. You can't definitively connect the dropping-the-building-into-the-stream thing with the running-away-from-Central thing." She made a sharp gesture with her fork, which Melanie then took out of her hand before she covered any more of the table cloth in sauce. "Are you doing anything, or have you done anything, that might have pissed him off that much?"

"Not that I'm aware of."

"Are you involved in this business at Central?"

"No, this is the first I've heard of it."

Nicky nodded. "You said that you thought that he might have been pressured into luring you there. That requires someone else to be involved. Who else have you been annoying lately?"

"Nobody – well, not enough to make them want to do that to me anyway."

She gave me an unnerving glare, a sort of judicial version of a Paddington Hard Stare. "You need to think about that really hard."

By this time we had finished eating and we decided to call it a night. Nicky paid for all of us, which was kind, and we wound our way back to the farm, speculating in a lack-lustre way about what was going on and failing to formulate a plan that didn't involve spirituous liquor and being sleep.

*

It came as no surprise that Clara was asked to go to Central the next day. The search for Oliver Gunn had also now become official police business, given a higher priority by Nicky's intervention. She was assisted by two DC's we never met and a DS called Keene, who wasn't. Once more our university studies were suspended while we got this sorted out, something that we were sadly all too accustomed to doing.

We all had to give proper statements about the building collapse to DS Keene. It took bloody hours because we had to explain the magic parts to someone who wasn't entirely convinced that magic was real. Nicky had made notes on what we'd said in the restaurant; it seemed that Amy wasn't the only one with a prodigious memory. Once we'd done our part Clara and I went to London.

Central was just the same as usual, apart from the area that Oliver had been working in, which had all its hatches battened down and the sort of security you would expect for the visit of some preening panjandrum. I couldn't even get into the general area he'd been in, and nobody but specialists were allowed into the room where Oliver had been working.

Nadia was acerbic going on furious. "Bloody Oliver. I'm sick of that stupid bastard. What the bloody hell is that fucking idiot playing at?" Nadia was clearly asking the air in her office, not expecting an answer.

"Still no clues?" I asked, trying to swim against the flood of invective.

"No. He paid the bill at the hotel he stayed in before he came to see you, but he hasn't used his credit card or mobile phone for three days, and he hasn't gone home either."

"How did you find that out?"

"As soon as your DCI Inglis got him listed as a person of interest in the destruction of that building she was able to informally give us access to all sorts of interesting stuff."

"Good. How much cash did he withdraw from the bank?"

"Three grand."

"Damn. That will be enough to hold him for a few weeks. Has he done anything that's actually illegal?"

"If we can't prove he made the building collapse, no. Everything else may be stupid and irresponsible but isn't strictly illegal."

Clara nodded. "So he can take himself off without let or hindrance because he's an adult and he can do that if he wants to."

"Afraid so."

"So what happens if he doesn't come back?"

"We'll have a problem," said Katherine, who had been sitting in the corner so quietly I'd barely registered that she was there. "No, we'll have *big* problem."

"There's got to be something that will give us a clue about what's been going on," said Nadia.

"When I first met him he told me he'd just sorted out something in er... Bristol and had driven up that morning," I said, hoping that might help. "Could it be something to do with that?"

"Bristol?" Katherine said, startled. "He came here from Marlborough two days ago. He was staying in a hotel in the town centre."

"He said he'd got up at five to drive to Nottingham that day," I said slowly, hoping I'd recalled his words correctly because sometimes context means a lot – there is a significant difference between 'let's eat, grandma' and 'let's eat grandma.'

"What? I spoke to him in his hotel the evening before he met you. Why would he...?" Nadia trailed off.

"He was dressed very oddly too," I added.

"The grey man?" Nadia asked and I nodded. "Yes, I've seen him do things like that before," she said. "I never could work out why he feels the need to do that. He can be quite odd sometimes."

"I assumed it was a disguise," said Clara.

"Why would he need a disguise if he was on official business?" I said. I told them the explanation he'd given me and it didn't make sense to them either. "Maybe he's planning on doing things people don't want him to?"

Nadia smiled. "I don't need a disguise when I do that."

"Only because you use the equivalent of 'obliviate' to make people forget that you've done it," I said.

"No she doesn't," said Katherine with a grin. "She just doesn't give a stuff what people think about her."

Nadia laughed, which seemed incongruous, almost improper, under the circumstances. That's one of the things I like about Nadia – she doesn't stand anywhere near ceremony, let alone on it.

"So we have to find Oliver so we can get this *erreka* shut down. And we also need to find out what the hell is going on," she said.

I think Clara nodded, but I was remembering things. Something Oliver said, a phone call… "Nadia, do you have records of all the power drain events? Not just the ones we've been involved in?"

"Of course."

"Can you see if one has even been recorded in Wiltshire, at West Kennett?"

"Sure. Kat, could you…" It took Katherine about twenty seconds to find that nothing of the sort had been reported and that, as I suspected, Avebury was the only significant source of power in the area.

"So why would Oliver invite me to go to Wiltshire with him," I said slowly, "if there hadn't been an event?"

"You've no idea?" Clara asked. She sounded confused.

"No. I mean, I did wonder if he, you know, maybe he fancied me or something." Nadia raised an eyebrow. "Oh come on, it is possible."

"Sure," said Nadia. "Some people get turned on by little old men with bald heads or little wobbly jiggly things, so why not?"

"Don't be mean," said Clara. "He's lovely." She meant me. At least I hope she meant me. "Not my type of course, but..."

"Yes, all right, it was just a passing thought. Anyway," I added, with a slightly theatrical bottom lip, "Amy thinks I'm all right."

"Ah," said Nadia, "but she fell in love, which always compromises the reliability of her judgement." I looked at her curiously. There had never been a suggestion that she had a spouse, partner, or even a pet gerbil. "Not just now," she said with a grin, "but I've had my moments."

"How jolly nice for you." I wished I was having one of those moments right now, but I was stuck with these two while Amy was indulging in some creative fabrication with a sceptical DS at a police station in Nottingham.

"Anyway..." Nadia began.

I held up an imperious hand. "Coffee."

Because they know me they conceded without demur and grabbed drinks from the Central common room. "So how are we going to stop the *erreka*?" Clara asked, once we had returned to the conference room. "Or, more importantly, how can we help you to stop it?"

"I need you to talk to the source, to persuade it to cut the connection," said Nadia. "Nobody has a relationship with the earth like you do, and I don't think anyone ever has. So if anyone can do it, you can."

"OK," she said with slow caution.

"I'll help," I offered.

"Thanks," said Clara. "We will need to have another plan ready in case it doesn't work, of course."

"An even bigger cork?"

Nadia glared at me. Her eyes are a rich deep brown that you could easily get lost in, but I wouldn't advise it. There's something in there that's scary and powerful and not quite fully under control. "I told you we've already done that."

I looked out of the window at the Thames, sluggish at the turn but still full of power. "Can you extend the *erreka*?"

"Why? As in, to what purpose?"

"Can it be extended out of the building so the power drains into the river? It's been taking all the crap we've throw at it for thousands of years and it's still just going along."

"We technically could do that, but if we released the power that way the blast could flatten half of London."

I grinned. "Which half? If it's got parliament and the snivel service in it then don't let me stop you."

Nadia laughed. "Don't tempt me."

"What can we do if this plan fails?"

"I don't know. I've got a lot of people working on this." That's one thing about Nadia she always seems to be fully in control of the situation, but over the time I've worked with her I've come to realise that occasionally, despite appearances, she isn't, and when she isn't she *really* isn't.

She sends folks like us off to do things, and always gives you the idea that she's perfectly capable of doing it all herself, but she's too busy, or too bored. In fact she often couldn't do it, especially the bits where being magically active as she is would have made things worse. That's what she needs mugs like me for.

"Can we just pump the energy back in?" I asked.

Clara and Nadia exchanged one of those looks that makes the average person feel about half an inch tall without even knowing why. "It doesn't work like that," said Nadia. This is high level *kemen* stuff, a subject about which I know three quarters of sod-all.

"Once it's passed through the *erreka* it has to be used or dissipated." Excess energy, from whatever source, is usually channelled into a magically powerful location that can soak it up without effort, like emptying an overtopped bucket into a lake. "But just too much of it has built up already. If we could clear that lot we might be able to control the flow, but..."

"Can we, I don't know, burn it off somehow? Use it up?"

"Not quickly enough. If we wanted to cut another channel for the river, maybe..."

"Can we store it?"

"Technically, but how much? That thing you broke could have held maybe 25% of a year's output from the Dragon – but here it would last less than an hour."

"So how long is it before everything goes bang?"

"A month, at best. We have reduced the flow for now, but the pressure will just keep building up, like a stood-on hosepipe. Oliver has got to come in and use his power to shut down the spell or the whole thing is going to go to rat shit in a big way."

On that cheery note she and Katherine left while Clara and I just looked at each other. I felt like swearing, because something was shouting at me, dragging at my mind, but I couldn't quite make it out. I registered that I was tapping my spoon on the table like an inept drummer.

"*Ki sa ki wivé ou?*" Clara asked. I gathered that this was the St Lucian 'patwa' – presumably the local equivalent of 'patois' - or whatever the local language of the island was called, but I had no idea what it meant. "What's is it?" Clara asked, but whether this was a translation I'm not sure.

"I'm missing something."

"Probably..." her voice trailing off as if something else had caught her attention. She was distracted in a way I recognised, so I fell silent and watched her.

At first her face looked still, but then I realised that it was moving very slightly, small frowns and twitches and occasional miniscule turns of the head that suggested she was listening to something she couldn't quite make out. Her face is quite slim and her eyes seem to be laughing when you do something stupid, even if her face doesn't move. Right now I could probably have done naked cartwheels while playing the tuba and she wouldn't have noticed. Er... don't dwell on that image, because I can't play the tuba.

Her breathing shallowed, then deepened and she seemed to drift away toward sleep – while sitting bolt upright with a glass of water in one hand.

I knew better than to even try to move it; all that was happening to Clara was going on inside her head, so her body had gone into a kind of stasis while she sorted out something that involved the higher magical functions of her brain. I'd seen Amy do this for more than an hour once, and she had been so still that I'd thought she was paralysed.

Clara was absent for maybe half an hour. I'd exchanged texts with Amy, alerted Nadia, gone to the loo and watched sunset fall across the river before she came back. I took her glass from her as she flexed her stiffened fingers as her own personal universe came back into alignment with this one.

"Um," she said when I put a coffee down in front of her.

"Take your time."

She blinked slowly, like a sun-stunned lizard. "Long time?"

"Best part of half an hour."

"OK." She rubbed her hands over her face and dragged her fingers across her cornrow hairstyle. "Fine. *Bon.*"

"Anything useful?"

"Yes." She slurped her drink and stood up, a bit unsteadily. "You and I need to have a conversation with a cathedral."

8

London may not be the city that never sleeps, but I don't think it ever does much more than take a quick nap. Even though the rush hour had faded into something a little less relentless and snarly, the city was still alive with light and people and fumes and oh so much of the detritus of the modern world; drifts of litter around empty rubbish bins, vomit-coated drunks communing with lampposts, dead eyed and desperate druggies and so on down the scale of decent human beings to politicians and other varieties of wastemen and criminals. What was below them I didn't want to contemplate meeting.

Clara and I walked up to St Paul's. It's barely five minutes from Central up Sermon Lane and she said that she needed a little more thinking time. The darkening office buildings loomed over us, but we paid them no attention. A well organised pile of glass and concrete is not a threat in and of itself; it's only when it's occupied by the vicious, the greedy, the thoughtless and the indifferent – i.e. most people – that it represents a problem.

St Paul's was lit and looming, and we could feel the energy rolling off it like a prefect surfing wave, poised but never actually breaking. There was a bit of a queue at the ticket booth, and while we had to pay over £20 each just to get into the place, there was no disguising or ignoring the soaring magnificence of the building. It's all white and gold and high and makes you feel like an ant below the glorious vault of heaven – which was doubtless Christopher Wren's intention when he designed the place.

Clara and I paid no attention to the suspended deity but instead headed for the crypt, full of the renowned dead and their less momentous hangers-on. The stairs brought us down opposite Wellington's tomb. To our left were the less reverential areas – toilets, shop, café and so on, so we turned right once we'd circled the mosaic-floored and be-pillared hub of Nelson's last resting place. The white-painted ceiling and clever lighting made it feel open and almost airy, but I wonder what it would have been like when it was only lit by candles and oil lamps – 'stygian' would probably have been an understatement.

We wove past the resting places of Nelson, Wren, Turner, Millais, Florence Nightingale, Lawrence of Arabia and then Nelson again. OK, so we got lost – the crypt has the same footprint as the actual cathedral and was partial built by prisoners. I'm not sure if that last actually matters, but it's something that got stuck in my head.

In the end we found it – a blocky and inconspicuous tomb tucked away in one corner, not far from Christopher Wren's surprisingly modest resting place. It was completely plain apart from the inconspicuous Latin inscription *'cor magicae'* on the base. Some visitors are a little surprised by the number of seats near the 'tomb' – more than a dozen – but nothing more than curiosity happens. Would you bend the ear of the Dean and Chapter of St Paul's about a few extra chairs?

They were comfortable and very supportive, and we sat in the oddly quiet corner and looked into the surface of the stone. Most visitors see polished black granite, but if they looked properly, and had the eyes to see, they would realise that the tiny flecks – normally mica, quartz and one of two kinds of feldspar – are actually moving, albeit everso slightly. Other than when it's all hot and runny this is not the normal state for rock.

"Shall I keep guard?" I asked softly.

"No. I need you with me."

"OK, but why?"

"*Ahots*," she said. Of course. The Dragon had appointed both of us as it's voice, and if we were going to negotiate then we need to bring the biggest set of guns that we could muster. Peashooters compared to what I thought we might be facing, but it was the best we could do.

I dropped a shield over the pair of us, just in case someone felt like relieving me of my wallet, as I felt Clara open a big hole in the universe and we dropped out of the world.

*

I've mentioned what's in a person's magical head space before – crystal caves, buildings, landscapes, all sorts of stuff. This wasn't like that; this was vast and resembled St Paul's Cathedral in the same way that a shoe box resembles a football stadium. It was fucking huge, and it contained exactly nothing, not even colour.

And then, gradually, it didn't. There was a thread of sound, a high pitched noise like a whistle but without the whole drilling-into-your-head aspect. Think top of the scale for an oboe and you'll be as close as I can get. Or possibly a clarinet – anyway, one of those stick-shaped instruments that makes you look like an overfed hamster when you blow into it.

The sound made a spiral in the air, winding down through the vast space and taking on colour and form as it did. It landed as an amorphous lump of glowing greyish silver and quickly became a creature inside a cage. Like the room, it was huge, it's head vaguely equine and every limb tipped with claws the size of a canoe. It was extremely ugly and apparently cross.

"*Hwone?*" Its voice thundered through the space, *basso profundo*, and rolled over us. It sounded like a dog being curious about something, but if we had been in the real world the force would probably have knocked us over. It occurred to me that this thing, which was probably about 100ft high, could never be aware if we spoke because our tiny vocal chords would be making noises too high pitched for it to be able to hear. It would be like trying to hold a conversation with a bat. I also had no idea what it was saying, and I was very glad that it was caged because it looked very scary.

Clara, by contrast, wasn't the slightest bit concerned, which is probably a more sensible approach than mine. "Hello," she said calmly.

"*Hwa béon uncer?*"

"Dæl ágenspræc cwæ."

I had no idea what they were talking about; I didn't even recognise the language, so how the hell Clara was able to have a conversation with it was completely beyond me. Then I realised that she wasn't – she was talking and the language was somehow sorting itself out. They could have been speaking Elfdalian, Ingrian or Vepsian for all I knew.

"Of course," said the creature in a very cultured accent. "I do apologise. It has been an exceptionally long time since I have been able to converse directly with anyone."

Clara smiled. "That's perfectly all right. I'm just glad that we are able communicate at all. Perhaps you could er, shrink a bit?"

"Gegnunga." There was a shimmer and the whole thing, cage and all, shrank until the creature was only slightly larger than us. No longer having nostrils like railway tunnels helped, but there was no way it was going to be considered attractive by anyone blessed with the gift of sight. This thing looked like it had been built by Herbert Frankenstein, the younger and less talented brother of the more famous Victor.

"I'm regret that my appearance does me er… no favours, but my intentions are unchanging," it said.

"That's nice," said Clara. I wasn't so sure – that sounded only superficially reassuring but I was still uneasy and while they talked I walked around the creature. The back of it was no more attractive than the front, but it was consistent. So was the cage, apart from one small area where the iron banding seemed blurred. It wasn't pitted or corroded, it just seemed to be slightly out of focus. I had no idea if this was a problem, an advantage or even a concern. I wasn't sure if, in a place like this, it was even a thing.

The creature, who had introduced itself as Deroc, was talking to Clara with grave seriousness, respecting her position as *ahots* without indicating it was specifically aware of the Rockingham Dragon. I wasn't too surprised about that because there was no reason why it should be.

Anyway, Deroc was being gentlemanly but unhelpful because it said it was unaware of Oliver's efforts to drain power from it. This stuck me as unlikely; Nadia had said that the drain was enough to level a whole city block, and while there was a huge amount of power here I doubted removing that much of it would go unnoticed by anyone.

Clara caught my eye and signalled me over. "It seems that our idea that the power is being drained from here is inaccurate."

I have known Clara for years and I know when there is something going on that she isn't saying. I also knew that however far away we moved the ugly brute in the cage would be able to hear us, and that changing languages would make no difference. "I see. Should we go home now?"

"In a moment. I have a couple more questions." I nodded as she turned back to the thing in the cage and, with them busy, I began to think about what was actually going on in here.

While they had been talking the space had slowly and unobtrusively taken on colour and shape. The roof was now slightly domed and there were sketchy patterns that might have been decorations, and the walls, although no closer, were now definitely walls. I casually looked back at the cage and puzzled at the blurry bit. Now that the room was definitely a room, I could see that the blurred bit wasn't really blurred but more *smeared*, like still-wet paint that's been swiped by a careless sleeve.

The elongation of colour led off across the floor to a part of the wall that seemed to be equally out of focus. I crouched to look and, as I got closer, I felt a presence that seemed to be in, or to be part of, the wall. I poured in some power and visually it firmed up a bit. Having conversations with architecture is not generally considered normal, but just then I had no idea what else to do. "Hello?"

The warm chuckle appeared in my head without troubling my ears. "I hear you. Your suspicions of Deroc are indeed justified."

"Yeah, the cage was a bit of a clue. So what's the story here?"

"It is a parasite, and it wishes to dominate this place."

"And you caged it."

"It was caged," replied the voice with a troubling lack of precision.

"Who are you?"

"I am Kadira, and you are within my scope." His voice was a deep gravelly rumble that would have earned him a fortune doing the voice-overs on trailers for routine and clichéd action movies.

OK, it's getting a bit cryptic now but, based on the only other example of sentient power I'd come across, this seemed to be how they normally talked.

"You are correct to be concerned about this," Kadira said. I knew that he meant the apparent thread that led from Deroc's cage to the wall.

"Is this the energy drain?"

"One of many, *ahots*, but most of them are of no concern. My power is here to be used by the magically capable. It is wholly regrettable that when this peculiar and ill-formed channel was opened Deroc was nearby. The drain will allow the liberation of Deroc if it is not soon halted."

"Can you stop it?"

"No." It paused for a moment. "It is as if I am a fish living in a tank with a leaking tap on it. I cannot leave the tank to close the tap from the outside, and if I try to block it from within I will be hurt."

"I understand that. How long do you have – rather, do *we* have - before it's too late?"

"It will be around three weeks before Deroc can attempt to escape. It will try to speed the drain of power because that will give it the opportunity to flee sooner. It will try to dupe you into doing that for him."

"Is it trying to destroy our world?"

"No, but it must pass through your world to escape, and it would do very much damage in doing so." There was a long pause. "It would also destroy me in making its escape into its own realm."

"You can't throw it out? Send it straight home?"

"Would that I could." It sighed. "I have held it for a such very long time – the third Henry charged his wisest men to restrain Deroc, lest he do more harm, and they passed the responsibility to guard it to me."

Henry III was king from 1207 to 1272, so Deroc was probably speaking Old English when we arrived. Time passes differently in places like this, but it had still been caged for the thick end of 800 years. No wonder it was pissed off.

"Thank you." I glanced at Clara. "I think we need to leave now."

"As you wish. Go well, *ahots*, and leave me in comfort to maintain this place."

I looked around. "What is this place?" I didn't expect Kadira to answer, but he did.

"This is the reason that your capital is where it is, for this is the seat of its power. Your Dragon has the power to protect its castle and the surrounding lands. The spirit of *Innis Metcaut* can encompass the whole island. I am the power of this city, and I have been forever. I am the reason the city is here. It is 600 square miles and I can cover it with just one hand. I invite you to imagine what would happen if Deroc were able to liberate all that power in an instant. It would create the Nightmare City."

The way it said that made it sound like a real thing, a tangible location, but I'd never heard of it. I don't know if it caught the scepticism in my thoughts, but Kadira decided to show me what it meant by the Nightmare City. I nearly shat myself.

*

It was London but it was grey, almost motionless and there were no people. But it wasn't like a black and white picture because there was lots of colour, but it was all shades of grey with deep black in the lee of the buildings, even though the sky was a flat pale glow without any sign of the sun. I shivered.

It was cold and a bitter wind blew down the river without disturbing the single thin trickle of water that slid down the centre of the embanked canyon like a venomous snake without the energy to strike.

All the buildings were dying, the glassless blind-eyed windows staring into the emptiness, the few curtains remaining sweeping like eyelids trying to blink away tears that would never stop. Some had fallen to time and other thieves, and the Shard was just that, a sherd of its former glory. From there, at the north end of the shattered Blackfriars bridge, I shouldn't have been able to see St Paul's, but I could. The dome was gone, not collapsed but sheared off leaving a shape eerily like a teacup. I could see parts of the roof flaking away, bizarrely falling upwards even as I watched.

The most striking thing was that Central was entirely missing. In its place, and reaching along the north bank and much of the way up to St

Paul's itself, was a castle, an honest to god castle. Amy would have known at a glance, but I thought it was probably Norman or something like that.

It looked very blocky, with two open courtyards contained within three or four storey walls with rooms inside them. Three turrets framed the side that faced the river, and there was a pier extending out into the water. It was empty, and there seemed to have been a fire because there were soot stains around the windows, like mascara smeared by weeping.

There was a small boat tied up at the end of the pier, but it was sagging, held up by its rope as the stern dipped into the mud of the riverbed.

Nearer, lower, buildings were being torn apart by a wind that owed nothing to the air, the tops pushed sideways like candle flames being threaded out by a breeze. The fragments fell in slow motion through the sickly air, tumbling lazily until they smashed into the surrounding buildings with crushing violence.

My heart froze. The flatness of the light and the lack of shadows made it even more surreal, and the eerie silence was like a physical force as it rolled down the empty roads. No dystopian vision could convey the sheer bleakness of it because in them there were always signs that people had once been there - abandoned cars, random bits of paper blowing around like urban tumbleweed.

But this was not a city that the people had left; this was a city where the people had been *removed*. Humanity had not fled, nor been wiped out by a pandemic or a war; here they had been erased, every mote, every iota, in a single instant. Humanity had risen and at the height of its existence it had simply ceased to be.

There were no dogs either, or stray cats or even birds. Those trees I could see were as broken and bare as bundles of barbed wire. Humanity wasn't the only thing erased - everything alive had been deleted. It had obviously been some time before, and the lack of any sign of reoccupation suggested that more than just this city had been affected.

I shivered again. This was London with all the life removed, all of it, from the highest to the lowest, from the pigeons that flock Trafalgar Square all the way down to the has-beens and never-weres of parliament. All dead. No, all gone. Including, I realised with a lurch, Amy, Sam and Clara, and mum and dad and everyone else I knew. I was totally alone, even more alone than Mark Watney because I had nothing to return to. I wondered if there had been people on the space station who had watched the world being sterilised and helplessly waited for their food to run out.

I felt fear, despair and a terrible pain in my soul. No, it was in my *gogoan* and the paved streets slowly became the familiar black sand and distant, impossible mountains defined by a skyline previously lost in the distance. But this version was no more stable than the sterilised city, and my black sand landscape started to come apart after only a few moments. At that instant my fear became genuine terror because I had thought I was viewing a possible future, seeing it as an observer, but whatever the hell had happened was now affecting me directly.

Which could only mean that not only was this real, but that I was actually here. Was this Deroc's reality? I saw my hands leave trails in the air as I moved them and the building opposite Blackfriars tube station cracked like it had been hit with an axe and fell toward me. I couldn't move, even though every iota of me was screaming for me to flee. Then the ground gave way and I fell into blackness.

*

I blinked and realised I wasn't under a falling building, but was exactly where I had always been. "Now you understand why it must be stopped," said Kadira.

"Certainly."

I stared at the place where the smear of power from Deroc was leaking out of Kadira's realm. It didn't seem to be a special place, or much of a place at all, but I raised as strong a barrier as I could, attaching a spell to it so that the power from the drain would keep it going. It seemed that being *isilak*, and so powerless, didn't apply here, and I briefly wondered why not.

It took a huge effort to create the barrier and while I knew it wouldn't stop the energy flow completely, I hoped it would slow it a bit more. Once completed I leant back, panting with lungs that, strictly speaking, I didn't have.

"Is it the only parasite you have to deal with?"

"The only one not... trivial," Kadira replied. "Now go. You have a lot to do. I will help you as much as I can." I felt something shift inside me and shivered. "Do not return unprepared," the voice warned me. "Deroc will be waiting for you and, as powerful as you are, you could not stand against it."

"I have no power," I protested.

"To use your current vernacular mage, 'you have no idea'. Once you have found your *jatorri* you may yet prove to be the strongest. Now you must go."

Clara and I left at the same time, returning via an unspecified but definite spot in the vastness. Deroc watched us with hungry eyes, as if trying to work out how we did it, but a shimmering barrier dropped between us and then we were gone.

*

We woke up still under St Paul's, but now with a small gathering around us, including Nadia, Richard Slater, Anne Collister and Bev Hinch.

"Unk." I tried to speak but that was all that came out. Richard handed me a bottle of water. As I drank I noticed that the area was now screened off and the shuffling tourists that glanced across quickly looked away.

"What...?"

"It's fine," said Anne as my eyes got used to the light and Clara drank from the bottle that Bev was holding. She appeared at best semi-conscious.

Then I felt a warmth on my hand and realised that Amy was there, and Sam too. This confused me – they were supposed to be talking to the police in the midlands. I think Amy felt the question.

"You've been here for nearly 18 hours. Richard sent a car for us."

"Oh."

Richard moved into eyeshot. "We need to get you back to Central as soon as we can. You've been through a lot, and other things have been happening." He didn't elaborate. We were helped to our feet and taken to the chapel of St-Somebody-Or-Other and into the back entrance of Central, the one that Sam and I had used when we first came here what felt like a million years ago.

It was all a bit of a blur and once we had been cleared by Lionel and his team they fed us and put us to bed. Clara was very drained but I was feeling itchy and unsettled as well as utterly worn out. Amy later told me that I talked in long semi-coherent sentences for about 5 minutes, then said 'lobster' in a tone of surprise and fell deeply asleep. I have no memory of any of it.

*

"Well, the good news is that thanks to your efforts the energy flow has been further reduced. We now think it's going to be about 3 months before we get any problems," Nadia told us when we were up straight again. "The bad news is that you two nearly gave us all a bloody heart attack. We didn't know where you were – I had to contact Sam and Amy before we could even find you."

Clara and I were sitting in comfy chairs in the small conference room on the topmost floor of the building, one normally reserved for Healers discussing patients and treatments, who is sleeping with who and why on earth they thought that was a good idea. We were being monitored by Bev who was, quote, 'not very fucking happy with you', unquote. It seems that my respiration had gone down to less than 6 breaths a minute, when it should be closer to 15.

"I was concerned about oxygen starvation damaging your brain – if I ever manage to find one," she'd said. I've known Bev for ages and she is a brilliant Healer – and a doctor too – but she was definitely down the pub when bedside manner was being handed out.

I felt fine. So did Clara. The only people who were worried were, well, everyone else. Some people were even cross with us, which I didn't understand; it's not like we did this on purpose, at least not all of it. The meeting was less than entirely harmonious but we still had a lot to say, so Clara and I just ploughed through the base narrative and fielded questions afterwards. I quickly got bored of saying 'I don't know' and 'I didn't ask'.

"So the further slowing of the drain is because you partially closed the hole on that side."

"Yes."

"Why didn't you close it completely?"

"I had nowhere near enough power." I'd almost passed out doing what I'd had, but apparently that wasn't good enough.

"Wasn't there anything else you could do?"

"If Kadira couldn't close it there was no way that I could. It also told me, very firmly, that we mustn't go back unless we are 'prepared', whatever that means." They'd heard this already, but I felt I had to repeat it so I didn't get a kicking for failing to do something I couldn't have done in the first place. I did my best but I'm not bloody Superman.

I was getting cross, despite knowing that they were only doing this because they were desperate. I put my hands flat on the table in front of me and concentrated on slowing my breathing while I identified and relaxed muscle groups all over my body. I don't know how Clara was feeling, but she looked ready to punch someone. Apart from being deadly tired we were both obviously unsettled, and I realised that I'd been feeling like this for a considerable period – weeks, possibly even months.

Amy put her hand on my shoulder. "Breathe. Relax," she said in a soft voice. "There's nothing here to fight." At that moment I realised that my flattened hands had balled into fists without my realising, the knuckles white with pressure. I exhaled and opened my eyes again.

"What can you tell us about Deroc?" Nadia asked.

Clara stirred. "It spoke Old English at the start and Kadira said it was sent there at the time of Henry III."

"I looked into that," said Amy. "I think its confinement dates from somewhere around 1230," she went on. "It was probably during the period when Ralph Neville was Archbishop of Canterbury – there are some ambiguous records from around that time - but they had five Archbishops in three years so it's hard to be sure. Deroc said that it was 'entombed' by the words contained in the *nigoþa agan* of the Ancrene Wisse, the *'wyrgung'*."

I enjoyed the looks of utter confusion on their faces as clearly none of them knew what she was talking about. OK, I didn't either, but I still let a faintly superior smile touch my lips. Afterwards Amy said I looked like I was supressing a burp.

Nadia sighed. "Go on then," enlighten us.

"The Ancrene Wisse is a book of instructions for Anchoresses which dates from around 1231," said Amy, our history expert. "'*Nigoþa agan*' means the ninth part, which is lost; all the extant versions only have eight. *Wyrgung* means 'banishment'." Thank you Wikipedia, I thought.

"So what the hell is Deroc then? You make it sound like a demon, not that demons actually exist, of course." Nadia sounded annoyed. She likes to know what's going on.

Clara sighed, a long, controlled exhalation that passed over my hands like a cooling breeze. "Kadira claims to be an earth power personification, like the Rockingham Dragon, only for the whole of the city of London."

"Bloody hell," was all Anne managed to say.

"Yeah."

"So where did Deroc come from?"

"I don't know, but it mentioned the 'confessors bones'," said Clara.

Richard stirred. "So probably Westminster Abbey. Henry III was responsible for the structure that's there now, but the original building was put up in 1060 by Edward the Confessor, or on his instructions at least. They're both buried there too," he added.

"So why was Deroc caged?"

"It told me that it had been removed and sent to be guarded by Kadira because it was a rival."

"Do you believe that?"

"No," I interjected. "Kadira described Deroc as a parasite. I suspect that the one in the cage was lying, even though that's the sort of thing Kadira would say if it was true."

"I agree," said Clara. "It's sometimes hard to tell the difference between simple hyperbole and genuine boasting. Deroc reminds me of a serial adulterer who is affronted that anyone could object to him doing whatever he wanted, irrespective of the harm he does to other people."

"So Kadira is probably a power like the Dragon, but I'm sure that Deroc isn't. I don't know what it actually is," I added, "but if we can't stop the drain that Oliver started then Kadira is convinced that Deroc will escape. He insists that it would not only destroy him but will also do massive amounts of damage to everything here too."

"And as Kadira is the personification of the power of London," said Richard softly, "it's destruction doesn't bear thinking about."

"But sadly we have to," said Nadia, glancing at him, "because we can't be certain that we can find Oliver in time. And even if we can, I'm not at all sure we can compel him to close the portal. He's set this up to create a huge explosion and do the maximum possible damage, so I haven't the least idea how we could persuade him to defuse his bomb."

"Well, I could threaten to rip his bollocks off." I said. "He's tried to kill me already, so I'm not all that kindly disposed toward him right now."

"That might work," Nadia conceded with a shrug.

"Or I'll just make sure that he's standing right beside it when it detonates. Self-interest is a remarkable motivator in these circumstances." There was a long silence in the neutral space of the room.

"Would you want to stay there to make sure he doesn't leg it?"

"I can make certain he can't run away," I said darkly.

"I assume you've had no joy with the track and trace?" Clara asked after a moment. 'Track and trace' is a basic magical technique that can be used to locate almost anything most of the time. It's used most often by the emergency services and is extremely useful when it works.

"Nothing, as you'd expect," said Anne. "He's shielding himself. Oliver could be in a flat in Shoreditch or on a boat off the coast of Canada by now."

"Do you have any idea why he's doing this?"

"No."

"Any idea how the whole Rockingham business is related to this?"

"I'm not even sure that it is," she replied.

That didn't ring right with me, but I couldn't explain why. "So what the hell do we do now?"

"Well, that's the problem," said Richard. I don't think I'd ever heard him sound so weary, so defeated and Nadia reached out and squeezed his hand. Despite the age gap – over 10 years – they are *erdikide* and even though their relationship was genially combative, the affection between them was evident when things got difficult. But right now something was infecting everyone with a corrosive despondency, and mutual support seemed to be the only way through.

"Either we have to find a way to close the drain ourselves – which we have no idea how to do – or find Oliver – same problem – and get him to do it. I can't see how we are going to make either of them happen."

"It's OK, Richie, we'll sort it out," said Nadia softly.

"You've plenty of very senior mages available, haven't you?" I asked, trying to be reassuring. She seemed to have an endless supply of experts that she could call on at the drop of anything that even vaguely resembled a hat.

Nadia looked at me oddly. "Mike, how many Talents above *Jaun* 5 do you think there are in this country?"

I thought for a moment. Best part of twenty Colleges, each with a Professor for each Talent, plus spares, so maybe a 150 there. Then the ones at Central and the equivalents in Scotland and Wales, plus the retired and Nadia's endless specialists... "Six hundred at least, I suspect probably nearer a thousand."

"Mike, there are aren't five thousand at that level on the whole planet. There are fewer than two hundred in the country."

"I'm confused. You seem to have so many on call."

Richard turned his head. "You know that there are significant points in a mage's development. *Iksale* 4, when you start doing serious spells. *Ikasberri*, when you're apprenticed to a senior mage." He paused. "I know that you weren't, which may be part of the problem. Then it's *Jaun* 1, and the next is *Jaun* 4. The vast majority of mages don't get to the *Jaun* grades at all, and even then they get stuck because the control, knowledge, precision and sheer bloody power required to go beyond that is phenomenal. Anne, Nadia and I are all *Jaun* 10, and there are barely two hundred people of our level or higher in the world." He sighed. "So while we do have senior mages available, we don't have nearly as many as you seem to think."

I stared. I hadn't thought about it at all. "But you always have so many specialists on tap," I said to Nadia. My voice sounded weak, almost pleading.

"They aren't all above *Jaun* 5 Mike. Several of the really specialised ones aren't even *Jaun* levels. Do you remember the one who opened the safe at that art gallery?" I nodded – he'd been an innocuous looking elderly man who had displayed extraordinary levels of power and control. "*Iksale* 2, but hyper-specialised." She sighed. "I can't think of anyone better suited to deal with this than you four." She smiled, still holding Richard's hand. "Today, you're my specialists."

The meeting broke up not long afterwards and we headed back to the farm. Once we were on the train and clear of London it was Sam who voiced the idea that the leakage from the drain was effecting everyone at Central. We'd never seen them so negative and defeated so I called Nadia, who I almost had to shout at to get motivated, finally agreed that Central needed to either be evacuated or to have the shielding around the *erreka* significantly increased. It was disturbing that they hadn't realised that they needed to that themselves.

*

Back in the empty spaces of the farm we had a chance to take stock. Sometimes you just need to pause, to take a moment, even when time pressure is a constant concern. Finding Oliver was a mounting headache because while time *ticked* away, Oliver could *run* away. All he had to do was stay hidden in a B&B in Liverpool, a hotel in Lincoln or a caravan in Llandudno until it all went off and then do, well, whatever he had planned.

But apart from an act of wanton and pointless destruction, none of us could think what the hell it could be. I mean, what possible advantage could he gain from wrecking Central? It couldn't be something to do with the people, or something that was kept there, because he could be certain that the building will be emptied well before anything happened. Once it's empty Central is just another building, and I knew that Richard had already started looking for a new place to set up shop, possibly annexing part of our college in Nottingham as a last resort.

He told me that the current favourite, if they stayed in London, was the old American Embassy in Grosvenor Square. It had been mostly empty since the yanks decamped to that thing that looks like a Borg Cube that's crash landed in Nine Elms. But it's only about 3 miles from Central so he was looking further afield, even contemplating Bristol or Leeds.

Work, study and ordinary life loomed, getting in the way of this business, but all we thought about was finding Oliver Gunn and saving Central. Even listing him as an official missing person hadn't helped, since his car was still in its garage and his house had been packed up just as you would for an extended absence. He clearly knew what was likely to happen, but none of us could work out why.

There were other things to consider as well, not the least of which was why the Dragon had thought that Sam's skills would be needed soon. Maybe we could close the *erreka* with a lightning strike? No, probably not.

I needed to think about this, but away from anywhere where things might be interesting or noisy, or provide any other form of distraction. A lot of what we thought Oliver was doing didn't seem quite right, didn't seem plausible let alone reasonable. We had no sense that he was irrational, delusional or psychopathic, but we seemed to be basing our assumptions on several premises that I was no longer certain were reliable. Or, as Sam so eloquently put it, 'what the fuck he doing?'"

One thought was that I wasn't completely clear about was what all the consequences of failing to close the *erreka* would be. A large scale disruption of magical stuff would be one thing, but if the explosion was of the 'bits flying everywhere' variety, that would be another. Was there something else within range of the blast that Oliver was targeting, rather than Central itself? I hadn't the energy to explain my thoughts to Nadia, so I sent her an email outlining my concerns. I didn't expect an answer soon.

I couldn't even be certain that whatever was behind this was real, was something that even existed. There is a class of magical items, extremely rare, that are termed 'theoretical objects', and they can create all the effects of something real without actually being there. It's like seeing something cut through a piece of paper without there being a knife present. They're tricky things, theoretical objects, because you can end up stabbing yourself in the leg with something that, strictly speaking, doesn't exist.

Amy came up with an interesting thought - just because we can't work out what he's trying to do doesn't mean that he isn't doing anything. There's an old archaeological dictum – 'absence of proof is not proof of absence'; or, in English, just because you can't find something *now* doesn't mean that it was never there.

A bit like Oliver, the slippery git. So we played the hypothesis game, of 'what if' without any constraints of probability or common sense.

Idea one: *He wants to destroy something in or near Central, or Central itself.*

Idea two: *He wants to neutralise something magical in or near Central.*

Idea three: *He wants to release Deroc.*

Idea four: *He wants to destroy the St Paul's place of power, or even the Cathedral itself.*

Idea five: *He's a nutter (or, as Sam said, 'he's not got all his oars in the water').*

Idea six: *He's made a huge mistake but he's running away rather than own up and getting help to fix it.*

Idea seven: *Any or all of the above, but at someone else's behest.*

Idea eight: *He's gathering power for something, and instead of trying to free the Dragon, it was him who set the jar in the first place (although we couldn't see how that could tie in the with the dampening thing in Norfolk).*

Idea nine: *He's doing something that we haven't thought of yet.*

As a summary, it was a pretty good way of clearing my head, but I'm not sure it moved us on at all. One and two depended on what Nadia said - I knew that Central was an outrageously ugly building but it isn't so bad you'd want to blow it up. Three was unlikely because we had no evidence that anyone knew that the damned creature existed until Clara and I found it. Four... possibly, but we couldn't think of why. Five didn't seem likely, but couldn't be ruled out. Six seemed equally improbable, but again couldn't be ruled out – I mean, if it was true, why wouldn't he just ask for help? It's a completely ordinary and unremarkable thing to do. Seven, god knows. Eight had a feeling of being at least reasonable, but there were several things that spoke against it. So, on balance, nine seemed to be by far the most likely.

I'm leaving out Clara's suggestion that he'd been taken over by a *Goa'uld*, one of those worm things from Stargate, and Amy's that he was being directed by a mind-control ray from an alien spacecraft. We also mooted an evil twin brother, flashbacks from past lives and direct substitution a *la* Invasion of the Body Snatchers. All of which entertained us through a long dark evening, but didn't actually get us anywhere.

*

We got two messages the next day. One was a detailed 'shopping list' of the probable fall out if the *erreka* was not closed in time and it made for very uncomfortable reading. The backlash would fry the brain of every magically capable person, whatever their level, within about 10 miles. That could mean hundreds of people being abruptly slammed into a fugue state, which is what happens when a mage becomes trapped inside their own mind. Nobody ever recovers from a fugue, so they are never put on life support.

The physical damage just didn't bear thinking about. According to Nadia the explosion would destroy everything from Temple Gardens in the west to the Millennium Bridge in the east. It would raze buildings as far as Ludgate Hill in the north and the blast would travel south over the river, wrecking Blackfriars bridge and the railway station, and it would probably flatten everything all the way to the Founders Arms on Hopton Street. St Paul's and the Tate Modern would be completely destroyed, the Globe shattered beyond recovery. That's a radius of about a mile – so $4.5km^2$ of destruction, with a lot of very serious damage much further out than that.

The Embankment would rupture instantly, and because the blast would be spherical rather than circular, it could knock aeroplanes out of the sky and dig a fucking great hole. Not the full half mile down of course, but certainly enough to drain the Thames and shatter every water pipe, gas line, electrical cable and data link as well. What it would do to the tube system I couldn't calculate – the Circle line, District, Metropolitan, Central, Hammersmith, Thameslink... most of them probably beyond economic recovery. It would probably be easier to list the lines that wouldn't be damaged.

So, no pressure to find Oliver then.

The second message came from Gerard over in Norfolk, asking us to contact him as soon as possible. While Nadia was totally absorbed with being a Cassandrian Prophet of Doom, Gerard might have something useful to tell us, so I called him. I hoped that it wasn't bad news about Patrick, who had been very wan and weak the last time I'd seen him.

Thankfully it wasn't, and I ended up speaking to Patrick himself. He sounded remarkably chipper, although I wouldn't use the term 'hale'. Not that I was likely to anyway, but still. Once we had exchanged pleasantries we got down to business.

"Now then dear boy, I may have a tiny bit of news for you."

"OK. Relevant to what?"

"That silly business at Morston and your troubles in London. You know that Central has put out a message because they want to locate this Oliver Gunn chap?"

"Yes." We don't have something like Magicweb, our own internet system that's powered by fairy dust, but we do have emails and an alert system that can be pointed at Bookface, Twittergram or whatever incarnation of vacuousness is most popular this week. Nadia had put out the equivalent of a 'wanted poster' for Oliver, with photos.

"Well, he was here."

"Where?"

"Here. Two weeks before you came."

"What was he doing?"

"Hiring a boat."

9

The implications of that left me extremely confused. My carefully numbered options had all gone the way of the dinosaurs – disappeared in one great big bang, but probably with fewer singed feathers. And if Oliver bloody Gunn had set up the whole power drain thing at Morston, everything made even less sense than I'd thought it did.

"I won't ask if you're sure," I said to Patrick, "because you wouldn't be telling me if you weren't, but do you have any additional information?"

"Of course dear boy." He coughed. "I've had a lovely time being Sherlock Holmes."

"With Gerard in the role of Dr Watson?"

He laughed, then coughed again. "He's more like Billy Wiggins. He's good at being inconspicuous and of course him being a local boy helps."

"I imagine so. How did you find out this information?"

"Well, I saw that email from Miss Hussain a few days ago, and we decided to go and have a bit of an investigate." His voice was light and joyful, but I could hear that it was rasping a bit, which was a sound that I didn't like.

"So where did he get the boat from?"

"A boat yard here in Wells."

"How long did he hire it for?" I spoke in a very measured tone, trying to slow him down, and I could hear him sipping something. His voice grew stronger after a moment.

"Three days. You don't need a licence to hire a boat but he convinced them he knew what he was doing, so they let him have it."

"And it was out for the whole time?"

"Away from the boatyard yes, and he returned it undamaged, but what he was doing..."

"Do you have any idea where he went?"

I could hear a tiny smirk. "I think we can work that out, don't you dear?"

"Fair enough," I conceded with a chuckle. "Do you know if he went anywhere else?"

"Well, he returned it with a full tank of fuel as required so that doesn't help and, of course, they don't have a milometer." He paused. "Or should that be a 'knotometer'?" He chuckled, a damp and breathy noise.

"I think I can hear the word 'but' creeping towards this conversation," I said.

"I knew you were a quick one," he said hoarsely, stopping to drink again. "Oh, there's a joke in there somewhere, but... anyway, Gerard spoke to the local lifeboat crew. They even spotted him down as far as Salthouse, and they think he came ashore at Blakeney too, probably to have lunch."

"Interesting. So do you think he..."

"Of course he did. He could easily have planted all those silly things in a couple of days. But he would have had to make them all in advance, of course."

"Of course. Any idea how long that would have taken him?"

"Ages, I'm sure, absolutely ages. There was a lot of planning behind this, and he would have had to buy all the bits to make them too."

"It adds another whole layer of premeditation to this if he had to spend that much time preparing for it."

"Indeed it does, dear boy, indeed it does."

"Is there anything else?" He was sounding breathless at this point.

"Only that he came back here again very soon after you left."

"After we left? How soon?"

"Not even two days." He paused to let the implications of that sink in, but they just floated by me.

"Fucking hell. Any idea what he did?"

"He was seen going up the High Street." He made it sound like he was descending into the very depths of depravity.

"Er... sorry Patrick, I don't understand the relevance of it being the High Street."

"It's just a road, silly, the one that goes inland from the quayside in Blakeney."

"Any idea where he went after that?"

"No dear. One of our friends just happened to see him, that's all. Face on him like a thundercloud apparently. We've no positive sightings after that, at least not that we've heard of yet."

"Is there anything noteworthy up that road?"

"Oh yes, plenty, but not that's relevant to this matter. I could show you some things..."

"If you could look into..."

"Don't worry dear boy, the North Norfolk Irregulars are on the case." He paused to drink once more. "Please can you all come and see me when this is over, if it's soon enough? I think I may have something for you." On that appallingly cryptic note, he cut the connection.

*

All of which was very interesting but didn't get us much further, other than in terms of Oliver's movements. The Rockingham business happened, and then he set up this whole stupid thing in Norfolk, no idea why, then he tries the West Kennett phony, whatever the hell that was about, then attempts to drop a building on me – it was hard not to take it personally.

Then he abandons the *erreka* project and does a bunk. What fits these pieces together? What is the coherent narrative that connects these things? An incoherent one would do. What single motive or desired outcome could possibly explain them?

I had no idea, so I asked the usual collection of brains to get together for a discussion. Granted, that meant another trip to London, but as that was where it was all going to go to rat shit in a few weeks anyway it was probably a sensible place to go, if not necessarily a clever one. Especially if we came up with a brilliant idea that could solve everything. OK, there wasn't much chance of that, but you can always hope.

*

The train journey, as different from the last one as one of a pair of socks is from the other, bored me, so I won't repeat the details. The tube was the tube, now so familiar that we were rising from our seats before the car had even started to slow. Blackfriars Bridge was heaving with people, as always, but now I looked at it with the eyes of desolation; you never value anything quite so much as when you are in danger of losing it.

I was in a sombre mood when we were met in reception by Katherine Duncan, who wordlessly escorted us to Conference 10, which is where we always seemed to end up, probably because it's the largest. There are about fifteen of the things – mages talk a lot, and when serious magic is happening they have to be in the same room. This is because magic has a significant emotional content, and the higher level of the spell the more there is. You can't do it by phone, Skype, Zoom, email, smoke signals or anything else -

you have to be nearby. It's been tested and proven time and time again, and it's a major pain in the arse.

Conference 10 could easily have been our incident room, with whiteboards covered in lines and photos and smelling of stale coffee and frustration. It actually smelled of fear and the sweat of people who had wanted just one more cigarette before they started, which was odd because nobody in the room was stupid enough to smoke.

Richard chaired as usual, but the conversation just stuttered around going nowhere. We all knew what the facts were and none of us could make any sense of them, so it became a Mobius conversation about what Oliver did and why. I became increasingly certain that they had called this meeting because they couldn't think of what else to do.

"Enough," I said after about 10 minutes of this gale-force buggering around. "I was afraid of this."

"What?" Nadia asked shortly. The extra shielding around the *erreka* had helped but everyone was still on edge.

"Finding that fuckwit and working out what the hell his motivation is should not be our priority."

"If we can't find him then we can't get him to shut off the *erreka*," Nadia pointed out. "Try to keep up."

"Yes, I know that. I once asked if we could divert it, but you said that it was too powerful."

"Yes, and it could get even worse if this Deroc creature continues to push against it."

"So I wondered, in my ignorant way," I said, "if there was another way of reducing the flow so it would be safe to divert what is left of it."

"Not with Deroc involved. Without that we might just have managed it, but, well, it may only be a parasite but it's well powerful," Nadia replied. "I had to get Tanya over at the Archive to look out some very obscure references to find any mention of this sort of thing happening before."

"That was where I was going," I said. "If we can get rid of Deroc we stand a chance of at least delaying it further, if not preventing it altogether."

"Yes. Six months, maybe longer," Nadia replied.

"Good. Now, Clara is certain that Deroc is a creature of air. For some reason I seem to be able to interact with the material structure of wherever the hell we are, so this is the proposal."

We had discussed this on the train, earning us may curious glances from other passengers until they decided that we were gamers and turned their attention to other people's conversations instead.

"Sam, Clara and I will go back into their realm. Sam, being of the air, helped by Clara and with my usually fruitless attempts at assistance, will eliminate Deroc. Then I'll close off the leak as much as I can, hopefully with the cooperation of Kadira, and then we will all come back. That should give us plenty of time to find Oliver Gunn and pull his toenails out one at a time until he closes the damn thing."

There was a long silence in the room, a combination of surprise, amazement and probably despair. "You know," said Richard in a conversational tone, "I could list everything that's wrong with that plan but I'd have to stop halfway through to shave."

"Like?"

"In no particular order: if Kadira has to hold Deroc in a cage that means he's incapable of destroying it, and if Kadira can't, what the hell makes you think that you can? Second, how will you block the hole? Are you going to stick your finger in it, like some sort of metaphysical Dutch kid? Third, it's insanely dangerous. Fourth, if you don't succeed you're likely to ruin what little control we still have over the drain. Fifth... it's suicide, and a suicide that can only make everything worse. We really can't let you do it."

"Do you have a better plan?" That earned me a steely glare and another long silence.

"Well, it could work," said Katherine quietly.

"It could get them all killed," replied Nadia.

"Yes. And?"

Nobody wanted to say anything just in case we did end up getting killed. For once, Nadia had nobody else to send, no handy expert to step in and provide all the answers. Nobody except us, and we were...

"If this is to stand any chance of working, you'll need something you've never seen before," said Anne eventually. "You going to need access to old magic, magic from the blood and bone, the power that everything else is built on."

"*Kemen*? I'm not..." I began, then fell silent as she shook her head.

"I'd better explain. We think that the first time people used magic was probably during the Neolithic period, so about 8,000 years ago. Their spells would all have been to do with survival – the Shaman who was a Healer, the wise woman who could make fire with a touch, the children who could make the crops grow whatever the conditions, the hunters who could track animals for days without stopping. It didn't become significantly more developed than that until people stopped thinking that anything they couldn't explain must be demonic and the era of burning witches was over. It only really steadied down once at least the basics of science had been grasped."

I nodded. This was something that first year mages studied to give their magical muscles a rest – the history of magic. Generally the professors never went further back than written records because before then it's all uncomfortably speculative. I was still vaguely amused that the last prosecution under the Witchcraft Act, in 1945, was for *not* being a witch rather than being one.

Most first years, superior beings that they are (and I include myself in this sorry collection of nitwits) found tales of early magic quite funny and quaint, especially some of the complex and bizarre spell casting rituals.

I have often wondered how these hyper-complex rituals were developed. Multi-step incantations, peculiar objects, burning herbs – if it was vital to do all these bits in that precise way and in that order, how the devil did they work it out? How many false starts were there and how many dangerous failures? How many times did they give up on something that could have worked if they'd stuck at it? And, in most cases, why the hell did they bother?

I'll give you an example: Say you have a piece of metal that you needed to make very strong, to make a sword for example. Conventionally you would heat it, fold it and hammer it over and over until the crystal structure has been broken down and then re-formed with much smaller crystals, which makes the metal stronger. This technique, called 'pattern welding', was common practice during the European Bronze Age and Samurai-era Japan.

But by the late 18th century, mages had somehow decided that a better way was for the billet of iron to be coated with a paste made of Dittany, Rue and Samphire for two days. Then it had to be placed on a large lump of polished granite (which is actually quite sensible) and have two pieces of raw copper placed on it, with all of it lined up strictly north-south. Then torches had to be lit around the chamber and ritual chants had to be ritually chanted. There was probably some specification that this had to be done by lightly or partially clad girls in their older teenage years, but such distasteful details have thankfully been lost.

The next part had to be done by at least three mages, one of which had to be a 'grand master', whatever that meant. I warn you, the more you get into the history of magic the more you discover that they seemed to have been a bunch of pretentious tossers.

Then some Grand Master or Witch Queen or whatever would intone a spell of tongue-stumbling complexity and strike the billet with a wand made of silver. All this took some hours. After that there was a lot of milling around before they did it all over again. They had to do this half a dozen times to achieve the same effect as they could have had ten minutes in the hands of a competent blacksmith.

These days a *kemen* Talent – and they only have to be *Iksale* 2 – just touches it and casts the spell *indarra-aima*. This creates something stronger than the very best pattern-welded steel and only takes about two minutes. It is perfectly possible to have scantily clad people present, if doing so is mutually agreeable, but it will have no effect on the efficacy of the magic, although it may on the spell caster's concentration.

When people discover that the first aeroplane flight covered less distance than the wingspan of a 747, they sort of dismiss it. What's interesting about Kittihawk when you can read about stealth fighters? What's really interesting isn't what they did, but the kind of mind required to conceive of it in the first place. Steam engines, aeroplanes, dams, medicines – they're all largely improvements on a basic principle, and that's excellent and laudable, but it takes a genius to invent something that a clever engineer can improve on and a competent artificer can copy.

Anne waited for all this to go through my mind before speaking again. "It won't take very long but it will be difficult and you will all have to do it. And we have no idea what the consequences will be. I'm talking to you in particular Mike," she said, taking my hand, an unexpected, tender gesture. "Be aware that in your current state it could shut down all of your magic."

"Or open everything up," added Nadia.

"You'll recall my observations about this being insanely dangerous?" Richard asked. "This could make it worse."

I looked at Amy, Sam and Clara. I was sure they could do this without me. I didn't have to put myself in the way of this additional danger but the thought of not doing this with the ladies made me very uncomfortable. Man the Mighty Hunter Protecting The Little Woman Back Home, real proper Neolithic thinking. But this wasn't about my ego, this was about what would work, irrespective of the consequences to my archaic male sensibilities. But I couldn't help but want to protect them. I looked at Nadia.

"Could they do this without me?"

"No. The fact that you are *euste* across five Talents is the only reason this stands even the faintest chance of success. You probably won't have to do anything in particular, but once you've got access to this stuff you just being there means you should be able to close the wall. The old magic will just make success far more likely."

"How much more likely?" Nadia shrugged. "You have remembered that I'm still *kea*, yes? Lost in the smoke."

"That won't matter," said Anne, "because when you get down to the basics, the real fundamental stuff, *kea* doesn't have any impact. It only influences the higher functions of magic, the way that it comes from the mage and interacts with the outside world. It's even possible that this may free you of the smoke, because we'll be stripping down your magic to its absolute simplest form and then rebuilding it."

"That sounds painful," I said. "Why haven't we tried this already?"

"Because it's very difficult to do, and with the least misstep your magic could get fried, and it could just as easily kill you. So it's not something we would do unless no other option – including letting you carry on as you are – presents itself."

"Is it that dangerous for the girls as well?" The idea horrified me.

"No. Only for you."

"Why am I not surprised." I shook my head. "And if we don't succeed then half a dozen square miles of central London will be destroyed and hundreds of people will get put into a fugue state," I said, my heart sinking.

"It's a calculated risk," said Richard. "If you do nothing it's destruction and fugues all round. If you go to Kadira and fail you'll all be injured or possibly killed, and the destruction could be worse. If you go to

Kadira and succeed there will be no fugues, much less damage and that postponed for months." He offered a bleak grin. "No pressure."

It wasn't necessary to ask the others – we had already discussed this in general terms and we all knew what had to be done. Don't get the idea this was any version of heroism, the steadfast facing of death for the greater good. I was properly scared and I knew the others were too. None of us *wanted* to do it, but we knew we were the only ones who could and we couldn't just run away.

I know plenty of people who would, but I'm that special kind of idiot that can't. This was being a 'have a go hero' on an epic scale, but it was no more than any member of the emergency services or the armed forces who run toward trouble rather than away from it. I didn't feel like a hero for doing it, but I would have felt like a coward if I hadn't.

"So when do we start?" Amy asked.

"You're all bloody mad," said Nadia, "but thank you."

*

I've met some odd people in my life, not least of which is Gronk, but I have never met anyone quite as fucking weird as Abraham Croft and Amelia Bond. They were the people who were due to train us in the old magic while everyone else continued to play 'Hunt the Oliver' in the hope that we wouldn't need what they taught us.

They lived in a building on Little Sanctuary, midway between St James Park and Westminster Abbey, not far from the Supreme Court. We walked into the house and the outer door swung gently shut without us touching it, thankfully muffling the penetrating traffic noise and the melodious clang of the bells of the Abbey.

Little Sanctuary is a classic London urban oddity; framed by ornately turreted buildings, the road is a grand total of 162m long and got its name because it used to be a place where prisoners could flee to for sanctuary from the law. There is even the original entrance to Tothill Fields Bridewell prison partway down, although it doesn't lead anywhere there days.

Not far from Parliament Square, the building was notable for its overblown and under-maintained grandiloquence, and extreme scruffiness. The inner door opened as we approached, revealing a hallway encrusted in ephemera. It coated the few items of furniture like barnacles, or a particularly stubborn kind of moss. It wasn't filthy or rat infested or anything like that, it just looked like it hadn't been tidied since the war – I swear I found ration books on the hall table. It reminded me of Sir John Soane's house in Lincoln's Inn, but without the gift shop or the charm.

Nadia had – well, I was going to say 'briefed us' but it would be more accurate to say 'warned us' - about these two. Later she had to reassure us that their oddness wasn't the result of dealings with the old magic, but the other way around.

They stood side by side to greet us, both of them tall and a little too slim, about 25 years old and dressed in clothes their grandparents would have considered a bit old fashioned. Some people, like Clara, smile naturally and when they do they light up the room; others do it quietly or reluctantly, but these two did it like they'd read about it in an instruction manual but hadn't quite understood the instructions.

"Hello," said Abraham.

"Do come in," said Amelia.

"I'm sure that," said Abraham.

"Mrs Bell can," said Amelia.

"Organise some tea," said Abraham.

"Or something," said Amelia.

"Hello," said Nadia, quite loudly. She introduced us, but their eyes never left her. I later discovered that Mrs Bell (who was actually eight people, three of them male) was as much a carer as a housekeeper, because these two could barely get dressed without assistance and anything more complex than eating was met with truculent incomprehension.

The hallway lead us to a very large room that, in total contrast to the rest of the place, was completely empty. The pale wood-panelled walls showed darker patches where paintings had once hung, and the horizontal dents and scratches on the wood spoke of decades of chairs being carelessly pushed back against the walls when no longer needed. The floor was scratched parquet, the windows tall and without curtains and framed with shutters that looked like they'd been installed by a gibbon with a mallet.

Actually it wasn't completely empty; there was a big circle of metal, about 6 inches wide, a good 20ft across and probably made of brass - inlaid into the floor.

"This is where we," said Abraham.

"will help you," said Amelia. I'll stop writing them out like that now – just assume that the first half is Abraham and the second Amelia, or the other way around. It doesn't seem to matter.

"Can you help all of them at the same time," Nadia asked, "as we asked?"

"No." "Not him." "The others together." Amelia pointed to me. "Not him."

"Oh. Ladies?" Sam, Amy and Clara, with considerable trepidation, stepped into the circle. The weird twins stood on opposite sides, raised their arms in perfect synchronisation and formed a dome of pale light over the women and then started to mutter, the same words at the same time. Their voices even sounded the same. I sidled over to Nadia.

"What is it with these two?"

She sighed, very softly. "We think they may be the same person," she said quietly.

"Like some sort of multiple personality disorder?"

"The exact opposite actually – that's several personalities in one body. This is a single personality in two bodies."

"How the hell did that happen?"

"No idea. We've had people studying them for years, and the current project leader's latest conclusion is 'shit happens'."

"Are they twins?" I could kind of see how that could have something to do with it.

"No. There is no consanguinity at all. He was born in Golders Green to Jewish parents; she was born two years later in Manchester – her father is highland Scottish and her mother is a local."

"So how come they can do this stuff?"

"We don't know that, but I think there's something that allows them to reach below the normal level of the *gogoan* to the root of it all, into the old magic. Or they're immensely powerful but barely controlled *kemen* Talents." She trailed off.

"Or shit just happens." She nodded. "Are they happy?"

"We try to make sure they are," said Nadia sadly. "They're such a valuable resource that we give them almost anything they want."

I looked back into the hall. "So why is everything so old fashioned? The decorations aren't something you'd expected to appeal to people in their 20's. Is it something they both favour?" It didn't seem likely.

She glanced at me. "I said that they were both one person – I didn't say it was either of them."

"Oh." The thought made me go cold. If a third person was 'running' both of them, that put it well beyond weird. And where were they in the meanwhile?

The dome shimmered out of existence and the silvery light that had filled the room subsided into the normal autumn daylight that was seeping in through the unwashed windows.

None of the women spoke. They looked confused and pale, shivering slightly as they left the circle and Amy, oddly, wasn't limping.

"If you would," "step into the circle," "we can help," "you," "now."

Without a backward glance, but not without trepidation, I did. The dome formed itself, solidifying in place rather than rising like the cover of a hinge-topped chafing dish or sliding sideways like an astronomical observatory.

OK, this is going to be hard to describe, so bear with me; I'm trying to tell you about something that I hardly have the words for inside my own head, let alone out loud. The first and overwhelming sensation was of being extremely cold, although my breath didn't mist when I exhaled.

From inside the dome I couldn't see anything of the room; I could, however, see two figures, neither of whom were Amelia or Abraham. They were the just the suggestions of figures, as thin as a Giacometti statue and as blank as an artist's mannequin.

I watched with nervous curiosity as they firmed up into slightly more in-focus versions of what I'd seen before. I had no idea who or what they were, and I still don't because they did absolutely nothing the whole time I was there and nobody else saw them.

"You may find," "it easier if," "you sit down."

I sank into a comfortable kneeling position just as the whole world went fucking mad. It was like having an LSD flashback while drunk and looking at two kaleidoscopes with different patterns going in opposite directions. I'm told, never having done anything like that, of course.

It started with the sensation of water, the brush of liquid across my skin; the slipperiness and the way it coats your mouth when you're drinking after a deep thirst; the faintness and the ache behind the eyes caused by dehydration; then desperation and desperate supplication, and the way the soil darkens when it becomes damp; sere vegetation greening and the sound of fast water tumbling over rocks; and behind it the profound knowledge of water, not for what it can do but as a thing in itself, connected to all other water, an endless single ocean; river to cloud to raindrop to shaking hands cupped with muddy liquid and drinking with the desperation of the dying; the soothing rhythm of rain and the bell-like sound of drips in the cave mouth; the children no longer crying, livestock no longer dying; no more fighting for the last, lost, precious drops – and all because you have learned to control it.

That faded and I was left cold, slumped and stunned on the dusty parquet, more alone than I had ever felt before. Nobody existed in that universe except me. And then fire happened. I remembered pain and the fear of the dark, and the terrors that hide in the night; sickness from raw food wrested from scavengers and dying in a landscape layered in snow for decades. The comfort of light; the glow that fights the night and the cautious approach of wild animals wanting to share the heat's bounty.

And so it went on. Air was the fear of the weather, unknowable, mysterious and deadly, storm, flood or drought. The sick feeling of the moments before thunder arrives and the icy bite of the wind when it blows from the white mountains in the north. Winds that push harder than a tree can resist. Sweat in the thick air of summer and the way the sky breaks into pieces and lies, crisp, on the ground in winter.

Earth was dying crops, poisoned waterholes, no food, nowhere safe, livestock failing as their food died under their feet; dry soil crumbling and the terror when the earth shakes and rivers change course. The moment the cliffs surrender to the sea and pain of the crops lost to the greedy ocean, or when the ground shatters and the earth runs in burning rivers over the land. Harsh and unwelcoming, spurning the urge to cower below ground, or soft and welcoming caves that hide terrors and horrors that come upon you unsuspected.

Healing was grief, sadness, pain and the despair of loss; the horror of recognising something incurable in a loved one and the joy and confusion of an unexpected recovery. Understanding beyond knowledge, the urge, the need to help, to stave off loss and grief and pain; the burning need to restore what was gone, to make it be not gone.

Kemen was juggling with the lightning, moving rocks with a thought, knocking down prey with a gesture, then the heady glory of power and the fear when it becomes too much and more than you can explain or control and having to flee or die, branded a demon or a witch, brought down by something you have no ability to control even if you could find the desire to.

Then there was a huge aching silence, empty apart from the thin howl of a distant wolf, a deep silver silence I'd never experienced before, as if something was trying to reach me, to connect with me and had obliterated everything else in the process. If I had been capable of anything resembling coherent thought I would have considered this an integration phase, a period when a new understanding is sinking into my mind. But I could no more rationally consider this than I could have juggled the freezing fog that enveloped and encompassed me.

But then there was a tiny thing, a burning diamond point of light that came toward me. I wasn't sure if I was supposed to be afraid; I could equally well have needed to be bright yellow or smell like a pigeon. I watched as it made progress from there, wherever the hell that was, to here, wherever the hell *that* was, and settled in front of me. It was at this point that I recalled that I had a physical body and that the floor I was kneeling on was cold and hard. Then, to my utter astonishment, it spoke.

"You are welcome in this place." The words just appeared in my mind, which is not unusual in an altered state like this.

"Where am I?"

"You are in you," it replied gnomically, which didn't help much.

"What's happening to me?"

"He has found a way to open the old magic in you, to go beyond the *jatorri*." *Jatorri* means 'origin'. It's the term for the access routes to the source of a mage's power, usually a specific location within the *gogoan*.

"And who are you?" I asked, wondering if the question should actually be 'what are you?'.

"I am what is beyond that." I was, of course, confused. "I am what was here before the fire and the wheel, before the night was a terror, before healing, before power and all the other manifestations of me."

"Are you god?"

"No. I am magic, magic in the bones and the soul, in the heart of being, in the heart of the earth. I am all of your power, all of your knowledge, all of what makes you yourself. Without me you do not exist, cannot exist. I am *ama lurra*. I am magic."

I just stared at the tiny spark. *Ama lurra* means 'Mother Earth', but it was so much more than just a noun. I had no idea what to do. Should I bow in supplication, or try to capture the light? No and, of course not, in case you were wondering. This was no demanding deity, nor was it just a spark. I realised that this was just my brain putting an image onto something that had no physical form. This was what Kadira, the dragon and all the other places of power were just aspects of, something whose existence had been theoretical up until that moment. I knelt, stunned by understanding, for an unguessable length of time.

"So what happens now?" I was tingling like I was leaning on an electric fence. I felt like I was too big for my own skin.

"Will you accept me?" The voice was a profound whisper, as deep as a submarine trench and nothing at all to do with sound.

"Yes." No thought, no hesitation.

"Will you take my mark?"

"Yes," I replied without hesitation. I had no idea what the implications of that were, but I had no doubt about doing it.

"And will you honour what this both grants and demands?"

"Yes."

"I accept you, *ahots*. I am magic and you are part of me now."

A searing pain struck my entire body, then an acid burn on my upper arm; I felt a flash of intense cold, a flush of nausea and that was all.

*

I woke up in hospital, wondering why most people's magical development leaves them with not much more than a headache, whereas I almost always end up in the medical wing of Central. It was getting boring, to be honest.

Fortunately this time it was more like a pastoral visit, because I only stayed there for a couple of hours. Once I'd proved that I knew who I was, where I was and what the square root of nine was they shoved me out with an almost indecent haste. They said they had just wanted to make sure I wasn't suffering any ill effects.

By way of greeting Amy punched me on the arm, reminding me of the pain, and then hugged me. "Will you stop doing that," she said. I was about to protest that I hadn't done anything, and ask what she meant, when she leant back from the hug. "Why can't you develop your magic like ordinary people? I just end up with a powerful urge for a stiff drink and you end up flat on your back. Again." She smiled. "'I don't think', 'he has taken this,' 'very well'," she said in an eerily accurate impersonation of Amelia and Abraham.

"What was it like for you?" I asked when we were in the common room again. Sam and Clara were sitting rather wanly next to Nadia, who was frowning, as Amy and I sat down.

"We all got shown the roots of our Talents. We've now got second Talents that could be activated."

"Really?"

"This is fairly normal for people as gifted as you lot," said Nadia. "Almost everyone has a vestigial second Talent, but they normally have too little power to be of use. Yours are more powerful and development than that, but not very much. They could be activated, but it would take a lot of work and it could be quite risky if we tried. We will if you insist, but…"

"So what Talents have you got now?" I asked, sipping my tea.

"Water and fire," said Amy.

"Earth and *kemen*," said Clara.

"Air and water," said Sam.

"So mostly what you'd expect," said Nadia. "It doesn't make you Dual Talents, but knowing what your secondary is will help you to develop interactions that are more... fruitful."

"Could we become Dual Talents?" Clara asked.

"Yes," said Nadia slowly, "but it will take a lot of work." She sipped her coffee. "Ugh, it's gone cold. Could you?" She looked at me.

Without much thought I put some warmth into it. Everyone looked at me as it started to roil. "What?"

"*Isilak* is it?" Sam asked.

"Oh." From the glint in her eye I realised that Nadia had done that as a test.

"You need to tell us what happened Mike," said Nadia in an oddly distracted tone, "because you really are different now."

"Different? How?"

"Well, you're drinking tea for a start." Which, for a famous coffeeholic like me – also known as a javaphile – was a bit of a shock.

"Oh. OK."

"Conference 10 in half an hour. I need to gather some people."

"Gather away."

"Oh, and you'll need these." She handed me a packet of paracetamol. "You're going to get the great grandfather of a headache," which explained why Sam and Amy were looking so glum. She was too late, however, because the headache had already arrived. Clara was staring out of the window. "So take those now and try not to do anything too energetic." She looked at us. "What is it with you lot and the super-fast gathering of magical power? We might have to look into that a bit more, when we have time." She shook her head and left.

I searched for a witty comment, an uplifting thought or positive spin, but I could find nothing. We had been given the tools we needed to deal with Deroc, and as Oliver remained as absent as ever it looked like we were going to have to go through with it. I couldn't even find a smile.

I just rubbed my arm and looked blearily at them. The people in the room swirled around our table, but nobody spoke to us or even caught our gaze. Some of them looked away when I glanced at them. I thought I understood why. Apart from researchers or visiting mages most of the people who work at Central are administrators of one kind or another. Don't misunderstand me – they are vital; every organisation needs people who know how paper clips work.

But we are Nadia's specialists, so this was like being in a Pay Corps office when four heavily armed members of the SAS arrive – doing the same job but not really, and way too unpredictable for most people. They valued us and what we did, just as we did them, but we made them uncomfortable. I think most of them wished we would just go away, so we did.

10

The meeting started with the women recounting their experiences in more detail. They closely matched mine, and the revelation of their buried second Talents was already disturbing us because they were already making themselves felt.

"That's not unexpected," said Nadia. "It seems likely that the circumstances that lead to the first practitioners being able to use magic were moments of desperation, and that the magic came through as it could. Your primary Talents have increased in power considerably, which has pushed your secondaries forward." The last Talent to be positively identified was *kemen*, which had been suspected for a long time but it wasn't formally recognised until the 1930's. They're now suggesting there might be another one, but I don't know any details about it.

While this was interesting I didn't really care, and I don't think the others did either. We knew we were heading for an encounter with Deroc and we just wanted to get on with it. But Nadia, and by extension the whole 'top table' of British wizardry, wanted to understand the last reckless but unavoidable thing we'd done before we blundered off and did another one.

Nobody was the least bit surprised by my account of events until I mentioned the two faceless figures. There was a suggestion that they might have been the actual Amelia and Abraham, but I suspect most of them thought they were just a by-product of my occasionally deranged imagination. They weren't, but as they could have been almost anything we decided to stop talking about them and move on to the really interesting stuff.

I described it in as much dispassionate detail as I could, because I didn't think that my being overwhelmed, scared, overawed and bricking it all at the same time would add anything to the discussion.

Nadia was very quiet when I finished, frowning and turning her head slightly as if trying to catch a very faint sound. After a few seconds she stood up and reached for the phone that was on the table by the window. She very deliberately pressed some buttons and then listened for a few seconds before speaking.

"Yes. Yes we do. Can you bring her?" She listened again. "He may well,." She said, glancing at me. Then she hung up. "We need someone in particular," she said in an oddly quiet voice. It's rare to see Nadia out of her depth, but right now she looked like she needed oxygen bottles.

"This is a bit coincidental," said Clara sharply. "Yesterday you didn't know we'd even be seeing the weird twins, and yet today you just *happen* to have an expert on tap?"

"No," said Nadia, her hands raised in a position of surrender. She seemed almost hunched. "We asked for her when we understood that Deroc existed and what Oliver had done. She's the only person alive who has experienced something similar and is still able to talk about it."

This suggested that not only were there people who had experienced this and weren't still alive, but also that there were people who were still alive but couldn't talk about it, which was something I didn't particularly want to hear.

"Right," said Clara. "If she's here because of Deroc then why is she only joining us now?"

"Because she really understands old magic. They kind of go together."

The door opened and Richard ushered in a slim, elderly lady in a very stylish cream outfit. She leant lightly on an elegant walking stick and had a coiffure that most ladies-wot-lunch would have killed for. I thought knew her face from somewhere, but I wasn't entirely sure. Clara did, or at least the way her chin nearly hit her chest suggested that she did.

The lady looked at us and offered a smile. *"Buona gionata. Sono Sophia Jilani."*

I nearly fainted. If Nadia *et al* were the pinnacle of British wizardry, then Sophia Jilani was the *éminence grise* of all the mages from Trafalgar to Tbilisi. I never thought I'd meet her. She was pure magical royalty and had been involved in some of the most important magical events of the last half century. She looked to be in her fairly healthy late 60's, but I knew she was actually nearing 80.

European magic is organised, if I can use that word for something so bloody ramshackle, by every country being responsible to the countries they abut for what they do. Such oversight keeps many an unreliable regime good. Countries are also assigned to larger regional groups, such as the North European Group which includes Britain, France, the Benelux countries and Ireland. It sounds really well structured.

But the organisation that actually does the work is the *Jakintzaren Gizarteko*, an informal network of senior mages that get together and sort everything out. Meanwhile the bureaucrats and people who hug slights to themselves like their favourite teddy bear get mired in swamps of their own making. Sophia Jilani was not part of the formal groups but exerted a level of power that made the lovers of rules very uncomfortable.

"Hello," I croaked. Richard made the introductions while she tried very hard not to laugh.

"Don't worry, I will not turn you into *torexàn*." She saw my mystification. "*Piccione*. Er... pigeon," she said, finding the word.

"Thank you." I knew she was Italian, but the first word she used didn't sound like it. I left that confusion to stew for a bit while she disposed herself elegantly in a seat, accepted a cup of coffee from Richard, and regarded us all steadily.

With some older ladies I have found that it pays to be stately, correct and a bit formal. Others reacted better to a mixture of roguish and avuncular, although in most cases that would mean being dead. But almost all of them, and this includes most older men too, like things to be said clearly and unambiguously. It seems as if their minds are so full from being alive for so long that anything that is less than completely clear gets lost in the vastness of their experience.

But ask me about that when I'm ninety, if I survive that long, and we'll see if I've got that right. If longevity really is just being frightened of dying for longer than usual then this was a slight price, and one I was willing to pay.

"*Signora* Jilani," I began, but she waved me into silence with an admonitory finger that shut me off like a mute button.

"Is *Signorina*, but you will call me Sophia."

"*Grazie*. Has Richard explained what has happened?"

"*D'aspàrte*. He has told me what and why, but not how it has taken you, as affected you." She sipped her drink, sighed and set it back on the table. I knew she wouldn't pick it up again, not having any spoons that needed cleaning just then.

Trying to keep the explanation simple, I ran through what had happened when I was under the dome, including having a conversation with a point of light that claimed to be magic itself. I knew it sounded odd, but the day before I'd been talking to a wall that didn't exist, so maybe this was just my new version of normal.

"This is interesting," she said softly. "This light, it had no *accento*?"

"Accent," Richard translated. I shook my head.

"What else?" Sophia asked.

"It was very complicated," I said "It is very hard to describe."

She raised her hand. "*Mailegatu-memoria.*" There is a well-known spell, *mailegatu-begi,* usually shortened to '*mail-beg*', which means 'borrowed eyes'. It allows a mage to literally see through the eyes of another. '*Mail-mem*' is a variation of that which allows glimpses of the other persons memories, but they are always vague, like blurred photographs. I nodded my consent.

I've done this before, we all have. It's disconcerting, viewing the past through another persons' eyes, even if it isn't in technicolour and 360° smelly-vision. Sophia didn't do that – she 'downloaded' my memories in a single disorientating rush and then broke the connection. Previously when I'd accessed memories they had not been clear and I'd had to watch them in real time, including an embarrassing trip to the toilet that I refuse to recount. This version of '*mail-mem*' was Jaun 9 at least and it will take me ages to learn how to do it, if I ever do.

She sat quietly for several minutes, her eyes distant, muttering in something that sounded sort of Italian. "It is *cuòr de magia,*" she said finally, lifting her head. "This is truly the heart of magic – all mages come into contact it when they first use magic for a purpose. It is not usual to do it er… with you voice." She tapped the floor with her cane. "Not usually *possible* with the voice. And the sound of the wolf is… very interesting."

"Interesting, but it might not mean anything?" I asked, trying not to sound relieved.

"*Così così,*" she said, rocking her hand in a 'maybe' motion. "It does not now, although the mark, that is a new thing. In the future, I think the wolf will..." She shrugged, a small but expressive movement. "I think it will come to the... forward sometimes. It could be important, perhaps."

"That's interesting, that's good," said Nadia, sounding not the least bit relieved. "What about the rest of it?"

"It is a little strange. I have never seen so many Talents er... *scoperto.*" She waved her hand as she struggled for the word. "Visible at one time. I think perhaps there will be strange interactions later. You should do this... thing soon. The power will fade too fast."

She rose, slightly creakily, and walked carefully over to where the ladies were sitting. She reached out and touched Clara gently on the face, looking deep into her eyes. "*Voce del drago.*" Sophia turned to Sam – the same touch, the same intense scrutiny. "*Voce del cielo.*" Then Amy. "*Voce del mare.*" She turned to Richard and Nadia. "It is good that they can receive this so quickly. And yet strange that they can accept the old magic so easily."

I raised an eyebrow and, despite my being behind her, she still saw it, and smiled. "*Voce di tutti loro,*" she said.

"Am I free of the *kea*?"

"*Sì.*" She turned and rested her fingertips on my chest, just over my heart, for a moment. My chest felt like it was being pierced with icicles. "You are free of it."

"He's *mamua*?" Nadia asked sharply. This means someone who is full power in all the Talents.

"No. Magic does not come out of him as normally. He is... something else. He is... *unico e pericoloso*. He is a new thing - call him... *zubi*." She leant on her stick and turned to the door. "I will see you again when Deroc is defeated." She paused, her head bent in thought. "I do not think Deroc... I think it is trying to steal the power, not destroy it. I have seen this before, an *ecrisar*."

"Eclipse."

"The sky became dark but the reason was *secreto*, a secret, a hidden thing. I reached into the *vécio magio*, the old magic, to find out the cause."

"And the cause was?"

"*Ànema*, a spirit like this Deroc. It was not doing this for malice, not planning to hurt."

"Was it sentient? Could you talk to it?"

"No. I *tanagiá, dirèto* to the *cuòr*."

"I gathered it up and directed it to the heart," Richard supplied.

"I change it to flow it away, to not get in the way."

"Did it actually block the sun?"

"No. It *ecrisar* the power, the power in the place."

"Where?"

"*Il sga*, the lagoon."

"It was Venice," said Richard, "it was threatening to flood the city."

"Flood the city? It wasn't just the *aqua alta?*"

"It was too much than normal. It would have flooded," said Sophia. She seemed sad, as if remembering a huge effort and perhaps a loss that was hard to bear. "Perhaps you will use it for another reason, in another place." And on that sententious note she left, albeit rather slowly.

"I think," I said into the ensuing silence, "that would have made more sense if I knew what she called us."

"'*Voce del drago*' means the voice of the dragon," said Richard. He pointed to Sam. "Of the sky." Then Amy. "Of the sea."

"And me?"

"Voice of everything. Unique and dangerous. *Zubi* is 'bridge' in Basque." The home of magic in the western world is those chilly Pyrenean lands, so that's the language used by the magicians of Europe and the English speaking world.

"Oh, right. So, now what?"

Clara stood up, magical energy crackling off her. "Now we go and kill a parasite."

*

We didn't need to go to St Paul's again because part of the advanced control stuff they'd set up allowed us to gain the same access without leaving the relative safety of Central. Plus the buildings are less than ½ mile apart, an irrelevant distance in terms of what we were hoping to do.

So we went to the workshop where Oliver had caused all this trouble and found ourselves some comfortable places to lie down. Last time they'd had to prop us up otherwise we'd have ended up falling onto the chilly stone floor of St Paul's crypt, which would certainly have broken our concentration, if not some bones.

Nadia had given Clara several options on how to get rid of Deroc – funnily the idea of restraining the bloody thing was never raised. *Ebaki*, disintegrate, was ignored, because Deroc could re-form in an eye-blink. *Suntsitu* – destroy - was also left out because it would kill all of us as well and probably Kadira too. *Eten,* disrupt, would have been no more effective than *ebaki*, so they settled on her using *xahutzen*, dissipate, which breaks down the target at a quantum level and renders the energy non-coherent for long enough to prevent the damned thing from re-forming. Richard told us that, according to Sophia, if Deroc was reduced to such a random mass of energy, Kadira would be able to absorb it quickly and without much effort.

This time Sam was coming into Kadira's world with us while Amy stayed nearby, to be our communications link to the outside world and to provide reinforcements should we need it. We'd all had a drink, we weren't hungry and we'd used the toilet. We made sure we were comfortable and wouldn't be too hot, or too cold… OK, we were putting off the moment of going because suddenly it was very real and more than a touch scary.

As I settled I could feel the other people around us – Nadia was with us, as was Bev, who was monitoring us. Richard was close by, but the person I could feel the strongest was Sophia Jilani, and it felt like she was waiting for something. That was very odd because from here she hadn't felt powerful at all. Then I realised she was damn near *lotar*, probably because of her age. It was her knowledge and experience that were so immensely valuable.

"Let's go," said Clara.

*

Even through the grey swirl of transition I could feel Deroc watching us like a waiting predator. I thought I should have felt scared, but I didn't, just oddly immune, as if the previously overwhelming sensation caused by being there were now muffled.

For some reason I didn't go straight to the home of Deroc and Kadira. Instead the Nightmare City rushed towards me like the scariest ever science fiction special effect. Even though I knew it was only in my head I still flinched backwards away from it. This time it didn't stop and I was rushed, jolting, through the history of the city, the buffeting bad enough to make me lose my grip and get lost in the past. I wondered if we were all going to have to pass through the Nightmare City to get to where Deroc was now.

I saw Baynard's Castle built, growing from the embankment like stacked books and the White Tower snapping into view shortly afterwards. With barely a pause for breath the first stone bridge tied the north and south banks of the Thames together like a single stitch, and then the first Great Fire of London, in the 11th century, swept by and destroyed much of the city. The Blackfriars Priory was barely complete before another appeared in Southwark, and Lambeth Palace grew like a mushroom not long after. I was starting to get lost in the passage of time, but then the Globe Theatre sprang up and then burned down, which told me I was in the 16th century.

Heat and smoke and the second Great Fire destroyed the first St Paul's and Baynard's Castle. Wren's St Paul's was towering in seconds when Buckingham House punctuated the Mall and the second stone bridge chained the city together forever. I got a confused glimpse of the deep trenches of the underground being built before there was a final blurring and I was back in the Nightmare City that I'd seen before.

It was the same grey and shattered landscape, the buildings like a mouthful of broken teeth, but now it was night and it felt like it was waiting for me, or something in it was waiting for me. It made me very nervous, with a flutter of real fear behind it, and my new magical abilities felt like no protection at all.

But the sky wasn't the same pearlescent white that it had been before. Now it was dark and studded with stars that glittered like diamonds dropped on a black carpet. The constellations were familiar, but no more than familiar, because the positions of the stars were subtly different. Alnitak, Alnilam and Mantaka, the stars of Orion's Belt, no longer lined up properly and it looked like a giant hand had smeared the constellations downward toward the horizon. Ursa Major was now a perfect square and The Pleiades glowed like a giant luminous thumbprint.

The air was icy but very still, the only sound the distant turgid rumble of the river and a deep metallic groaning. I looked across at the sticky vacancy of the riverbed. Lying on its side a little upstream was what had been HMS Belfast, a floating tribute to the fortitude and courage of the sailors in my world, but now a rusting hulk. The prow was propped slightly up by the barrels of the 6 inch guns which had dug into the riverbed. But as I watched the turret mountings finally gave way and the ship dropped onto the mud with a resounding crash. The impact snapped the hull in two and remnants spilled out onto the riverbed. It was an incredibly sad sight.

Unlike the last time I'd been here none of this had an impact on my *gogoan*, and I wondered why. But wondering was all I could do because I had no idea and there was nobody to ask.

I turned to look toward the castle that sat where Central should have been. It was intact again, the stonework bright and tight and the roofs in one piece. That seemed odd, especially as I had seen it burned down just moments before. Why was everything else in neglectful decay but this building wasn't? Especially as it – Baynard's Castle - had been built on the junction of the river Fleet and the walls of Roman London in about 1080.

And then I was right outside it, looking at the sturdy wooden door, the ragstone walls and the unpopulated windows.

The windows may have been unpopulated but the building wasn't. I could hear someone – perhaps something - moving around inside. It wasn't footsteps but a rustling like the sound of leather wings and the click of metal tapping on stone. It struck me that this could be where Deroc came from. If Kadira's home was the City, with its centre at St Paul's, then this might be the equivalent for Deroc, and as their territories overlapped - I can't think of a better way to describe it - this could be the reason for the conflict.

There was so much magic here that I could feel it like a static tingle under my hands, and realised that could easily be the reason that Central had ended up where it was - an area so suffused with magic couldn't help but be attractive to people who use the stuff every day.

As I thought this a crack appeared in the wood in front of me and I glimpsed the open courtyard interior. There was a huge noise, a wordless howl that filled the sky, and above me the heavens flashed once and then the darkness returned. Alnitak had vanished. Another sound, another flash and now Mintaka was gone. Deroc was howling the stars out of the sky, and if something as relatively small as Deroc could do that, what could something the magnitude of Kadira accomplish?

A final moment of magical pressure and I arrived in the huge empty space again. It was mere seconds before Deroc arrived. We'd used *mail-memoria'* with Sam so she knew what to expect, but I'm sure that it was still a bit of a shock. Even caged it was huge and it was doing its best to be terrifying, but I was not impressed. In fact I was cross. Without this damned thing this would not be a dangerous job because Kadira would have been able to support us.

"You will grant me my freedom," it roared.

"Says the one *inside* the cage," replied Clara calmly.

"Oh, it's you." Deroc shrank. "I knew you'd come back."

"Yes. But we haven't come to let you out."

It moved its mouth. I suspect it was trying to smile, but it was hard to tell with all those teeth. "You will, because I am not alone."

Fading in from the formless surroundings were several other unprepossessing creatures. Fangs seemed to be a major feature, and claws were much in evidence, and all of them on something about the size of a small dog of the 'rat on a rope' variety. So like a dangerous Chihuahua but without the flat-faced belligerence and unassailable stupidity.

"You will free me or they will attack you."

Sam raised her hand and a huge wind rolled through the space, bundling the creatures into the dimness in a confusion of limbs.

"They will return," said Deroc smugly.

This time Sam reduced them to ash with a single glance. They came again, swarming like rats, and soon Sam and Clara were busy with them, so I profited on this distraction. The girls didn't need me disturbing their concentration so I sloped off round the back of Deroc's cage to do my bit. It ignored me just as it had before and I wondered if it even registered that I was there, and if that was because I was not really a magical being.

I could see that the weakness at the rear of the cage had grown and the surrounding bars were more displaced. The lines joining him to Oliver's canal were now gouged into the floor – which, suddenly, was a mosaic, Renaissance rather than Roman, just like the one in St Paul's.

I examined the hole in the outer barrier that the power was flowing towards. Maybe it was Kadira trying to help, or perhaps I was seeing things in a new way because of what Amelia and Abraham had done, but now it looked like a wall that had been partially disassembled. I just needed to put the key stones back and most of the flow would stop. I glanced at Sam and Clara, who seemed to be having a lovely time reducing the things to dust. Deroc was shaking its cage as they swept them away without effort, howling with frustration or anger. I had no doubt that was its plan, of course – it could keep the creatures coming indefinitely, and the ladies would tire eventually. I wasn't sure if there were hundreds and hundreds of the damn things, or just the same ones coming back over and over again. Then I noticed that the girls had, as agreed, changed their tactics, Clara leaving Sam to deal with the little critters so she could focus on Deroc itself. Now it's attention was fully occupied it was time for my part.

I concentrated on the wall. Kadira was, oddly, absent; I had expected him to help me or something, but there was just a huge silence, and that made me wonder just how much power Kadira actually had – being a discorporate entity didn't make him incapable of lying. I wondered if perhaps he was busy helping Clara by restraining Deroc. Not that it mattered much because she was giving it a really hard time now. I tried to move a block to close the gap, but I couldn't shift it. I added more power, felt a growing chill and it started to move only but slowly. Behind me I could hear Clara swearing.

"It's the damned cage," she said, "it's blocking spells in both directions."

"You'll have to break the cage to get at it," said Sam. Her hands erupted in green fire and the encroaching hordes vanished again. They were thinning now; I hoped that meant that she was finally beating them, but it could equally mean that they were massing for an all-out attack.

"Let's do it now," said Clara. "No point in waiting."

Even as I pushed the stone I could feel the build-up of power, with Sam shoving all that she could spare into Clara. In here the Dragon couldn't help, so we had to rely on our native abilities – which in the girls were considerable – plus what we had gleaned from the weird twins, and what help Sophia, Nadia and the others could give us from the outside.

Yes, Sophia was there too, providing me with a line of subtle strength and, more importantly, guidance. It wasn't like anything I'd experienced before. I recognised that this was true magical power, which is so much more than just the ability to cast spells. I drew into me as much of the knowledge and emotion of it as I could, felt it filling me up and I almost wept with the joy of experiencing it. Now the blocks slid into place much more easily.

Despite this manifestation of me having no pain sensors I could feel a deep and penetrating cold gripping me. Deroc suddenly went quiet and I thought it must have guessed what we were trying to do, and that it's one chance to escape would be in the instant between the cage dissolving and Clara blowing it to tiny pieces. The air, to use entirely the wrong word, crackled with tension, and then Sam struck.

A sudden percussion roared through the space and the cage started disintegrating into spiralling fragments. Clara held her hands ready for the killing spell - no, not 'evading kenaveral' or whatever it is. Deroc seemed to have been expecting this, planning for it this since Oliver's blunder had weakened its cage.

At the moment the bars started to let go the horde of things returned. Sam turned her attention from the still mostly complete cage to blast them, but before she could turn back Deroc broke out of the weakened back corner and surged for the only escape route. It shrank as it ran, the better to fit through the gap, and its howl of triumph was painful to hear.

All I could think of was that if it got out the devastation would be appalling, and in destroying Kadira it would certainly kill all of us, and many more besides. And the only thing that stood between everyone and that was a hole slightly larger than a suitcase, and me. There was no way I could get the last block in place before it arrived, so I filled the gap with the only thing I had left – myself.

In the real world this would be like volunteering for hand to hand fighting with a pissed-off tiger, but in here it was different because everything was probably an expression of an energy state, or it could equally have been to do with the colour of my socks or the smell of mutton sausages. I don't know.

So I made myself as resistant as possible – and so cold that the image of a glacier came over me -and waited for Deroc to arrive. I knew that I just had to hold on until Clara could finish it off. I couldn't let it escape. This, I suspected, was not going to be any kind of fun.

It pulled up short when it saw me, which I thought was very odd. I had expected it to just run me over "Move or you will be destroyed."

I couldn't be bothered to answer. Holding a powerful shield like *horma* is hard enough outside, but in here it was bloody murder, old magic or not. The power to create it was being drawn directly from my body and I was now so cold it hurt. It slashed at me and its claws skittered across the shield. I heard Sam swearing in Mandarin, Italian and fury as she shredded the tiny creatures that were trying to stop Clara her casting her killing spell.

Except that she couldn't, because Deroc was directly between us. Normally *horma* would protect me by stopping any spell so she could have cast, but Deroc's second strike had cracked it and the energy had leaked out in a flourish of light, leaving just me and the much weaker *armarria* that I had raised behind the *horma*. Now that it could reach me Deroc slammed one clawed hand into my shoulder, pushed me aside and, howling with pain from breaching the *armarria*, headed for the opening.

I grabbed at it, managing to trip it so it fell against the wall, then tried to regain my footing. It lashed out with its leg, knocking my feet out from under me, and I went down like skittles, rolling into it so that it toppled sideways. Its claw had just reached the opening in the wall when Clara's spell arrived.

"*Xahutzen.*"

Deroc screamed – there really isn't any other word – and it came apart, cracking into fragments like a glass figurine breaking. The energy of it spilled out, soaking into the walls and the floor. I could feel Kadira absorbing most but not all of it; a good chunk of it hit me square on. I used the last of my strength, garnered from I have no fucking clue where, but certainly refined by whatever Sophia was doing to me, to slam the missing block into place.

As Deroc ceased to exist I felt the terrible city flow past me like a gritty storm of hatred and despair so I tried to focus on the bright land that I wanted to preserve. The Nightmare City pulled at me, unbending my fingers one by one until I felt I had no strength left and it started to pull me in.

I had about two seconds to be grateful that this representation of me was not equipped with pain sensors as the force burned away my body like a leaf in a furnace. My last thought was that I was going wake up in Central at any moment. And then I died.

You'll realise that I didn't actually die, not in the world of bus tickets, chip shops and jet fighters, but in this realm of power I did. I'm disappointed to recount that there was no tunnel with a white light at the end, no life flashing before my eyes, no benign or tetchy deity asking me to account for my actions, and certainly no kindly relatives waiting to greet me. I just had time to think '*ah shite*' before it all went away.

*

"Well, that didn't go exactly according to plan," said Nadia as I opened my eyes. Amy was sitting by me, looking pale and slightly cross, but Sam and Clara were still elsewhere. "How do you feel?"

"Numb in some places and sore in others. Bloody cold." There was considerable discomfort where Deroc had hit me and an odd tightness across my scalp. "I also have a headache you could use to stun a rhino."

"I'm not surprised."

"I'm going to give all of you a thorough check up once you feel up to it," said Bev.

"OK."

"Can you tell me what happened?" Nadia asked.

I did, in detail. While I was speaking I felt more pain, but this time around my right shoulder. I mentioned this to Bev when she noticed me wincing.

"Not to worry. I'll check everything."

I looked towards Sam because I could feel that she was still casting spells but without expending much energy, which was unusual. I could also see that she was twitching and straining, her movements tiny but powerful, apparently echoing her actions in the other place.

"I can see why my muscles hurt."

Amy smiled. "You nearly punched the wall a couple of times. Nice balance in the first defence. The second one, not so much."

"Thanks." I shook myself, aware that something external had been grinding me down, infecting my thoughts into a downward spiral that was hurting everyone around me. But as I came back from wherever the hell we'd been, I felt something burning away inside me and a great lightness flowed in. The room came into focus again and I found myself smiling in what felt like an utterly inane manner. I looked at Nadia. "What's happened with the energy flow?"

"I'll find out." She lifted her mobile and spoke a few sentences. I barely heard what she said because I was wondering why Clara and Sam were still in there, seeing as how Deroc was now no more than a bad memory and a headache. "It's dropped to 10% of what it was. You've brought us at least nine months."

"Well, that's good." I looked around. "Any chance of a drink?"

"Sure," said Bev, handing me a cup as Sam and Clara came back in a rather calmer and more dignified manner than me, and clearly not in the same level of pain and distress as I was.

I had expected water, but it turned out to be barely diluted whiskey. I coughed a bit, and then smiled. "That's better." Bev and Nadia turned their attention to the others for a moment, so I was left alone with Amy. I tried to ease my shoulders but it didn't help.

"Sometimes you amaze me," she said, I hoped fondly.

"Why?"

She touched my arm, her face almost abstract. "Because most of the time you're just Mike. You cook and push a trolley round the supermarket and, occasionally, wash the cars. You don't live your life in a cloud of fireworks or a fountain of rainbows. Most people don't know you well enough to know how exceptional you are, mostly because you usually don't talk to people about what you do. To most people you're the most ordinary man alive."

I wasn't sure I understood where she was going with this. "Yet since I've known you, you've survived one of the most intense magical battles in modern times, despite being terribly injured. You walked through a spell storm that should have killed you but just made you cross. Then you volunteered for hand to hand combat with an *izain* in a place that didn't really exist."

I eventually remembered that the word literally means a leech, but it's used here to indicate something that sucks magical power from anything it comes into contact with. No wonder Kadira had to keep it in a cage. It was only at that moment that I really understood the danger. If Deroc had decided to attack me properly rather than focus on escaping it could easily have killed me for real and always. I wondered again why it had stopped when it did, rather than just running me down and escaping.

"How did you know that it was an *izain*?" I asked, largely to distract myself.

Nadia turned to us. "As soon as we had a date and a name I set someone to locating the records."

"That was quick work."

Nadia looked at me steadily. "You were in there for nearly 16 hours." Which explained why I was busting for the loo when I surfaced. "Excellent researcher, as you know."

I looked at her for a few seconds. "You are kidding me. Gronk?"

"Best there is," she replied, smiling. Today she had given up on her usual sweatshirt and jeans pairing and was wearing a man's dress shirt and dark trousers. Bev then decided that everyone should stop taking up space in the work room and piss off somewhere else – apart from me, of course, because it was time for my check-up.

So they all obligingly headed to Conference 10, again, where one of Nadia's minions had organised coffee, food, analgesia and other comforting things. Meanwhile Bev hauled me up to medical and gave me the promised once over. Having ascertained that my pulse was pulsing in a satisfactory manner, my lungs were causing me to respire rather than expire, and that all the parts of me that should be attached were, she decided to help with the muscle strain by giving me a back rub. Bev's hands were wonderful, filled with warmth and power, and the energy flowed into my muscles like a balm.

I remembered the magic spark and the pain it had caused when she prodded me in the shoulder. "Let me look," she said after I yelped. I took off my shirt and she peered at my arm. "Um, what is that?"

"What's what?" I turned to look and found what appeared to be another tattoo, but this one a lustrous silver that pulsed and shimmered like oil on mercury as I moved my arm. "Oh. I don't know...," then I thought about the thing that Abraham and Amelia had introduced me to, and explained it to Bev.

"I see," said Bev.

"What is it?"

"No idea. Stay there." She left, coming back two minutes later with Nadia, Richard and Sophia Jilani, who was smiling slightly.

"You knew this would happen," I said to her, trying not to sound accusatory.

"*Può essere.* I think it might," she replied, touching my arm. The discomfort in the tattoo, a wide uneven line about half the length of my upper arm, faded a bit. At the same time the Dragon tattoo on my left forearm started to ache.

"What's happening?"

"Is *aderire*, a joining. This is the mark of the *bihotza magia*." She slipped her jacket off and lifted her sleeve – she had a very similar mark, although hers was somewhat faded.

"So I'm sort of connected to all of..."

"I know. *Tutti*."

I looked at Nadia. "What's *bihotza magia*?"

"Heart magic, below even the old magic that you used on Deroc. It means that you are in contact with the very basis of magic, what everything else flows from, what is behind even *kemen*." She didn't look very pleased about it, and she caught my enquiring look. "I've only heard of it happening a couple of times before, ever."

"So what do you do now?" Sophia asked.

"I can't do anything."

"Why not? You are an earth Talent and Healer."

"I am *ahots* to the Rockingham dragon."

She nodded. "Of course. I had forgot. Anyway, *caio*," said Sophia. "I go. Good luck *giovanotto*. You are *un uomo di talento silenzioso*. Call me if you need." She left, heading back to Italy and a presumably less exciting life, to be replaced by Sam, Amy and Clara.

Richard blew out a long breath. "Well, she likes you," he said, looking at me speculatively. "I look after her whenever she comes to this country, and that's the first time she's given anyone permission to contact her directly. You should be honoured."

"Er... what was the other thing?" I thought I really should learn more Italian, but as I have the linguistic skills of a bucket of custard I knew it wouldn't work.

"A man of quiet talents."

"Oh."

"Fucking amazing," said Bev, who seemed to be having an entirely different conversation to the rest of us.

"What?"

"Look at this." She indicated my arm. The silver was fading as the line narrowed, revealing symbols that were attached to the sides of the by-now very thin silver bar. At the same time the details of the dragon tattoo on my left forearm started to be highlighted, picked out in silver, like metal being inserted painlessly under my skin.

"What did you do?" Sam asked. I shrugged. Clara was looking at my dragon and then the mark on my shoulder and frowning. With a single smooth movement, she pulled off her shirt and twisted to look at her own tattoo, clear below the sleeve of her t-shirt. It was going the same way as mine, but she didn't have the silver etching on her arm.

Bev frowned. "Clara, where did you and Mike get those tattoos done?"

"A place in Nottingham, not far from the college."

"Do you think that the person who did it was a Talent?"

"Not at all," she replied, putting her shirt back on. "He was just a geek with some serious artistic skills and a steady hand."

"He certainly did have that," said Richard. I realised that this was probably the first time that he had seen Clara's tattoo in full, and it really is a splendid piece of body art. "Did you feel very strongly connected to the Dragon at the time?"

"Yes, but even more so when I was setting out the images." Clara is a very good artist and had designed our tattoos herself.

"Hmm. Interesting," Richard said thoughtfully, but he wouldn't be drawn further on the matter.

"So now what?" Amy asked.

"Unless you can cut off the *erreka*, or know where Oliver is, I suggest you go and relax. Sleep. Drink heavily. Run around screaming. Do whatever you feel like – but no magic," Nadia added firmly. "And going back to see Kadira is out of the question, however tempting it might be."

"Damn right," said Bev. "I can see your auras and they're deadly unstable."

"You can see our auras?" I was surprised because she'd never mentioned it before.

"Of course – it's one of the reasons that I'm such a good Healer."

"Do I need to learn...?" I asked.

"You either can see them or you can't," she replied with a shrug. "It's an innate ability, not a skill that anyone can teach you."

"What do our auras look like?" Amy asked.

"Yours is normally smooth, a rippling blue light that's sort of egg shaped. It becomes red and turbulent when your hips are hurting, like they are now." Amy just looked at her.

"Sam, your aura is white and angular, like a suit of armour made of... well, to be honest it looks a bit like a stormtrooper's outfit from Star Wars." Sam, our Warrior Princess, looked vaguely pleased.

"Clara, you have a purple-bronze layer about an inch clear of your whole body that sparkles like diamonds." She paused. "Mike, yours keeps changing. When we first met yours was routine, just a vague encompassing light,. It's now usually a very dark greyish-silver and shaped rather like Sam's." I had no idea what to do with this information, so I just filed it. "But right now all of you look like you've been coated with crackle glaze. You need to protect yourself because in that state it would be easy to damage it."

"Why is Mike's so dark?" Amy asked. "I thought most of them were bright,"

"They either go dark or disappear if the person has suffered a life-threatening illness or injury, or has had a near death experience. Mike has now died er... three times to my knowledge, so it's amazing he has any aura at all."

"Right," Amy replied. "OK, let's go." She had clearly decided we were leaving, and when she's in that mood she's as decisive as a two position switch, so none of us argued.

"I need to sleep," said Sam. The fight and giving Clara all that power had really taken out of her and I had nothing left to help her with.

"I'm going to swim," said Amy. There was a hydrotherapy pool not far away that Central had access to, and floating was good for aching hips.

"We're going for a walk," said Clara, grabbing me by the hand and hauling me to my feet. "I have some ideas about that idiot Oliver that I want to talk about."

Richard, Nadia and Bev watched us go. I could no more see their auras right then than I could see the colour of Richard's underwear, but I could tell that they were very troubled.

11

The relief at disposing of Deroc was like a huge weight being lifted from my soul. I was sure that Kadira would be very grateful for it, even if he hadn't showed it yet. Plus Central wasn't going to blow up any time soon, at least not from Oliver's *erreka* anyway - otherwise there was pretty much the same chance as always. We had survived everything, got in touch with some new magic, and now officially had some time off, even if my head felt like it was full off bubble wrap and everything in the world seemed to be about 3 inches to the left of where it should be.

Clara and I decided to walk west down the river in the direction of Somerset House and Temple; the brisk air made my head clearer than it had felt for days. This was a time to breathe, a time to think, a time to talk about nothing very much. Clara is very good company and, as Amy's *erdikide*, immune to any advances I might make – not that I had any intention of making any, you understand.

We watched the boats and the gulls, then spotted a bird of prey, probably a Peregrine, flying off the supports of one of the bridges. I looked around at the clatter of pigeons as the movement of a crisp bag in the breeze sent them off in a panic. The relentless drone of the traffic underpinned it all, with the occasional burst of music banging out of a passing car – why is it never Mozart? – and the deeper grumble of the buses. This was the sound track of much of my childhood, because my dad's a Londoner and we used to visit his family a lot when I was growing up. Mum's from a very old Nottinghamshire family, so visiting them was a boring ride in the back of the car not an exciting expedition on the train. Dad would never drive in London, and having had to do it several times I saw his point.

We wandered, arm in arm, into the beginnings of dusk. I could feel that Sam was now deeply asleep and Clara told me that Amy was safely drowsing in the hydrotherapy pool. I didn't feel like sleeping – I felt like spinning and jumping and shouting and enjoying just being: I'd died but I was alive again, which was cause enough for a celebration I thought. But I was also profoundly exhausted, so it balanced out in the odd giddy moment, enough to get us noticed but not enough for anyone to get official about it. Clara just smiled a lot, and we told each other silly jokes and shared memories and I got her to talk about Ben as dusk touched the sky.

"He was a nice enough bloke I suppose; he wasn't always particularly kind but he was never really mean. He could be thoughtless at times, and was frequently selfish, but I think was from stupidity rather than malice."

"Sounds typically male," I hedged.

She nodded. "You mostly can't help yourselves, so don't worry about it. We enjoyed being together at the beginning, but I suspect that if things had got... sweaty... it would have been a bit... vanilla." She smiled, and so did I. I knew exactly what she meant. It was like me and Amy – the earth doesn't move every time, but it doesn't have to.

"But…?"

"You know, his whiter than white friends, the way he would oh so very carefully avoid what were clearly habitual remarks, ones that were not… politically correct, and his unswerving assumption that he was always right. It was painful to be around, and soon the idea of sleeping with him made me feel slightly sick. I ended up not wanting him to even touch me."

"Presentism," I said, nodding. "Figures of speech you were bought up with that sound shocking now. Nobody should have to apologise for having used them in the past." I felt slightly light headed. "There was an Afro-Caribbean family next door to us in our first house. We had no problem with that of course, but Leonard's skin was properly black, not dark brown like his wife, and Simon and I knew we had to be careful about how we referred to him." I chuckled. "Me being a very sophisticated 10 year old I used to refer to him as a 'tinted gentleman' which, fortunately, he found hilarious. My dad tried to apologise when Leonard heard me say it, but Len said that he'd repeated it to his mates down the pub and they all thought it was brilliant. They called him 'Mr Tint' for a while."

"What did Simon say? Something tactless, knowing him."

"He called them 'the black man and the brown lady and their mixed up kids', but his best mate was Len's son Darius, so there wasn't any harm in it. And he was only six."

"Shame Simon grew up to be such a dickhead," Clara replied.

"Yeah, well, but what can you do?"

We got coffee from a van on the embankment as the night thickened and all the knots in my muscles finally unwound themselves. I felt like jelly melting and it was lovely to be like that after so long as tight as a clenched fist. I wanted to keep that sensation because it meant that now I could sleep, so I looked at Clara. "Taxi?"

"Taxi."

We joined the small queue at the nearest taxi rank, couples chatting, a lone man lost in his headphones, an older lady scanning a very dense book on her kindling or whatever those things are called, and an older, bearded man watching everyone with hooded eyes.

Taxis arrived and departed and we all dutiful shuffled forward to wait for the next one. This went fine until it was our turn. Just as the taxi drew up a group of three white boys in their late teens walked straight in front of us and made to climb in. I held the door shut with a simple *oreka* balance spell before I spoke.

"This is ours. Go join the back of the queue." Several people behind us were looking annoyed but nervous. These three had a collective IQ slightly smaller than their shoe sizes and a belligerence that nobody without body armour would voluntarily confront.

"Fuck off," said their spokes-gorilla. I kept the door closed, even though he kept pulling at it.

"Yeah, fuck off," said the other one. This one had very little hair and apparently the same amount of brain. The third one never spoke. I just stood there, knowing that they couldn't get the doors open whatever they did and certain that they would get fed up of being humiliated long before I get bored. I had been feeling soft and warm and content and I resented them for disrupting that. The gorilla wrenched at the door handle again, with an equal degree of success, and several people in the queue started to snigger.

Then the taxi just drove away, leaving the brainless trio flat-footed in the sodium lights, and now very cross.

"That's your fuckin' fault," shouted Gorilla 1. It didn't bother him that he couldn't work out what was happening. He had wanted something and he hadn't got it, so now he was going to hit somebody.

I sighed. "Just take your turn."

"You fink I'm gonna get out of the way for you and that nigger?"

Clara's face was like stone. "Well, yes," I said slowly.

"I ain't lettin' no nigger bitch go in front of me, so you can just fuck off." He sneered. "You can't tell me nothing. I never shagged no nigger, you dirty bastard monkey fucker."

I suppose if I'd been sleeping with Clara it might have been different, because he was trying to suggest that having sex with someone who isn't Caucasian was automatically a bad thing. I considered it, under mutually agreeable circumstances of course, to be a perfectly splendid idea.

Another taxi started to pull in, so Clara turned around and spoke to the nervous couple behind us. "You take this one. We'll deal with the brain donors – you don't need to be involved in this." They nodded gratefully and the taxi driver, catching the vibe, wisely pulled up short of the brainless ones.

Then Clara, seemingly unaware of the concept of de-escalation, stepped forward. She peered at the one who was capable of speech with the same expression you'd use on a parrot that's learned to play the piano. She looked him up and down, like she was assessing a horse to see if it's confirmation was sound.

"What're you..." brainless began. Clara waved her hand and his words cut off. It looked like she'd learned that mute button thing from Sophia.

"Well, I'm not surprised," she said eventually, at least notionally to me. "Don't think any of them are much of a man, and certainly none of them are man enough for me." She looked at him. "Don't worry white boy, a failure like you wouldn't get to fuck me even if you wanted to. You'd need to be a real man, not a silly little boy who spends his time drinking pissy lager and wanking over pictures on the internet. Now run along and play so the grown-ups can get on with stuff that actually matters."

Where I come from that's fighting talk, and several of the people who were watching applauded, which just made it worse, especially as at least half were videoing his humiliation. *'Viral won't be the half of it'*, I thought.

"I'll fuckin' do you, I will," said the thug, going red in the face. He tried to loom, to intimidate, but the street lights were shining straight at him and I could see an odd expression – sputtering outrage plus a tiny bit of fear. People, I suspected, were supposed to be frightened of him, so to be treated with such easy contempt in front of his mates by a woman, and a black one at that, was incomprehensible. He probably wanted to say 'you can't talk to me like that' and wouldn't understand why everyone was laughing at him.

By now you're probably wondering why I hadn't done anything about this. I hadn't because I didn't need to. I could feel what Clara was thinking of doing, and I knew she was in no kind of danger. It was quite fun watching, and I could always step in if it was needed. Starting the whole thing had been unwise, but what he did next was just plain stupid. He tried to punch her.

You can shape a shield spell almost any way you want to, and I could see that Clara had made an *armarria* in the shape of a closed tube. So when thugo tried to hit her she slipped it over his arm. His fist hitting the end probably broke a couple of his fingers, but then she twisted it – she had extended the *armarria* most of the way to his elbow – so that he was driven to his knees in front of her. She kept her palm over the end of the tube to make it look like she was twisting him to the ground with only one hand. I almost laughed.

His mates tried to join in, but I blocked one of them and the other was prevented by the hard looking guy with a bushy beard who would have made three of me any day of the week. He was also trying hard not to laugh.

Once the thug was on the ground Clara let him go. "Now stop being a silly little boy and run back home to mummy so she can kiss it better."

He charged at her, but she'd put the *armarria* back up, this time as a screen at around head level, and he ran into it face first.

"Dear me," she said as his feet went out from under him and he landed flat on his back on the wet pavement, his nose bloody and not quite straight any more. "Can't even stay on your feet. Has daddy been letting you sniff the cork of his gin bottle again?" She was starting to enjoy herself, and I knew I'd have to stop her soon or people with blue lights on their cars were going to be asking us to assist them with their enquiries.

That was when he pulled his knife, which made it a little more serious, but he was using his off hand because several of the fingers on the other one weren't pointing in the normal direction.

Clara took a step backward, but not because she was afraid. I don't think I can remember a time when she'd been properly frightened. Annoyed, upset and occasionally startled, sure, but not frightened.

"I'm gonna fuckin' kill you, you bitch," he shouted, waving his knife at her. He'd gone white and his lips had thinned, going from a blustering bully to someone intent on causing serious harm. Only Clara wasn't going to let him.

She didn't feel her cast a spell as such, but she pulled up something that Abraham and Amelia would have approved of, and pushed an extraordinary amount of heat into the metal of his knife. It went from stone cold to hot enough to blacken his flesh in a second. He screamed and dropped it and Clara very carefully kicked him in the bollocks. He gasped and slumped, vomiting.

"I think that should do it," I said. His mates were mutely staring, unmoving.

"Not quite," she replied.

"No, that's definitely enough," I said firmly and grabbed her arm. She tried to fight, registered it was me and sagged. A moment later a very plain car drew sharply up beside us. The driver was Katherine Duncan and she was bloody furious.

"Get in," she snapped.

Clara glared. "I was going to…"

"Haven't you done enough damage already?"

We climbed into the back. "What about him?" I asked, indicating the shape huddling on the pavement. It appeared to be crying.

"He'll be fine," said Clara vaguely, sounding like she was slightly drunk.

"And he deserved it anyway," added Katherine, cutting through the traffic like it wasn't there. A grim-faced woman who I recognised as Polla Bashir sat silently in the front and I knew that if she was there then her oppo and *erdikide*, Bill Hanson, would be around somewhere. They're two of Nadia's top fixers for when things get properly rough. She didn't look at us, her eyes restlessly on our surroundings. It's rumoured that Bill was an SAS officer before his magic became active and I imagine Polla had been something similar.

"How did you know where we were?" I asked. Clara slumped bonelessly against me, suddenly pale and limp.

Katherine paused, her eyes flicking to Polla for an instant. "We have both your *erdikide* at Central, so we knew what you were doing," she said. "You couldn't have been more magically conspicuous if you'd been using a fog horn and a klieg light." She glanced at me in the mirror. "Make sure she's breathing."

"What?"

"Just do it."

I put Clara into something like the recovery position, being careful where I put my hands as I maneuvered her almost dead weight. "I don't understand."

"What was the last thing Bev said to you before you left?"

"Oh. No magic."

"Right."

"I mean, I did…"

She waved her hand dismissively. "You just used a balance spell, didn't you?" It wasn't a question. "That's a tiny thing, especially for you.

She," I had no doubt she was talking about Clara, "has burned more magical energy today than she has in months, what with fighting Deroc and the amount to took to receive the old magic." She shook her head. "And I thought she was sensible the one."

"What the hell are we going to do when this ends up all over social media?"

"It won't," said Polla, still not looking at me.

"There must have been fifteen people filming it on their phones."

"And when they try to post it they'll all find that for some reason nothing got recorded. Funny that," she added.

I wasn't sure how she'd been able to do something that subtle from a speeding car, but it turned out that she hadn't. Bill Hanson, who had been the man holding the other thug, had taken care of it, plus calling an ambulance and blurring people's memories until they weren't entirely certain what had happened.

*

Bev was waiting for us, and Clara was stretchered upstairs while Nadia applied coffee and questions to me until she understood what had happened.

"You should have stopped her," she said. She was clearly cross.

"How? She was using serious magic, she was so full of anger and I wasn't sure she wouldn't have used it on me by mistake. So, short of hitting her on the head with a brick, what was I supposed to do?"

Nadia was quiet for a few moments. Richard and Anne were watching, and it was Anne who broke the silence. "Fair point. And there's never a brick around when you need one," she added, trying to lift the atmosphere.

"I wish we could take it back," said Nadia heavily.

"What?"

"The old magic," she sighed. "This sort of thing has happened before. I know you couldn't have defeated Deroc and dealt with the *erreka* without it, but now this particular genie is out of the bottle we can't put it back, however hard we try." Anne added. "Thank goodness it wears off."

"Why is it such an issue?" I asked. "Wasn't this a good thing?"

She sighed. "What spells did Clara use?"

"Um... certainly *armarria* and... I don't know, actually. They weren't ones that I recognised."

"You're both earth Talents, and you're the same level as her, but you didn't know what the spells were?" Her voice was flat with something like disbelief.

"I can't recognise all of them, can I? My memory isn't that good."

"Don't flatter yourself – there's nothing wrong with your memory," Anne snorted. "I'm guessing you didn't recognise the spells because she wasn't actually using spells. That's what the old magic is Mike, the source of power that magic springs from, not shaped into anything as formal or organised as you are used to. There are no spells as you would know them, just wishes and needs and a terrible, terrible cold fury."

"Could you do it?"

"No. None of us can, at least not any more, I'm glad to say."

"Glad?"

"It is neither subtle nor stable Mike. Most of the time it's barely rational. It's a blunt instrument that flows from anger and want and fear and desire. It is a child of desperation and passion and, as a result, it does not know any form of restraint." She sighed. "Imagine being able to do almost anything you wanted to just by thinking about it. Forget about acquisitiveness, this is what's behind the rise of tyrants."

"Oh."

"It can make people act way out of character when the power starts to take them over. Can you imagine Clara doing something like that two months ago?"

"Unless it was directed at that idiot Ben, no. I thought... well, truthfully, I didn't actually think about it. It seemed like she was just letting out all the stress of the Deroc business and splitting up with Ben." I paused. "That's rubbish, isn't it? That isn't how Clara is. She'd normally have just decked that idiot and walked off, not shredded him in front of everyone." I thought about it for a moment. "There was just so much *anger*."

Anne nodded. "That's typical of the old magic. Desire and anger and the need to punish those you think it, but without the restraint to ensure that they really do, or that the response is proportionate."

"Sounds bloody dangerous."

"It is, and you've got it in you too. Fortunately you seem to have it under control, at least at the moment."

"Am I actually still *kea*? Is that why I'm able to control it?"

Anne looked at me for a long, uncomfortable, time. "No Mike, you aren't *kea*. We no longer have a word for what you are, so we'll use Sophia's word - *zubi* - for now." She paused, looking deeply concerned. "You have become... unique. Nobody has ever managed to gather and integrate as many things as you without either going nuts or dying." She sighed. "You just don't conform to any developmental pattern we've ever seen before, and nobody can work out why or what the route of your developmental will be." He sighed. "We have always believed that you got your high levels of power from Sam, as she got her control from you, but now I'm not sure about that. Richard and Nadia don't agree, but I think you could be at least as powerful as she is. Time will tell on that one."

"So what now?"

"For you, rest. You haven't used your magic enough to create a problem, so that's shouldn't be an issue, but it's obvious that you are profoundly weary. I was amazed when you and Clara elected to go out – I thought you'd fall asleep face down in your dinner. That's why we had someone keeping an eye on you."

"Why?"

"Old magic," she repeated wearily. "Someone had to stay awake all night to keep the fire going so the tribe weren't taken by animals, but still had to be able to hunt the next day. They found out that some people could."

"Oh. OK. So, sleep then."

"Yes," said Richard. "We need to find out what Clara has done to herself, stabilise both of you and then get your magic under control. And then after that we still need to find Oliver and get the *erreka* shut off. Individually, Sam has to learn how to use the old magic in her air spells – the understanding she'll gain from it, even after the power itself has faded, could make her a global meteorological resource. Amy has to do the same with her water Talent - anyone who can create a watertight bubble 50ft under water just by thinking about it is never going to be short of things to do. Clara is… less clear. Her second Talent is *kemen*, and if she can use old magic to combine the two things it could get very interesting indeed."

"What about me?"

Richard rested his hand on my shoulder. It was the first time I could remember him touching me. "I have no idea what in Hannigan's Hell we are going to do with you," he said softly. "Now go and get some sleep."

*

I woke up in our usual room in Central late in the morning to find myself alone. Amy's side of the bed had been slept in but was already cold, so I guessed she'd gone for breakfast some time before. Sam was already awake somewhere nearby, but all I got from Clara was a great big silence.

After a quick shower I decided to find them, but only once I'd had coffee. It was a good choice because I found Amy and Sam collecting mugs in the canteen.

Amy smiled. "Hello sleepy. Grab yourself one – Nadia wanted you to join us when you woke up."

"OK. Where?"

"Next to her office," said Sam. She still looked dead tired but now her energy felt clean, which is how it's supposed to be.

I followed them into the room two minutes later, coffee in one hand, huge bacon sandwich in the other, to be met by a disapproving glare from Hugo Swithering.

"Hello," I mumbled, proffering a smile.

"Perhaps if you finished your breakfast first you might be more intelligible," he sniffed.

"It never normally helps," muttered Amy, which made Sam laugh but just confused Hugo. He had that pinched look I associate with religious zealots who have discovered that, blasphemously, someone is actually enjoying themselves.

"I beg your pardon?"

"Never mind," said Nadia. I knew that she had still been working when I crashed out, yet here she was, up before me and looked as fresh as a daisy – a daisy in DM's, jeans and a baggy sweatshirt with something rude written on it, but still sufficiently daisy-like to... OK, I'll stop digging now.

Anyway, we spent a while rehashing everything that had gone before. When we are solving these puzzles we are a lot like the police – we bring together huge amounts of apparently unconnected information to try to see how – if – it means anything when you put it together. The police have got this amazing thing called HOLMES 2, the updated version of the Home Office Large and Medium Enquiry System, to do it for them. I bet they had to work really hard to make the acronym fit.

But we don't have HOLMES; the closest I could get was 'Wizards And Talents Search Organisation *something beginning with* N.' But we didn't even have WATSON, we just have long wandering conversations around a big table, and we tend to reach conclusions only when the coffee runs out or someone gets a headache and loses their temper. That was usually me.

I lasted barely half an hour this time, because nobody was talking anything other than around in bloody circles.

"Right. Enough." They all stopped and looked at me in silence, apart from Hugo who opened his mouth, doubtless make a disparaging remark, but caught Nadia's eye and wisely closed it again.

"Speculating about how Oliver did this and why, is all very lovely, but unless we can use some of these ideas to find that bugger it's all just more bloody hot air. We... I... I... just need to *do* something." I wasn't fizzing with energy but I couldn't just sit still.

"Do you have an idea Mike?" Nadia asked carefully.

"Yes. Well, a bit of an idea anyway." I started to explain but all the things I'd dreamt up seemed a bit tenuous once I started to speak, but carry on regardless, eh? "Firstly pretty much everyone who knows we've damn near sealed the *erreka* is in this room, yes?"

"Yes, that is correct," said Hugo, "although doubtless more serious practitioners within the scope and demesne of the entity you call Kadira will be... aware... that..."

"Thank you for that concise answer," said Amy, who seemed to have grasped what I was going for. "You think we can use that as a way to find Oliver?"

"I doubt it," said Richard. He was looking even greyer than normal after the last few weeks. His partner Jill was in equal measure concerned and exasperated with him, to the point that she was threatening to drag him off to see a doctor. "He's expecting an explosion, but when he realises that we aren't starting to evacuate he'll know we've manged to at least forestall it, and he's not going to come rushing back to see how we managed it, is he?"

"OK, that's fair enough, but presumably he still wants to blow something up," I said, sipping my coffee, "so I'm guessing he'll try to find another way to do it. Is there one?"

"Not now there bloody isn't," Nadia replied sharply.

"OK, so how about we offer him one, something that isn't directly related to his Talent, but something he can still use, then grab him when he tries to use it?"

"You mean you want to set a trap?"

"Yes."

"Although there are questionable moral and legal elements to that proposal, I have to say it seems an eminently practical and sensible course of action." This was Hugo, of course, and I was surprised by his enthusiasm, however it was expressed.

"So you think it's a good idea?"

"That's what I said," Hugo muttered, looking sulky.

I gave him a flicker of a smile and turned back to the others. "Does Oliver have a second Talent?"

"Yes – air, but it's largely vestigial."

"It's enough," said Sam. "I think we make that trap. Him *húdùn*." This is not a polite thing to say – the best translation is 'bastard' - but I didn't feel I could argue.

"And what will you do once you've caught him?" Nadia asked. "I'm OK with setting a trap, but I'm not sure I can approve of some of Mike's more... inventive ideas about coercing him."

Richard chuckled. "Oh, I'm sure we can find a way to persuade him. Or Polla can." I nodded. Everyone is frightened of Polla. She scares me even when I'm asleep.

"Good. And if that doesn't work, maybe we could just set the wild Clara on him." Several people chuckled at that.

"Speaking of who," Amy went on, "how is she?" It was odd that, being her *erdikide*, she didn't just know.

"I'll find out," said Nadia.

Bev joined us on speaker phone a minute later. "She's asleep again. She says she has no memory of what happened, which I'm not sure I completely believe. But as I'm certain she isn't especially proud of what she did I'm not pushing it. She'll probably be up and around tomorrow."

"Thanks," said Nadia and ended the call. "So, have you come up with any plans about how to trap him?"

"Yes," said Sam before I could voice any of my astonishingly vague ideas. "Maybe. We think we wants to destroy Central, yes?"

"Yes."

"So we need something he thinks will be a threat to Central, but actually isn't."

"That's *not* a threat to Central. Why... er...?" Hugo was confused.

"Because it would be too bloody obvious," Amy snapped.

He dipped his head in acceptance of the rebuke. "Such as?"

"Lots of building and digging in the City, yes?"

"Yes. Most of it seems to be either Crossrail or someone building yet another unoriginal glass and steel cube. I wish they'd design something that's worth the effort of building it," Richard added sourly.

"It a lot of work to keep the water out of the tube system," said Sam. "There have been flood gates on the District Line around Embankment and South Ken since the 1930's and there's hundreds of pumps running all the time. They normally remove about 6 million gallons of water every day, and with these storms we've been having lately I have no idea how much it is now. So maybe we say that in one location the water ingress is almost out of control and we're having to use magic to stop it flooding."

"That would be easy to set up," said Richard, "but how will that entice him? A soggy tunnel wouldn't be a threat to us."

"Consider the Crossrail workings," said Sam. "They're 26 miles long, and the tunnels are around 6 metres across. So if they flooded that could easily be 350 million gallons of water, something like a billion litres, which would weigh maybe one and half million tonnes. How much magic would be needed to keep that lot out?"

"That much weight in motion, I couldn't even guess," said Nadia. "If it was moving at more than a snail's pace it would overwhelm any *oreka* spell." What we do may be magic, but it's always subject to the laws of physics. Well, almost always.

"So we say that because a certain tunnel is in danger of flooding we are going to put in an air ram, just in case it lets go. We are going to base it on an object that Oliver can easily steal and could use against Central."

"Couldn't such a thing actually do substantial damage to Central?" Hugo asked suspiciously.

"No." She didn't add 'you idiot' but we all got the message. "The air ram will remain dormant until it's needed. I can feel when it's set off, so I'll use the old magic to divert it when it happens."

"You understand the old magic well enough to do that?" Nadia asked.

"Yes," said Sam carefully. I could feel that she was rather insulted by the suggestion she might not.

I should explain what an air ram is. It's a very specific spell, one that's hard to cast and requires prodigious amounts of power because the effect has to be delivered almost instantaneously. It's used as an emergency measure and they are put in a place where there is a serious potential danger. It sits there doing nothing until the dam breaks or the avalanche drops or whatever. At the moment the water comes it pushes back with equal force, holding it in place until the break can be fixed or the snow diverted. The power in an air ram drains away after about a month if it isn't used, so there aren't nearly as many available to the emergency services as they would like.

It's probably the most extreme example of the *oreka* class of spells (the word means 'balance') where forces, temperatures, pressures and the like are exactly matched by the reaction, neutralising one without creating a danger because of the strength of the response. At a small scale they are very easy to control, as it was with the taxi door, but really big ones like an air ram (it would be *'aire pistoi'* in Basque, which sounds a bit prissy, so we generally call it an air ram) take a lot of creating, a lot of maintaining and can be insanely dangerous if not used very carefully.

If one of the size that we were planning to use let go it would be more than enough to turn Central and most of the surrounding square mile into a pile of concrete, rubble and damaged people. As a latent air Talent, and also quite powerful, Oliver shouldn't have much trouble nicking it and using it against Central. An air ram has a release function to allow the spell to dissipate when it's no longer needed and obviously this has to be hard to activate, but we were sure he would manage.

In a horrible sort of way it made perfect sense, and because Central had helped Crossrail with various inconveniences already they would have no problems going along with it - provided the flooding story didn't turn out to be true, of course.

12

A lot of the time I feel like I don't know anyone who isn't a Talent or a medical person of some kind. I don't mean the small change interactions of everyday life, but friends and close associates. Apart from my family, there's Amin and Billy and the others at karate, who I don't get to train with as often as I would like, the staff at college, who are very much 'in on it', and outliers like Nicky Inglis. Most of them know the score intimately, so it was odd to meet someone who knew about magic, wasn't quite sure he believed everything he was told and had no interest in it apart from what it could do for him personally.

His name was Zayyir, one of the senior engineering managers with Crossrail, and a more charming, cynical pragmatist you would have to go a long way to meet.

"Oh, right, Michael is it?"

"Yes." We shook hands.

Zayyir was a solidly built man with a trimmed greying beard and the hands of a piano player. "Our bosses 'ave been talkin' you know, plottin' to make things 'arder for all of us."

I nodded. "They do that."

"If we're do this it's goin' to disrupt our diggin', isn't it."

"Yes, but if that's what they've organised..."

"Right, well, let's go and 'ave a look." You might be thinking that I'm sounding a bit subdued; I was, because I was submerged in a sunken subterranean world that I substantially did not seek out.

We were at the bottom of a great big fuck-off hole, 40-odd metres down in the London Clay. The weight of rock, soil, office buildings, sewer pipes, electric bikes and gorgeous little restaurants above us didn't bear thinking about, but that didn't stop me thinking about it.

Sam, who was born and raised halfway up a bloody great mountain in China, didn't seem to be the slightest bit bothered. Cow.

Zayyir provided us with ill-fitting hi-vis jackets and hard hats that made me look like a disco tortoise, then took us to see the tunnel that was supposedly going to be in danger of flooding. Because this was Sam's gig she had to be there, and I was apparently tagging along to provide moral support, or comic relief in case things got a bit tense.

There were two tunnels running parallel. In one we could hear the tunnelling machine grinding through the rock face, whereas the other was silent. Zayyir nodded to it. "This'n's the one. We're shuttin' it for a week, for whatever the bosses 'ave got planned. We're goin' to use the time to do some maintenance on the drill, isn't it."

"Will the other one keep working?" Sam asked.

"Got to, don't it? It's going slow enough as it is, yeah? Can't afford to stop both, whatever the bosses think."

I guessed that he didn't know exactly what was going on and was working hard to find out what it was. *'Well, not from me friend,'* I thought, *'because if your boss wants you to know, he'll tell you.'*

"How far do you drill in one week?"

"The average is around 14 metres a day, right, so 'bout a hundred a week. Goes quicker sometimes. They managed 72 metres in one day up Stepney way a few years back. They got some soft rock, didn't they. We ain't, we got some Lambeth deposits and it's like cuttin' through a car tyre with a butter knife." He sounded gloomy about it.

"I can help," I said. Although the tunnels were light, well ventilated, totally secure and even smelled quite pleasant, I was not enjoying being down here, and I hoped this would allow us to leave all the sooner.

"Oh yeah? Got your pick and shovel, 'ave you?" He laughed a lot at this remark, and I was pretty sure I wasn't the first person he'd used it on.

"No, but I can make the ground easier to cut."

"You sure? We got 300 metres of this damned stuff. You reckon you can help?"

"Yes." I didn't mention I could punch the tunnel out in hundred metre lengths just by thinking about it, because it would be pointless – without the rigid concrete lining that the tunnelling machine was putting in place, my burrow would last, oh, several seconds before collapsing.

I turned away from him and felt the ground ahead of the digger. "Straight line, yes?"

"Yup."

There was a good solid formation ahead, with hard compacted layers. I gathered that it wasn't that the layers were too hard – nothing short of 100m of battleship steel would stop these tunnelling beasts – but that the hardness differed across the diameter of the hole, making it prone to collapse and all sorts of unfunny stuff like that. Making it easier to cut through was actually quite straightforward, but it would need a lot of power. Which I currently had.

I reached out, feeling the now familiar chill creeping over me, sliding the edges of the spell down the line of the tunnel, then pushed it forward until I felt the rock soften and become a more consistent density. The last thing I wanted was to cause a collapse, so all I did was send a shiver down the line (yeah, dead technical me) that broke the rock into lumps. If you could see it, it would look like parched mud. This made the drill sing and speeded up noticeably.

"Hope that helps," I said.

Zayyir's radio crackled and he listened for a moment then looked at me. "Sure has. We should be able to do about 30 metres today now. Cheers."

"You're welcome. Now we have to…" I gestured to the other tunnel.

"Yeah, right, sure." The tunnels are oddly different to the ones we were familiar with on the tube, and I realised it was partly because they were so light, the concrete not having been darkened by the smoke from the steam trains that originally pulled the carriages – which should actually be called 'cars', if you're being pedantic about it.

The tunnelling machine, a Herrenknecht, was huge, fully 150m long, weighed the best part of 1,000 tons, was worth about £65 million and Crossrail had eight of the things. Zayyir clearly loved the machines and would have happily talked about them all day, but thankfully it wasn't that far to the one that was being 'taken down for maintenance'.

It had been withdrawn from the face by about 10 metres to give us a large safe space. The dozen or so people who worked in the machine looked at us curiously but made no comments. What they thought of us I have no idea, and I didn't really care.

Sam had put the air ram onto an aluminium box that was not much bigger than a briefcase. It had spikes fitted on the bottom and it took only seconds to drill the holes to drop them into.

"OK," said Sam. "We're done."

"That's it?" Zayyir said. "All this for a metal box, is it?"

"Not the box," said Sam, "it's what the box can do. You make sure nobody touches it. That would be bad."

"I'll put some barriers around it."

"Good. Someone will collect it in a week if nothing happens. If it does we'll be here sooner, of course."

"That's all right. You goin' off now?"

"Yes."

"Come on then."

I don't know why we'd had to go down there. Any junior mage could have done it – one of the canteen staff could have done it. Because the activation was built into the spell, we didn't even need to be there. I suspect this was Nadia having a go at me for something.

If the bottom of a tunnel sounds a bit remote for Oliver bloody Gunn to get hold of the box, don't worry. These particular workings were part of the regular tour that Crossrail offered to other engineers, concerned members of the public and the incurably nosy. Absenting himself from the tour for long enough to grab the case would be as easy as a very easy thing for him and he could use the spell like *adigabezia* (distract) to make sure nobody realised he was doing it. I had faith in him, oddly, but not necessarily the kind he might have hoped for.

When we emerged we were in Kensington. While this is the sort of area that has residents rather than denizens, we could tell that we weren't welcome; people like us occasionally rattled the Meissen, so we were definitely not to be encouraged. Zayyir helped us shed all the gear and we left the Portakabin compound like any other member of the public. I hoped Oliver wasn't watching us.

We joined the tube at South Ken amidst clouds of school kids leaving the museums and rode the seven stops to Blackfriars in companionable silence. I've known Sam so well for so long that this kind of silence was a form of communication in its own right – these moments are the closest thing that *erdikide* get to reading each other's minds because telepathy is not a known magical ability. Sam was very calm, but previously that peace had been a veneer above a seething emotional turmoil, caused mostly by her mother being ill. But thanks to a bit of creative accountancy by Amy and I we had managed to get Bev over to China not long before and she had been able to Heal her.

Then there had been the whole business with her former boyfriend Sho, who I would cheerfully strangle for all the grief he put her through. I love Sam to bits, but in a familial rather than sexual way, like you would with your children. You would kill anyone who hurt them, and you try to stop them from getting hurt in the first place; it doesn't always work, but that doesn't stop you trying nor feeling the pain when it doesn't.

I could hear voices, boisterous and loud, before we even got to the escalator, and they got louder as we rose from the depths of the earth. There was a group of youngsters, mid-teens probably, just playing around on the station concourse. There was no anger in them, no attack, no harm. They were just being a mild nuisance, I suspected simply because doing that allowed them to make some sort of mark on a world that was basically ignoring them. I found their antics funny if a little loud, and was happy to bypass them with a smile.

One boy, mixed race, with bright, intelligent eyes, was pretending to surf on the wide surface between the up and down escalators while his friends filmed him. There was a long horizontal part that allowed him to do it safely, and he was shuffling forward so that it looked like he was standing on the hand rail. And then he was, or at least one foot was, and he slipped and fell onto the rising escalator, landing directly on top of us.

I grabbed the moving handrail, twisting around as I struggled to keep my feet. The lad landed head down on the steps, stunned and bloody. Somebody had the wit to hit the emergency stop button as I got a grip on the boy's jacket to stop him sliding any further, then looked around for Sam.

She was lying half a dozen steps further down, her face and head splattered with blood, showing the loose-limbed immobility of the totally unconscious. A man in a suit was stepping around her with a look of superior distaste on his face, not stopping to help. I sent a shaft of intense pain into his legs, dropping him to his knees, dirtying his lovely jacket and getting blood on his hands and cuffs, then grinding his knees into the hard-edged metal steps enough to shred his skin as well as his suit. I only let him go when friendly hands relieved me of the weight of the boy and I was able to get to Sam.

She was a mess. She had been thrown onto the edge of a step by the force of the boy landing on her. There was a serrated gash spanning her left cheek that ran across her temple then up into her short dark hair. It gleamed in a way I didn't want to look at too closely.

I reached out with as much Healing as I could, but nothing happened, not even the welcome chill of the old magic. My brain was too stunned to be able to do more than speak. I dared not move her for fear of causing spinal damage, so I sat with her until the ambulance arrived, holding her hand and giving whatever help I could offer.

I was numb throughout the 20-odd minute journey to University College Hospital, with Sam lying on one bed and the lad who had fallen, currently failing to respond to the name Henderson, on the other. It was a grim journey and I stayed out of the way while the paramedics stabilized them, endlessly checking their cervical collars and telling me not to worry, which I couldn't manage.

I texted Amy once I knew where we were going but I could barely find the words. I felt sick, dizzy and confused, which is a fairly normal reaction when your *erdikide* has been seriously injured. I felt so bad that the paramedics started treating me as a casualty too. I assured them it was just shock and I would be better after a little while, some reassurance about Sam (and Henderson, who I was now feeling guilty about not catching) and some coffee. Or whiskey. They recommended that I stick to coffee for now, and one of them gave me a sugar-heavy mint to suck.

At A&E we were whisked past a waiting room full of patients because cardiac, respiratory, spinal and cranial trauma cases automatically go to the front of the queue. One person made to protest but then subsided when he saw the blood on Sam's face and the sickening dent in her skull. I have no doubt that his obviously broken arm was hurting him a lot, but if he had to wait there would probably be no lasting consequences but if they delayed treating Sam she would almost certainly die.

The paramedics, who had grilled me for details of the accident on the way, hurried off with the stretchers as soon as they were unloaded, leaving me standing, flat footed and bewildered, in the reception area.

One of the WRVS volunteers found me about two minutes later. "Are you Michael?" I nodded. "You come with me now," she said firmly.

She was like the favourite auntie I'd never had, with iron grey hair swept back into a ponytail and an expression that said it would be a bad idea to argue with her. She reminded me strongly of Ambrose' mother Dzifa, who I think is utterly wonderful and who I definitely wouldn't want to pick a fight with.

"Where are we going?"

"The doctor wants to see you."

"Why?"

"You'll need to ask him that," she said, guiding me firmly toward the door by force of personality alone.

The doctor was waiting for me. "Mr Frost?" I nodded. "Dr Sarakam. Your friend has gone off for an x-ray and preliminary treatment. I need to ask you some questions."

"Whatever I can do to help."

Dr Sarakam made me describe the accident in minute detail, guessing distances and angles until I was drowning in the memory of it. It didn't take long before I was crying, and the same nice WRVS lady came and took me to a room where I could gasp out my shock in an undignified stream of tears, snot and swearing. Her name was Rose, she said, and she stayed holding my hand and hugging me until I'd recovered myself. Sometimes the kindness of strangers amazes me.

Once I'd got all that silliness out of my system I felt a lot better, so I went back to reception where Amy was waiting for me. We had to wait for another hour, which felt like a sizable chunk of forever, before one of the nurses came and found us. That was also when Henderson's father arrived, looking grim, and was taken away by a different nurse.

When he came back about ten minutes later he told us that although Henderson had a concussion and a nasty scalp wound, he was otherwise unhurt, beyond some spectacular bruises. He thanked me for helping, apologised for what had happened and then left for the ward where the boy was being kept overnight for observation.

We were taken back to Dr Sarakam, who looked like he was trying to be positive in the face of insuperable odds. "I don't want to frighten you, but Samantha's injuries are very serious. The worst is a depressed skull fracture, which we are treating, a broken cheek bone and a dislocated shoulder, which has already been reduced. Beyond that she has a nasty laceration across her face that runs up into her scalp, plus other cuts and bruises that shouldn't present any long term problems."

"Is she going to survive?"

"Yes."

"That's very decisive," I said curiously because doctors are rarely that definitive.

He looked at me. "If you'd asked me if she was going to be all right, I wouldn't have been able to be so positive."

"Oh."

"The problem is the fact that she was lying head down on the escalator." He held up his hand. "You were absolutely right not to move her – her spine is undamaged, but you absolutely couldn't take the risk. Gravity meant that the blood pooled in her head, which wouldn't normally be a problem for such a short length of time, but it increased the inter-cranial pressure around the depressed fracture to dangerous levels."

"But she won't die?"

"No."

"When will you know how bad the damage is?"

"I'm not certain."

"Can we visit her?"

"Well, you can't see her right now because she's in surgery, and we are going to keep her in an induced coma until the swelling in her brain has gone down. That could take days, probably longer. We won't be able to say much more until that happens."

"I guess she won't be awake at any time during this?"

"Not at all. Brain injuries like this can be very distressing for the patient if they're conscious. It's frightening and confusing for them, so we let them sleep as much as they can. It also gives their bodies the best chance to heal as well."

"OK." I thought for a moment. "Um, please don't take this the wrong way, but you may be contacted by a neurologist called Beverley Hinch..."

He smiled. "It's all right, I know Bev. In fact I trained with her and, yes, I know all about her... particular talents. She's already explained about the peculiar relationship between you all, so I've included her in the team. I've also sent her copies of all the reports and she's agreed to come here when we need her. If we need her." I felt relief wash over me like the best detergent you've ever seen, only without the bubbles. "Do I understand that you are similarly... talented?"

"Similar, yes," said Amy, "but not exactly the same."

"I see. And how are you feeling Michael?"

"Shaky."

"I'm not at all surprised." He turned to Amy. "Please take him home, feed him whiskey and chocolate and then put him to sleep by any means you think appropriate. We are likely to need his ability to communicate with Samantha in a little while, and he'll be of no use to us if he's wandering around like a zombie."

And on that cheery note, we left. Central had sent a car with Amy and it was waiting for us in one of the car parks. I don't know how long it took to get back to Blackfriars, but nobody had to spell me to sleep.

*

I won't bore you with my dreams that night; they involved blood and falling and losing people and all that other cheerful shit, and I wouldn't want to inflect it on anyone else. Truthfully it was almost a relief to wake up. It certainly was for Amy who said I'd been talking in my sleep half the night. So as soon as I'd showered and dressed she told me to go away and let her catch up on her beauty sleep. I told her she didn't need it, which I thought was a bit gallant and tactful, but she just called me a creep and threw a pillow at me, so I left.

I wasn't too upset to eat because I knew that starving myself wouldn't help Sam in any way, and I was certain that I would be needed to help her at some point. I was slowly working my way through a breakfast I wasn't sure I wanted when Anne Collister found me.

She put a mug of tea down on the table, sat opposite me and waited for me to talk. Nadia is very bright, quite aggressive and impatient with most people: Richard is more considered and considerate, and is very good at slow, careful planning. Anne can appear to be quite soft hearted, but I once saw her remove a car that was obstructing an ambulance showing blue lights by crushing it to the size of an office desk with a gesture and then throwing it across the road.

After a couple of minutes' silence, she opened her hands as if fanning a pack of cards, then held them out of me. "Pick a banality."

"Sorry?"

"I know what I want to say, but every time I start I know that whatever I come up with will either be a platitude or a cliché."

"Try harder."

She sniffed. "OK. It's shit, what's happened to Sam. I really wish it hadn't. We'll do whatever we can to fix it. I am sad that this has happened to you. I would like to help you, but I don't know what you will accept from me. Plus all the 'you only have to ask' stuff that usually finishes these conversations."

"Not bad," I conceded, nodding thoughtfully. "Nice brisk start, good pace through most of it, but a bit unsteady on the dismount. The French judge has only given you an 8.5 because you missed an element."

"Damn. What?"

"'I'm here for you', or some variation of that."

She nodded. "I'll give you that one. So, how are you feeling?" She held up her hand. "Don't say 'worried about Sam' – that's a given because you aren't a psychopath – but in terms of the impact that your *erdikide* being injured has had on you directly." Anne started out as a Healer and it shows at times like this.

I won't go into the detail of why your *erdikide* being injured can be so serious because it was to do with energy flows and what are called 'spot breaks', the places where the shared energy of *erdikide* working together, or at least not working contrary to each other, have a profound impact on both.

The consequences of these things can be big, loud and obvious or arcane, complicated and subtle, but the impact of such things when interacting like this is much the same.

I was saved from the very worst of the effects of Sam being hurt because we four are all connected at some level. This meant we were able to share the impact, if you see what I mean. As Anne started to pick at the impact on me in the most minute detail I realised she was trying to distract me. I was afraid to ask why because I would know instantly if Sam died, so I concluded that Anne was trying to stop me *feeling* her.

"What's going on?" I asked into a brief pause in her interrogation.

"Sam's in surgery again. Bev said that she wanted you otherwise occupied because if they start doing things to her mind – as opposed to her brain, you understand – then it could be bad for you as well."

"I can't just sit here," I protested.

"What else would you do?"

"Go to Amy."

"That wouldn't help," said Anne, "you'd just be worrying in a different room."

I closed my eyes. My brain felt like it does when I have a heavy cold or I'm very tired, sort of fuzzy and full of cotton wool and nettles. I reached out to Sam and there was nothing there. Nothing at all. She hadn't died, because a mage always knows when their *erdikide* dies, however and wherever it happens, but this was the next thing to it. I shivered.

"You see Bev's point," said Anne softly, holding my hand.

"Could we not use the old magic in her to fix this?" I'm sure my voice was plaintive, and I felt like a small child asking for someone to make everything better.

Anne shook her head. "I'm sorry but no. From what Bev has been able to discover the old magic in Sam has gone, along with much of her ordinary magic, but she's certain that Sam will get that back when she recovers."

"Could we...?"

"No. Clara has virtually none of it left either and Amy has no significant Healing abilities. If anyone could it would be you, but Sam being your *erdikide* means that your brain is so scrambled right now that you can barely work out which shoe goes on which foot."

"So technically I could Heal her but I won't be able to until she's recovered enough that she probably won't need it."

She nodded again. "And you are either going to be overwhelmed by irrational urges or, more likely, be mostly asleep until then."

"Yes," I said faintly. I did feel like I wanted to go to sleep, but I knew the moment I lay down my brain would be going in fruitless circles at a thousand miles an hour, and that's one thing that's absolutely guaranteed to stop me sleeping. "Where is she?"

"You'll need the tube to Warren Street," said Anne dryly.

I have no idea how long the journey took, who I met on the way or if I even spoke to anyone. I went into the hospital reception and kind people directed me to a room where I could wait.

I wasn't alone. In another chair, his face carved from granite, was Sam's brother Zhang Wei. He must have got the train the moment he heard about the accident. We shook hands, but I couldn't think of any words that were even vaguely appropriate. The silence was such a big glutinous thing that every comment or observation got stuck to before we could voice it.

It was over an hour before they came to find us.

*

"Well," said the doctor, a neurosurgeon still in scrubs, "as far as it's possible to say at this stage, it's good news." I started to breathe again, unaware that I'd stopped. Zhang Wei rubbed his hands over his face.

"We have done all we can to the damage to her skull – we've moved the bones back into place and repaired the blood vessels. Her brain is still inflamed, and it's going to be some time before that improves. Thankfully there's no longer an issue with the intracranial pressure. The surface damage to her face is quite bad but that will heal. We may be able to do some cosmetic work on that later." I was sure that our Healers could make that unnecessary.

"Can we see her?" Zhang Wei asked.

"Yes. Well, you can look through a window anyway. This soon after cranial surgery we have to keep her in as sterile an environment as we can. She won't be awake for a long time. You can wait if you like but it would probably be better if you leave us your mobile numbers and we'll text or call you if there is any news. Or when she wakes up."

We thanked him and went to look at her. Lying still with a huge covering on her head, she looked about twelve, childlike and vulnerable, and I felt my heart soften. Zhang Wei was crying, his face still, as if he were unaware of his tears.

"She hurt her head before," he said. His voice was lost in the depths of memory. "When she was small. She looks just the same."

"What happened?"

He glanced at me and nearly laughed. "It was such an ordinary thing. She stood up quickly and hit her head on a cupboard door. Silly accident in the kitchen. There wasn't a doctor we could afford, so we went to the village healer, who turned out to be a Healer. It's what woke the magic in her." I nodded. I hadn't known what had done it for her, and I still had no idea what had done it for me. For a moment I wondered if it mattered that, for me, it hadn't been a single identifiable, event.

They gave us ten minutes, that lasted about thirty seconds, before quietly ushering us out of the room and then out of the building. Zhang Wei shook my hand again, briefly, then disappeared into the crowd. With no idea of what else I could do, I went back to Central and Amy and all the complications of that world.

I felt torn; Amy is the person I've chosen to live with and it almost felt like a betrayal to be so concerned about Sam. I suppose it makes sense if you consider your *erdikide* as a member of your family, someone you are 'stuck with', for better or worse. So even if I considered Sam as my sister it was emotionally confusing, and I really wouldn't like to explain it to someone who didn't understand what *erdikide* were.

*

Either Zhang Wei or I were there almost the whole time for the next four days. Sometimes Clara was there too, sometimes Amy. Zhang Wei's fiancée Lian came down the next day, and they set up in her uncle's house near the Ecology Park in Greenwich.

One evening they took Amy and I to eat in the best Chinese restaurant I have ever been to. It wasn't not the usual flashy gold and red everything, but the sort of place where the menu isn't in English, we were the only non-Chinese in there and we were only accepted because we were with Uncle Fai's niece. I also had my few badly pronounced words of Mandarin, but whenever I tried to use them there was a great deal of respectful amusement, so I suspect I was tolerated rather than accepted.

The food was completely authentic and wonderful, apart from the pickled chicken feet and the Tuna eyeballs, and it spoiled us for our local takeaway for ever. We had just finished eating on our second visit when the hospital called – Sam had woken up.

13

'Woken up' turned out to be a generous way of putting it. We all piled into the hospital and up to her room, expecting at least a few words, but when we arrived I could see no change apart from the fact that Bev, in her guise as Dr Hinch, consultant neurologist, was in attendance.

Sam, on the other hand, didn't look any different. "The text…" I began, but Bev raised her hand.

"Was accurate. She was unconscious, but now she's just asleep."

"So can we talk to her?"

"No."

"Did she say anything?"

"Sort of. She was muttering but it was in Mandarin, so I've no idea what she said."

"Is there anything we can do to help?"

"No."

"So why did you get us to come here?"

"I thought you'd like to know that she was improving."

"We were halfway through dinner," Zhang Wei growled, his voice clipped and disapproving. "Please contact us again only if she actually wakes up, not just when her brainwave trace changes." Zhang Wei and Sam are part of the rump of the Chinese nobility, and it was times like this when it showed. Sam, our Warrior Princess, has the same hauteur available, and they can both switch it on like a hosepipe of disdain.

"As you wish," Bev replied a little stiffly, then vanished into some medical fastness, leaving us flat footed.

I reached out to Sam but I got only the lightest connection, an impression of her mind like the print of a feather in fine dust. I couldn't feel fear or distress, nor any suggestion of pain, which was good, but there was some confusion. But mostly it was a not-quite-untroubled sleep, and was heart-achingly familiar.

I felt a soft touch and a gentle hand wiped away tears I didn't know I had shed. I had expected it to be Amy, but it was Lian.

"You're a good man Mike," she said softly. "We know you love her like family, maybe a little more than family." I didn't reply. "You need to be strong for her so she can heal without concern for you."

"Thank you." I couldn't think of anything else to say and we left in a gentle rush. Clara, Amy and I went back to Central, while Zhang Wei and Lian went back to Uncle Fai's house. I think I slept a little – I know that Amy did because, unusually, she was snoring. That isn't me being tactful because she really doesn't snore unless she's got a cold or something.

I wish I could report that great insights came to me in the night, but it was just incoherent horror stories as my brain played out every worst-case scenario it could come up with. I didn't try to shut them off because I learned a long time ago that the only sensible thing to do is to let them play out. Trying to cut them off or deny them life just means that the stress surfaces in some other way. I did not enjoy the process, but somewhere in the back of my mind a small thought started gently clearing its throat, unobtrusively trying to attract my attention. It failed, blocked out by the cacophony of fretting.

By dint of careful movement I managed to get up, go for a piss and get dressed enough not to get arrested without waking Amy, then slipped out of our room. Magic is a 24 hour thing and sometimes it occupies all of those 24 hours, so there is always some part of Central that is awake, and that included the drinks machines in the canteen. The coffee was, admittedly, vile, but it was better than nothing.

That was my objective but I never got that far because I was intercepted in the corridor by one of the Healers. They are very adept at detecting broken sleep and without so much as a 'by your leave' he cast a delayed action sleep spell on me and told to get back into bed immediately or I would wake up on the floor when it wore off. I made it to bed, just, but I was groggy for most of the next day as a result. There was no change in Sam.

*

The gentle thought that had been trying to get noticed gave up being gentle and punched me in the head at lunchtime when I saw someone eating from a sandwich box. This associated with other boxes I had known and thus, by a series of mental steps of astonishing vagueness, I remembered that Sam and I had stuck an air ram at the bottom of a Crossrail tunnel a week before and I had no idea what had happened to it.

The answer, it turned out, was 'bugger all'. The box had remained untouched and undisturbed, even by curious Crossrail staff. As Nadia said 'we laid a pretty good trap and that little shit Oliver signally failed to oblige us by stepping into it'. *'Dammed unsporting,'* I thought, *'but what can you do?'*

I started to get cross then, not cross with the world but with bloody Oliver sodding Gunn, the author of all this misery. It was like I could feel that something was going to change about him, but I had no idea what or why or when. Recognising this I closed my eyes and let my mind drift. Being psychic is not a mage thing, but sometimes stuff can seep in. Nadia silently watched me from the other side of the room.

Sometimes you can feel something coming because the person involved is thinking very hard about you. Someone associated with water was thinking hard about me: I knew it wasn't Amy and I hoped it wasn't Gronk. It took a little time, but it finally occurred to me that it was probably Patrick Ashe. Our visit to Norfolk seemed like it was a thousand years ago. Nadia said she'd find out, and invited me, Amy and Clara into a room with a speaker phone when Patrick called back.

"Well hello my dears," he said, sounding vigorous and cheerful, which was nice. We chorused a reply of some kind.

"I have some interesting news. I set my Gerard to finding out what that horrible Oliver man was doing back in Blakeney after you went. Gerard spoke quite *firmly* to a couple of people – I know, he's such a darling you wouldn't think that he could, but I've seen him shut a restaurant down with ten words – and he found out who Oliver has been talking to."

"Excellent," I replied. Could this be the thing we needed to crack it? I could only hope. "What did he find out?"

"He was talking to some crusty old sailing type who most people call 'Captain Haddock'. His real name is Henry Cole, which is a very local surname and suggests his parents were paddling in a fairly shallow gene pool. It seems that Oliver was talking to him about renting one of his boats."

"Why would he have being talking to Haddock *after* we'd retrieved the device?" Amy asked.

"Because he'd spoken to him before, and seems to have arranged to hire one of his boats for your little jaunt."

"Was this the one he picked up in Wells two weeks before we arrived?"

"No, that was a decent boat. This Haddock is a bit of a… character, and he doesn't look after his stuff very well." He paused, suddenly taking a deep, shaky breath.

Nadia sighed. "I'm sorry Patrick, could you get to the point please?"

"Oh very well, spoilsport. He arranged to hire a ruinous old boat from Haddock with, I suspect, a view to sinking it while you were out trying to retrieve the device. Haddock would get the insurance and Oliver would get… whatever it was he was after."

We sat in a thoughtful silence, because that made very little sense. "Why would he want to sink the boat when we were all in it? I mean, he'd even checked to see if all of us could swim. Why would he do that?"

"That might explain why he was so cross when Gronk turned up with his little wasp," said Amy. "Otherwise – what the fuck?"

"Well that's all I have for now darlings," said Patrick. He sounded very tired now. "Now you promise that you'll come and see me once all this is finished?"

"Yes Patrick."

"I do hope Sam gets better soon – she's such a lovely girl," he said faintly.

"Yes she is," I replied, with feeling.

"Bye bye." He cut the connection and we sat and looked at each other in silence for what felt like minutes. Eventually Nadia stood up.

"I have no idea. We need to get someone to have a little chat with Henry Cole about dodgy boats. He might even have contact details for Oliver that we don't know about."

Then she went off to do other stuff and the rest of us went back to the hospital. Sam was resting more easily, all her bodily injuries well on the way to a clean recovery thanks to Bev and the Healers. We now just had to wait for her brain to stop swelling so she could wake up.

*

In the end it was just Amy and I that went to Norfolk, leaving Clara at Central to keep an eye on Sam, eat Uncle Fai's wonderful food and do some research – she'd said that she'd 'had a bit of an idea' and needed to work on it. She declined to be more specific, however much I hinted.

This time we met Gerard in a café on Westgate Street in Blakeney, where he conspicuously failed to catch our eyes while we talked. Patrick, he assured us, was fine but tired, so he would be joining us later if he felt up to it. We chose not to comment on this comforting fiction.

In his guise as a chatty local, as well as the Captain of the North Norfolk Irregulars, Gerard had found out that Captain Haddock was in the habit of propping up the bar in one of the local pubs, scrounging drinks and telling tall stories to anyone who was stupid enough to listen and gullible enough to believe him. We decided to go to the same pub, early doors, doing our best to look like tourists. We didn't introduce ourselves, of course, and Gerard ignored us and made hasty inroads into a pint of Moongazer.

Haddock wasn't the clichéd hoary old sea captain with nicotine stained whiskers and a jaunty cap; instead he looked like a crumpled, middle aged man in a battered waterproof and stained jeans. He also seemed to have a raging thirst because he was already three pints down when we arrived and it didn't seem to have touched the sides.

So how could we start to ask questions about something dodgy without giving the game away? Gerard had clearly recognised the problem too and had found someone who could raise the matter without Haddock suspecting anything. This proved to be a young lady who dressed like she lived on the water and probably knew Haddock better than perhaps she wanted to.

"Henry," she said, "I saw *Rocinante* up on the jetty. I thought you was going to get rid of that pile of junk."

Haddock brushed away the question like it was an irritating insect. "Never you mind about that. I had a plan, but..." He shrugged. "I'll find a way to deal with it, you watch."

"You told me you'd got someone who'd do it for you."

"Yeah, well, that didn't work out, did it."

"What, he didn't want to take that heap of lumber away?" She laughed. "Can't imagine why."

"There's nothing wrong with *Rocinante*," snapped Haddock.

"Oh come on Henry, it ain't been caulked any time this century and it'd sink if a lobster sneezed on it."

"Shut up Josie," said Haddock shortly. "Don't need none of your lip."

"Drink your beer, you old gouger," she laughed as he pulled on his diminishing pint.

Haddock went to the gents to dispose of the first couple of pints and Josie looked at Gerard, who smiled, then looked at us and winked. Amy and

I continued to play tourist, looking at leaflets and chatting about places we might visit. Haddock came back, claimed the pint that was waiting next to his chair by the bar and drained it with more relief than relish. He signalled for another, but the barman shook his head.

"That's all Henry. No more money on the slate."

"Just one more."

"No. Just one more always turns into just three more, then you owe us money you don't got and someone ends up taking you home in a fucking wheelbarrow." His tone was one of wry familiarity and resignation. Haddock accepted this with ill grace and stomped off into the night.

I turned to Amy. "I can see why he was the perfect person for Oliver to get a dodgy boat from, but I'm wondering how he found Haddock in the first place. I mean, he's not exactly going to be advertising, is he?" I turned at Amy's warning glance to find Gerard and Josie standing behind me.

"You got what you needed?" Josie asked.

"Yes thanks," said Gerard. She leant over, gave him a peck on the cheek and left the pub. "My niece," he said. "She works the boats all up and down the coast and gossips like a fish wife."

"What did you find out?"

"Haddock is permanently broke. Whenever he gets any money he either drinks it, loses it on the horses or something equally stupid," he said as we took seats at a corner table. "He can't sell his house to incomers because it's falling down and nobody will pay him the amount that he insists it's worth. He's already claimed the insurance on one boat that got wrecked when it 'accidentally' broke loose from its moorings in a storm. But he was given the gypsy's warning by the local agent after that."

I nodded. I let you get away with it this time, but don't try it again.

"He buys old boats, does them up just enough to sell them on and then he drinks the profits, the silly bastard. The best we've been able to work out is that Oliver was looking for a proper boat to hire and stumbled on Haddock and his wreck. It seem that they came to an arrangement where Oliver would sink the boat and Haddock would get the insurance."

"Do you think he would have any contact details for Oliver?"

"Seriously doubt it," said Gerard. "Do you want to ask Oliver directly?"

"Not unless we have to," said Amy. "If he has a way to contact him I have no doubt that he'd warn him the moment we asked about it."

I stood Gerard another pint. There was a lot of tension in his body that I hadn't noticed until it faded as the alcohol unknotted his muscles.

"So you think that meeting Haddock was just happenstance?" He nodded. "But you've still no idea why Oliver wanted to do this?"

"I did wonder if he was trying to drown somebody. I don't imagine Haddock's life jackets would be any more reliable than his hull."

"Why would he want to drown one of us?"

"Maybe it's something that he doesn't want bruited around the place," said Gerard after a long draught. "Or he doesn't like the way Amy wears her hair. How would I know?"

"Fair enough. It's a start, an explanation of at least some parts of this bloody mess."

Gerard leaned back against the chair and closed his eyes, as if exhaustion had caught up with him, but it didn't stop him raising the glass to his mouth again. "I love Patrick dearly, but sometimes it's just nice to have an evening off."

I nodded, feeling the sweat of recollection touch my face. My grandmother – Nonna – had lived with us for the last five years of her life, mostly in a wheelchair and increasingly suffering from dementia. I had seen the same strain on my mother, seeing it getting worse and worse until I finally managed to persuade her get some respite care. Eventually mum let me take a few day time shifts every week and that was when that I got my mother back. I hadn't realised how much I'd missed her. It seemed that Gerard was drinking his respite.

"A couple of friends are with him now," Gerard said. "I sometimes feel guilty when I leave him." I thought he might cry.

"He sounded very positive when we spoke on the phone."

"Oh yes, he can be very up sometimes, but when he does fall, he falls so far."

"Er… it may be a bit tactless to ask, but…?"

Gerard sighed. "Patrick used to get sent to naval bases around the world for his work; sometimes even onto ships or submarines. He was in... a very hot place... when he caught some nasty local bug that screwed up his immune system for several weeks. That wasn't the problem because the local medics had seen it any number of times before, so he recovered from that fine. No, the issue was that while he was in the hospital he picked up another bug and that one damaged his heart muscles. It's called..."

He used a very long word, with the things 'cardio', 'sino-atrial' and 'atrophy' in it, plus a lot of other syllables. Written down it's about six inches long and looks like an explosion in a scrabble box. I was certain nothing good had a name like that.

"So no transplant then?"

"The doctors said the operation could easily kill him, so he refuses to let them even try. He says that a donor heart should be given to someone with a higher chance of survival and with more need for a future. He's only 43." He stopped for a second and drew in a damp breath. "Why doesn't he want to have a future with me?"

'My god', I thought, *'I don't think I could ever be that good a man'*.

"So do you know how long it will be before his heart fails?" Amy asked softly. Unasked, the barman brought Gerard another pint.

"Not long. Every time I'm out and my mobile rings my pulse rate goes up. I've given Patrick his own ring tone so I can I answer it immediately."

"What is it?"

"'Crazy Little Thing Called Love'." He smiled. "I like the base line."

I nodded. Amy and I had done the same thing – her phone plays the introduction to 'That Man' by Caro Emerald when I call. Mine plays 'Gone to Pieces' by Nik Kershaw when she phones. Sam has the Tardis noise from Dr Who and Clara the opening bars of 'Night Boat to Cairo'. Ambrose has a punk song by Wayne County and the Electric Chairs. I'll let you look it up.

"So now what?" Gerard asked.

"We give you a lift home," said Amy. "We'll head back to London tomorrow morning to chuck all this information into our great big thinking machine and see what comes out."

"Um, I just had a thought," he went on. I sipped my orange juice – I was driving and Amy had been matching him pint for pint. "You don't think that he set up that thing in London, do you? That Sam was another target of his?" It seemed very unlikely.

Then his mobile rang – thankfully not Patrick's ring tone – and he fumbled the buttons as he lifted it to his ear. "Hello?" The phone made scribbling noises for a few seconds, then cut off. "It's the people who are with Patrick. He's awake and he's asking for me, so I have to get back."

"Of course. Let's go."

We drove most of the way in silence. They lived in a modern two storey house with softening touches that made me want to look inside, but not right now. Gerard levered himself out of the car, then leant back to breathe Moongazer fumes all over me.

"You know," he said, slightly indistinctly, "I reckon this Oliver bloke must really hate one of you."

After that startling observation he wove gently to the door, which was opened by a woman who greeted him with patient exasperation. She looked so much like Josie that she could only be his sister.

We went to our hotel – this one was in Brancaster rather than Blakeney, just in case - and held each other tight. We had been shown a world where no amount of love, skill, devotion or effort was going to make any difference to a truly horrible outcome. We had not that long found each other and, like most people in their 20's, couldn't understand, on an emotional level, that it could be over in an instant and nothing to be done for it.

That night, leaning on our balcony and looking out over the moonlit landscape we decided that, happy though we were, we needed to make the whole thing a bit more formal and legal and all that. No snivel partnerships for us – we were going to get married. We had no idea when or where, and although people say that marriage is a community consisting of a master, a mistress and two slaves, making a grand total of two, that didn't matter on that chilly Norfolk night.

*

"That all makes sense, but it doesn't actually help," was Nadia's observation on what we found when we spoke to her back at Central shortly afterwards.

"The actions are clearer," added Richard, "but the motive remains opaque," which didn't help much either.

We had reached the all too familiar 'bored of talking about it' stage, so I refused to participate more than I absolutely had to. I wasn't feeling too well, even though Sam was resting easier every day and was even showing signs of waking up, plus I didn't feel that I could add anything useful.

But they insisted that I was there, so I sat back and let them go over it all. I wasn't really listening, and I certainly wasn't paying much attention. Like I said, mages talk a lot and I suspect that it was because I wasn't joining in that my brain finally had a chance to start working properly.

"It's all bloody Oliver, every bit of it," I said abruptly, startling everyone, including me. "Any money you like that he set up the device at Rockingham and all that 'defensive spell' crap was just a bullshit attempt to stop us going there."

"Why do you think he crashed his car?" Richard asked.

"The Dragon either spooked him, or possibly attacked him. Or maybe he just cocked it up and stuffed it. I can't imagine Oliver being the sort of person that would admit that he'd made a mistake like that – everything is always someone bugger else's fault."

Nadia nodded. "Yeah, that sounds like him."

"And one of us must have discovered something, because everything he's done since then has been aimed at getting rid of whoever knows whatever it is he's trying to hide – the collapsing building, the fake thing in Wiltshire, the stupid business at Morston..."

"Not..." said Nadia quietly. I think that the loudness of Nadia's voice is inversely proportional to the insight behind what she's saying. "You told me that he invited you – just you - to Wiltshire?" I nodded. "And that he was not happy when Clara turned up at that building in Ironville?"

"That's right," said Clara. "He asked me if I wanted to stay in the car and rest. It seemed unusually thoughtful of him."

Nadia sat in silence for a moment and there was no sound except the clicking of the air conditioning and the muted rumble of traffic outside the building. "It isn't just someone Mike, it's *you*. This whole thing started when you wrecked the Rockingham device. You discovered something that he doesn't want anyone else to know about."

"Oh shit." I sighed. "Trouble is I have no fucking idea what it is."

"So it's probably best if you don't go looking for him," said Nadia. "If he can't find you, he can't hurt you."

"Yes, I know, but someone still needs to locate him – otherwise the whole *erreka* thing will have been delayed but not solved," I said.

"That's true," Nadia conceded. "So I'll set some more people hunting while we try to work out what it is that you don't know that you know."

I stood up. I knew that she was deliberately using the word 'hunting' rather than 'searching'. "Great. Let me know how you get on with that. I'm going to see Sam." They knew better than to argue.

*

Zhang Wei was sitting outside the room when I arrived; he looked distressed, and Lian was holding his hand, her slim face an image of misery. My heart sank. "What's happened?"

"You see her," she replied. Zhang Wei didn't say anything, just shook his head.

I went to see her. She was sitting up in bed, sipping some water from a small cup. She seemed alert and much more herself, although I couldn't feel anything from her.

She turned her head stiffly and looked at me. There was a flicker of a smile. "Hello," she said. "Who are you?"

14

I could understand why Lian and Zhang Wei had been so distressed. I tried not to react despite the frisson of horror that made me quake inside.

"Hello," I said, trying to sound cheerful. "My name is Mike. What's yours?"

She nodded stiffly at the nurse standing attentively by the bed. "He said it's Sam, Samantha, but... I'm not sure. I can't remember. Why can't I remember?"

I smiled. "You banged your head. It can have that effect."

Her eyes drooped a bit, conspicuously more on the left side than the right. "My head does hurt." She touched the swathe of bandages around her skull. "I shouldn't be... too surprised."

The oddest part of this was her accent – she wasn't speaking the way she had ever since I'd known her. It made her seem even less like her, and something clenched in my gut.

"Do you mind if I hold your hand?"

"I suppose not." I took her hand and put as much *indar* into her as I could spare. She didn't react, apart from a small frown that could barely move her face because of the pressure of the bandages around her head. I tried to make contact with her as an *erdikide* would, but there was almost nothing going on in there, at least magically. Her hand twitched and I let go.

"Thank you."

"That felt very strange," she said, then frowned. "It's odd; when I look at you I think I can see a… farm? It's blue, and there's a… pond?" She was clearly uncertainly about her own memory, which was distressing.

"That's good. I do live on a farm."

"But I… it's not really a farm. The barn is full of cars. And… someone who died?"

"That's right. Do you remember me?" I tried to say it gently, but there was an edge to my voice I couldn't suppress.

"No, I don't. Should I?" Another pause. "I… you have been at the farm… or near the farm… for a very long time." She frowned. *"Shìjì."*

The word meant 'centuries' in Mandarin, and that didn't make any sense, but I wasn't going to push it just now. "It doesn't matter. You rest."

"I will." She smiled sleepily and closed her eyes, so I left her being eased under the covers by the nurse. I managed not to cry until I was well away from her room.

*

As you can imagine this upset me. Actually it made me cross, as in seriously fucking furious. I must have been radiating rage on all wavelengths because there were people waiting in the reception area of Central when I returned.

"What are you planning?" Richard asked. Nadia's face was a picture, one that would give you nightmares if you looked at it for too long.

"I'm going to find that bastard and rip his fucking heart out."

"You sure he wasn't forced to do this by someone else?"

"Oh yes. All this smells of pure Oliver."

"OK," said Nadia. "How?"

"Well we've got to find him first, obviously."

"How?"

"I'm going to scan the area where he lives."

"We've already done that."

"Not the way I'm going to do it," said Clara.

*

Oliver's home was near the River Og in the splendidly named Ogbourne St Andrew, about 2 miles from Marlborough in Wiltshire, near the equally wonderful Wet Pits Lane. The building was dark and cold, but we'd been fooled by places that were apparently empty before. In fact the last time I nearly got killed, but that was under very different circumstances.

I did the pointlessly polite thing and knocked on the door, but with no expectation of a reply. As there was no response I reached out with my mind and used the spell *hoztu* to freeze the lock until it was brittle. Then I shattered it with a kick and pushed the door open. I've talked to entry specialists – admittedly a conversation over coffee rather than on a training course – so I knew better than to turn on the lights. I wouldn't put it past a shit like Oliver to wire a bomb to such a handy source of switched power.

Before I even got in the door I knew he wasn't there, but we still needed to look for something. Or rather Clara did, because even without the Rockingham Dragon on call, she had been able to access all sorts of earth Talent things, further bolstered by the last knockings of this old magic stuff. It was a heady combination and with the Dragon involved she was almost unstoppable.

We rolled through the house like a thundercloud, and Nadia elected to stay outside while Richard hovered in the doorway, just to make sure we didn't do anything especially stupid. There were another couple of women with us too, but I don't know who they were – a red haired *kemen* who reminded me somewhat of Katherine Duncan, and a skinny, intense Healer with a very thin face. They just watched and I assumed, if I thought about it at all, that they were specialists that Nadia was training.

The house showed signs of a hasty but not panicked departure; mostly orderly, but the cupboards weren't properly shut and dust was starting to build up on the flat surfaces.

"Have you found it yet?"

Clara shook her head, scanning the living room with a spell which made magical items glow dark purple. The thing I was expecting – hoping for – wasn't in there, so we moved on to the next room. We eventually found it in the box room, dropped on a table, mixed in with a great many bits of magical equipment, detritus and other miscellaneous stuff.

"Got it," said Clara, carrying a small box out of the house and letting the rest of the team in.

"What have you got?" Nadia asked as Clara very carefully put it on the bonnet of the car.

"It was with his tool kit, the one he used to make all the devices. It damn near glows in the dark."

"Yeah, I can see that. So?"

"So I'm going to use this to trace him."

"How? All you'll get is his *esku*; I don't know how you can use it to find him more effectively than the usual track and trace," said Nadia, for once genuinely puzzled.

Clara grinned, feral and excited. "Watch me."

*

Nadia insisted that we adjourn to the local college to do the work because the building, or at least parts of it, would be magically shielded. I expected we'd go to Winchester but we ended up in Marlborough, in one of the half dozen or so college departments that are not part of their main campuses - the Healers Centre for the Hereford college, for example, is six miles away at

Credenhill and the *kemen* department at the Swansea college is in Gorseinon, which is even further.

This one was buried in the local council offices, on the odd figure of eight roads of Oxford Street, Kingsbury Street and the A4. The staff did not seem pleased to see us, but they were certainly familiar with Oliver Gunn. We chatted while they got everything ready for us.

"You're looking for Oliver? Have you tried his girlfriend's house? It's in Clench Common," said one of the technicians in a rolling local accent.

Nadia nodded. "She promised that she hasn't seen him for weeks."

"And you believe her?" The head of Marlborough, which was a rather small operation, was a tall, cheerful fire Talent called Gillian Moylan. I had bumped into her once at a conference, unfortunately while she was wearing a cream suit and I was carrying a glass of red wine. She didn't appear to recognise me, for which I was grateful.

"Of course not," Nadia replied. "We had a quick look around," she said, clearing her throat in a pointed manner. "There was no sign of him, nor any sign that he had been there since all this rubbish started. I'm pretty sure that she's spoken to him, but that isn't enough to allow us to start poking holes in her memory."

"Pity."

The other technician, a man in the traditional white lab coat – and slightly less traditional light pink suede shoes – signalled that the room was ready, so we all made our way deep into the building, ending up in a part that most people don't think is connected to the offices, if they think about it at all.

There were the usual stainless steel workbenches – steel because it's fire proof, doesn't react to most chemicals and doesn't mind getting very cold – and a scattering of chairs, tables, whiteboards and other paraphernalia of all kinds.

The only thing that actually interested me was the thing clamped securely in the middle of the bench. It's a specialist mage's tool, strictly called a *batu* (which means 'join'), but it's usually referred to as a 'splice'. Its function is to take something magical from one thing – be it power from a mage or, more usually, a spell from an object imbued with one – and move into another. They are very much like a flash drive used to manually transfer data from one computer to another, and they're often used, if you'll pardon an outrageously weak metaphor, when a mage wants to 'change the batteries' on a device they've made without the spell failing because there isn't enough power to sustain it.

This one looked disappointingly like a small screwdriver and I would have missed it if Clara hadn't been doing a magical search. Gillian and Nadia managed to watch in silence for nearly two minutes.

"Explain what you're going to do please." Gillian said eventually.

Clara didn't look at them. "You know that a normal track and trace operates by scanning for a person's *esku*, but that won't work for finding Oliver because he's shielding himself."

"Yes."

"The thing is that no shield is perfect."

"Of course not. It isn't possible," Gillian agreed. "And?"

"If you push it hard and in the right way, you can still pick up the *esku* of the person who cast it."

"Well, yes, in theory," said Gillian. "And while I'm sure it would work if he were in the next room or a similarly proximate location, the man could be absolutely anywhere."

"And," said Nadia, "you can't do it with raw power because it would burn out a lot of magically sensitive things and you would get swamped by all the signals left by everything he's ever done."

"All true," Clara interjected, "but right now I can tell the difference between 'live' *esku* and a residual trace."

Gillian looked startled. "That's a *Jaun* 9 reading. I can't manage it."

"I have the power but not the skill," Nadia added. I had neither, so I decided not to say anything.

"It's level 1 with old magic." Clara shrugged. "Well, level 3 maybe."

"So how will you...?"

"We're going to set up a scan, Mike's going to map the results. Then we'll find him."

"Good," said Gillian, sounding sceptical. "Then what?"

I looked at Nadia. "Unless you actually want me to rip his heart out, you'll need to grab him first."

"OK, you find him and I'll organise the rest."

"Mind out though," said Gillian, "if you literally do that he's likely to call the police and claim he's being kidnapped or something. Would you want to explain all of this to one of our local plods?"

There was a short, thoughtful, silence but then Nadia shrugged. "I'm sure we'll manage something."

"Good," said Amy, gratefully sitting one of the softer chairs. "Now I suggest we all shut up and let Clara do her thing."

The five minutes of silence that followed was an object lesson in focus, and I could feel Clara drawing power from everywhere. I gave her all that I could spare and Amy squeezed my hand as Clara cast something over the splice and the room was filled with light and movement. I felt a deep stirring inside me that was nothing to do with the curry we'd had the night before, and a map of the country appeared inside my head.

Amy had already taken one of the rolls of maps that all colleges keep for track and trace work and laid it out on the map table. You can't do it for more than a few seconds on electric maps. I'm not sure why.

I moved my vision until the map in my head overlaid the one on the bench, a glowing 3D representation of a flat reality. I touched the paper map and Amy marked it with a red highlight pen; another glowing point came into my mind, and we mapped it again, then another and another. After a while they got a detailed map of the local area and we populated that with a large number of contacts. The one for London was much the same.

Please don't get the idea that this is a commonplace technique – it's extremely difficult, requires prodigious amounts of power and almost never works. It can also give you a death-dealing headache unless you're really careful and this was the only time I was able to do it. It also went on for ages, and the paper became more like measles than a map. Oliver had been a very busy boy.

"*Wi*," said Clara in a strong voice and a final spot flared on the map in my mind – she'd managed to locate Oliver's active shield. Talk about clever – he'd hidden in the middle of one of the most powerful power sources in the country – Avebury stone circle, less than 10 miles away down the A4.

*

Oliver Gunn may be a bastard but he's also quite a powerful mage, so this wasn't something that we could do without support. Nadia made a couple of calls she wouldn't let us overhear and we were met by a group of very nondescript people in a café in Beckhampton, just a mile north-east of the circle. A couple of people lurking innocently on the outskirts of Avebury made sure that Oliver didn't leg it while we were tooling up. I suspect that it was probably Polla and Bill, or their local equivalents. Whoever they were they reported that the trace was stationary, so we knew we had time.

Nobody introduced anyone, although they all obviously knew Nadia. That said, there are lichens on churchyard walls in Stockholm who know Nadia.

"This is a snatch," the largest of them said to the others. "We identify, contain, neutralise and restrain. This is not a killing job." That startled me because I didn't think that mages did that sort of thing, at least not as a matter of cold policy. In a fair fight – or even in an unfair one – things can happen… but… "Questions?"

There were plenty, all to do with arcs of fire, how to deal with civilians, level of force permitted and related things. If these people weren't soldiers, or hadn't been soldiers, then they'd been watching far too many military films. Once that was finished we decamped into a very plain minibus and lurked just inside the village while things happened.

"The observers will wait at point one until we're done, then we'll call you forward." Translated into English that meant that none of us would be involved in any way until the excitement was over, which wasn't what I'd imagined. I had been expecting to do something vaguely heroic, peering around corners, dashing from cover to cover, that sort of thing, but what we actually did was sit in a minibus in the car park of the Red Lion, in a fog, listening to radio chatter that started out in plain English, graduated to guttural jargon and ended up with swearing.

Avebury consists of a circle of around 30 stones – there were originally 97 of them – surrounded by a 430m diameter circular bank, with a road running through the middle of it and a village next to it. We couldn't see a damn thing, just the verdant, soggy countryside, stark bare trees, dark and jagged like cracks in the sky, and the ragged and time-worn inside of the minibus once we'd pulled up in the car park of the Red Lion.

Once they started it took barely 3 minutes, but it still felt like a sizable chunk of forever. The radio said something I didn't catch, the driver started the engine and quickly drove further into the village They'd found Oliver's hideaway quiet easily – a holiday cottage on the western outskirts. The front door was standing open and looked a little worse for wear, but the man guarding it indicated it was safe so we went inside. We got out and met the leader of Nadia's little group, who gestured us to go with him.

If Oliver Gunn had been living in the house then he must be the tidiest person in the universe, because there was no sign that anyone had done much more than breath in and out in any of the rooms. Well, not quite. On the dressing table in the second room was a wooden box. When we opened it – I didn't let Clara blow this one up first – we found another splice, this one the size of a paperback, which gave off so much magic it glowed in visible light.

Clara looked at it. Sometimes, when she gets excited, she will break into the creole of St Lucia, which I had recently learned is based on French. I think that was what she was doing this time because I didn't understand the words, but I could see that she was cross. I think people in Scotland could see that she was cross.

"That bastard," she said. "It's a decoy. He knew we'd search for him so he set this up for us to find."

Nadia, meanwhile, had called the police and advised them that we had found the last known location of a person of interest, and suggested that perhaps they might want to find out how he'd rented it and so forth. They said they would, ma'am. Nadia can be very scary over the phone.

"So the *esku* search didn't work. I thought it wouldn't," said Nadia. She sounded rather irritated.

"Oh it bloody worked," Clara replied. She pulled out a pen and, in the best 1970's cop show fashion, moved the splice to one side.

I nearly vomited. In the bottom of the box, surrounded by things that contained a lot of magical power, was the tip of a finger.

"*Esku* that strong can only be given off by the physical presence of the mage," said Clara. She looked grim. "Or part of it."

*

Then it got rather complicated, with a lot of people rushing around creating a certain amount of irritated confusion. The police took the box with the finger in it so forensics could confirm that identity of its former owner and how it had been removed. I knew that bit - he would have used a hyper-focussed push spell called *bultza-moztu*, literally 'push-cut' but it would still have bloody hurt. Nadia carefully made the magical stuff vanish before the police stuck their size 9's into everything. I didn't know much about this and I didn't care, because suddenly I was pretty sure I knew where Oliver was, and I told anyone who would listen.

Amy, Clara and I got a lift to Swindon and then sat on the train for an hour to get back to Paddington, to be with Sam, more to carry on trying to find her. Sam was, I knew, still in there, looking for a way out, and she needed me to help. Well, that's what I had persuaded myself anyway. I thought I was right. I didn't want to be wrong.

Lian was there; Zhang Wei had gone to get some sleep and Sam was awake, seemed brighter and in less pain, but her memory had not improved.

I had been reading my Healer text books; I got to keep them even though they'd chucked me out of the class back in Nottingham, and I'd been learning from every Healer I could as I went along.

One of the things they all agreed about was the value of talking to people when they were in altered states of consciousness. Coma patients do respond to familiar voices, even though they aren't supposed to be able to hear anything. In mages these altered states can often be less traumatic than a full coma, but the contact can still help to bring them out.

I was also thinking of attempting something that was probably going to be horribly dangerous for me, and possibly for Sam as well. I also knew that if anyone found out – especially Bev – they would almost certainly render me unconscious rather than allow me to even try. Amy and Clara, I knew, would be of the same mind, so I could only do it when I was there alone with Sam.

Only somehow I never was, at least not for the next few days, and it always seemed to be with people who would detect a spell that complicated before I'd finished even preparing it. Sam did improve, but not very much and not very fast. I wanted my Sam back, my Yu Ying Li, my Warrior Princess, the other half of me. I now really understood why your *erdikide* dying is such a traumatic thing. I was suffering the same level of shock and withdrawal and horror as I would if she had died, but while still being able to see her and talk to her and hold her hand and try not to cry. It's probably worse than them actually dying, like your wife leaving you for someone else but still coming to your house all the damn time.

In the end it was Lian who came to my rescue, if that's the right word. She and Zhang Wei are not Talents, but he had grown up with them – Sam had showed her first signs of magic even before she was a teenager, so Zhang Wei was used to it. He treated it the same as having a sister who was a prodigy on the flute or at clog dancing or juggling eggs.

But while he *accepted* it, Lian *understood* it. In fact she felt it, and I was fairly sure that she had some magic of her own buried somewhere. Not that I was about to liberate it, you understand – I'd done that once without consulting anyone first and I had loosed upon the world a senior police officer who had too much Talent to be mundane but not enough magic to be anything more than a bloody nuisance. I'd been spoken to very firmly about that little cock up.

Lian brought coffee while we watched Sam sleeping restlessly, babbling in Mandarin. Lian said she wasn't saying anything particularly coherent, just phrases and single words that didn't form coherent sentences. Sam was also speaking English and Basque and another one that we couldn't identify but Lian thought might be one of the Tibetic languages. It turned out to be a patois from rural Hong Kong and because Lian was born and brought up in the UK so she hadn't recognised it.

"What are you intending to do?" I was brooding when she spoke, and it made me jump.

"How did you…?"

"You're not a person to sit aside and do nothing Mike. You have a lot of magical power, even though you can't always get at it." I nodded. Sam must have been talking to them about me before the accident. I'm always amazed that people do that because I'm really not interesting. "So what is it that you want to do?"

"Well, Sam is still here, but she's locked inside her own brain. I think I can connected to herself again by putting an image of herself on the burned-out bits." I have no idea why I told her like that.

"How?"

I explained about *mail-memoria* and how I'd worked out a way to make an image of her, as my *erdikide,* and my plan to drop it into her brain, into her mind, in the hope of rebooting her, of restoring her psyche.

"This is dangerous." Lian knew enough from sharing a house with Sam to not make it a question.

"It could be," I prevaricated.

"Could it make Sam worse?"

"I don't know."

"Then don't do it."

"But I have to do something."

"If there's any chance it will make her worse, don't do it," she said firmly.

"I have to."

That was when I discovered that either Lian does some kind of martial art, or perhaps has lots of older brothers, because she hit me on the shoulder hard enough to make my whole arm go numb.

"No," she said sharply. "*Nîbù gân.* You do nothing that might hurt her more. You leave healing to the doctors." She was very cross, but then she let out a big sigh and the fire went out of her eyes. "You love her like I do. If you love her you will not do anything stupid that could hurt her. Now you leave."

Cowardice being the better part of valour, I did what I was told. I had no doubt that she would be telling Bev about my hare-brained idea within minutes, so now there was no chance that I would be able to do it. Maybe they were right, maybe it really was a spectacularly stupid idea. I spent most of the journey back to Central glumly sitting in the tube staring at the floor or trudging along the familiar and dimming streets.

I should have been paying more attention because that kind of posture marks you out as a victim for people for whom street crime is a way of life. To give these three credit at least they didn't start by attacking me. The leader, a skinny man with fevered eyes, started with a genial conversation, which was almost worse.

"You look like a sensible bloke," he said when I looked up. "There's three of us and one of you. We want yer phone and yer wallet. Give us them an' we'll leave you alone." He lent in. "An' you really don't wanna argue 'bout this, 'cos we ain't got a problem with doin' it the other way."

"Yeah, right, I get that." I felt like setting them on fire or something extravagant like that, but I knew that wouldn't be a good idea. So I used *horma* instead, but encompassing them rather than just in between us.

"Trouble is," I said, "there's people who'll go for that and people who won't. I'm one of the people who won't."

"Your funeral," said the one in front with a shrug, then tried to grab me. Sadly for him, *horma* is an impenetrable shield at the best of times, and when it's fuelled by burning anger, fear and, above all, heart magic, it really can be bad news.

The shock on his face when his fingers crumpled against nothing was almost enough to make me smile. He drew another breath, probably to shout something, but his face showed a thread of panic when he couldn't draw a full breath. He wouldn't know why, but he and his grubby little friends were using up all the air in the *horma* bubble.

I stepped away as they started to gasp. Then I called the police, who undoubtedly would like to have a word with them. Then I did something very mean - I increased the gravity underneath them until they were all about 40 stone – that's around 250kg for people with metric heads – when I decided to stop and released both spells. They lay, blue-lipped and gasping, unable to move.

"I'll fuckin' kill ya, ya freak," grated the first one. It took him several breaths.

I was about to do something unwisely vicious, to vent my anger by hurting them even more, but then I realised I was doing my own version of what Clara had done in the taxi queue. I also realised that by now she would be dragging me away before I crossed a line I could never come back over. So I put just enough of a shield on top of them that they couldn't leg it.

I could have just walked away of course, but the need to take out my fury on something was terrible. I had seen the fourth member of their little gang getting out of his car when I didn't immediately surrender but then retreating when he saw what was happening. Before he could get back into the car I let loose a spell that I knew but I'd never used before. The spell is called *hankapetu* - the literal translation is 'crush', and for once it's a bloody accurate one. With an astonishing amount of noise their getaway car was reduced to a flat outline maybe three inches deep. The ground was covered in shattered glass and metal and petrol flooded out of the ruptured tank. I made that inert, a routine exercise for an earth Talent, before casting *ezaxolatu* on myself.

It's a spell we use a lot – it doesn't make you invisible, just persistently unnoticed. I carried on not really being there until the police arrived. I gave them a brief statement and promised to give them a more complete one later. Then I faded away while they had a conversation with my assailants that was probably going to end with words like 'detained' and 'interview'.

I went back to Central and shakily describe the events to Amy, Clara and Nadia. They were cross, understanding and scornful respectively. With no prospect of Sam leaving hospital in the near future it was decided – not that I was consulted about it – that we should go home. As Richard put it 'I'm not certain the undesirable elements of London could stand much more of you two'.

*

It was a relief to be home, away from air you can slice and a river you could only say was full of water because sludge doesn't flow that quickly. Actually that's not fair – compared to what it used to be like the Thames is wonderfully clean, but still I wouldn't want to drink it.

The farm was quiet, so quiet that I wondered if I'd damaged my hearing. Amy, who seemed to have been least affected by what had happened, set about organising things, unpacking and doing washing while Clara and I sat in the kitchen torpidly watching her. I can only assume it was the encounter with Kadira, then all the business with Abraham and Amelia and the trauma of Sam that made us like this. Or, according to Nadia, it was because we are bone idle.

Over the next two days I walked a lot. It's about a kilometre from the farm to the bottom of Quarry Lane by the school, and barely another 100m from there to the pub, although that wasn't always my destination. I've always liked walking, even when I lived in a drably twee suburb of Nottingham with my mum and dad. These days I'm more likely to encounter sheep and tractors than dog walkers and delivery drivers, but I liked the silence and the time to think without the nagging feeling I should be washing up or cooking dinner or, god help me, ironing.

Some days the ladies would come with me but mostly I went alone. I could still feel the old magic burning in me, tainted by whatever I had been hit with when Deroc had been destroyed and again it felt like I was too big for my own skin.

It was about a week after we came home, and everything had become a good deal calmer, that we found ourselves on the higher ground to the rear of the house. We could see Jim, the actual farmer, tending to his sheep in the pasture down the other side of the hill while his wife Helena tried to coax their ratty old tractor to life again.

Near the top of the hill were the ruins of an old building, some disintegrating baronial hall or other. A lot of the farm buildings were made from bits of robbed out stone, which was why the doorway of the cow shed was framed by a fireplace surround you could have easily walked a cart horse through.

It looked like it had been a middle sized manor house built in the 17th or 18th century 'conspicuous consumption' style, stricken with ogives and curlicues that demonstrated that having enough money to build a place like this was no guarantee that you have good taste. The core structure had fallen to time and other thieves, but the wings had been systematically removed so little but the foundations and one chimney place remained.

We had walked through the remains many times, tracing the floor plans and discussing what it would be like to live there, imagining ourselves the lords of the manor. Amy would then patiently remind us that they didn't have televisions or infrared sensors or a helicopter landing pad. There is a small stand of really old trees just below the crest, and we sat down on the edge of it to look out over the valley that stretched all the way to the glimmer of the city. The wind nosed around us like an inquisitive puppy, and we sat, silent in our heavy coats, for a long time.

"I hate this," I said, even though being up on the hill always made me feel a bit better. "I know Sam is going to recover; I'm sure Oliver will eventually surface and Richard and the others will find a way to close off the *erreka*, but I get the idea that there's something there that's more than just that, something we haven't identified yet. It's frustrating." I shivered and rubbed my cold hands together. There is a spell called *ukita beroa* which you can use to warm up specific parts of your body, but I was so uncertain with my power that I didn't want to risk melting my watch strap.

"It's more than that." Amy touched my face with a chilly finger. "Mike, you aren't letting us down just because you haven't managed to fix this yet."

I blinked. Telepathy is not a mage skill, but Amy seems to be able to read my mind. "This whole thing has been a bloody mess since the word go, and I'm glad that it's over."

"Except it isn't," said Clara, her voice distant. "You know that the old magic is starting to fade for Amy and I. I don't know about you," she said, looking at Amy, "but it has had a lasting effect on me. Sam lost her access to the old magic when she was injured. It isn't likely to come back according to Bev." She shrugged and the rustle of her waterproof jacket was like a small creature in the undergrowth. "And you're just in bits. Since Sam's injury you've been flapping around like a flag in a hurricane. We may be partial *erdikide* Mike, but the Talents that you have that Amy and I are connected to are muffled, so you've lost all your anchors in the magical world." Sometimes I forget that Clara is an experienced psychologist.

I couldn't argue because that was exactly how I felt. I had no control and I was confused all the time. In fact, it was like I had virtually no magic. Sam had given me power and I had given her control, but now it was all gone. It was like being drunk, but from the point of view of the beer.

I needed to talk to someone who had gone through this before, but I knew of only one. Anne Collister, whose *erdikide*, a full Triple Talent, had died when she was just 20. But there was no way I was going back to London until it was time to bring Sam home.

Meanwhile Amy had been looking at the tumbled stones and the partial walls of the building below us. "This really was a seriously large building," she said, offering a distraction. "Two full wings, a central courtyard and almost certainly a substantial stable block. And I think there may have been a walled garden as well." She gestured to some unusual plants on a flat area behind us that I hadn't noticed before, or if I had registered them I hadn't realised what I was looking at.

"The home of a noble?" I asked, grasping at the distraction with both hands. "Old King Cole or something?"

"No, something lower down the social scale than that. Anyway, Coel was the King of Rheged, which is in Cumbria, and about 1,400 years too early to have lived here."

"I wasn't being serious dear," I said.

She smiled. "I know. Can't help it, I'm afraid." This was true. Archaeologists are historians with dirty trousers and bad knuckles and the most important word in their vocabulary is 'why?' because they are guided by Locard's Principle just as much as any police officer. "I think I might try to find out more about the house, see if there was anything interesting going on and why it fell into disrepair." She's been threatening to do that ever since we moved in.

I nodded. "It's funny, I away got a little magic from around here, but it's like there used to be a lot more of it but it's sort of faded. Maybe there was a really powerful magical object here that was removed." Something Gronk had mentioned nudged me but I just couldn't bring it to mind.

"Possibly. And that removal might have been a bit... exciting." She pointed to a couple of walls that looked like all the others to me. "Most of these walls fell down because of neglect, but these two, the way they are lying, they remind me of what Oliver did to that building at Ironville."

"We do still need to find Oliver," said Clara. "Once we've done that we can concentrate on Sam's recovery."

"We've tried to do that," I said. We started walking in a dot and carry one sort of way down the steep hill. "He cut off the top of his little finger to avoid getting caught."

"It would have been better if he'd cut his dick off," growled Amy. "Don't want a bastard like that breeding."

"Very true," I replied, trying not to wince at the thought. "So how the hell can we find him? The police got nothing from the booking of the house in Avebury – cash in hand, no questions asked."

"He does have a way of finding dodgy people," said Clara.

"Takes one to know one," Amy muttered, skirting a steep bank of red soil with a wall fragment on top of it. "Actually he's been a suspicious bugger since forever."

"How do you know?"

"I had a chat about him with the people at Central. There's been concerns about his behaviour for a while now, and a lot of people said they no longer trusted him. He was even excluded from the Archive because there was more than a suggestion that he was misusing the information he found in there, whatever it was. He was originally described as an 'odd duck'," she went on, "but nowadays he's mostly just odd."

"When was he excluded from the Archive?"

"Er... last year some time. Why?"

"Was that while Gronk was still there?"

"I think so." We'd reached the track that Jim uses to get the sheep to the tops and crunched down over the patchy cinder surface while I mulled. "I wonder if that's why Gronk came over to Morston," said Amy. "He didn't trust Oliver so he thought he'd help, but he did it in his own particular way."

"I guess," I said. I could feel that we were on the edge of something, but I couldn't work out what it was yet. "Does Oliver have any family?"

"Are you planning to take them hostage?" Clara asked with a grin.

"I know his parents died when he was a teenager and he was brought up by his elder sister," said Amy. "She absolutely doted on him and gave him everything he wanted, even when it was to her own detriment. So basically she spoiled him rotten. She died of cancer about... three years ago, I think they said."

"How does that timing of that line up with when he got a bit strange?"

"Um, I'd have to check, but it sounds about right."

"I know the type," I said as sour memories painted unwelcome pictures into my memory. "He's a taker, the sort that expects other people to support them while they do whatever they want." I sighed. "That type tend to either abandon their family or run away when their supporters aren't there to pander to them anymore. And then suddenly he's got nobody in his cheering section anymore," I said, stopping by a displaced buttress that I had passed I don't know how many times before without really noticing it. Now, in the slanting sunlight, I could make out two letters – an 'e' and an 'a', although what word they were within I had no idea. "How come you know so much about him? You couldn't have got all that from a casual chat."

"They let me read his file," Amy replied. "You two were stuck in the hospital for quite a while and I had to do something."

"Oh. OK. Did someone mention a girlfriend?"

"Yes. Pavinder Kohli. She's a software optimiser who lives in Clench Common, not far from the airfield."

"Are we sure Oliver isn't there?"

"Nadia is. Why?"

"Because we got an awful lot of reaction from there when we were scanning." I shrugged. "But that isn't any kind of surprise, of course."

"So what are you thinking?"

"We went to the wrong place because we were tracking the amplified *esku* from his finger. He's shielded himself and was carefully not doing any magic while we were looking. I think he's at his girlfriend's house, or he was, anyway."

Amy didn't look at me as we trudged down the edge of the farmyard. "Fair enough, but I'm not going to go all the way to Wiltshire to test that theory. I'll call Nadia and she can send the heavies in. If he's there, Bill or Polla will find him." Knowing them I didn't doubt that for one second.

"OK."

We went back inside, out of the wind, and sat down by the low-banked fire once we'd shed our coats and Amy had propped up her sticks in the rack by the door. "I wish this was over, that we could go back to a normal life. Whatever that means."

"There's a thought," said Clara. "What would Oliver do if he thought this was over? That all is forgiven. I mean, what's he actually done wrong?"

"Won't work," said Amy, stretching out her legs and wincing slightly. "Even if we could pretend we've shut off the *erreka* and he's been forgiven from running away – he couldn't have known that bloody Deroc was behind that – there's still the small matter of trying to murder you two by destroying a building when you were inside it. That one he won't believe we could be forgive him for – and anyway, the police are after him for it. Apart from the whole 'attempted murder' business, the owners of the building aren't too happy with him either."

"Good point."

"I'll send Nadia an e-mail about the girlfriend's house and then I'm going to have a lie down."

"OK." I have to confess I nodded off on the couch not long after she left. If I'd known what Clara was going to do next I'd have probably tried to stay awake.

15

Amy and I woke up at much the same time to find that Clara was no longer in the house. It was raining outside so we knew that she probably hadn't gone for a run and then I noticed that her car was missing. No answer on her mobile, of course.

"She's driving," was all Amy could tell me, which was simultaneously a 'well, yes, and a reassurance that she was at least moving of her own volition.

"Is it worth following her?"

"How could we? She's got an hour's head start and I've no idea where she's going."

"Track and trace?" She just looked at me. Of course not. I wouldn't be able to think of anything magical that Clara wouldn't think of too and block instantly. "Call the police?"

"And say what? Our friend has gone for a drive without telling us she was going, so we want her found." Her tone was gently scornful.

"How about if we explain to Nicky?"

"She'll give you the same answer."

"What do we do then?"

"Nothing. Drink coffee. Tell Nadia, I suppose. I mean, Clara could have decided to go to the shop to buy some apples and a bottle of wine."

We knew that wasn't the case because the magical miasma that hung over the house tasted like burnt tin and blood. This was anger and old magic, deep magic, heart magic and, importantly, the anger of the Dragon.

"Oh crap," I said, realising that the feeling was familiar. I suddenly knew what Clara was doing. "She did something like this when we... lost you. She went to the Dragon and used its power to find you, but she never explained how she did it – and I was so focussed on finding you, I never pursued it either..."

"What did she say?" Amy asked in a small voice. She sounded scared, which Amy almost never is.

"That she used the power of the earth to find you."

"Oh my god. I need to talk to Anne." She vanished to the telephone and I, as suggested, made coffee. She came back and put the call on speaker.

"Amy's filled me in," said Anne. "Are you certain that's what she's doing?" From the background noises I guessed that there were several other people in the room.

"No, but it's the only thing that makes sense," I said. "I mean, she hasn't gone to a yoga class, has she?"

Anne sighed. "But if she could find Oliver that easily, why didn't she do it before?"

"I don't think that she could. When she did this before she was in a highly emotionally charged state and I don't think this will work unless she is." Magic has a significant and unavoidable emotional component, which is sometimes a damned nuisance.

"And she was looking for her *erdikide*, which would have made it easy. Well, easier anyway." That was Richard. He sounded cross and frustrated, and I knew why. They had been trying to copy Clara's technique ever since she first used it, but with very limited success, mostly because she refused to help.

"Um…" I said, feeling my way around an idea. "Are we convinced that if she finds Oliver she's going to be in danger?"

The response came out as a long, reverbative 'yes'.

"Good. That means we can call Nicky Inglis and ask for an ANPR request to locate her for her own safety, and to prevent the commission of an offence."

"I'll do it," said Nadia. She actually called Tony Addison, Nicky's boss, and within twenty minutes her car was flagged on ANPR systems across the country. Not that it did any good, of course, but you have to try, don't you?

*

Amy got the first hint about where Clara was about 2 hours later. "She's stopped," she said in a faraway voice. We were snuggled up on the couch, and I'd wondered why she'd suddenly gone distant on me – hopefully not because of something I'd done, or hadn't done, as the case may be.

"Any idea where she is?"

"South, quite a long way south. She knows the area. I can't feel any uncertainty, but she's definitely looking for something." She stood up, settled her clothes and then stared blankly out of the big window that looked down the valley. The sky was doing a typical sunset, so clouds on fire or any other cliché of your choice, but the view really was lovely.

But she wasn't seeing it as she started muttering and clenching her hands lightly. I didn't have to ask what she was doing. I recognised the precursors to *'mail-beg'* – borrowed eyes - without having to be told. After a little while she grunted.

"She's let me in." I didn't reply because there was nothing I could do or say that would be anything other than a distraction. The communing lasted about two minutes, and at one point Amy held her phone up in front of her face but didn't press any buttons.

During that time I very quietly straightened up the room and put some stuff in the dishwasher, and when she'd finished she sat down heavily in her high seat chair and breathed out hard.

"She's in London."

"Can you be more specific?"

"I'm not sure. I think she just wanted me to known she was OK. I don't think she's reached her destination yet."

"Did you see any buildings or street names?"

She frowned. "I'm pretty sure she's somewhere near the Royal Academy of Dramatic Art."

"That's on Russell Square, not far from the British Museum. I'll call Nadia." Which I did, and she promised to get someone to look for her. I suggested it not be Ben.

"Don't worry, I sent him to the college in Swansea, teaching defensive techniques to a group of students from the Gambia." She chuckled and I hung up.

"One other thing," said Amy. "She's suddenly not completely certain she's doing the right thing, or that she's doing it right."

"Does she need our help?"

"What help could we offer?" She sighed, glanced at her watch and swallowed a couple of pain killers. "She needs our help like a dolphin needs a life jacket."

"I was thinking more of moral support than practical help."

Amy was silent for a while. During the *mail-beg* she would have absorbed an awful lot of information other than the purely visual, and it can take a while to sort it all out.

"I think she used the last of her old magic to find him, but because it's now wearing off she no longer certain that she can beat him." Another pause. "She's afraid he's going to kill her."

"Shit. We have to go."

"I know."

"Now."

"I know."

*

For the first time in I don't know how long we drove to London. I have no problem driving *to* London, but I have deep reservations about driving *in* London. It's too easy to get lost, or cross, or both and the congestion charge, if you can work out how to pay the damned thing, would bankrupt an oligarch.

Anyway, we got to Central a lot faster than we probably should have, but it was still nearing ten at night when I managed to squeeze into the underground car park without playing pedestrian dominoes. The drive there had actually been fine, but in the fields of red dragon's eyes that are the fields of rear lights in central London, we had completely lost track of Clara.

Richard met us and gave us our room number. He didn't have to say that they hadn't found her; he didn't have to say that they hadn't found Oliver; he didn't have to say anything. When things get bad I look stubborn but Amy radiates crossness like a physical force, and Richard could feel it. We knew they would wake us when there was anything to do, say or understand, so we went to bed. I don't think I slept, although Amy assures me I did. I suppose I must have done, because I wasn't overwhelmed with the urge to drop-kick somebody down the stairs the next morning.

We decided not to see Sam unless we had good reason to; the lack of her as her had caused a vacancy in my head like a broken tooth you can't stop poking with your tongue, and I didn't want to make it any worse. And anyway, I was here to do violence to the person of Oliver friggin' Gunn, not to try to restore Sam's memory.

But first we had to find Clara, hoping that she had found Oliver. I wanted to ask her was why she had decided to fly this one solo – none of us would normally have done that if there was any choice. I mean, with the 'firepower' of all three of us available, why would you?

But Clara was off the air again, and Amy was getting nothing except that she was still in the city and was near the river. OK, that meant she probably wasn't on Kilburn High Road or in Euston Square but as the Thames is seriously wiggly and more than 60 miles long just within the city, that was only of limited use.

It was mid-morning when I finally had an idea that I should have had some time the previous day, a way to usefully fill the time we would have to spend waiting for Clara to make herself known. To implement it I needed a powerful *kemen* Talent, so I contacted the strongest I knew, a half Japanese girl called Marika who studied at the Southampton college but was currently at Central. I knew her slightly, admired her skills tremendously and lusted after her in the abstract.

News of our adventures with Deroc and Kadira had set off a frisson through the ranks of the *kemen* Talents, and Clara's connection to the Dragon had become a matter of even wider discussion, but almost nobody knew about my partial connection.

Marika was interested in what had happened because the general understanding of *kemen* hadn't changed much in the last few years and what had happened recently had challenged a lot of basic assumptions. And the fact that it had been happening to a wierdo like me, someone who is not a *kemen* Talent, made it even more interesting.

She spent a lot of time examining the silver-stained tattoo on my arm and muttering, much of it in German. There's no point in trying to repeat these as I would almost certainly get them wrong, and it could just as well have been her reminding herself to buy some milk on the way home as some great magical revelation.

After a while she touched the tattoo with one finger, she said something with some power behind it, and the lines began to glow slightly. "You do know that this isn't just a tattoo?" I'd already explained about the silver that ran through it, so I nodded. "No, not that, not the silver. The original tattoo."

"No, I didn't. I know that it responds when I interact with the Dragon, but..."

"I'm sure it does. That's not what I mean." She raised a sceptical eyebrow, folding her arms over a t-shirt that claimed that she was Sauron's big sister or something, topped by a cardigan my grandmother would have approved of. At least her pale grey jeans didn't have creases.

"Give me a clue," I said wearily.

"This really isn't a straightforward thing. The simplest assumption is to say that Clara was strongly in contact with the Dragon when this inking was done, so part of the energy of the Dragon has been permanently tied to the image."

I knew that something like that had happened, but not this. "It's not just a connection?"

"No, there is an actual movement of power."

I had noticed that my mate Ambrose sometimes reacted oddly when I wore a shirt that left it visible. It happened even more strongly when Clara did the same, but I suspect that his responses were modified by something that was more to do with his trousers than anything magical.

"OK. It's not actually a surprise, I suppose." I hadn't got time to think through all the implications, of course, but something disturbed me when she said that. "Clara's connection is much stronger, of course."

"Of course. I have long suspected she's in permanent contact, at least at some level."

"That's interesting, but how does that help us to find her? I thought I could use the fact that we're both in contact with the Dragon to - I don't know what, make a link to her or something. That's why I contacted you."

"A reasonable thought." She sat back on the chair and ran her fingers contemplatively over the tattoo, it's beautiful swooping lines now marred by a scar that separated one claw tip from the rest of it. It was the result of the deep cut that I'd got in the woods at Rockingham, which hadn't healed cleanly. I found her touch sensual without being too overtly erotic, which I'm sure she knew.

"Close your eyes."

I did, and drifted away for a few seconds. All I could hear was the brush of fabric as her arms moved against her sides, the soft sound of wool, the rasp of denim and the clunk of sensible shoes on the carpet. Then I heard someone – several someone's in fact – come into the room. None of them spoke but I knew one was Amy and that her hips were hurting again, and far more than she was letting on, which was typical.

My tattoo started to... I was going to say itch, but that isn't quite right. It began to feel the way muscles unaccustomed to hard work do when you've been using them all day. It almost felt like the tattoo was moving and then I realised it actually *was* moving and it bloody hurt. I clenched the muscles in my jaw and pulled in a deep breath.

"It will pass," said Marika softly. I hoped so, because for a few moments it had hurt like hell. She touched my hand and it faded slightly.

When I looked the tattoo had changed, with the silver from the now faded heart magic tattoo concentrated on the eyes and claws of the Dragon. "Why is..."

Marika grinned. "I couldn't resist doing that. I had to make a change, and I thought that I could make it look better while I did." She shrugged. "I mean, why not?"

"Well, yes it does, but I'm not sure…"

She touched my hand again. "Nadia said that you were a new thing but I didn't realise how much of a new thing. So I had to do something I've never done before, and it wasn't easy. I'm sorry if it wasn't done perfectly."

"It's OK. What have you actually done?" I asked.

"I have made it so that, for the moment, you will now be able to communication with the Dragon and through it, Clara."

"Is this going to have any consequences?" Nadia said, apparently reading my mind.

"No," said Marika. "It's temporary, but your reactions are likely to be a bit abnormal while it lasts." I closed my eyes. Marika hadn't understood that I just wanted to find Clara. Or maybe she had.

So now I was all over the place again. Everyone in the room was looking at me the way people do when they meet a bipolar person who's having a bad day. It isn't fear or hatred or anything like that – it's caution, a hesitancy to say or do anything because you're not sure how it's going to be received. And then suddenly I didn't care because I knew, with chilling clarity, exactly where Clara was, and where bloody Oliver was too.

"Water?" Amy asked, catching a drift of thought from me. "They're near water?"

"They're facing each other across water," said Nadia.

I frowned. "How...?"

"The image in your mind is so strong that it's leaking."

"They're in St James Park, by the lake." I said. "Clara is watching Oliver, but he hasn't seen her yet."

"We can be there in ten minutes," said Nadia.

*

We dumped the cars on The Mall, risking the displeasure of traffic wardens until another car could turn up with spare drivers to take them away.

We met Clara at the St James's Café, a slatted wood pavilion at the eastern end of the park with big glass windows. It served food and drink to tourists who wanted to be able to sit down and still watch the fountain and the wandering crowds. She looked drawn and tired, but still gave us bone-crushing hugs.

Amy took her hand. "Why did you come all this way without us?"

"Background noise." Clara had mentioned things like this before – if she's trying to 'listen' to magic, she needs to get away because the rest of us being too close makes it harder in some way. She didn't do this before the Dragon arrived, so I suspect that it was related to the higher level skills their contact had created and possibly our enhanced contact levels.

"OK." Nadia and Anne were there too, but Richard and Marika had decided to stay at Central in case Oliver went there – although why they thought he might I had no idea. "How did you find him?"

"I had his *esku* from finding the splice and that was enough to give me the focus to locate him."

"Clever," said Nadia, sounding uncertain. "So where is he now?"

"On the Blue Bridge."

"What's he doing?"

"Nothing. Staring at the water. Watching the pelicans."

Anne frowned. "How do you know that? You can't see the bridge from here."

Clara smiled. "I tagged him."

"What did you tag him with?" Anne asked.

"Blood."

She gasped and went the colour of old parchment. "What the hell did you do that for?"

"I'm not losing him again, not after all this." The few tourists that came out of the café walked away down the wide path, peering through the dense trees toward the water. The whole place was alive with pigeons, tree rats and all sorts of birds I was too anxious to consider identifying.

"That's really dangerous Clara," said Anne. "If he knows that he has your blood…"

"He hasn't got my blood - it's in his hair." She held up her arm – there was a deep scratch across the Dragon tattoo, in exactly the same place as mine, an oddity I would look into later, if I remembered. "He never even noticed that I did it."

"How did you manage that?"

"On the tube. The idea was that he would think it was someone's rucksack." It's part of the etiquette of the underground that you pay no attention to such small, accidental contacts.

She closed her eyes for a moment, her face going slack, so I touched her hand and poured as much *indar* into her as I could spare. She smiled softly and took a deep breath.

"Let's get him," she said. There were a lot of questions I wanted to ask, but now was not the time - Oliver Gunn was a powerful earth Talent, and a serious git, and I was positive the bugger wouldn't come quietly. Truthfully I don't think I wanted him to.

The western end of St James' Park is only a short RPG shot from Buckingham Palace, so it's riven with police and innocent strollers who also carried guns and radios. If we started in on Oliver directly they would have no way of knowing that we were the good guys – for any given value of 'good' of course – and they were just as likely to jump us as our target. Normally Nadia takes care of the whole 'chain of command' thing and the police often look away or become amnesiac or just happen to not be in the area just then, but there hadn't been time to make that happen.

The Blue Bridge is halfway down the length of the lake that Henry VIII had installed in the middle of his deer park in the 16th century. Oliver was standing right in the centre of it, looking toward Buckingham Palace, which was just visible through the trees. Nadia and Anne approached on the south side of the bridge, their backs to Birdcage Walk and the Wellington Barracks. Clara and I were on the other, and it was toward us that Oliver turned when we broke the cover of the trees.

"I was wondering when you'd turn up," he said conversationally, leaning nonchalantly on the railing. "I've been waiting for you."

I didn't speak. I didn't want to. I just wanted to punch his lights out. Anne started to cross the bridge but ran into a *horma* so solid that it almost bent the railings.

"Not yet," said Oliver smugly. "You can stay there until I say that you can come closer." He paused. "I'm curious - how did you close the *erreka*?"

"We didn't," I said. "We reduced the flow so it won't be a problem for some time – but we still need you to close it."

"And if I refuse?"

"You won't," said Clara softly, "because whatever else you may be Oliver, you aren't a monster. I just don't know why you didn't close it sooner."

"No, you don't," he said in a totally flat voice.

"In fact," I said in an equally cold tone, "we don't know why any of this happened."

"If you can't work it out, nobody can," he sneered. "And because you can't I'm now leaving."

"If you're just going to run away," said Clara, "why did you come here at all?"

"I like the pelicans. They've been here four hundred years, you know. They don't treat me like..." he stopped. "Because it was the only way I could be sure of meeting you again Michael."

"You could have just called me," I said, but he didn't respond.

Instead he turned, raised his hand and sent a crackling bolt of energy like a missile straight at me. Without conscious thought I crouched, touched both hands to the ground, then stood and raised them, like an earth bender or something. A shield that was not the product of any spell I had cast formed in front of me and the fire washed over it, setting the bushes to crackling even though the leaves didn't actually burn. The boom was soft, not percussive, but it would certainly attract attention.

With the gulls rising in a cackling storm he loosed another one, this time at Anne. It passed through his *horma* but failed to penetrate Anne's, and it remained in between the two, broiling and roaring, creating a wall of fire that neither of them could get through.

I started to walk my protection forwards across the bridge, but I found I couldn't move it anywhere above the water. It could have been because of something Oliver was doing, but it was more likely because it was an earth-based spell.

Clara looked at me. "How the hell is he planning to get away?"

"Into the water?"

"Amy's stopped that. He would have known that she would do that."

I couldn't see what Amy had done, but I took Clara's word for it. "So now what?"

"I'm going to go and get him," I said.

Oliver rolled more fire toward us, but that rebounded as well. "Come on then Michael," he shouted. "Prove you're a real man – face me alone."

"Fine," I shouted back. "Come out from there and I will."

He laughed. I wish I could say it was maniacal laughter, but it wasn't. He just seemed to find it funny. "No way. You've got to come to me."

"It's another trap," said Clara urgently. "Screw this up and there won't be enough of you left for Nadia to bollock. And I still don't understand how he plans to get away."

"I'm going to stop all this rubbish," said Amy, and the lake leapt over the railings, killing his fire barriers and frightening the life out of enough waterfowl to repopulate a small nature reserve. It was clearly a nasty surprise for Oliver and Clara was sprinting down the bridge before the splash had subsided. Unfortunately Oliver was quick and his rebuilt wall of fire was racing toward her in an instant.

I saw the flame hit her, felt the shock and then the pain. Without thought I channelled the Dragon - serious head rush – laced the energy with Healing and poured it into her. She didn't stop, and even though her clothes were smouldering and her skin was blistering and being Healed even as it burned, she actually went faster.

Oliver's face was a mixture of shock and terror – Clara was bearing down on him like a burning zombie, insensible to pain and bent on fiery revenge. Nothing he did changed her approach – every damage was Healed instantly, although it must have been agonising – and all his spells just bounced off. The run took her about seven seconds, which must have felt like forever. Clothes burning and trailing smoke, she crashed into him, bowling him over onto the wet floor.

He tried to get up but Clara delivered a beautiful snap kick that drove his head back into the railings, and he slumped unconscious.

Anne reached them a couple of seconds later, with the rest of us only moments behind. Clara was slumped in a puddle, clutching her arms around herself, her eyes red from the smoke, her mouth tight.

"Fuck me, that hurt,' she gasped. I tried to Heal her again, but I had lost the Dragon somewhere along the way. Anne took over while Nadia and I dealt with concerned members of the public and several coppers who had run towards the commotion.

"We need to get everyone back to Central," Anne said, carefully stepping on Oliver's fingers. He didn't stir. "Good work, by the way."

"Thank you. Are you going to tell me not to do it again?"

"No. In fact, I want you to explain to me what you actually did."

16

We did eventually get back to Central, with a police escort, mostly because Bev turned up with her official 'doctor and scary person' hat on and Nadia started getting official all over them. The coppers were only too happy to hand everything over to her, especially once the boss of Special Ops, a Superintendent, had rowed in. We had to promise that we would go to the cop shop at Charing Cross to give proper statements later. I really must get around to that someday.

  We left the park in a state of confusion. One or two ducks might have got slightly baked and several did get singed, so the official Birdkeeper started making suing noises. The park maintenance people also wanted a word about the state of the bridge, but we had just legged it as fast as we could. Central has an entire department for dealing with the legal fallout from large scale damage and, in this case, a diminution of the avian population.

  We ended up on the hospital floor, of course, with Oliver in a 'restraining room', which is a space that is physically impossible to break out of and that is immune to all forms of magic. Sadly we have to have these places because sometimes mages can just lose it, despite everyone's best efforts, and when they do it can be in big, dangerous ways. There can be lots of uncontrolled and uncontrollable consequences to these outburst, so these rooms were created as much to protect the ailing mages as anyone else.

Clara had been put in a normal hospital room, from which I was politely but firmly removed. When I objected it was pointed out that they needed to examine all of her skin for burns, lesions or other changes, and while they were sure I would enjoy the view, they weren't so sure that Clara would feel the same.

I conceded with as much good grace as I could, and ended up being shunted back to the bloody coffee shop again. I was getting really sick of that place, and of being gently interrogated by Richard Slater.

"I understand the mechanics of what has happened," he rumbled, "but it's how it was done magically that I don't understand."

"I blocked the fire with a shield. It felt like I pulling it up out of the ground." He nodded. "Clara started to run at him but I couldn't get the shield out onto the bridge." He nodded again. "So I tried to minimise the damage by running continuous Healing on her."

"Good. How?"

"I did what I would normally do to give someone *indar,* but I put Healing into it instead."

"And you weren't near her."

"No. We were about five feet apart when I started and probably closer to thirty feet when I stopped."

"You do know that it isn't possible to do that?"

"Er... beg to differ."

"Hmm." He was silent for a moment. "Anyway," he said, standing up in his slightly creaky way, "let's go and see Clara. Then we need to look into Oliver's mind."

"That won't be hard – there's plenty of empty space."

Clara was recovering nicely and we were politely requested to piss off, so we did.

In most stories, if the bad guy hasn't already given everything away in advance by inadvisable bragging, they usually tell you everything at the end, just to satisfy the demands of narrative structure. But Oliver wasn't interested in narrative structure and he refused to say a word. No, that's not true; he did talk, but he said nothing about what he'd done or why he'd done it. I think he enjoyed the frustration that we let him see.

Nadia wasn't concerned about anything except shutting down the *erreka* - the rest he could take to his grave for all she cared. We could have threatened violence but mages are not outside the law and *habeas corpus* still applies if you're holding someone officially, or the rules on unlawful detention (i.e. kidnapping) if it's unofficial. The best we could hope for was something very like sectioning him, but we all knew that it would be a form of judicial fiction which we didn't want to test, at least not on him.

Oliver didn't ask for a solicitor, he asked for tea and a cheese sandwich; he didn't ask to be released, he asked for some dry clothes; he didn't ask what would happen next, he asked if we could let his girlfriend know that he was all right. So we were stuck.

Then Amy came up with a very clever idea, one that really shouldn't have worked. In the time we'd had the old magic available we'd all done things that shouldn't have worked, so while nobody was surprised that she'd dreamt up something like this a lot of people were very dubious about it working, especially as the amount of the old magic she had available continued to drop sharply.

"Your *esku* is a part of what makes you a mage, yes?" Amy said. Richard nodded. "We know that this is, in fact, a very basic part of magic, this old wild stuff." Richard nodded again. "I can still get at the old magic, although it is definitely fading, so I thought I might use what's left to shut down the *erreka*."

"I don't believe that will work," Richard replied hesitantly. "*Esku* is like magical DNA – everyone's is different, so you won't be able to replicate it. And if you can't replicate it you won't be able to effect the *erreka*."

"It has to be worth a try," Amy said.

He shrugged. "OK, I mean, what's the worst that can happen?"

"It could actually make things a lot worse."

"That would be bad," he agreed gravely. "So we need to take some precautions to make sure that nothing very bad happens."

Amy smiled. "Don't worry, Mike and the Dragon will be with me while I do this. If they can't stop it I don't know who could."

"OK," said Richard, "let's get on with it."

*

It took ages to set it up. Amy had to fully understand Oliver's *esku* in order to override it. His *esku* was not a twisted thing, tainted and evil, but neither was it the epitome of purity. It was just an *esku*, and no different from any other. Amy had to find the place where Oliver's *esku* was still controlling the flow of energy from the realm of Kadira and change her own so that it matched Olivers.

It didn't take her very long to find it. He had made no effort to conceal it because he had no reason to think that anyone would look for it. I was there when they did this and for all the power and complexity involved the difference was very subtle, but still extremely scary. *Esku* is as much part of the person as the colour of their hair, and Amy very subtly wasn't herself while she was doing this.

The level of magic used was so intense and complex that it had needed a level of skill far beyond mine to make any difference at all. Nadia, Richard and Anne had all rowed in, and specialists were brought in from mainland Europe. To nobody's surprise, one of them was Sophia Jilani.

Amy told me that the place she found was a fair analogue of the wall I had tried to seal on the other side. She had tried to close it using no more than her own skill and identity but that had no effect, which is what we had expected. So she dredged up what remained of the old magic, changed her *esku* to closely resemble Olivers and basically forced the final part of the *erreka* to close. Her bland description of what she did made it sound fairly easy but later she told me that, magically, it was probably the hardest thing she'd ever done.

Coming back from it, Amy told me, was very hard, but my steady image of her reminded her of who she was and she was able to slip back into herself. It was several days before she was normal again, and her magic was unstable for more than a week. In fact it had been so hard that Bev had to sedate her and force her to stay in bed for 24 hours to start her recovery.

It had several consequences, apart from the obvious. It had burned out all the old magic that was left in her; people who had been labouring to keep the *erreka* under control were finally able to relax, and you could hear Oliver swearing halfway to Norwich.

The *erreka* had been his bargaining tool. He had decided that he would risk getting caught just to have a chance to get to me, and that he would be let out, unpunished and immune from further action, in payment for shutting off the *erreka*. Not that it would have worked of course, but by then we knew that Oliver was a perfect example of the smug, self-satisfied type who thinks they should be able to do whatever they want and that nobody is clever enough to stop them. Donald Trump, Elon Musk, Dracula… you get the idea.

But even with the *erreka* gone he still wouldn't open up. He didn't explain to us why he had done wat he did. In fact he clammed up even more, so we left him to stew for a few more days. I wanted to hurt him. Richard wanted to offer him some kind of deal. Nadia wanted to do the whole 'boot, bat and bastinado' routine.

Anne was more subtle, playing on Oliver's ego (which was huge), his self-awareness (which was tiny) and his common sense (which was pretty much undetectable). So she got him talking to someone who was also resident in the secure section.

Her story was that she had failed to integrate a very late-emerging second Talent and was staying at Central until the Healers could make it safe. This was not very unusual, but as the lady in question was Marika, who Oliver didn't know, this was obviously not true.

Marika made sure that she conformed to all of Oliver's egotistical expectations, but it still took her two days to get him to open up, two days of pandering to his ego, agreeing with him and never, ever, challenging anything that he said. In the end it was all so simple, far too simple for us to accept without Marika assuring us it was true.

Oliver had started the whole *erreka* thing as a legitimate research project, as confident that he could make it work as any other mage doing research. However he failed to correctly calculate how much power would be required; to be fair his original calculations had been largely correct but Deroc had overwhelmed him.

Sadly he wouldn't admit that things had got out of hand and soon he was out of his depth and sinking because people like Oliver are never wrong and never need help. Instead he decided to acquire the power to do what he needed from another source.

With his ego and arrogance preventing him from asking for help he'd set up the drain at Rockingham, a source that was being much discussed at the time. He hadn't know about the connection to Clara which had led me to find and smash it. He should have known that the poxy little device he was using couldn't have stored enough power to hold Deroc at bay for ten minutes, let alone be enough to close the *erreka*, but overconfidence beats common sense every time.

But of course now he couldn't own up to being behind the Rockingham business either, because then he'd have to explain why, and like so many people who are caught in such circumstances, he wasn't wise enough to own up and take his lumps. Instead he hid it and tried, with increasing desperation and an equal lack of success, to dig his way out. But he just succeeded in digging himself in deeper, and then I'd ruined the only thing that he'd tried that had even vaguely worked.

It hadn't taken him long to decide that everything was all my fault, that if I hadn't destroyed the Rockingham device it would have been fine. He tried to get me to go to Wiltshire so he could stage a car accident. Morston was an attempt to drown me. The building in Ironville – well, you get the idea - and all the time he was waiting for the *erreka* to rupture. He didn't much care that there would have been a lot of magical damage. Once it had happened he could say it was nothing to do with him and carry on as before. It was pathetic and troubling, but sadly understandable, and I was glad I didn't have to decide what would happen to him now.

There was a lot of fuss about what to do with Oliver. But there are no magical police and no magical prisons, and a conventional prison hasn't been made that can hold a *Jaun* level mage for more than half an hour. It was decided, at a European level no less, that he hadn't committed a magical crime serious enough to have his abilities permanently removed, so a specialist was flown over from Portugal to apply a fairly vicious variation of the spell e*seki*. This loosely translates as 'suspend', and it stopped all his magic working, and would continue to do so until it was lifted.

It wasn't something that could be done without the extra support that had been brought in because the spell is a big, serious thing and not something lightly done. Sometimes people go insane, fall into a fugue or even die when it's used on them.

The police weren't much interested in anything apart from attempted murder by means of demolishing a building with me and Clara still inside it. After an odd trial where a lot got glossed over he was sentenced to 10 years in prison – five of those in custody and five out on license. He will have to prove himself reliable after the license period is up if he ever wants to get his magic back. If he can – reversing *eseki*, I understand, doesn't always work.

With the *erreka* closed, Oliver neutralised and the Dragon once more untrammelled, I still had a few things to sort out - in no particular order Sam, Jerry, Ariadne and Patrick.

I have a small confession to make here. When Clara and Amy reported the old magic had left them I had remained silent and everyone assumed that I had been affected in the same way. But I hadn't. Sure, the old magic, the power that could fry a tiger or create a cave with a thought had mostly faded, but I had been left with the knowledge of the old magic and a powerful and enduring connection to heart magic.

I knew I could use it only once more, or maybe twice at a pinch. I had hoped I could use it to help Sam, because I missed her terribly and I wanted her back. Being with Sam was still painfully like being with my grandmother. She'd lost her mind to Alzheimer's rather than because of an injury, but the effect had been the same: someone you've known and cared about for years no longer has any idea who you are or what you mean to them, or they to you. I found my eyes filling with tears just at the thought.

But Sam was improving every day, although she was still exhausted by the least effort. Great chunks of her memory were coming back as her physical wounds healed, and had been Healed, and all she was left with was a scar that was only visible because it didn't tan like the rest of her skin.

"Hello," she said when we came into her room. She reached out to hug me, even though her dislocated shoulder was still sore. She had no memory of the accident, even after I showed her the CCTV images, but at least now she knew who I was most of the time.

Her newly created memories were fine and her magic was indeed returning, but there were big, oddly specific gaps in her past. She could create a waterspout in a teacup but had to be reminded which road she lived on. Zhang Wei told me that her Italian accent had changed, now being more Venetian than Roman, and she was no longer fluent in French. She also described almost everything using colours, sometimes had trouble creating coherent sentences and when she was very tired she became synaesthetic. The Healers still wouldn't let me help her with anything much more than headaches and muscle strain, which upset me even though I knew they were right.

Marika came to see us a few days later. "Take her home, back to the farm," she said. "Take her home. She needs space and peace in familiar surroundings. Her memory needs gentle stimulation, but she cannot be exposed to the clamour and demands of being in the city. The jaggedness of the magic in the college would harm her." I could have cried with relief, but once we had all resettled back at the farm I left Clara and Amy to deal with it because now I was free to keep two promises that I'd made.

*

The first was the wedding of Jerry Denton and his best beloved Ariadne, and this was especially important as Jerry had asked me to be his Best Man. That had meant digging out my one and only suit, which I found didn't fit any more so I had to buy a new one, and writing a speech. I found the speech easier to achieve than the suit because I hate shopping.

The day was delightful and the ceremony was held in a posh hotel overlooking a wooded valley populated by deer, badgers, clouds of songbirds and other things of a rural bent. Ariadne looked stunning in ivory silk decorated with dark blue roses, and Jerry proved that even the scruffiest nerd will scrub up nicely if someone exerts themselves enough. His suit didn't fit any better than mine.

Ariadne had asked her best mate Samira to be her Matron of Honour, and she brought her husband Jonah and their children. Amy and I spent ages playing with those kids after the ceremony so that their parents could have some grown-up time with the happy couple. I reckon about half the guests were doctors and the other half were mages of some kind or another.

An air Talent arranged for some towering theatrical clouds to add some drama to the wedding pictures, but he lost control of them quite early on and they turned into a thunderstorm. I suspect Ariadne would have preferred some nifty work in Photoshop rather than having her shoes full of water. A lot of women from the college were giving me and Amy speculative glances, which I responded to with a warm and friendly blank stare. Amy met them with a small smile that would have been quite agreeable if it hadn't been quite so calculating. Don't misunderstand – I would marry Amy at some city centre registry office tomorrow, but I have a feeling that she has something a bit special in mind.

Sam wasn't well enough to come, of course, so we got a nurse to stay with her while Clara brought Ambrose to the wedding. He looked like he'd won the jackpot right up until she left when Amy and I did, but without him.

I like Ambrose but I think he's a bit too much of a Bethnal Green wide boy for Clara. I guessed he'd be around our place more often than usual, at least for a while - with Jerry, his *erdikide,* swanning around Greece on his honeymoon he was going to be at a bit of a loose end. I didn't mind because he's known us all since we started at the college, and it would be nice not to be the only bloke in the house for a while. With him around I would also doubtless learn some new swearwords – he speaks perfectly good English but he has a habit of swearing in Akuapem Twi. Yeah, I've got no idea either.

*

The other promise took me to Norfolk. "Hello. Come on in," said Gerard, stepping aside and gesturing me toward the kitchen. It was heavy with pale wood and shiny stainless steel units that should have been incongruous, but somehow worked in the space.

"Your face answers my main question," I said.

Gerard nodded sadly. "He will keep trying to do things that are quite beyond him now. It's almost as if he wants it to happen."

I rested my hand on his arm. "OK, blunt question. Am I right in thinking that he doesn't have long?"

"You are." He blinked back tears. "It could be as little as days."

"Well, I've got something I want to try. I can offer you no guarantee of success. It might work but it equally could have no effect at all. It could even…" I didn't need to finish the sentence.

"Anything, even if all it will do is ease his passing." I cannot describe what his face looked like but the only word I can think of is 'destroyed'.

We went to Patrick's bedroom, a converted downstairs lounge with a view over the coast. He was lying very still, his limbs displaying a heavy immobility that reminded me uneasily of Sam on the steps at the tube station.

"Hello dear," he said, his voice faint and his lips slightly blue, "have you come to say goodbye?"

"Perhaps not. I've an idea of something that might help you." I repeated the caveats, but he waved them away. I don't think he had enough left in him to even listen properly– nobody with skin as dark as his should look grey.

I sat quietly by his bed and put my hand on his chest, resting it gently over his heart. I could feel it fluttering and struggling, the weary muscles burning themselves out as they tried to make up for those that were lost. I felt his blood flowing, sluggish and irregular, and heard his laboured breathing. I felt sick, scared by what I was about to do, and there was a flutter of panic on the edge of my mind that I couldn't still.

I hadn't been wasting my time while I had been sitting in the hospital with Sam. I'd made a point of not only learning more Healing spells but how Healing actually worked. I'd talked to many people, doctors and psychologists, about Patrick's condition, trying to understand what they could, and more importantly couldn't, do. All that the medical profession had been able to offer was a dubious prognosis from an equally dubious transplant. Healers would have been able rebuild his heart, one step at a time, just like they had with Amy's hips, but doing that would have put so much strain on him that he would almost certainly have died in the process.

But I had one thing that none of them did – access to the old, wild power, the roots of magic, power born of need and hope and control born of the fear of loss. I had enough left for one really big jolt, oddly thanks to Deroc. I hadn't been able to decide if I should use it to help Patrick or Sam, but Marika and Lian had been very clear about not using it on Sam. So here I was and it genuinely never occurred to me to use it to get myself out of the smoke. And yes, I really am that special kind of stupid.

"Hold his hand," I said to Gerard. "This going to be hard and he will need the reassurance of you being there with him."

I reached deep within myself, found that last surge of heart magic and combined it with every scrap of Healing I could find. I felt my skin tighten and my breathing became shallow and painful, but before I could do anything the power was hugely augmented. I thought that perhaps Marika had been wrong when she said my connection to the Dragon was temporary, but this didn't feel like it came only from the Dragon. I decided that I would look into the source of the power when I had the time, which was not now. I struggled to direct it to where I needed it.

The human body renews itself every so often - all of your skin is replaced every 28 days, and most parts of your body within 7 years. But with the heart the replacement rate can be as little as 6% each year, but even then none of the replaced tissue would be the heart muscles that had been destroyed, because dead tissue isn't renewed.

With my mind I pushed into Patrick's chest.

After a few seconds I realised that I wasn't seeing his actual heart. Instead I was within his *gogoan*, or at least on the edge of it. Mine is a landscape of black sand, but Patrick's is a castle, one made of a rich stone like polished granite but shot through with red like veins. It was truly beautiful and I could have run my hands over the surface for hours despite the flat, powerless light. But I didn't have hours.

The whole structure was the representation of Patrick's life, his future and his love for Gerard, and I knew I had barely minutes before it collapsed. I didn't dare rush this, but I didn't dare fail either.

I fed my Healing into the castle and watched as the dimness around me started to pulse very gently. What brightness there was contrasted with the trembling, pervasive darkness around his damaged heart. It took me a moment to realise that this trembling was Patrick's final heartbeats.

I slowed them until no more than a flutter remained, just enough to sustain his life. I could feel his heart muscles straining, so I calmed them, felt for the weaknesses, the dead and dying tissue, the failing heart in its last struggling moments.

Then I found a flaw deep within the weakened walls, the representation of the damage Patrick had suffered, and I poured in my power, my fury at the cruelties of fate, my hopes for the future, my tears for all the suffering I could not prevent. I felt a sudden release, like a dam breaking, and the magic flowed, and then it was me who was empty, a sere reed with the heart gone out of it. I slowly pulled myself away from the glowing castle, watching as it was rebuilt, one glorious, glowing fragment at a time.

I don't know how long it took, days or seconds or a large part of forever, but I felt his life coming back, his strength growing as his surging blood took energy and oxygen, and magic, to his brain.

Patrick passed out almost as soon as I started. Please don't ask me exactly how I did it – Bev does every time I see her and I still can't explain it to her satisfaction. I'd had the power and the will and it had worked, but fuck me it hurt. By the time I'd finished I barely had the strength to carry on breathing myself, and every part of my body hurt. I was shaking with the cold, I knew that I was crying and I made no effort to stifle it. I actually got a slight case of frost bite on the hand I had placed over his heart.

We had to get an ambulance to take Patrick to hospital in Norwich immediately afterwards, but within days his heart was as strong as it had been before he was first ill. He was mute and tearful with gratitude, and Gerard insisted on kissing me goodbye when I left the hospital, still feeling shaky and a bit sick.

I had arrived as *zubi*, the bridge, but when I left I was *kea* again. I knew that I had lost any chance of getting myself out of the smoke when I used the last of the old magic to save Patrick. And I didn't care. When I got home I found three tearful women waiting for me. They knew what I'd done, knew what I'd sacrificed so that Patrick, a good man, a better man than I'll ever be, would live. That was enough.

I was so tired, so bone weary, that it wasn't until the next day that I realised that Sam hadn't just come to the farm to recuperate – she'd moved in. Zhang Wei and Lian could have their house to themselves, and I wondered how long it would be before Clara came to live here too.

But meanwhile there were fires to be laid, meals to be prepared, a life to be lived. I didn't know it then, but as I watched the flames in our open fire dance a man was dying, crushed by a tree that had no reason to fall over, and that would pitch us headlong into something that we had no reason to be involved in. Sometimes I think the universe is out to get me.

Printed in Dunstable, United Kingdom